IRON TOWNS

This paperback edition published in 2017

First published in Great Britain in 2016 by Serpent's Tail,
an imprint of Profile Books Ltd
3 Holford Yard
Bevin Way
London
WC1X 9HD
www.serpentstail.com

Copyright © 2016 Anthony Cartwright

1 3 5 7 9 10 8 6 4 2

Designed and typeset by Crow Books
Printed by CPI Group (UK) Ltd, Croydon CR0 4YY

A CIP record for this book can
be obtained from the British Library

ISBN 978 1 78125 539 1
eISBN 978 1 78283 201 0

IRON TOWNS

ANTHONY CARTWRIGHT

SERPENT'S TAIL

We come through our black labyrinths, massed shadows. The fires are all out now. We are the smoke that patterns the brick. We are the iron roar that you thought you'd silenced. We sing to twisted metal and down long, flooded tunnels, across empty water and fields of rubble. We sing of better days.

'Dee Dee, that you?'

She knows who it is before he speaks, with what she takes to be the line's prison hiss, in the energy of a phone ringing when it shouldn't have. All these years spent willing it not to ring.

'You know it is,' she says, and walks down the hall, through the empty bar, chandeliers catch the morning light through a half-closed curtain, out into the yard. Red sky at morning over dead cranes at the Lascar docks.

'I wanna see her, Dee Dee.'

'Where are you?'

'I wanna see my baby.'

'You can't.'

'I wanna see my girl.'

'There are people here who'll kill you. You know that, don't you? Understand that?'

She thinks of her uncles, the way they used to sit around a table in the back room. She'd watch them through the blue smoke, the half-open door. There has always been a look that comes when people find out who she is, the people she is from. Their power has long gone. There is no one to kill him. He knows that full well, wherever he has been. And she has no intention of conjuring up a vanished world now. Back at school there'd been kids who'd said she was a witch. There have been plenty of times since she has wished it true.

'I'm gonna see her.'

'Where are you, Goldie?'

'I stayed away, Dee Dee. I kept away.'

'You stay away then, you hear, you keep it that way.'

It is hard to breathe. She thinks of the rattle the asthma pump makes as you shake it, the fizz of life as your lungs open. The pump is in the bathroom cabinet, feels a long way off.

'I'm already here,' he says, and she steps forward with a jolt into the rosy brightness of the yard. The smell of bleach rises from the concrete, a sense of things wiped clean. She looks at the jagged glass stuck in concrete atop the wall, half expects to see him come over it, his face, spiteful and handsome, across nearly twenty years, counting.

'You try anything, I'll kill you myself, I swear to god.'

Then comes the old manic glee in his voice.

'I'm already here Dee Dee, I never went nowhere. And I'm coming now, you mind that, darling, eh.'

Upstairs, the bureau is open in the spare room, dark wood against the yellow wallpaper. A square of sunlight comes through the net curtain and onto the wall. The furniture in here is all her nana's relics. Alina works at the bureau sometimes, sitting in the high-backed chair, face illuminated by her electric pad's screen, some art thing she's carried on with even though she's finished at college now. Dee Dee wants to ask her about it, holds back.

There is a photograph on the desk's green inlaid leather. There are photos stuffed in all the drawers, snapshots from when Dee

Dee was a kid, a posed portrait of her great-grandad wearing a turban and salwar kameez, with a waxed moustache, in sepia, is propped against the wall. She has intended to get a new frame for years. Alina told her that they made the colour by grinding little sea creatures into a paste.

She pauses for a moment. A passing lorry rattles the window-frame, she sees the roof of the 29 bus slide by, and is startled to see herself twenty years ago in the picture on the desk, though she has never made any effort to hide these photos. She sits with her arm in Sonia's. Their hair touches as they lean into each other. They wear identical outsized T-shirts, Dee Dee's yellow, Sonia's blue, which fall off their shoulders. The boys are standing, moving. Mark Fala and Goldie lean in the same direction, each with a foot raised as if to run or dance. They grin, the edges of their bodies blur with movement, a little out of focus, as if they are not fully there. Liam is caught in the act of rising, unfolding his long arms and legs, his skin unmarked. He looks at Dee Dee.

She looks away. The flyover in the distance creates a bar across the window, a horizon. In the mornings there is the dark shadow of the hills beyond. The afternoon sun dissolves them. She looks back.

They are on the roof at the flats, you can see the Lascar cranes in the background. The Falas' flat was in Stevedore House. She could lean out of the window now and probably make out this same block, this roof. *Is*, not *was*. They used to sunbathe up on the roof; it would be a good day for it today. She hasn't been down there for years, a distance of a mile, no more.

There was always the five of them back then. Who took

3

the picture? A shadow cuts across the frame. It is Mark's mum. Within a few months of taking this she will be dead. Within a few years, Sonia too. Goldie is looking somewhere off the roof. She is struck by how he and Liam look so similar in this picture, like her and Sonia. Her hand shakes. She wants to push Goldie, to send him running over that low wall and down to the ground below. Everything would be different. Everything is different now. His cracked voice across the years has changed the light in this room. If she had pushed him Sonia would be here. Alina would not be. Dee Dee considers this. This is why she does not look at old photographs, tries not to answer the phone. Everything would be different.

.   .   .

The Anvil Yards football ground. Irontown Football Club. An empty dressing room, the middle of summer. Out of season, out of luck. The sun shines through a narrow open window, onto the wooden benches, the bare treatment table, the tiled floor. The room smells of fresh paint and disinfectant, but linger, and underneath that is the smell of ancient liniment and sweat and thick winter mud that has soaked into the wood through the years.

The thin window shows an oblong of pitch. Gulls peck at the centre circle. They think it is a beach, perhaps, miles inland. They are the descendants of the birds who would follow the boats up the estuary and river and canal to the Ironport. Now they live on the council tip out towards Burnt Village, under the motorway. They hang in the dust that rises from the middle of the pitch. The club has opened the iron gates at the Greenfield End and run a car boot sale every Sunday since May. The sun has baked the mud.

The handle of the dressing-room door turns and turns again. From behind it there is a bang, a grunt, a sigh.

'Ted, Ted,' calls a voice. 'He's only painted this door shut.'

'What?'

'The door's slammed shut and the paint's dried. I told him to wedge it open. It won't budge.'

'Give it some iron.'

'I have. It's tight shut.'

The door handle rattles again.

'Jesus. The lads'll be here in a minute. The gaffer's here already. I've seen his car in the car park. He's got to meet them Portuguese. They've got that kid with them, the triallist, he looks about ten years old, I swear to god. They'll have him for bloody breakfast. I've got to get this kit laid out. We can't look any more of a shambles than we already am.'

'Liam's here somewhere. He's signing shirts in the Players' Lounge. Liam'll save us.'

In the empty room the men's voices fade as they move away down the tunnel. There is the occasional rattle of a seat in the grandstand above. Footsteps sound along the walkways. There are the ghost sounds of thousands of feet in the aisles, the ghost cries of great crowds, echoes of old songs, the clang of metal, the roar of a furnace, rattle of a tram, a siren across the docks.

Silence.

A clock ticks and then more voices come, clear now from behind the door.

'I'll have to force it.'

'Do what you've got to do, mate.'

There is a thud and the wood around the door handle splinters. The door is locked. The bolt twists and shreds the wood and the door bursts open into the room. Liam Corwen stands there in the light, rubs his shoulder, blinks.

Two men, half his size almost, crouch and haul the kit baskets into the room across the splinters.

'I thought you said it was stuck? You just needed the key.'

'Ah, well.'

'Don't worry about it, Liam. Thanks our kid.'

'Thanks Liam. You've saved us.'

He shrugs.

'You playing today, Liam?'

The big man shrugs again.

'Up to the gaffer. He says I need to rest, my age. I tell him I ain't got much time left, Ted. He might as well play me.'

'Good lad, Liam, good lad. Enjoy yourself if yer get on.'

Liam Corwen's is a face from a cigarette card, though they have not made them for forty years. They had something similar in boxes of teabags for a while when Liam was a kid, went the same way as the Austin Allegro and Saturday teatime wrestling.

In the dressing-room quiet Liam flicks back and forth from the magazine's cover, *Human Animal: People, Culture, Places, Trends*, to the pictures of him inside. He sits under his number 5 shirt on its peg, captain's armband slung on the hook. He doubts that he's starting, but sitting here, in his usual spot, will put him in Ally's eyeline and that might remind him to get him on at some point. It is possibly a good game to miss, all triallists and kids against a team of part-timers.

In image and biography, he is the acme of the modern footballer, Liam reads. *Body art, brushes with the law, two ex-wives, his first, Dee Dee Ahmed, former rebel in girl band Aurora and backing singer for nineties bands such as Massive Attack and Ocean Colour Scene, the other a Scandinavian underwear model. A career that failed to live up to its early promise (he holds the record for the shortest ever international career: less than a minute as an England substitute when he was eighteen). Now he's playing out his last days at Irontown, after returning from the obscurity of FC Kallevelo, of the Finnish Veikkausliiga. His hometown club, for whom he has made more appearances than anyone in their proud but luckless history, and for whom he has the extraordinary record of converting thirty-nine successive penalties across nearly twenty years, has fallen on the hardest of times.*

Look closer at those tattoos, though, and a different picture begins to emerge. Not the gothic script or Native American warriors of his contemporaries, but an entire history of football inked on his impressive frame. Great figures from the sport's golden age, such as Alfredo Di Stéfano and Eusébio, sit alongside more personal choices, from a chipped penalty that made Czechoslovakia European Champions in the seventies, to now obscure greats from before the First World War.

Why do it?

I'm a football man. I wanted to show myself as that, to celebrate it. It's been my life.

The photos make him look good, he gives them that. The

words don't matter. No mention of Tony, though. Tony has done every one of the tattoos except the one of Jari Litmanen. He got that done in Finland. Tony added the other Ajax players later. Edgar Davids autographed it after he'd played against him last season. Tony went over the signature that same night to make it part of the piece.

The piece. The work. That's what it's become.

'It's a piece of work, that,' is all his dad had said when he'd gone swimming with him at the Heathside Lido when Greta and Jari were here in the summer.

He wonders for a moment what Greta would make of being described as a Scandinavian underwear model. She'd probably just shrug. I did model underwear once, she might say. He doesn't know. She might have. She is hard to read. She is not his ex-wife. They are still married. He doesn't want to think about this right now. Dee Dee never sung for those bands either. Finland isn't even in Scandinavia. They never get it right.

As for brushes with the law, one driving ban and a caution for indecent exposure after pissing in a plant pot at the Hightown casino the night they won the old Division Three – a hundred points, a hundred goals – does not make him Ronnie Kray. It does not even make him the Ahmeds or Goldie Stone. And how has that memory drifted into his thoughts? He spends a lot of time not thinking about things. He stuffs the magazine under the bench out of sight. All reading material is banned from the dressing room.

. . .

The air parts for him as he runs, this kid. Defenders chase him like hounds after a stag in a medieval tapestry. Di Stéfano is just about old enough to be his dad, feels like it right now. It is two years since Hampden Park, might as well be twenty. Another European Cup Final, another northern night, Amsterdam, and the sky a darkening blue beyond the floodlights. The ball skims the turf, see the soles of Eusébio's boots as he hurdles into a follow-through. The ball flies inside the post. The crowd call his name. On the touchline a thin Dutch ballboy tries to move just like him.

A look goes between them, Di Stéfano and Eusébio. Some torch passed? Maybe this is the night, Di Stéfano thinks, his legs heavy as he strides back up the pitch, tries not to show it, two nil up, five three down. Maybe he thinks nothing of the sort. Great men, and the not so great, always believe that they have one more act, one more victory in them. But maybe this is the night he becomes an old man. An old man, who for a long while has been the best footballer in the world.

. . .

Joseph Stalin Corwen likes to drive up out of Black Park and above the Far Valley on the back road to get to the ground. He drives past the end of the terrace where his dad still lives, shored up with props against the lee of the hill, the house he grew up in. Joey knows all the lanes that web the hills, learned them twice over, as a boy and then in all his years as a postman. Up ahead are the Cowton high-rises. He knows them too, shudders at the thought of the November wind funnelling down the estate walkways, feels it now in his hip, and smiles at how he manages to conjure ideas of winter from a blue sky. White butterflies pattern the hedgerow.

His old man Eli refuses a lift to the match, refuses to acknowledge football at all until the cricket season is done with, has complained about the overlap for as long as anyone can remember. In some distant past football began the week after the Oval Test Match. Joey saw him this morning, left him sat in a deckchair by his back step, listening to the start of play on the radio and watching his cabbages with a glass of home-brew. Joey feels his dad's presence in the car, there in the passenger seat. Liam's too, as a boy, and more recently. Since Liam's driving ban Joey has ferried him around. He has no idea how he is getting to the game today, has not had any reply to his texts.

'Has he still not been in touch?' Liz asked him. 'Always the same, that boy. I don't know what went wrong.'

He pictures Liam riding there on the bus or the tram, can't quite put it past him, as if some Brylcremed ghost. Half the team used to travel on the 29 bus when Joey first started going to matches, 56-57. That was the year they played the Busby Babes in the cup. Same year they played Bishop Auckland six times with all the replays. It's why they're playing them today, a tradition revived. You can think what you like about Ally Barr, and Joey does not think much these days, but he likes to follow tradition.

Back then they would walk up out of the valley to Wrexham Road after his dad's shift had finished, catch the bus to the castle, then squeeze on the tram, the old tram that clattered through busy streets, through the Lowtown Bull-Ring and Lascar and across the river into the Anvil Yards. The air became heavier, wetter, as you came down the hill, closer to the rivers. The tram windows would steam up. When the works were open the fogs were worse. There'd be half a dozen Saturdays every season when you'd descend into it. He'd watched games when you could only see a third of the pitch, Stanley Matthews come slicing out of the gloom like Excalibur from the lake. There are moments now when Joey thinks they have all outlived themselves, him and his dad. Liam too, truth be told, still playing at almost forty, kids old enough to be his sons alongside him, skipping by him.

. . .

There is no Iron Town.

They are plural – Anvil Yards, Iron Towns – but the years have reduced them.

Back in the seventies the authorities made them singular, an act of rationalisation, enclosure.

You used to see the letter s graffitied on signs along bleak slip roads on the way out of Cardiff and Birmingham and Liverpool. Older people would scrawl addresses in bold: Anvil Yards, Iron Towns, and that used to make Joey Corwen smile on his post round. You don't see it so often these days. The Anvil Yards are close to empty. Joey is retired. The anger has died off, turned inward, assumed a hundred thousand different forms. Take the shiny new tram that goes nowhere in particular, from the Spider

House to the Heath, and see the messages on the bridges and the crumbling Victorian brick.

Lascar Intifada, Ddraig Pengwern, Kowton Bullet Krew.

The people of the towns tell themselves they have greater concerns than an abandoned letter s.

There is Hightown, with its cliff and ruined castle keep that looks west for insurgents who never come. There is Lowtown and its Spider House and markets. Oxton and Cowton, with their Rangers and Celtic supporters' clubs, high-rises of third genera-tion Glaswegian families who once thought they were moving south for a better go of things, the Sheep Folds beyond them where the roads run out. There is Salop, and Calon, with their avenues of sycamores and 1930s villas. And pit villages all along the Far Valley and Welsh Ridge. There are no pits. The villages are emptying out. The Iron Towns are shrinking. Lascar and the Ironport have their vacant docks and rusting cranes, Chaintown has its dark terraces that have dodged the wrecking ball. There's the Pengwern estate, a lost pebble-dashed valley edged by canals and scrap. Then there's the Heath, remnants of wildness and witches and common land, and the long roads of Heathside on its fringes, with its golf club, and Tory councillors, and dreams of a different England.

And there along the valley bottom, between the two rivers, is the Anvil Yards, a maze of ancient works and roofless brick fac-tory buildings. The blocks of the old Greenfield Ironworks stand at its heart like some secret kaaba. Names from the glory days of a revolution appear on road signs and raised in metal. Newcomen and Stephenson and Darby and Boulton and Watt. And there at its edge, hard against the bank of the River Chain, is the football ground, built to look like one of the factories, still going, creaking into life for another season, one more year. There is talk of tearing it down, that the club will fold soon, the same talk there has been during all its years in the wilderness, much of the last hundred years. But it's there for one more season. And even now, people come through the spaces between the empty factories, just not so many of them any more. They shuffle up the remaining terrace and sit on clacking seats in the stand, huddled, laughing and grumbling against whatever might come next.

. . .

'Are you Dee Dee Ahmed, pet?'

She drops the tray of freshly washed glasses at her feet. They clatter across the lino behind the bar and by some miracle don't break. Not one. There are half-hearted cheers from the few drinkers in the lounge.

'Sorry my love, I'm sorry. I never meant to startle yer.'

The man leans against the bar and talks in a soft north-east accent. Dee Dee looks at him, realises he is not some ghost come to haunt her, but just a man standing at a bar early Saturday afternoon having a pint before the football.

'Yes. Yes I am,' she says, wipes her hands on her apron, bends at her knees to crouch and put the spilled glasses onto a shelf.

'Someone told me you ran this place.'

She nods. Sun comes through the pub's high windows.

'I saw you sing,' the man says, 'a few times I think. I was a roadie for a bit. Charcoal, The Carnations. Newcastle bands, you know?'

Dee Dee nods again, not quite sure where this is going, folds her arms. He does not look like a friend of Goldie's, not at all, in his Hendrix T-shirt, tugging at his earring.

'I don't sing any more.'

'Well, life moves on, I suppose. King Tut's, I saw you. Then that Primal Scream gig in Newcastle. I don't have much to do with it either now. Not at all?'

'In the shower, maybe.'

He looks down at his pint and smiles. She thinks he might even be blushing above the start of a beard.

'Well you had a lovely voice, Dee Dee, pet. I'm sure you still do. That's all I wanted to say.'

He sees his drink off and looks at her and smiles. Warm, she thinks, kind.

She mumbles thanks.

'You take care of yourself.'

'I'll try,' she says, 'I'll try.'

He's already gone. There's a group of them down from County Durham for the afternoon from what she can tell. The man's companions get up from their table by the door. An old bloke in a flat cap, maybe his dad, and a young lad in a blue-quartered football shirt, his son, she reckons, a couple of other men, short sleeves and tattoos, different ages. It's a long way to come on a summer's afternoon, for a pint in the Salamander and a game of football at the Anvil Yards. It happens all year, though, from places like Rochdale and Hartlepool and Mansfield.

Names from the football coupon. At least they can enjoy the sunshine today.

She keeps her arms folded across her chest. Running a pub is no way to hide yourself.

. . .

The club was founded by bearded Victorian men, Methodists, cricketers after some winter training. They stare out of old photographs like Marx and Nietschze. The only Anglican of the group, the fifth James Greenfield, heir to the Greenfield Ironworks, was an old Etonian. That's why the club's shirts are Eton Blue. Ted hangs them on the dressing-room hooks. Eton Blue is pale green against wood panelling.

The gas lamp under which Iron Towns Football Club was formed in November 1874 had been preserved until the late sixties, when the square on which it stood was demolished to build the flyover. Mount Zion, the chapel, was taken down brick by numbered brick and reassembled a few miles down the road at the Heritage Museum. There is talk of doing similar to the closed East Stand and its iron railings, a joke that they might have to do the same to Liam Corwen.

. . .

Where the lane meets Wrexham Road Joey hears drumming come like squalls of rain across the fields. At the junction he winds down the window. He sees a police girl, a wisp of blonde hair astray across her cheek. She walks in the middle of the road, her right arm up to slow the traffic. In front of her Joey sees a broad back and a bowler hat. The Orangemen, of course. He's forgotten all about them. It's still marching season. They linger on past all thoughts of the Boyne and into early August here. Everything goes on too long, Joey thinks.

He recognises the bulk of the man who limps out in front, sees him in profile as he turns his head. Pink veins mark his face, comb lines run through his steel coloured hair. His white shirt collar has rubbed a red line on his neck. Joey gets a strange sense of looking at himself. Not that this kind of thing is his cup of tea.

The sash my father wore, they sing, tuneless and lost in the wind.

It's Billy Kerr, he knows him from years back. Billy's dad had been a miner, worked the same shift as Joey's at Black Park. The sun shines on Billy's Brassoed ceremonial chain. He walks like he's got corns. Half a dozen others straggle along with him. An old boy limps with the flag held out in front. A handful of kids march along the verge. They wear berets. There's a boy on a drum, a boy on a flute. A handful of scattered spectators stand on the corner by the shops. A woman comes out of the butchers' with a bag of square sausage, puts her arm out for the bus, oblivious.

'To see my British brethren all of honour and of fame.'

Joey looks at these men, red blotches the shapes of empire on their faces.

The road dips away here and the Iron Towns spread out beneath them. The castle stands bone white against its hill and the ground falls away again beyond it to a patchwork of dark buildings and the green bowl of the hills. There is a glimmer of the rivers and the canal and docks at the Ironport. Joey tries to pick out the floodlight pylons at the ground. From here it all looks the same as it ever did. No smoke, no fire, of course, but the shape of it is the same, more or less. He can see all the way to the Goat Wood, past the training ground, at the far end of the Heath, where when he was a kid they said witches met in the clearings, where the people killed a German parachutist during the war, stuffed his body in an old mine shaft and never told anyone about it. His ghost joined all the others. There is no noise from the valley like there once was, carried up the rivers on the wind, just the notes of a flute and rattle of a drum drifting off into English summer air.

'If the call should come we'll follow the drum, and cross that river once more.'

He has no doubt they would, despite their ragged look. Under the castle, there in the wall that marks the boundary with Lowtown, is the Crusader stone. It's where they met to leave to go to Worcester and follow the Lionheart on his holy war. Joey likes his history. The stone itself is much older, left by Druids on their exodus west, patterned with lichen and faint Ogham lettering. They say Manawydan forged shields on it. This had been one of the cities of the legions, its name lost in time. The Pals Brigades would touch the stone for luck before they left for the First World War. They would have looked just as ragged, men and boys full of a strange anger, dreaming of Jersualem and Mons, followed by patient crows.

A few cars line up behind his. A horn sounds. The police girl follows the heavy union flag into the turning for the shops and the Cowton Orange Lodge, which sits flat-roofed on a car park of sparkling broken glass. She waves everyone down the hill. There is nothing more to see.

. . .

The city and the country Eusébio was born in are no longer there. Or rather, their names have changed, as has so much else with time and war. They are different places. It used to say *This is Portugal* high up on the dock buildings, and in the look in people's eyes, for better or much, much worse. It wasn't, of course, wrong continent, wrong hemisphere, except in some ways it was. Such is empire.

That night in Amsterdam, the shooting at home is soon to start, has already begun in Angola, where his dad was born. His brother is ready to lift his gun. Eusébio has left the hammering sun and the glitter of the bay of Lourenço Marques. *This is Portugal* he would see as he ran with his feet barely touching the ground.

And Barracas, Buenos Aires, too is changed utterly, transfigured by rust and the years of the generals. Di Stéfano remembers being taken to see the old iron bridge pulled down. The men spoke in hushed Italian dialects. His dad was from the island of Capri, his mother was German, Irish. Europe was finished for them. He is Argentinian, becomes Colombian, becomes Spanish. Barracas is a place of shadows now, empty factories and stock yards. Trains clatter through, don't stop.

But these are men of movement, do not look back, keep the world spinning with their footsteps.

. . .

Paul, her bar manager, puts his head round the corner of the lounge.

'You've got a visitor at the off sales, Dee Dee.'

'What?'

'Don't worry. Just your usual Saturday dinner gentleman caller.'

She doesn't know why she's kept the hatch open. She tells herself it was what her nana would've liked, but times change. Dee Dee used to sit on a stool in the space between the bar and the lounge on long ago Sundays and watch her nana serve at the hatch which opens onto Meeting House Lane. At 3 o'clock they'd lock the doors and she'd always do a song or two in the empty lounge bar under the chandeliers before they went upstairs for dinner.

Mark Fala stands at the counter. He's spread a pile of change across it. No more than a pound, she can see, runs her hand over it. There are a couple of washers, an old Italian coin. Lira doesn't even exist any more. She can't tell if he's serious, pulls a bottle of sherry from the shelf and some cans of cider from the chiller nevertheless. She takes down forty Superkings too, her own, not even the pub's, although it's the same thing she supposes. She bought them at the new Ukrainian shop.

'All right, Mark,' she says.

'Thanks Dee Dee. I appreciate it.'

'You take care of yourself,' she says, looks at the shadow under his eye, can't decide if it's a bruise or not.

He doesn't move straight away, sways a little, as he arranges his bottle and cans into his plastic bag. He stuffs the cigarettes deep into his overcoat pocket. He used to go weeks without speaking at all. He has always shown up here though, always early in the afternoon on matchdays. She wonders if he used to walk down here with his dad when he'd been a kid, something pulls him back, not just a few handouts. There are plenty of people who'll give him them.

'You got anything for me dog, Dee Dee?'

'Your dog? I didn't know you had a dog, Mark.'

He shrugs.

'Sometimes.'

She reaches to the back shelf, pulls a couple of bags of scratchings off the thin cardboard display.

'Thanks, Dee Dee,' he says, 'thanks. I'll see you soon.' And he turns and limps away. She'll get him some shoes, she thinks, but doesn't know if he'd accept them. He doesn't have to dress like he does. He's not down and out. She knows he still lives in the flats, although they're slated to come down when they begin the work. When he turns the corner at the sagging wall his shadow angles across the road and a smaller, lower shadow follows.

She has kept the hatch open for Mark Fala, of course. That's how things work. People do things for him. She stands and catches the sunlight on her face, mouths a song to herself, slow and quiet, hears the bell ringing for service in the lounge.

. . .

There is no match traffic. There isn't when the season is in full swing, so certainly not today. Clouds move up the River Anvil, high and slow over the cars and floodlights and cranes. An ice cream van has pulled into the kerb by the car park entrance. Joey considers buying one. A lone figure stands nearby with a pile of new copies of the fanzine. New season special! The fanzine is called *46 seconds*. It angers Joey every time he sees one. His boy played for England and all people do is take the piss. They say he never touched the ball, even, but he did, he won a header, a flick-on. People never get anything right.

He puts his hand up to acknowledge the seller, a young, balding man, prematurely aged, wears a hearing aid, and whose name Joey can never remember, with the new away shirt spread across his belly. This shirt's official colour is chocolate, another legacy of the Greenfield family. James Greenfield played cricket, briefly, for Surrey, and the shirt is the colour of their county cap. Like dog shit on a lawn, Ally Barrr once said when the team had been given a hiding somewhere, Plymouth or Yeovil was it? Some team in green. Everyone says they hate these brown shirts, but they are the only thing at the club that turns a profit. They get orders from Salt Lake City and Mannheim and Daegu, men young and old buying a piece of football folklore.

Joey turns in through the club gates. In front of the offices, a couple of Mercedes shine in the sun and Ally's BMW, a new car for the new season courtesy of Lionel Ahmed, who had probably intended it for Liam. The Mercedes must belong to the Portuguese, already here. Joey decides against pulling into the space marked *Club Captain/LC*, drives instead across the tarmac to the unpaved ground under the fence by the canal. He sits in the meshed shadow for a while, thinks about moving the car to the shade. It looks cool under the solid end wall of the old Watkins Cylinder Works. Ivy has grown and spilled down a length of the wall. Elder branches arc over the towpath. Everything is still. From the tunnel of branches comes a man, limping, limping and swaggering in equal parts. He wears a long overcoat in spite of the weather and a football boot on his left foot, an unlaced brogue on his right, a carrier bag of drink swings from his wrist. The shoes account in part for the limp. His face stays in shadow but Joey knows full well who it is.

Mark Fala's walk has retained some of the old character it used to bring to a football pitch, although he's not stepped on one for nearly twenty years. Wasps swim out above the water, zigzag against the pattern of the brick, as if they move for him. Joey would not bet against it. That boy. Mark drops his head and disappears from sight under the bridge. Joey sits for a while.

A fox walks along the towpath in the same direction as Mark, nose up, a patch of grey-orange fur missing from its flank and its ribs sticking through, but shiny eyed and alert. Following him, Joey thinks, not just chance, trotting along there with his nose up, on to a scent. Joey tries not to believe in bad luck. They say there's a curse on the ground. He missed that fucking penalty on purpose, for one thing, is what Joey thinks. The fox goes on its way into the gloom under the bridge. More thoughts of carrion.

. . .

They are not Portuguese. None of them are, even the young lad himself, Luis, who is from Cape Verde.

'This is Liam Corwen, club captain,' Ally says. Liam shakes hands with the two men who have stepped from the Mercedes. He sees himself and Ally reflected in their sunglasses. Another man sits in shadow in the rear of one of the cars, does not move. Liam turns to the young kid who stands next to them in his green tracksuit. His hand feels like a little boy's. Liam thinks of Jari, thinks of his hand in his.

'Liam, these are Luis's representatives.'

'I'm sure they are, gaffer.'

Ally gives him a look, but what to say?

Ally worked at Sporting Lisbon, coached there under Malcolm Allison, so this Portuguese bit at least sounds true. The rest is a mystery. One thing Liam is certain of is that only he and this slight boy he now leads down the corridor's torn lino to the dressing room are not set to make something from this little pantomime. Steve Stringer's absence only adds to Liam's suspicion. The club secretary holds the place together, haunts it in his baggy, grey suits, invisible most of the time, filling out forms and talking on the phone in his office, which sits gloriously out of time, with stencilled lettering on frosted glass, inside the West Stand. The directors meet every now and again for some sausage rolls and a chat about the season. The club is owned by the last of the Greenfield family – Dorothea Greenfield-Carter – who lives out her old age in the Madeira sun. The last of the line, she refuses to invest, or sell, or do anything at all with her absolute control of the club.

Liam knows the look that comes from behind the glasses. Older men watch much younger ones and calculate what they might make from them. Reflected glory, reflected youth, cold, hard cash. Not that Luis's representatives, as Ally calls them – Ally is good with the jargon – are that old. Liam is maybe even giving them a few years, smooth skinned men in expensive suits, the world shining in their glasses. They are of indeterminate ethnicity, a phrase Liam read in the paper, but then aren't we all, he thought at the time. And the boy looks about fourteen. What must he make of this, on his route from Cape Verde to Lisbon to who knows where via the Anvil Yards? Liam ushers him towards a corner of the dressing room.

'You know Eusébio?'

'Eusébio?' The kid has no idea what he is talking about.

Liam untucks his shirt and lifts it to show two men inked onto his right flank. Eusébio and Di Stéfano look at each other at a moment of passing, the 1962 European Cup Final, Benfica 5 Real Madrid 3. Eusébio has just scored.

'Eusébio,' Luis grins, says the name again but it sounds different this time.

'He played here, you know. Trained here. Three times. For the Rest of the World, for Portugal in the World Cup, and with Benfica, before the cup final against United. Played here.'

'Here?'

Luis looks around at the dressing room, widens his eyes. He is quick, Liam senses. He bets he can run like water.

'Right here, yeah. You think I'm pulling yer leg.'

Liam smiles and so does the boy. The Eusébio stuff is all true. In the sixties the club was in the second division but the Greenfield family still had some say at the Football Association, told everyone that the Iron Towns were an easy drive to Wembley.

Liam points again at the picture.

'Real Madrid,' Luis says.

'Yeah, Di Stéfano.'

'And this one?'

The boy points to a dark-eyed figure, a glitter to his eyes and a toothpick clamped in the corner of his mouth, his gaze equal parts magic and menace.

'Billy Meredith.'

'And this one?'

The dark-eyed man looks at a pale-faced boy in an old-fashioned England shirt, his face open and innocent.

'Steve Bloomer.'

For a while he and Tony had concentrated on pairs, on great players as they passed each other on the way up, on the way down. There's one of Van Basten coming on as sub for Ajax, Cruyff coming off, holding his hand out to shake.

'I don't know this ones.'

'Old players.'

'You have Ronaldo?'

'The old one, the Brazilian one. I'm not allowed players who are still playing.'

It is true, but Liam sets the rules himself. He feels good saying it, though, like this was some bigger thing than himself.

Liam unbuttons his shirt, takes it off, stretches his arms out to the sides and turns to show Luis the image of Ronaldo between his shoulder blades, arms outstretched too, as Christ the

Redeemer above Rio. They copied it from a tyre advert but put him in his Barcelona shirt.

'I like Ronaldo. This one. But Cristiano is better.'

'You play like him?'

The boy laughs. 'More like Messi, maybe.' He grins.

Liam likes this lad. God knows what he is doing here.

. . .

The film is from a January morning. Alina has recorded so much now that she is months behind with what she watches. This one is possible, though. Although possible for what she is not sure, some exhibition that exists only in her head. When there was no cloud those winter mornings were good, better than the summer glare, something to do with the angle at which the sun comes over the hill at Burnt Village. To think she didn't know the sun rose at different places, from different angles, until she'd started this work. Hardly work, really. She didn't know what to call it, thinks instead of a word to describe the light and is left scratching her head. Sunrises, sunsets were not thought of as appropriate subject matter at art school, but still. The sunrise is not really the subject. We are flying through space on a giant rock.

There is a thin line of blue above the far hills. Yellow streetlights pattern the foreground, then there is the dark mass of the docks and the Anvil Yards. Venus shines bright above a black hill. The blue line broadens, lightens slowly. A red sun comes up into the blue band. Plane contrails form between what clouds there are. On the far hillside Burnt Village looks just that as the sun appears to swallow it. The outline of charred houses is silhouetted against the sun. Light and shade ripple across the valley, then the light evens, as the sun, golden now, rises behind clouds.

It's fine. It's OK. The light is good. The way it comes green down the hillsides might make you think of a time there were no towns here at all. But it's not what she wants.

Then she has a thought, simply plays it backwards. The sun sinks back towards the middle of England. The light fades, slowly, slowly, then fast. The hills burn again, then that last band of blue takes ages to disappear. But time has reversed, run back on itself. And it is so very simple. She wonders now if this is too simple, too easy, no soundtrack, no other explanation, nothing. But that is exactly what she wants: time running backwards, time lapsing, folding in on itself.

. . .

'Blisters, fucking blisters, but.'

The dressing room is hot and silent.

'Blisters. Unbelievable. Professional footballers who cannot think to look after their feet.'

They sit and stare at the tiles. Julius Williams has a wet towel over his head. Steam rises from it. Kyran Blackstock, one of the kids who has come up from the youth team, grins and tries to catch someone's eye to highlight this phenomenon. Liam gives him a look and he puts his head down, eyes to the floor. Kyran won't last five minutes, Liam thinks.

They are not all professionals. Ally's wrong on that

score. They're still playing triallists, got a couple of lads over from Ireland, an attempt to get a few more warm bodies in before the season starts.

They are two nothing down to a team of part-timers. The pitch is a moonscape. Ally needs something on which to focus his anger. Liam watches him. The man is chewing, red faced, as if sick of the world and the injustice of it all, but Liam can tell he is trying to work himself into this anger, moving his false teeth up and down his gums. He's had enough. This, with everything else, does not bode well for the season ahead. It's as if Ally knows what he should do, knows how he should be feeling, knows the rage these players expect and deserve, as he looks from face to face, but the anger isn't there. He's finished, Liam thinks suddenly to himself. Ally breathes hard, looks at the wall, pulls at his shirt collar. He's in his third spell as Irontown manager, is sixty-six now. One more season, he told himself, back in May, kidded himself if he could get a decent couple of players in they might be good for the play-offs, delusional. Finish with one last promotion. One last bit of pride. He is a man who believes he was destined for bigger things than this. He played on the fringe of the Lisbon Lions team, the Quality Street Gang after that, grew up in Finnieston, like Danny McGrain who always got picked before him, chased the ball on the cinders under the crane as a kid, a Protestant boy who played proudly at Celtic, like McGrain and Dalglish, like Jock Stein himself. He has half a team complaining about their feet.

'Fucking blisters.'

This is how Liam comes to get on that afternoon, not that things improve much. They let in another goal ten minutes from the end after a scramble in the six yard box following a corner. Liam loses his man, their big striker, and he hopes Ally does not see it in the dust storm.

The kid barely gets a kick. Liam has almost forgotten about him in the humiliation, the day's touch of glamour, this boy on his way into or out of Sporting Lisbon, as if, and somehow playing here en route. Then in the last minute Liam thumps a clearance from twenty yards inside his own half, more out of frustration than with any intent, and he is there, Luis, and sways into the ball, takes it on his right thigh, dead, swivels and flicks it with his left foot past the moving defender, takes a step, hits it on the volley, all in one movement, with his laces. The ball fizzes and dips twenty-five yards, as if it's a different object from the one that has bobbled around for the previous ninety minutes, clips the outside of the post with a satisfying ping and rebounds back to the edge of the box off the advertising boards with a deep thud before their keeper has even moved.

It was Cruyff who claimed he used to sometimes try to hit the post on purpose. Cruyff is the pale Dutch ballboy. He tries to move like Eusébio, like Di Stéfano.

Half the crowd have already gone. From the ones who remain, many weren't looking. There is a jolt from a few, and a handful of oohs and applause drifts across the pitch. Some of the young lads behind the goal begin to sing *Sign him up*. These are the boys who sometimes come to matches wearing a fez, a homage to an old newspaper headline 'Ally Barr bars baa baas', a reference to the time Ally tried to get the livestock market to close on Wednesday match days. That was in the days when Ally thought he could do anything, took the club from the bottom of the third division to that missed penalty kick in the play-off final away from the Premier League. He could do little wrong then. The market has gone for good now anyway. The boys laugh as they sing, because they know that there are bigger forces at work. This kid, listed as 'A.N. Other' on the programme, in a nice Edwardian touch, is not destined for the Anvil Yards.

Liam glances up at the grandstand. Spits out some of the dust. They don't know what they're looking at, most of them, the punters, he is convinced. If they see anything as good as that for the rest of the season they'll be lucky. The ref blows for full-time before they take the goal kick.

. . .

Di Stéfano traps the ball as it falls from the keeper's kick, rolls his studs over it (over *her*, he writes in a book years later called, *Thanks, Old Girl*). He turns to his right, with his back to goal he is moving left, but he keeps turning, almost a complete circle, away from the Eintracht player, and now takes a couple of paces. Strange how his legs seem longer when he has the ball. He feints, sways as if to strike it wide for Canário, but stops, almost entirely still for a moment. His opponent runs from him and he moves forward now, builds momentum, pushes it to Vidal, gets it back, has to check his run, but from his heels springs forward, slides it towards Puskás with the outside of his boot, looks to sprint for the return, but as Puskás opens himself the defender has nicked it away. The defenders are not often so lucky.

It is like this all night, *la furia*, changes of pace, of direction, unrelenting. Like this, he moves through people's dreams. When he gets the ball the blood quickens in the eighth of a million people inside the stadium. They have laid down their iron on the banks of the Clyde to come to see him in the European Cup Final, to see the great Real Madrid make it five in a row. He walks, he sprints, he stands still. Hampden is his time, his space, to do with as he wishes.

. . .

Liam sits on the bed in the room. He has lived at the hotel for three weeks now, since pre-season training began, since Greta and Jari went back, got a deal from the manager, Amir, an old school mate. He thinks he might never leave.

He stands for some time at the window, stretching his calf muscles, looks out across the Anvil Yards. A crow flies from the floodlight gantry to the East Stand roof. The gulls wheel over the empty dock water.

In a few minutes he'll turn on the laptop. The bedside clock blinks and tells him it is still too early. She said seven o'clock, nine in Finland. Long blocks of shadow fill the view. He imagines the white Northern light filling rooms; the light across the lake fills the house, Greta and Jari move through the rooms. She is combing his hair while he stands in his pyjamas. Liam's body aches. She lets Jari stay up when they're at the lake house. He can feel the grooves of the pine jetty under his feet. He has a blister on his right heel. He can hear the sound of the water lapping against the wood. You can't open the windows here in the hotel. He wants some air, wants to hear the sound of the gulls, the sound of traffic, of cars going somewhere else; the sound of water on a thin beach and the silence of great forests beyond. He cannot see a single human movement across the whole of the Anvil Yards, Saturday teatime, no one there. He looks at the ruin of the old Assembly Rooms, where his own parents met the year of the World Cup, talked about Eusébio. They used to hold under-age club nights there before the dancefloor fell into a hole. He remembers queueing up to get in on a summer night, Dee Dee and Sonia in the line in front of him, and Sonia turning round and looking at him over her bare shoulder.

'What a fucking mess,' he says, and his words colour the glass.

A dirty St George's flag that hangs from the corner of an old warehouse moves in a sudden breeze, pigeons rise and veer together across the old docks wall and away towards the Greenfield Ironworks. His face has caught the sun, his nose and cheeks have reddened. He enjoys the small burn of it. That pitch, a corner of which he can see here over the river and through the gates at the Greenfield End, is a desert. He pictures Laurel and Hardy in the Foreign Legion, going in circles. A helicopter comes down the line of the hills and river, angles in at the corner of the window, moves away to turn and head back up the valley towards Cowton or Oxton. He tries to make his mind as empty as the pitch, the dock, the long stretches of wasteland that radiate out from the old ironworks.

There is Greta on the screen. He can tell she's made an effort, has done her hair, some make-up. That's good, he thinks.

Something has happened to the sound, so he watches them moving in the patterns of the water reflected from the lake. Jari refuses to stay in front of the camera, Greta reaches for him, her arms bare. Liam sobs, lets it out now, leans away so he is out of the picture. One time last year he started, couldn't stop.

'Daddy sad,' Jari said.

'Never do that again, never,' Greta hissed down the phone a few days after that. It was when things had been bad, worse than now.

'Daddy,' Jari says. The boy's face, his hair. He holds a blue plastic robot. It's the one he chose on one of the last days of their visit when Liam's mum and dad had driven them out to the ToysRus by the motorway.

The small amount of English that Jari had learned is fading. Greta says she uses it with him but Liam doesn't believe her. He never learned Finnish. Greta speaks Finnish, Swedish, German, Russian. There'd been no need for him to learn, he picked up the odd phrase, he was always the Englishman, the big man, always set apart, in the corner of the dressing room, in the centre of the pitch. It had suited him, he thought. Now he looked at his son babbling away into the camera. They would not speak the same language.

'*Kaunis poika*,' he says, beautiful boy. He knows a few words, should get those tapes out again, god knows he's got enough time on his hands. They say it's one of the hardest languages to learn. Jari is a beautiful boy.

Then he is gone, there's just that flickering light from the lake and Greta, distracted, a quick goodbye, neutral. Just stay, he wants to say, leave the camera on, go about your business, I'll just sit and watch from here. They arrange to speak during the week.

He looks at the blue plastic bag on the table he'd meant to put in the bedside fridge. The cans of beer inside sweat, there are a couple of bottles of Lucozade and a packet of jaffa cakes next to the bag. He'll run the beers off on the Heath tomorrow, dress the blister, take it easy and stretch himself out for Monday's training. Archie Hill's got him on a special programme. The aches are starting. He can feel his heel, his hip, his back, all start to go. He'll watch the rest of the cricket highlights, read his book, about Real Madrid in the fifties. He can read about Di Stéfano, Puskás, Gento. He can do that. He can phone his dad to talk about the match if he wants to. He wonders about that boy, Luis. Ally's car is still in the car park. The Mercedes have gone. He stands at the window and watches the blue evening fade.

. . .

INTERVIEWER: But you are hopeful, Ally, for the season to come?

ALLY BARR: It's August. Listen son, in August there's always hope.

INTERVIEWER: Even in Irontown?

ALLY BARR: Even in the Iron Towns.

LIAM CORWEN (aside): Wait until September.

(Laughter)

. . .

A dead pigeon hangs in the mesh suspended from the giant concrete awning. The Lowtown bus station is choked with fumes and lit by yellow strip-lights, even though the sun shines brightly on the building's open side. Goldie waits for his bag, muses on the pigeon. He wants to feel something, something to make it all seem real. Twenty years can be a lifetime, as well he knows. Though the twenty years in his head seem longer than the ones that have passed here. Prison time lasts longer in some ways, in other ways does not pass at all. It wasn't like he'd been in prison all that time anyway, less than half if you added it all up. He had made a life in Birmingham with Nadine, and look what that had come to now, same as everything else. The pastel coloured murals, the daytime twilight, the food stalls, are all the same as the last time he came here. He remembers now, waiting for Sonia and Dee Dee to come back on the London bus from an audition, a Friday night not long after he first got a car. Excited, all of them. Liam and Mark were with him, must have been June, outside the football season, otherwise Liam would've been tucked up behind the net curtains in his nice Black Park bedroom. It might well be that he has come back to slit Liam Corwen's throat.

On Fridays a big van used to pull up on the waste ground outside, where the football coaches parked, and set off racing pigeons. They would rise with their wings sounding like applause. He'd had a row once, stupid, in the workshops at Winson Green about whether pigeons and doves are the same bird, different colours. *This is what it sounds like* . . . There was a Prince tape he wore out playing in the car and on the roof at Mark's flats. It was the one that was playing when they crashed. Pigeons can fly, he thinks, and wonders why these ones choose to stay here, pecking at scraps of burger and dying in the rafters.

'This yours, chief?' A Brummie accent, the driver wants to get a move on, has to go back the other way in twenty minutes or so.

'Thanks, mate.' Goldie hauls the kit-bag onto his shoulder, an army surplus, he bought it at a kiosk in the Rag Market. He thought it might make him look like a soldier back on leave. It just makes him look like who he is, what he is. He can see his reflection in the glass barrier. When he looks away he sees the departure board. Buses to Manchester, London, Holyhead/ Dublin. He has been to none of these places. He could head to the ticket counter, go for whichever bus comes first. He can do what he likes. He feels the same weightlessness he had that morning, walking down through Digbeth, leaving the city that had been his home in one way or another for much of the past twenty years, his adult life. He can go wherever he wants. But he knows what he's doing. He asked for a ticket to Lowtown.

'Return, love?'

'I ain't coming back.'

But coming back is exactly what he is doing. The bus only took an hour and a half, came the long way too. He is deflated by the paltriness of the distance, the way time collapses. In his head it is like the crossing of a great continent. There was traffic on the Hagley Road.

He wants this to feel like an occasion. He puts his hand to his jacket pocket. There's a roll of notes, a couple of half-smoked spliffs and a little tub of diazepam. One of Nadine's brothers must have borrowed the coat. Goldie hasn't smoked for years.

He doesn't need any more paranoia. He thinks they might come after him. He can sell the tablets. The place won't have changed that much.

There used to be a bar just here, been done out as a café now, you can see in through the windows and out to the market on the other side. There are plastic tables with umbrellas out on the concrete. The windows were blacked out in those days. The Eight Ball, it was called. Sometimes Stan Ahmed himself would sit there at the bar, his thick arms resting on it. A few times Goldie was told to call in there, get his instructions, explain himself. More usually it was at the bookies at the corner of the docks road in Lascar. Goldie tried to read the signs, what a meeting here or there might signify. He could never tell whether he was being spoken to because he had done something well or not, if he was on his way up or down.

He feels something now. He looks in through the window at the young girl serving, scans the faces at the tables quickly. Maybe that old man there, maybe, with his blue eyes staring out of the window towards the markets, is that a flicker of recognition? It jolts him. He knows that Stan Ahmed has long gone, to his villa first, and then a private hospital somewhere near Marbella. Stan's brothers too, sold up, moved out, or ruined, inside, or dead, a little bit of all these things in the aftermath of a fallen empire. Lionel's still around, he knows that. He is exposed here, looking at his own shadow. The old man stares through the window, takes a sip of tea, his eyes pass over Goldie, look through him. Something like disappointment makes him sag a little. He wants to hide, wants to be seen.

He wanders through the light and shade of the market edges. This is dangerous now, the Lowtown Bull Ring. Things don't change that much here. Maybe twenty years is not so long. The woman there at the fruit stand with the perm, didn't he used to collect money from her on a Friday?

'Tell him, he'll have the rest next week, chick.'

'He won't be happy, darling, I can tell yer that for nothing.'

And there at the taxi rank, where the drivers lean against their cabs and flick through the papers, stroke their phones, wasn't he one of Lionel Ahmed's little crew? The man turns his thick neck out of the sun, puts his hand on the car top, see: only three fingers. People said that Lionel had cut his mate's fingers off over a girl they both liked, but that was crap, a length of steel cable had torn it off at the Ironport. It's him. Goldie cannot remember the bloke's name, ducks his head, weaves between the shoppers. It all hits him now. He keeps his head down. Every glance now, he's like a kid in a story lost in a wood, faces in the branches stare out at him. And he feels the darkness creeping in at the edges of his vision as sweat runs into his eyes. There, and there, and there, and that girl in her summer dress just there, Sonia's face looks back at him. Sonia's face back then, still twenty years old and full of life. He edges past the man with henna in his beard, selling batteries from a pink plastic bucket, meets the fence, walks along it, away from the market, expects to hear his name called, expects footsteps behind him, feels the weight of the bag on his shoulders, although god knows what is in it for it to weigh like this, everything he owns, and the money from behind the panel at the back of the airing cupboard, and his knives. He worked in the kitchens at the hospital when he first came out on licence, was lucky to get a place doing anything, taught him how to use a knife. They will come after him. He walks with the market behind him now, lines of buses between him and the bus station. This road runs down into the Anvil Yards. And here, there's a gap in the fence, signs warning of dogs and security, but he'll take his chances. He slips through the gap, sun bounces off the bus windows, and he glances back at not a soul around, goes down a set of crumbling blue brick steps where nettles and dock leaves grow, and into the shadows again.

. . .

There are rooms in this house that no one has stepped inside for years. No one has ever been in that extension, she's sure of it, since the builders finished years ago. By the time that was done Dee Dee and Liam were already coming apart. Dee Dee chose the child over him and that was the end of that.

This is a family home. Liz looks out of the leaded window at the turn in the stairs, looks out at the green hills turning blue in the distance, the roses in the garden below. That lawn is dying. This house is more than most people dream of, she thinks, the kind of house people might climb the hill to get a glimpse of, drive past on summer evenings, on Sunday afternoons, and say one day, if all our ships come in, we'll live somewhere like this. Liam bought it from a consultant at the Bethel, Mr Jenkins, same one who'd operated on Joey's mum that first time, small world they said. Small world for sure, it was Mr Jenkins's replacement,

Mr Ali, who spoke to Liz in that hot, side-room off the ward and discussed procedures and ways forward and strategies to contain and then eradicate her cancer. You knew it was bad if they ushered you into those little rooms. They never used to use the word itself. Your nan is very ill they said to Liam and the girls when it was Joey's mum's turn; Molly is very ill they would tell people, and people would nod and understand.

Liam and Dee Dee were twenty-one, same age as when she and Joey got married, except they'd moved into his mum and dad's back bedroom, waited on the council list. She remembers having no idea how Liam could afford it, but he'd played for England, Dee Dee had been on *Top of the Pops*. It was the very start of those years when the banks lent money hand over fist. They had the money. They had everything.

This was the kind of house where children ran back and forth across the lawn, laughing and playing, protected from the Iron Towns by the high walls around the garden and the money in the lanes that led down to the stables and the tennis and golf clubs at the edge of the Heath. She has told him she'll just come once a week from now on. She gets tired now much more quickly than before, maybe her strength will build, but more because there is nothing to clean.

This was the kind of house that should be full of voices on a Sunday night, brothers and sisters and uncles and aunties and cousins and grandparents, laughter rising out of open windows and across the hills like those fire lanterns that have become popular now. She half expects one to drift down the valley from a birthday party on one of these lawns one Saturday and burn down the Anvil Yards. If only, she thinks, if only. She has spent her life getting away from the place and still only made it halfway up the hill.

Liam barely speaks to his sisters. Their girls have a cousin who they don't know, an uncle who takes no interest in any of them. He is not a good son, has not been a good husband.

The house could not have been colder when she was here with the boy. Little Jari, her grandson, her own flesh and blood, half a world away even when he was here in the summer. She kept speaking to him in their language, explaining what his nan and grandad had said to him. Finland. You may as well say Timbuktu. She knows Liam asked her to stay here with him. You think she'd be happy to move from the cold, the dark. He has mislaid two wives and a son now with this carelessness, that's what she thinks, but by the time she's finished the banister rails, she's back to lamenting how those girls were not good enough for him. It was they who refused him, her once beautiful blue-eyed boy.

. . .

She sings at funerals. That's what she could have told the man at the bar. A few through the years now, that's for sure. Her nana's, of course, a couple of her uncles'. Dee Dee imagines when Stan dies they'll fly the body back, can't arrest a dead man. She sang at Sonia's, at the wake, though, that she and Liam organised. The service had been plain, barely any ceremony, police stood discreet at the back of the chapel of rest. Sonia's parents had not wanted any of them there at all.

Liam drove back across the Heath after the service, pulled into a clearing off a back lane. She wore black tights too hot for a summer's day, torn them off herself, climbed in the back, only a few hundred yards from where the car had gone in the river, not even much of a river there. They tore at each other. She dug her nails into his arse, bit his neck. They froze at the noise of a tractor going past, animals in their burrow.

'Don't worry, it's nothing, just fuck me Liam,' she said. For years afterwards she felt ashamed of that half an hour or whatever it was, no longer than that, for sure, under the trees, the day of her best friend's funeral, the car roof sticky with sap. It made more sense as the years went by. She thought of it now in moments of quiet, one of the true things of her life.

Dee Dee loves that line from Dylan Thomas, *After the first death there is no other.* Not as a negation of what comes after, more that whatever comes afterwards simply amplifies the past. She tries not to think of Sonia at all, then looks at Alina, her daughter, *her* daughter already past the age at which she died.

Were they older then, somehow? Dee Dee was more certain of herself that's for sure, certain of the world, already married a year, of course. I'll take care of her, she said. It was years of hating him for not going along with it before she realised she had never even asked him.

She sings at funerals, likes Dylan Thomas, doubts every single thing she has ever known. She could've told him that, the handsome stranger at the bar.

'Are you Dee Dee Ahmed, pet?'

'I don't know, love. I honestly could not tell you.'

. . .

Mark Chapman: Of all tonight's ties, none are more
loaded with history than the one at the Anvil
Yards, Irontown against Wolverhampton Wanderers.
Redolent of another age. Pat Murphy is there for
us.

Pat Murphy: Yes Mark, it's thirty years or more
since a rather uncharitable former manager of
both of these clubs said that if the Wolves were
sleeping giants then Irontown were a comatose
pygmy. He had just been sacked, mind you, by the
once all-powerful Greenfield family, very much
absentee landlords these days. Dorothea Greenfield-
Carter, last of the dynasty, lives out her days
in Madeiran exile and refuses to sell or invest.
Nothing soporific about tonight, though, as you
can probably hear. The Anvil Yards is full. Its
capacity is just over ten thousand these days,
with the closure of the East Stand and other
health and safety issues. Gone are the days of
fifty thousand plus and the old 'iron roar'. The
crowd is boosted by a large contingent from the
nearby Black Country, hopeful of a new dawn under
Kenny Jackett. There used to be a big rivalry
between these two, of course, but they haven't
played each other regularly since they slid down
the leagues together in the dark days of the
1980s. One last thing, for those of you of a
certain age, Liam Corwen, he of England infamy and

```
     Irontown legend, forty next year, is on the bench
     tonight and is currently laying out cones for
     the warm-up, a rondel, Barcelona-style, in front
     of the away fans. The PA system is playing 'My
     Sweetest One', sung by his ex-wife's girl band.
     Perhaps he's wearing earplugs!
Mark Chapman: Thanks, Pat. Updates from the Anvil
     Yards and elsewhere throughout the evening . . .
```

. . .

This is more like it. His dad has even lifted his summer ban for the night. The Wolves at home in the League Cup under the lights.

One of the last great crowds here had been when they had the League Cup run in the early eighties. They'd played Liverpool in the semi-final, there'd been traffic all up to Hightown before the first leg, young lads scaling the walls at the Greenfield End. He remembered the way the ground used to look for those night matches, the glow of the floodlights, and the bigger glow of the Anvil Yards beyond, lighting the clouds that came up the river. The sound, the roar. And the lighting of the whole sky. If you came along the Monmouth or Wrexham Roads back in those days, from way out, looking over the hills, it was like you were approaching the crack of doom itself, matchday or not. The red valley they used to call it then. But then that couldn't be right. By the time of that Liverpool game the works were already closing. They had a red flag that filled the away end, sang *Dalglish* all night until they started on *You'll Never Walk Alone*. It was Rush, though, who'd scored twice. Liverpool had won three, four, was it? Won the second leg six-nothing. They were sat in line with Rush's second goal, he'd fouled big Archie Hill, clipped his heels as the ball was played and then left him for dead. Joey remembered Liam alongside him, eight, nine years old, screaming at the linesman to stick his flag up.

. . .

'We are English, Welsh, Black Irish,' Mark Fala's dad would say to him, tugging at his dark curly hair, 'pirates from the Spanish Main, gypsies at home in any hedgerow,' tell him stories of where their name came from. The stories would always start and end in the same way. A young man would leave his valley for the last time, sometimes with his brothers, sometimes alone, to the sound of wolves howling across the mountain snows or the sun coming patterned through the cork trees. His route, and all the generations that followed him, eventually brought him here on the road between the Ironport and the Anvil Yards, to the sound of iron being struck.

It would depend on how much his dad had drunk, how long and complex the way became, but there was always the flight from the mountains, from wolves and bandits and hunger and vicious landowners. And there was always a first glimpse of the sea.

Sometimes it was a fishing village set among the green cliffs, sometimes the harbour of a great city. One version had the young man arriving in Lisbon as the Armada massed, and signing up for a place on one of the impossible floating castles, bigger than the village the lad had left, that sat out in the estuary. Another longer, even taller tale had the man and his brothers join other ships and cross the Atlantic to the slave markets and jungles and great cities of gold. The man returns with jewels and chocolate and a tame crocodile but somehow loses all this and can't find his way home and is blown by a storm into the rainy north. There is always a storm and a shipwreck. In the Armada story, defeat and bad weather has the ships floundering off the Irish coast and just as the hull splinters on some rocks the man leaps and swims ashore, led by mermaids whose names are Estrildis and Habren, through the waves to a deserted beach, where he lies on the edge of the water half dead but still somehow escapes the soldiers who wait to kill him.

There is always Ireland in the story, in some guise or other. The man is his sons and grandsons and great-grandsons and so on. He is hundreds of years old. He moves inland through the mist and silent fields and peat bogs. He is chased like a fox by the English, goes out of his mind with hunger when the famine comes.

He sets sail again, to New York, to Australia, to the Liverpool docks or Lancashire mills or Midland factories.

'We are English, Welsh, Black Irish,' his dad would say to him, take a sip of his mild ale. He smelled of chemical soap from the works, and he'd look up out of the valley where he'd always lived to the limestone hills and appear every inch a man of the Iron Towns. A man made of coal and iron and wiry muscle.

The man in the story was a miner, a tinker, a docker, a pud-dler, a horse trader at the Stowe fair. Somehow the road would

wind nearer and nearer, merge somehow with the real, like figures stepping out of a comic book. Mark's great-granny lived
at Merthyr Tydfil. They would go and see her at Easter and he
would pull at his elasticated tie and look at cousins whose names
he could never remember.

And there they'd be, beside the River Chain, the man would
become his own dad, off to work at the Samson Foundry every
morning at six, a small black shape against a raging fire, that was
how Mark would see him on the few times he'd been down to
the work gates, kicking his tennis ball against the kerbs on the
way.

When he almost signed for Torino, the club had that money
to spend after selling Lentini, the whole thing was cursed, they
were going to take Liam with him, and he guessed Dee Dee
might have come too, the lawyer in the beautiful suit, his fat head
leaning forward behind his glasses across the contract like the
emperor of the toads spoke to him.

'Fala, a good name. Venetian, I think.'

Mark shrugged. 'I'm not sure, I don't think so.'

'Spain? America? Ireland?' His mum laughed whenever he
asked her. 'Your dad's never been further than the donkey rides
at Weston and you can only see the sea there when the tide's in.'

. . .

We came when you enclosed our meadows and drowned our
valleys. We came out from our little forges in the sun-dappled
woods. We came from fields of dead potatoes and soldiers, from

Clydeside tenements with the promise of work, we came no distance at all, our ways of life swallowed, harried off our land by your gamekeepers and lackeys. We are English, Welsh, Black Irish, Scottish. We were none of these things once upon a time, and we shall not be them again. We take many forms. Some of us once watched from ditches by the river, or from the higher peaks, waited for Roman soldiers to pick off one by one. We are patient as the stones.

. . .

The players are born within the sound of hammers. Whether a great boom across rivers and docks or the tap, tap, tap from backyard workshops, the sounds of metal and stone are always close by. The rattle of the railway and tram, the tapping of the nailyard, chainyard, pottery, the blasting of stone from quarries, the hacking of coal from deep underground, the roar of a furnace. They hold in them the energy of fire and dammed rivers. Di Stéfano and Billy Wright look out on their iron bridges, Beckenbauer's dad delivers his post through the snow and ash of ruined Munich while Jack and Bobby Charlton's father lies deep underground scraping coal. There are exceptions, sure. Pelé was born in a city of cows, where lanes filled with sacks of coffee hauled by mules, but he was soon off to the port.

In the end, they all come from iron towns.

. . .

'Liam, Liam, will yer sign this?'

He looks into the enclosure. They've split it between rival fans tonight. There's a Wolves flag hung over the wall, a line of people in wheelchairs behind it. He steps off the pitch and sees the hands holding an England shirt and a pen towards him, watches his step on the narrow gravel track in front of the stand. They are watering the pitch like crazy. It's turned to a kind of grey soup on top and then is still rock hard underneath.

'What they still watering for?' Julius mutters, struggling to trap a ball that skimmed off the surface.

'Suit our slick passing game,' Liam replies.

It's true that Ally does get them to try to play, to pass it out, play through the fullbacks, press. They do not have the players for it. He wants them to go after the ball too far up the pitch for a man nearing forty to leave an acre of space behind him.

Liam is not starting again.

'I've got a game in mind for you, son,' Ally said yesterday as they did a warm-down on the training ground at the Heath, stretching and looking across a yellow field. Liam watched a ball, tiny against the sky, as it climbed and fell, missed the fifth green at the golf club.

That might mean he will start on Saturday in the league game, which is how it should be. Or it might mean that Ally has some vague notion of a fixture in November when he thinks he'll need him. Anyhow, what's certain is he won't start against the Wolves, probably the last chance he'll have to play against them. He tries not to let his face fall, wonders what is coming next. 'When the pitches get heavy, that's when your season starts,' or something like that, he's heard all sorts of crap before. The truth is, he's still the best player at the club, no one will convince him otherwise. He should start alongside Devon at the back every opportunity, every time they're both fit. They should just defend deeper. It's their only hope of staying up this season.

'I've got a game for you,' Ally said, stretched, looked at the man hacking around the rough grass searching for his ball, turned to run back to the changing rooms.

Liam reaches for the pen with one hand, the shirt with the other. The pen is snatched back from his grasp.

'What would I want your autograph for, yer prick?'

The words come hissed and sharp like a slap. Liam looks across the wall to see the face of a younger man leering back at him. There's a chorus of laughter, jeers, from the seats around the man, the boy, who speaks to him. Faces crowd in, he sees knuckles whiten on a fist gripping the handle of a wheelchair. The bloke jerks back in his chair and tugs the shirt which Liam still has hold of. Liam leans across the wall, keeps his grip on it, knows he should let it go. 'Prick,' the bloke says again, his long face twisted in a grimace. The man brays like a donkey. Liam doesn't know if he's laughing or reviving an old taunt. Still he holds the shirt. He feels the mood of the crowd shift. Faces press forward now. Men stand three and four rows back.

'Give him his shirt, mate.'

'Give him his shirt, yer bully. Picking on a kid in a wheelchair, I ask yer.'

This last a woman's voice, high and shrill. Heads turn, there is the clatter of seats flipping up as the people stand now in this corner of the ground. Liam sees an orange-coated steward walk towards him, another move down the steps. He should let go of the shirt. There are other hands gripping it now. The same white knuckles from the wheelchair handle. He feels the shirt begin to tear. The steward is next to him looking into the crowd. Liam leans forward slowly, uncoils his grip and the shirt rests on top of the wall. He holds his palms up to the faces in front of him, smiles. Someone spits past his ear. The steward has his arm round him, pulls him back, just as carefully, as gently, as he let go of the shirt.

'What's going on here, Liam, eh?' the young man says softly, softly, he has a split lip pressed to Liam's ear. Liam thinks he recognises the steward from Billy Ahmed's gym, a good kid, Tyrone he thinks his name is, from the Pengwern. It is unusual to look at a man the same height, bigger under that padded jacket. He can still hear the woman's voice but can't make out what she says. The young man has turned him round. Liam faces the pitch now, starts a sprint to catch up with the others, who have almost reached the tunnel. He glances back once, thinks of Cantona, that moment when he crouched, cocked his ear and went charging into the crowd. Liam is surprised that it doesn't happen more often. His blood is an outgoing tide now and he laughs as he sprints through the floodlit glare. He can hear Dee Dee singing.

. . .

The men in the good suits come, puffing on their cigars. Eusébio is to join Sporting Lisbon. There is an agreement, Sporting

Lourenço Marques is tied by a colonial umbilical cord. That much is clear from the name alone. Di Stéfano will go to Barcelona and play with Kubala. An Argentinian and a Hungarian will shine for Catalan nationalism. The truth is that the players do not much care for flags. The men in good suits come. Samitier smokes his cigar, talks to Di Stéfano, parties, pours another brandy, although it's not clear through the blue smoke whether Samitier really is for Barcelona, or maybe now for Madrid. Nothing is clear at all. Di Stéfano shrugs and looks at the papers. Europe will be an adventure, a grand stage. The shirt he wears won't make that much difference. The game will come to him. He is sure of his footing.

They take Eusébio to a house on the Algarve. He runs to the sound of the sea. He runs the same, whatever the continent, the hemisphere, his feet barely touch the ground. The sea sounds the same. He gets his haircut, talks to Guttmann. The men in good suits come.

Behind them, invisible, the men in uniform.

Eusébio signs for Benfica, Di Stéfano for Real Madrid.

. . .

They are three nothing down inside twenty minutes. Ally tells Liam to lead the subs in a warm-up. The usual spot is in front of the enclosure, right in front of the kid in the wheelchair. He takes them the other way instead, trots towards the Greenfield End.

'Where's our Liam off to?' Eli says. The last communist of the

Far Valley has lifted his football ban for the evening. He sits next to Joey.

'Leading a breakout,' a voice calls from behind them.

'Come back,' pipes up another, 'you can't get out of it that easy!'

There's localised mirth and then a collective groan as the ball goes in the box again and almost falls to a Wolves forward.

Joey feels a tap on his shoulder.

'Why ain't Liam started, Joey, is he fit?'

Joey shrugs.

'Keeping him for Saturday, I expect,' says another voice and saves Joey having to invent an answer.

'I should bloody hope so.'

Joey knows that these voices are kinder towards his boy when he's not in the team, that he becomes several times the player when he is not out there. Plus, their voices soften when Eli is with him. If Liam makes a mistake when Joey is there alone it always seems to him that there will be some sense, in the silence or the comments around him, that he is at least in part to blame. He is responsible for delivering such an abject son to the football club. When Eli is there, it's as if they do not want to hurt him, this old man, the grandad, who is tougher than them all, Joey has no doubt.

Liam continues the run towards the Greenfield End. Noise builds. He raises his arms above his head, signals to no one in particular, into the glare of the lights, for the fans to sing up, to lift them somehow. He is applauded. *Iron Towns, Iron Towns*, they sing. The Greenfield End have never dropped the s. They segue into *One Liam Corwen*, which was not Liam's intention at all, and he knows he'll get a bollocking from Ally later on. If not from Ally then from his dad.

'What is he fucking about for?' Joey asks the concrete and chocolate wrapper and puddle of tea between his feet. He fears his son has always craved the attention. Joey fears that his son enjoys the idea of being a footballer rather than playing football and that has been his downfall. He pushes this thought away. Then takes it up in another form, his old man enjoys the idea of being a human, rather than being human.

They stretch on the far touchline, with the silence of the closed East Stand at their back. Liam feels like he is being watched. Not by the thousands of eyes on the other three sides but from the darkness behind him. Irontown have a rare attack but the ball bobbles through to the keeper. The noise at the Greenfield End keeps going. Archie Hill waves and points at them from Ally's shoulder. He makes a motion of dragging them back around the touchline. From this distance Archie looks like a man gesturing the installation of a noose. Liam glances up into the shadow and starts the half-lap back round the pitch.

. . .

This to win it, the cry of boys on darkening streets and scrubby fields all over, to be champions of Europe.

Panenka takes a run-up of eight, nine strides, as if he might try to blast the ball back to Prague, off the penalty spot, across the brilliant green pitch and over the concrete stands and Belgrade high-rises named for Partisans. He shapes to do so as well. The goalkeeper Maier moves before he makes contact, forward and to his left, sees how Panenka's body remains slightly open. When his foot comes down on the ball Maier is off the ground. And Panenka doesn't strike it, but digs his foot underneath the ball, stops it, so the ball springs up and floats in a gentle arc and everything slows down. The ball hangs a few feet above the turf. Everything stops, except Maier who accelerates, flies almost past his left-hand post, like one part of an experiment in advanced physics. As the ball slows, his momentum increases. Everything else is dead still.

There is all the paraphernalia of mid-seventies European football behind the goal, caught for that moment that the ball hangs in the Belgrade night. There is an orange running track in shadow, the crowd is miles away beyond it. Not that this huge bowl lacks atmosphere. They nickname it the Marakana when Red Star play at home. A line of photographers stands at an angle to the goal, there's a wheelie bin, temporary advertising boards, some in Dutch (the Czechs had shocked Cruyff and his beautiful blue-eyed boys in the semi-final). There they are, time stopped still.

Panenka accelerates now, surges into a follow-through so he almost catches up with the ball. Maier raises his right arm, hits the ground. The ball floats into the middle of the goal. Maier is already standing, he looks back at the ball, shakes his head, and Panenka turns and continues his run with his arms aloft. There he is, still running.

. . .

Liam plays in an area ten yards square in front of Devon and this young lad McLaughlin. His job is to protect them, the kid anyway. Devon's got his hands full dealing with the forwards and the crosses coming in and talking the boy through the match. He is not good enough, but neither is this midfield. Liam closes down, harries, runs short bursts, gets goal-side, barely even puts in a challenge, but stems the flow, stops them pouring straight through. There are no thoughts of a comeback. This is damage limitation. They defend off the edge of their own eighteen yard box, give no space behind them. When Liam gets the ball at his feet he kicks for territory like a rugby fullback. The intensity leaks from the game. The clock ticks down. They get through the second-half without humiliation.

'I don't know why he didn't play our Liam from the start, I'm sure I don't.'

'Two games in a week, Dad. It's tough the age he is. Anyway, that kid McLennon, he looked good in the reserves last week.'

'Two bloody games in a week!?' Eli leaves every other comment he could make hanging in the summer evening.

The game is drifting, the atmosphere of earlier has gone with it. People shuffle along the rows to get away. Eli changes tack. Both men have this conversation while keeping their eyes on their son and grandson who shuffles backwards a few yards to watch their right-winger, who steps inside to look for the scraps.

'You went to the reserves last week?'

'Yeah, they're playing home games up at Cowton, trying to save this pitch a bit.'

'You've got a wife to look after at home, you know.'

They stare at the pitch, their heads move in unison as the keeper kicks from his hands. Liam wins the header but it skews off his head and bounces out for a throw. Joey slumps. He feels heavier in his seat than a few minutes ago. A man stands up half-way towards the corner flag and begins an essay in bile aimed at no one and everything and the stewards move towards him.

'Give it a rest,' Joey says in the direction of the shouting man, quiet enough for him not to hear.

. . .

Panenka runs across Liam's left shoulder. Liam cannot sleep, lies there on the bed with the curtains open. He sees the floodlights go out with the shadow on the hotel bedroom roof. He thinks of Panenka as he runs up to take the penalty, thinks of Mark Fala, out there, somewhere in the night. He read somewhere that Panenka knew before the match that this is what he'd do if he got the chance, no doubt in his mind.

The room is too dark with the floodlights at the ground switched off and Liam reaches across to turn the bedside light on. A plane blinks against the clouds over the hills. Getting to sleep after a night game has always been a problem, but these days it's nearly impossible. He thinks of Panenka and Maier to ward off thoughts about Greta and Jari. Football will heal him. His body has started to ache. At least that means the adrenaline is fading and he might sleep soon. He should stop thinking. He tells himself that men who head footballs for a living should not think at all.

He turns the TV on again, flicks through the channels with the sound off, another cricket rerun, some tennis. One of the news channels plays a report from Australia. Aboriginal people have been thrown off their land for a giant open-cast mine, the usual story. He knows that he has seen all these pictures before. Drink cans scattered across the red earth, people with angry, bewildered looks on their faces. The young men wear vest tops with the names of Aussie beers scrawled across their chest, T-shirts with pictures of Michael Jackson and Ayrton Senna, and then he sees the faded chocolate football shirt, jolts upright. A long-limbed boy wears it, fifteen years old or so, he reckons, but a head taller than everyone else, the same shape Liam had once been himself. The shirt is long sleeved, and the sleeves only reach halfway down his forearms, but the body looks big on his thin frame. The shirt is dirty, smeared with red dust, the one with the name of the sponsors who went bankrupt, press studs at the collar, and he knows, a fraction before the boy turns in the searing desert light, that he will see in fading print on the back, the number 5 and the name Corwen. The boy's eyes look at him from the screen, staring back over his shoulder, a can of beer in his hand, utterly lost. Liam's heart thumps, scared to be part of the world.

. . .

When he came to the valley James Greenfield knew that this was the place. There's a painting which hangs in the Hightown Town Council chamber, a copy you can buy as a postcard at the Heritage Museum, of this first James Greenfield stood at the head of the valley like Moses. He has walked up out of the Sheep Folds, leans a hand against ancient oak. The scene is deep English pastoral. The brass plaque beneath the painting reads 1722. The rivers meet, cows drink from the banks, sheep drift along the steep hillsides. The glade in which he stands is where now the last of the Cowton estate runs out, where they trampled that boy to death, a shepherd's hut is just visible through the greenery. The shape of the Heath is clear in the distance where the valley opens out and beyond are the blue hills and the sky a lighter blue above that.

He already knew the valley well, of course. His family were farmers, smallholders, he had cousins spread across the Midlands and border country. His dad's family farmed land near Bridgnorth. When the family fame grew, a story attached itself to them that an ancestor of his mother's, a milkmaid, helped King Charles hide as he fled through Worcestershire. This country was no great biblical revelation. And it was not empty, there were mills all along the rivers, farmhouses and hamlets, forges out in the woods. Hightown Castle and the Lowtown markets which clustered below it came with the Normans, fortuitously beyond the crest of a wooded hill in the painting. The castle had been built on an old abandoned fortress; the earl's masons worked standing stones into the castle walls. Offa had contemplated his dyke here. Blue men had once watched columns of centurions appear through the river mist.

He'd been apprenticed to Darby at some point, had followed Chamberlain and Baylies out to the Dolgun furnace at Dolgellau, realised there were hundreds of valleys like the one at Coalbrookdale.

That the future was made of iron he was certain.

. . .

Alina gets the 29 to the bus turnaround at Cowton sometimes. There are often plastic flowers tied to the stile, the odd card in the spring, where the fight had spilled into the scrubby field. She can't remember the boy's name now but it had been a big thing at the time, he'd been the same age as her. She can't remember what he'd done or was meant to have done or if anyone was ever caught, which shames her every time she sees the shrine, and thinks to herself she'll have found out for next time, but still never does. She does not think they left flowers and teddy bears for her mum. She used to want to, pestered her mum, her mum now, would not let it drop one year. Was it the year that Diana died or was she still too young to understand then? To take her down to the roadside and lay some flowers. Dee Dee said no, wouldn't relent. Her mum had a plaque at the crem and a rose bush. They could go there instead. It was not what people did back then, the laying of roadside memorials, another of the many ways the actual fact of her death fell away into the past.

She walks the paths up where the fields start, looks for the place where the view becomes Greenfield's. It isn't there, of course. Or if it is, it is so changed you may as well say it was there in the next field, or under that line of trees up on the ridge, or exactly where the last kick ended the boy whose name she cannot remember.

Maybe there, because she sees herself taking pictures, posed portraits, like the one of her great-great-grandad, except he isn't, of course, because her mum, this mum, the only one she has known, is not her real mum, and he is not her real great-

great-grandad in his sepia waxed moustache and robes. Pictures of people in Congolese suits and Polish football shirts looking down the valley at the end of the bus route, trying to believe this place was their destiny.

. . .

'That is Liam all over. No mention of Tony in that article. No credit to anyone else. What, do they think he's carving them tattoos on himself? He is a piece of work.'

Dee Dee's free hand rests on the magazine. Nico, the new Vietnamese boy with the fringe, is doing her nails. They are at the front of her cousin Lily's salon. Her aunties, Gracie and Marcia, sit under the dryers through the back. Lily has resurrected the old fittings since she took the place on.

Dee Dee was in a video which used dryers like these when she was singing. It had a kind of fifties cold-war feel. Aliens were beamed to earth through the dryers. They looked like crocodiles, or people wearing crocodile heads. The whole thing was intended to look cheap. It was post-modern, apparently. Dee Dee appeared briefly, pretending to scream as the crocodile women walked down the street. She'd sung backing vocals they used on the twelve-inch and ended up as an extra in the video. It was when she was about to pack it in. She remembered standing waiting to give her details in order to get paid, stood in a draughty corridor of some warehouse on the edge of London. She could see Wembley Stadium over the traffic. There was a pile of crumpled prosthetic crocodile heads. She was getting the bus home, meeting the lads at the bus station, Goldie was probably going to give her a lift. She'd had enough, her band had split up, which hadn't been much of a band anyway, thrown together by the management company. She'd sacked her agent, the brief attention she'd got from being the girl who walked out of a chart act to sing backing for more 'authentic' bands had faded. Authentic, my arse, she thought, most of them. She'd got married, and although she didn't know it, was less than a year away from adopting her best friend's baby and getting divorced.

'Tony seems pleased,' Nico says.

'Tony's too soft.'

From where she sits she can just about see the small red neon sign that Tony had sent to America for. It says 'Tattoos' with a jagged arrow flashing underneath it. It hangs off the old snooker hall awning. Stan Ahmed owned all the buildings along this little stretch at one point, where Lascar runs into the Anvil Yards. His grandchildren and great-nieces and nephews pieced together what was left and were doing OK with the pub and the salon and tattooists and gym. Heads above water OK, not private hospital on the outskirts of Marbella, still on the run from the police OK like Stan.

Running a business, standing in front of the magistrates was one thing. They'd nod in that particular way when she gave her name, although even that was fading now with Stan and his brothers so long absent. Phoning the police to tell them about Goldie was something else. They wouldn't listen anyway. Alina is twenty-one years old. Dee Dee thinks of phoning Liam and watches faces go past on the street. There has been no word from

Goldie since that phone call, she has started to hope that nothing might come of it. There had been a few calls, years ago, when she took Alina in, just silence on the end of the line, not even breathing. But she knew he was safely out of the way then. In the faces in the street she looks for the Goldie from that photograph. God knows what he looks like now, then she realises that it was like he said on the phone, that he's never really gone, not really, always there in the shadows. She'll know him when she sees him that's for sure.

She wonders when Liam goes to see Tony, whether he goes during shop hours, or even in the season at all. There was a match this afternoon, of course. She thought of Liam, angry and pretending everything was OK in the days before a big game. By the morning of matchday he could barely speak, would sometimes throw up before leaving the house. She wonders if it's still like that. He must've got used to it by now.

She wants a cigarette. Nico works at her cuticle.

'I just think they should've mentioned him by name, that's all. Liam could've said, I want my tattooist acknowledged, they'd have put it in if he'd said.' She stops herself, 'It's our Tony's work, after all.'

Her aunties do not listen. Gracie looks to be asleep right now. Marcia flips through a TV magazine. She opens one eye, arches the painted brow.

'You seem very interested in what Liam's got to say for himself, Dee Dee, that's all I can think, love.'

. . .

Another iron town. Their club crest shows a fist which holds a girder with the word iron forged into it. The old badge showed a blast furnace and ironstone fossils. The town itself exists because of its steelworks. They play in claret and blue shirts, modelled on Aston Villa's, which for reasons that may now seem inexplicable, the people of Scunthorpe thought might bring them luck. Some say it was West Ham, though, another set of irons, echoing across the empty London docks, blowing bubbles over the car works at Dagenham. Liam has Hurst, Peters and Moore holding the Jules Rimet Trophy aloft tattooed on his right thigh. When the supporters pile out on the away car park in Anvil Yards, next to the yellow concrete of the bus station, the sun glints on the towers of scrap over by the canal, and they sing *Gyppos* and *What a fucking shithole*. Some of them take off their shirts. Their blond hair and white bellies move across the burning plain.

'Who are yer? Who are yer?'

'We are iron men, from the Iron Towns, come from the Anvil Yards, come from the Anvil Yards,' they reply from the Greenfield End.

Quieter, a low chant in the background, fewer people, they bang the corrugated iron at the back of the stand to create the sound of thunder, a storm coming,

'We are the Spider Boys, we are the Spider Boys, we are the Spider Boys . . .' into a sibilant hush.

The spider mythology did not begin with the building of the Spider House, that was just its height. The eighth James Greenfield joined the craze for zoo building in the 1930s. He had the arboretum landscaped and built the Spider House at its entrance. The visitors dwindled but it lingered on like much else in the Iron Towns. They still draped lights through the remaining arboretum trees every winter, decorated the branches with silver webs and plastic spiders.

The first mentions of the spider came with the Norman farmers, settlers. Young girls – it was always young girls, milkmaids and farmer's daughters – would report seeing the movements of long thin legs high up in the trees, curtains of silver thread draped the branches and hedgerows. The land was cursed in some way. Rumours and strange stories lingered on.

There is a game the children still play. Liam sees them through the rain-dashed tram windows, over the wall of the Ironport primary school. Girls and boys – always one girl, one boy – back to back with arms linked, four arms, four legs, staggering around, pulling each other this way and that, trying to catch their screaming, taunting mates.

The spiders had moved over the years, become subterranean. Liam remembers lying on the furry rug in front of his grandparents' coal fire. He could lie for ages, watching the shape of the flames, seeing mountains, dark tunnels, fathomless pit shafts he knew his grandad crawled through when Black Park was still open.

'There's summat down there, I don't care what they say.'

'What you going on about, Dad?'

'You watch what yome saying Eli, you'll scare the boy.' His nan's voice from the kitchen, the flames flickering blue-edged around the coals. He remembers the rough black finish on the scuttle handle. It still sits in a coal bucket in his grandad's out-house, lined with ancient dust.

'He takes some scaring.' His grandad ruffled his hair. 'All I'm saying is there's summat in it. There's none of you ever been down there, and a good thing too.'

'It's dangerous enough without talk of giant spiders. You know what you sound like?'

'I ain't saying what it is, whether it's the spider or what. Just sometimes you get the sense of summat else, that's all. I ain't even saying it's a bad thing, that it means any harm. Just that there's summat there. There's things people don't understand, can't explain, no matter how many degrees or bits of paper they've got, that's all I'm saying, so then they say there's nothing in it, it's just an old wives' tale, just to make thereselves look clever, everyone else seem stupid for thinking it.'

'You'll be telling us to say our prayers next.'

'You know what I think about that nonsense.'

That his grandad, who had dug coal from deep underground every day like his dad and his dad before that, who believed in Marxist dialectics and liked a pint of mild and a bet on a Saturday, a week in Llandudno and his October trip to the Prix de l'Arc de Triomphe, also believed a giant spider lived in the tunnels that dragged down the hills they lived on never struck Liam as that strange. You could hold plenty of different things in your head, he knew that even then. That you could be a good man who did bad things or a bad man who did good things, and that they might amount to much the same, was something he understood from somewhere deep within him, like the coal in the hillside.

. . .

The lad takes a touch, half-turns just inside the centre circle. Not here you don't. Liam is in. Takes the ball, man, everything. He hears the air leave the kid's body as he falls. First big cheer of the afternoon. Liam stays standing, above him, says nothing. The ref blows up. Calls Liam over and warns him, talks in a low, calm voice to him. Liam nods but doesn't listen. He would've booked him had it been any later than the second minute, that's for certain. It's a free shot this early in the match, the season. There's a voice chipping away at the ref. Liam stares straight ahead. The striker is on his feet, jogs forward, doesn't look at Liam. They stick the free kick straight down the middle. Liam is up, bodies bounce off him, heads it back towards the sun. Out they go. Out. Out. A deep-throated growl goes through the crowd. They sing his name.

. . .

That she is the great-aunt of the dreadlocked man who stands on the ladder, with wires trailing over his shoulder and down the other side of the bar, is something that fills her with wonder. She knows it's a trick of big families, this overlap of generations. They joke about it. She has not seen Nathan for a few years, she remembers a shy boy fiddling with an electronic game, half-hiding behind his mum, Natalie, Dee Dee's niece, though Dee Dee is four years younger. The joke doesn't seem that funny to her. As a kid she had great-aunts with silver hair that they always tied in buns, who could remember when they brought electricity to the villages up on the Welsh Ridge. Maybe she is those women now. Sitting in a high-backed chair, lips moving with no sound coming out, remembering times of darkness. She tries to work out what relation Lionel is to Nathan. Lionel is her uncle but not Natalie's, she doesn't think, can't remember for a moment.

'Thanks again, Lionel,' she says to him as he comes back in from the van. They sit at a table with a beaten copper top in the lounge in the net curtain light.

'Don't mention it love. I'm glad you've seen a bit of sense installing those cameras. We worry about yer, chick, living down here on yer own. It ain't safe, love. I wish I could say it was. It ain't the place it used to be.'

She doesn't know where else he thinks she could go.

Lionel sighs, sits back. He's enjoying this, this show of concern. The subtext is it ain't safe since your uncle Stan stopped keeping things in order down here and had to do a runner to Spain. 'When yer uncles was around,' she hears quite a bit from the drinkers in the bar, said in the same tone as 'When the works was open'. Nostalgia has replaced fear, a trick of time. There was a lot more to the collapse of the Anvil Yards than the demise of the Ahmed family.

Lionel is the last of his brothers still around. He runs a car yard and a security firm that won the contract to guard much of the abandoned works sites. He runs the men on the doors in the fancier pubs of Heathside and Hightown, sends someone to watch the pub doors on matchdays, even though Dee Dee never asks. He still sails close to the wind, but hasn't been in any trouble, except over VAT receipts, as far as she knows, for years. He prefers the quiet life these days, Sunday roasts up at the golf club and so on.

She can hear voices from the kitchen and thinks for a moment that Alina is talking to Nathan but he remains with his head through a missing ceiling panel and Dee Dee sees the other boy – when she came to think of men in their twenties as boys, she is not sure, finds her own ageing unbelievable in some way – who stands in his blue overalls smiling at something Alina must have said. She didn't even know she was in.

'I didn't know Alina was here,' she said and watches the boy as he nods and says something and smiles again. A lovely look-ing boy, tall, with clear, golden skin and long eyelashes she can see. This is good, will do Alina good, she thinks, to be flirted with by a handsome boy. Alina is too serious, although maybe there is plenty to be serious about.

Lionel dips his biscuit into his tea and there is a moment of quiet while Dee Dee decides to say anything or not.

'You seen Bobby?'

Lionel flinches at the mention of his son, knew it was coming though, and she can't tell how much that reaction is rehearsed or genuine. She does not have such a high opinion of her own family these days. There is custard cream smeared on Lionel's lip.

'I told him,' he says, 'I told him not to come back. He's upset his mother too much now, crossed the line. I don't know what's the matter with him. I've washed me hands of him, told him don't come back. He's had too many chances, should've been harder with him from the start.'

From the start of what, she's not sure. He doesn't ask her if she's seen him, which she hasn't, she was out on the morning Paul told Bobby he couldn't serve him at just turned eleven o'clock in the morning with Bobby all glassy eyed and looking for an argument and Bobby had smashed the glass in the bar door with the fire extinguisher. That had been a couple of months ago, but it would be nice to be asked.

'I look at you here, and Tony and Natalie with the salon now. None of yer had it that easy, one thing and another. He had everything he ever wanted and what do we get in return? Everything throwed back in our faces. No, I've told him.'

'What about if he got cleaned up?'

'He won't get cleaned up. I've told his mother, one day there'll be a phone call, a knock at the door, yer know. We've got to steel ourselves for it.'

'He's only a kid, Lionel.'

'Some people am no good.'

'Your own son,' she says quietly but Lionel is not listening.

He nods towards Nathan pulling the wire for the new cameras up through his dreadlocks.

'These two here, great workers. You couldn't meet a nicer lad than our Nathan. And this other kid's his mate. I was employing him over the Yards, security work, you know, and some stuff on the doors, but he's a fast learner, he's worth more than that. I've got him out with me on jobs some of the time now. You could trust these with your life. The kid, Tyrone, he's off the Peng, right, background you wouldn't believe, even for there, unbelievable. Yet, here he is, getting on with things. And then you've got our

Bobby. We spoilt him, Dee Dee, that's for sure. Hundred pound trainers for Christmas, remember? Florida and what have you. I told Gracie at the time, this is too much, he's out of control, this one. And then with the boxing, we should have held him back a bit more. He believed what people said about him. Would her listen? I've told him, don't come back this time.'

Words for their own sake, is what she thinks. Lionel's right about the spoiling. Bobby needed help and he got fancy trainers. But Bobby's not her problem, thank god. If he turns up here again and asks for a drink she'll let him have one. It was like digging at a scab, mentioning him to Lionel at all, like she wanted to hear the worst, his hypocrisy and blame. Maybe he was just being honest. They had spoiled him and now he wanted to forget about him. But just because Lionel's practised the words doesn't make them less true. He sold used cars for years, for god's sake, can't sound genuine even when he is being, charmed the magistrates and the tax man, has kept his detached house on Heathside, with stone lions and cameras at the entrance to the drive, after all. She wonders whoever said crime didn't pay.

The boy Tyrone is still smiling, looks daft in the sunlit doorway, his eyes following Alina hidden somewhere back in the kitchen. Dee Dee cannot begin to imagine what they are saying to each other, but doesn't need to, she supposes. She wonders whether to mention him to Alina later, decides not to. She's never teased her like that, never pried, tried not to show how much she worries, how much she has put in to being the girl's mother, this lovely, lonely girl, and sometimes thinks there is more than one way of spoiling a child, and for the briefest moment as the light shifts in the room and they hear a cheer from the Anvil Yards carried on the wind, that she has more in common with Lionel and Gracie than she would like to admit, and so maybe perhaps should not be so hard on them.

. . .

Dave 'Iron' Willis: Such has been Irontown's form in the season's first few weeks that to get to half-time goalless is some achievement. They've certainly tightened up since the League Cup mauling by Wolves, helped in good measure by the return to the back four of veteran skipper Liam Corwen. Dominant as ever in the air, he has even nipped in front of the Scunthorpe strikers a couple of times for clever interceptions and the odd foray into midfield. He has been ably supported by Devon Samuels. No spring chickens, though, these two, and in this heat — it's like a furnace out there on the pitch for both sets of Irons — the worry for the home team, without much threat going forward, must be whether they might wilt in the second half . . .

. . .

The sun has come through the frosted windows of the gents' and there's a hot, thick smell of pissed beer. The porcelain still radiates cool, though, and Joey is enjoying this moment, the relief for one thing, he cannot make it through a game any more without needing to go, and Liam's performance out there, and he reads 'Dudley' over again in light blue lettering tattooed into the white urinal slab, even thinks of Liam's tattoos without shuddering, when he hears the groans from above his head and knows that they've let one in.

He does not know what had made him feel so cheerful in the first place, pisses down his leg and onto his shoe in trying to finish, not knowing he hadn't finished, and wanting to get to the clamour upstairs. He struggles out the door, the sounds of anguish coming louder, and there's the sound of a few thousand people all saying no at the same time and the square of blue sky at the top of the steps. He walks up into the light to the sound of another collective howl and sees the ball sitting there in the Irontown net and their winger, the quick one, running away to the corner and their supporters. The keeper lies outstretched and looks at the ball. Liam walks back towards the goal, twenty yards from it. Devon Samuels is just behind him with his hands on his knees.

He's missed goals before, Joey, of course, having a piss or waiting for a pint. He cannot remember ever missing two in the same trip. His dad's seat is empty. Les Martin leans across to him as Joey slumps down. He smells of extra strong mints. He is one of those blokes who takes a perverse delight in the team's failings. If Liam is at fault in some way, he never quite comes out and says it, just has that glint in his eye. He owns a tool hire place in Lowtown, lives in Heathside somewhere, is worth a bob or two.

'First from a corner, free header, back post, one of their centre halves up, nobody near him. Keeper should've come but never. Next, we kick-off, give the ball back to them, ball over the top, we've pushed up too far, kid runs after it, linesman don't put his flag up, but he was probably on, two-nothing. Two in, what, thirty seconds?'

'Took it well,' a voice comes from behind.

Les turns, 'He did, he did, I'll give him that.'

'I've seen it all now,' Joey says.

'Well, except yer never did.'

'What?'

'See it.'

Joey looks down at Liam. He thinks for a moment that he will gladly never watch another game of football in his life if Liam packs it in. For Joey, there is something about Liam's size that has always made him vulnerable. He remembers watching him in the playground, blond hair bouncing head and shoulders above the other kids. Liam claps his hands and says something to Kyran, the young kid they've got at fullback.

He looks across the low barrier into the director's box, no one sitting there except Steve Stringer, who must live in this stand, scurrying in and out of his little office next to the toilets, trying to make ends meet, helping Ally get players in, players out, and Ally treating him like he treats everyone else, like he's there to serve the great Ally Barr. Steve had been a ballboy with Liam, but never in any of the youth teams, just a kid who hung around the ground doing odd jobs, taking the post and the like. His old man used to work at Greenfields, used to drink in the Salamander. Joey used to enjoy having a pint with him. That was before he had to stop going in the pub after the mess with Dee Dee and the girl. Liam was a stupid boy, giving her up. He raises his hand and Steve waves back, the worry etched permanently on his face. Joey reminds himself to ask him how his dad is at full-time. Probably not good news, not here, the whole place is cursed, Joey thinks.

'Surprised you're here, Les, not off on another cruise or whatever,' he says and keeps his eyes on Liam as he gets up to head the ball, thinks of how many hours throwing balls up for him to attack just like that.

'What, and miss all this?'

. . .

Goldie holds the knife at a shallow angle to the steel. He loves the sound that the sharpening makes, builds a rhythm with it, sees his shape in the canal's green water. The sound comes back off the factory walls that form the opposite bank. The wall bulges where the water must have got in and Goldie wonders how safe it is, when the wall will come down. Tree branches grow from it, long rust streaks pattern the brick. But he feels good all the same, away from anyone, time a bit to think, no one will have followed him here. He sharpens the blade with a flourish and it glints in the sun. He hears a murmur and then a shout from the ground, a ripple of applause. He would hear a chant in his cell sometimes, from the Villa or West Brom, depending on who was at home and which way the wind was blowing. Sometimes just a great shout, voices all mixed together as one, some roar of joy or anguished moan. It's strange that he used to like to hear it, it made him feel less alone, that and the sounds of traffic outside or of work going on, like the clang of scaffolding poles, to make him think of a world outside. But then when he was out, like when he'd lay awake and look at the fuzzy yellow light outside the blind when he lived with Nadine, he'd listen out for those sounds and think of his cell and almost feel better and able to sleep. Maybe he should head over to the ground, he thinks, when he's done his knives. He is a free man, he can do whatever he likes, and he smiles as he thinks this, something about it not quite right, a thought in his head asking, when are you ever free of anything? He is bare-chested. When he thinks the carving knife is sharp enough he pauses for a moment, holds the blade to his skin until there's the shallowest cut and a neat line of blood, touches his fingers to it and then puts them to his lips. There is another shout from the Anvil Yards. The thought hardens in his mind, sharp and clean like the cut. When are we ever free of anything?

. . .

The ball takes a crazy bounce on the baked pitch, loops over Kyran's head, and he's too far upfield anyway, trying to force it, nothing doing. Liam is across to it. It's the last minute and he's beating their forwards to the ball, he wants people to see this. Wins it. Sticks it high up into the empty East Stand.

There's no time for the throw-in. He hears the whistle for full-time, the cheers from the away end and a smattering of boos from elsewhere, lets his run wind down in the direction of the ball and kicks out at the old wooden advertising board. The clatter of it echoes back across the pitch. Something moves in the cool shade at the back of the stand. Liam stares for a moment. The linesman, assistant, whatever he's called these days, walks towards him to shake his hand. Liam's seen cats up there, leap suddenly through the missing panels at the back, or slink down the crumbling steps, a fox once. They used to get kids sneaking in, but that seems to have died off.

'Played Liam.'

'Yeah, some use, eh?'

He begins to limp back across the pitch, then he turns and looks back once more. It was a man, the shape of a man running away. Liam shakes his head. If the bloke paid nothing, he's still been robbed.

. . .

Tony lays out photocopies of paintings by Zurbarán, proud faces in dark shade.

'It's their faces, their faces you want,' he says.

And it is, but it's something else as well.

Zidane slices it on purpose, hits it with fade like a golf shot. This is the World Cup final. Buffon, the best goalkeeper in the world stands in front of him. People crowd around televisions in Papeete and Tripoli, Basse-Terre and Dire Dawa, Mamoudzou and Asmara. Millions of people watch one man. Seen from above the earth must throb with the glare of those millions of television screens. Liam thought he'd mis-hit it, in the moment, leaping forwards from his chair by the side of a Finnish lake. Then something in Zidane's face as he turned away made him realise. He was in utter control. Millions of people. He'd even made the ball clip the bar on purpose, Liam reckoned, just for the lovely drama of it as it fell those inches behind the line and bounced back out of the goal again. If you had power like that you would go nuts. Perhaps that's what happened later when he flattened Materazzi. Maybe. And Liam wants that too, feels both acts, the penalty and head-butt, to be the same thing. Or maybe the shape Zidane's body forms as he volleys the goal at Hampden Park, another Hampden night, Di Stéfano there in the crowd, looking on. Zidane will take some thought. Zidane you could think about for ever. His face on that wall in Marseilles.

'Chiaroscuro,' Tony says. 'Light and shade.'

'Yeah, you're right about the faces, and maybe do that on another one. Pirlo's got a beard now and we can't do him till he stops playing, anyway.'

'Zidane though.'

'Yeah, but what I really want from this is that moment when everything stops, you know?'

What he wants is that stillness, the ball in mid-air, following a gentle arc, the keeper the only thing moving, tumbling away from it. That still moment of grace, that's what he wants.

There was a split-second in the play-off final, nothing more than a split-second, when Mark Fala stopped his foot and stunned the ball softly above the thick Wembley grass, when Liam thought they had that moment. His stomach flips over. The keeper flinches and doesn't move. Time does not stand still. The ball arcs into the keeper's hands. He catches it. Catches the penalty, and he is already moving, and so is Liam, or trying to, turning one last time on this thick, spongy surface, and his legs won't work properly. And the keeper has already taken his strides and launches a kick – he's alongside Mark who just stands there, a yard or two past the penalty spot, could even then have stood in front of the keeper and stopped him kicking it. And the ball meets its own shadow yards into the Irontown half and bounces once and then a second time, in that channel that Geoff Hurst ran down for the last goal in the World Cup final. They think it's all over, again and again. That kid, he's thinking of him as a kid because he's slight and fast but he's older than Liam, is on to it and even though he's running with the ball at his feet now, Liam is going backwards, the kid is running away from him, and is into the box and now he's sliding it past Big Al in goal, who never plays again either, same as Mark Fala, retires back to his pub in Carrickfergus, a man who is too old and slow to fall on this one last shot and the ball is there in the net. They were 3-1 up what seems like hours ago now, have lost 4-3. The ref blows the whistle. Liam hears it through the roar. He can see he's blowing for the goal and he's blowing up for time. No more time. It's over. They have lost. Mark Fala stands just past the penalty spot. Liam hits the ground. He cannot get up. He tells himself he will never get up again. But even in this feeling he knows there will be more games, more seasons. He is young and the days stretch out in front of him.

Fal – Liam never called him that, always Mark, the older lads called it him – has already started to walk off, separate from the others, shrugs off Big Al's arm as he tries to console him.

'Head up, son, eh?'

He walks round the pitch on the pale gravel, Mark walks like a young man at the end of a long journey.

. . .

You cannot understate the fact that it is Germany, of course. When the men Panenka grew up listening to said 'the war' they meant the second one. The ball that floats through the air, a conjuring trick, a joke, is an act of the deepest resistance. Resistance against what? A lack of imagination, perhaps, against too great a seriousness, an absence of humour? Is it a last defiant act of the Prague Spring? If there is a message in it, it must be not to take life too seriously. We realise it does not matter whether the penalty goes in or not. It is the gesture, the joke that matters. But thinking about it all is part of the joke, because it is to take it seriously, far too seriously, grown men playing games, chasing a ball, other men looking on. The joke is either on the penalty taker or on the goalkeeper, or on us all, but the joke is there. The joke is in the way the ball pops up, floats lightly in the air, the way a child's balloon might drift in front of a tank.

It did not just appear in Panenka's head, just like that, fully formed, even if he was the first to do it. It came from some-where, not just from Prague, from the memories of the old Empire, buried deep in the minds of coaches like Jez̆ek and Venglos̆, back to Béla Guttmann, in the movements of players like Masopust and Puskás and Sindelar, layer upon layer, back and back, on pitches in Prague and Ostrava and Budapest and

Vienna, in countries which no longer even exist. Panenka's kick as a dream of Mitteleuropa, a stray idea from another vanished world.

. . .

Autumn in the Iron Towns, rust coloured, a slow drip-drip from a cracked pipe. The place leans in on itself, subsides, walls fall slowly and roofs sag, a slow motion catastrophe, a slow motion coup. Had it happened overnight, not across forty years, there would be soldiers on the streets, helicopters to drop relief packages all the way up the valley. Instead, it is quiet, moss and rust grow on factory gates. There is a long slow drift into silence.

One day, perhaps not so long in coming, the human world will be elsewhere. A few mossed over stones will remain, strange metal relics, chemical traces through the ground. There will be the myth of great ruined cities in the north and west of the islands, like the rumour of the giant spider, explorers will hack their way up narrow rivers, searching for a few lost tribes.

. . .

And these are men of great joy too. Do not forget that.

England v. Rest of the World, 23 October, 1963. A celebration. They play Eusébio and Denis Law as inside-forwards. Di Stéfano gets the number 9 shirt, the captaincy too, even at thirty-eight.

The only forty-five minutes Eusébio and Di Stéfano play as

teammates is goalless. Eusébio comes off at half-time for Puskás, a gentleman's agreement. There is a chance when Eusébio runs a diagonal, left-to-right, outside-in, and takes the ball on his right foot, fifteen yards out, turns the defender, but drives it with his left into Gordon Banks. Di Stéfano tries to get up alongside him before he shoots, can't make the distance, but then it is his dropping deep that has made the space for Eusébio.

He is the master of time and space, people move to his will, even now, this late in the day.

. . .

Liam cannot move. He lies on the bed. He has spoken to Jari, to Greta, sat and watched Jari playing with a set of wooden trains on the laptop screen. He lies still. He holds that picture of Jari in his head, Greta stands at the door and looks out at the lake. The light is falling now. He imagines the bed to be there at the lodge. He has that sense of sleeping close to water. He feels the flicker of light off the lake, believes he can smell pine woods. In a moment he will get up, walk into the living room, join Greta for a glass of wine and look at the water.

He buys two pricey bottles of Sauvignon Blanc from the Heath Vintners, the posh off-licence. George Best drank white wine near the end, that's what he's thinking as he chooses it. He is not near the end. His dad gave him a lift back to the house.

'Well played, son,' he said, when Liam struggled out, already stiffening up, 'see you tomorrow.' Liam groaned inside. Both his sisters and their families are here tomorrow. They are having

Sunday roast at his parents'. He will be expected to kick a ball about with his nephews and nieces.

He will never sleep in his house again, of that he is certain. When he is sure that his dad's car has turned the corner towards Black Park he walks to the row of shops at Heathside and then takes the long way back to the hotel. He considers buying a can to drink on the way but it is Saturday, early evening, there are people around. Someone sounds a car horn and he hears laughter from within as it goes past him too fast. A man walking hand-in-hand with his wife nods to him. They look happy, off to a meal at the Italian here. Liam wants to hide, could've called a cab, he thinks, too late, halfway to Meeting House Lane already. The pedestrians thin out as he comes down the hill, there's the occasional roar of a car that booms through the empty streets. The helicopter is up somewhere.

He thinks of rising, Sunday mornings. He and Jari run at the lakeside. The boy's hand is small in his, grips hot and tight. The boy laughs, 'Faster, Daddy.' Liam quickens his step and the boy half-flies along the track. They are barefoot. Their feet skim the packed earth, they feel the cool of the water on their left, the light comes through the trees and flickers, light then shade, light then shade, like old film run fast. Along the path they see the jetty, a blue boat against it. Greta stands on the veranda, waves and smiles as she sees them come through the woods.

Finland is a dream to him now. That was him. That was a life he had, somehow.

He lies on the bed alone and runs through the woods with his son.

. . .

'Albion, Albion, Albion . . .' The song echoes off the dark brick of Chain Street at the away end.

'Albion . . .'

Albion: the White Land.

'. . . Albion!'

The giants sing this as they approach Brutus' feast on the cliffs. The island has vanquished invaders since it became an island. Seas shift, land rises and falls, nothing lasts for ever.

The invaders are war hardened, Trojan refugees, delighted to find this empty white land. Brutus nods at Corineus. It must be done. The giants have grown soft in their isolation, despite their clamour and noise. They do not feel so much like giants, their arms and legs and heads scattered across the fields, their plump white bellies slit open.

They put Gogmagog in a cage. The bars twist to his shape but do not break, brand his flesh. He cannot move his head to look away from the ruin, from the feasting and celebration. They joke that they might keep him as their pet, tame him, lead him round on a collar. Brutus nods at Corineus again. He tips the cage over the cliff and Gogmagog is dashed on the rocks below.

'Albion, Albion, Albion, Albion, Alb-i-on.'

. . .

'Does he not want you in this morning, love?'

Alina walks into the kitchen, she wears a thin cardigan over her nightie. Her hair falls in her face. Groggy, she looks like she's had a night out, Dee Dee thinks, but Alina never goes out.

'No, he's opening a bit later he says, never anybody there before eleven.'

Alina works in Rob's record shop at the Lowtown indoor market, another of Dee Dee's cousins. He sells vinyl, reggae and metal and dance twelve-inches, scrapes by like everyone else. Dee Dee's voice locked in a groove on a record somewhere in the Lowton Bull Ring.

'Kettle's boiled,' Dee Dee says. 'Do you want some toast?'

'I'll do it, Mum.'

'Sit down.' There is suddenly not enough space for them here, with the leaves of the table drawn out. Dee Dee moves her widening hips through the space between the fridge and the back of the chair, feels Alina a head and shoulders above her. She thinks of her still as a gawky schoolgirl all arms and legs, and now she is this lovely long-limbed young woman. She thinks of Sonia, the way she could move hardly at all when she danced but everyone would still look at her, want to be her or be with her. Alina sits without saying anything else, pushes her hair back over her ear. She wears earrings with teardrop scales that shimmer in the light through the window.

'I like your earrings.'

'Thanks. They were yours, I think.'

Dee Dee puts her hand across the table to hold Alina's hair back herself. She cannot place this jewellery at all. They look proper silver on the undersides, a peacock blue inlaid on the other side, meant to be feathers or fishscales.

'I got them from one of the boxes upstairs.'

Always messing with things, this girl, poking into drawers and boxes, ever since as a sticky-handed toddler she found a photo of Sonia as a chubby little girl and pointed at it.

'Look, it's Lina,' she had said, 'it's Lina.'

'Might have been Nana's,' Dee Dee says and puts milk in the tea, gives herself a sugar, cannot get the energy this morning, barely dragged herself to let Roni in, banging on the door early, nearly half-seven, like the place needed such a thorough clean after a heavy Friday, when they had barely had half a dozen in all night, if they took a hundred quid they'd been lucky. This cannot go on.

'What about, you know, anything else coming up?'

'I don't know, Mum. What like?'

Dee Dee doesn't answer, puts the bread back down in the toaster, she can never get that setting right, doesn't know what to say. Twenty-one years old, no boyfriend, barely any friends it seems to her now. What happened to Donna? she wants to ask her. Do you not see Taylor any more, love? Nothing in response, not much anyway; seems happy enough in herself, but it didn't seem much of a life to Dee Dee, living in the rooms above a pub, bits of part-time work in your cousins' and uncles' – not even your actual cousins and uncles – shops and market stalls, not even doing much with her art now from what Dee Dee can see. When she finished college, Dee Dee thought Alina would do something else. She could've gone to university, something. The years start to drift.

'Just, thinking about the future, you know.'

'By the time you was my age you was married,' Alina says in

a neutral tone. Dee Dee isn't sure if she is taking the piss or not, chooses to give her the benefit of the doubt.

'Nearly divorced,' Dee Dee replies in the same flat tone, looks at her. There'd been some big blow-ups as a teenager, some big rows, but that was to be expected, just the two of them together under one roof, needing one another. Never, not once, any 'You're not my real mum.' Not once. The opposite, really. 'I don't care, I'm glad what happened,' she said once, when she was eleven, twelve, just going up to secondary school, 'otherwise we wouldn't have been together.'

'Don't say that, Alina, don't say that. Your mum loved you very much,' she said to her even as she held her tight. Maybe that was when they started to move apart. Maybe Dee Dee had pushed her away, for her own good she thought.

And she wasn't even sure it was true. Sonia had not wanted her, only as a little trophy, a little doll. When she cried as a baby, Goldie had been better with her, shushing her and letting her sleep on his chest.

'She needs changing,' Dee Dee had said to her one afternoon, early on, Sonia moping about saying she felt fat. Dee Dee looked after Bobby and Tony, plenty of other younger cousins.

'She'll get a rash, Son.'

'You do it then, if you know so much about it.'

And she had. Old style nappies with safety pins because that was what Sonia's mum knew. Dee Dee soon changed that when she got the chance.

'And what's all that rope doing in the yard?'

Alina has coils of rope sitting inside the back gate, too heavy to lift anywhere. Dee Dee has no idea where it's from or how she got it there, the kind they used to tie things on ships with.

'Where's it from, even?'

'It's for a project.'

'What project? For who? An art thing?'

'Yeah, an art thing.'

'Roni says it'll attract rats.'

'Roni's bloody obsessed.'

'Says she can't put her bleach down properly.'

They both smile at this, at least, look at each other for the first time that morning.

'What art thing?'

'Just something, I don't know . . .' Alina's voice tails off, then, 'Tyrone's collecting it in the van for me,'

'Oh Tyrone is, is he?' Should she ask, who is Tyrone and pretend not to know? Dee Dee tries to think on her feet, not as quick as she once was, she realises, understands that there's still a smile on her face that she should probably try to lose. The rope is an utter mystery.

There's the smell of burning, then a coil of smoke before the alarm goes off. She can never get this toaster right. The smoke rises from the grill and is drawn up behind the half-open blind, drifts across the ceiling.

Dee Dee swears, pushes the window open, grabs a tea towel to threaten the smoke alarm with. Alina scrapes her chair back, gets up.

'Is the water on? I wanted a shower before I go,' makes her escape, moves like the smoke through the kitchen door.

. . .

Like Zidane, Pirlo's expression does not change, not one flicker from start to finish. If there is anything, there is just the tiniest hint of self-admonishment. It's the face of a man who has been out and come back home and realised that he has forgotten to post the letter he'd meant to. He is wearied. He looks like he wants to sit on his arse and think about Dante. The English players chase the air between Pirlo and the ball. He passes it into the gaps between the players, it's simple, he says.

Hart is on his back, like some great insect trying to right itself, Gregor Samsa in a red goalkeeper's shirt. Maybe it's all some joke that swirls back to Prague. Still, Pirlo's face stays the same.

. . .

She tried it with wool before, had not taken the scale into account. Spent half a day deeper than she'd ever been into the works, part of Lysaght's, Greenfields itself, Alina is not sure of the demarcation line, the railway tracks maybe, heavy iron wagons sat in the sidings, grass growing in tufts around the wheels, tall thin reeds with yellow flowers that she does not know the name of grew between the wooden slats. She stopped to photograph them. There was the long wall of one of the sheds in the background, and the contrast with sun on the hillside beyond, a corner of the cemetery fairly indistinct at this distance, an angel's wings just about visible. So she had something to show for the day, they'd come out well. She wanted to do something with the colour, deepen it, heighten it. She didn't even have the language for this stuff. The material was too big, she thought. It would take a life-time to learn how to do it, how to say anything of what she wanted. There was a lot to learn. The scale, for one thing. She spent a couple of hours trailing the wool through what had once been rolling mills, the sound of pigeons from the roof, she was shat on twice. As she walked she thought she should record their sounds, the splatter of wings and shit, the vibrating murmur in their throat as they slept. Just the sounds, maybe pictures with it. This was more of a complete piece. Ariadne, she'd call it. And it was strange, because she never got scared in there, never, although she knew she probably should, but that day she had the feeling that every turn she took she would come face to face with the monster, some monster or other, anyhow. No one who came over here was up to any good.

It was wrong for the space. It wasn't a maze, not this part, this wide abandoned factory floor. The wool did not work. She'd wanted to suggest frailty, of course. You could barely see it in the pictures, just a slight thread, but then maybe it was good, maybe that was the point. When she started to think in this way every-thing just went in circles and she'd ask herself what was the point of it all, tell herself to get out of there. It was why she always took photos, there was always a fall back, and in the imaginary conversation she had in her head of what she was doing in there she would say taking photographs because it was clear, to anyone who looked at the place for more than a few seconds, really looked at it, that surely this was something worth capturing. But the Ariadne thing kept playing on her mind. Hence the ropes.

'You should watch yourself, wandering about them factories all on your own,' that was the first thing he said to her, she thinks, but he had a smile on his face as he said it and it was like he was setting her a question, like how would he know about what she did, where she went. Afterwards, she thought she should've been more freaked out than she was, his earring glinted in the sun.

'I'm taking photographs,' is what she said.

'What for college or something?'

'For meself. I was at art college, so sort of, but I've packed it in. This is my own thing.'

'But you do need to be careful. For real. There's people living over there, I swear. There was a kid in a tent last summer. You get all sorts. And the animals, a whole pack of dogs, foxes everywhere, skinny little wild cats. One of our lads said he saw a tarantula over there, it come up out of a pipe by the old docks. It's the blokes who end up over there you need to watch out for, though, obviously.'

She laughed. 'A tarantula?'

'That's what he said. Escaped from the Spider House, or left over from the days of the docks. Things would hide in ships.'

'They'd hide in ships, not canal barges come from Birmingham. People really believe them spider stories.'

'I didn't say it was true. But the people thing is. And you should be careful. You ever play that spider game, when you were a kid? Hey, where did you go to school?'

'The Ironport,' she said, 'then Lowtown.'

He was from the Pengwern.

'I'm off the Peng,' is what he said, ruefully, defensively. He started naming people he thought she might know and she didn't know any of them.

'But you're Nathan's cousin, right?'

'Yeah, second cousin, really.' That would do. Sometimes it was useful to be an Ahmed.

'I used to train with Bobby sometimes,' he said this sadly too.

'Do you ever see him now?'

'Funnily enough, over the Yards sometimes. I think he might sleep over there himself some nights. I don't know. I told Lionel. He wasn't so sure.'

'My mum looks out for him. I'll tell her. You tell him he can come here if he needs anything.'

'I don't know for sure, but he's sometimes around there, round and about. If he sees the car or the uniform then he runs off, even if he sees it's me. I'll give him sandwiches or something if he stops. Not money, because you know where that goes. He don't need money, though he acts like he does.'

She texted him the picture of the angel's wings, the one with sun and shadow, and he texted straight back. She asked him if he'd help her move the rope. He said no problem, and how about getting a pizza or something afterwards.

．　．　．

The second painting hanging in the Hightown Town Council chamber is from the same aspect, looks down the valley from the hills. They say de Loutherbourg painted it on his way to or from the Bedlam works but it is not attributed, hangs on the opposite wall to the other painting.

It is night lit as day by the furnaces which bloom along the rivers. The Samson Foundry is there, the Watkins Cylinder Works, the fires which form the first incarnation of Greenfields. Bridges span the rivers. Canal mania has hit and barges throng the cut and the half-built Ironport docks. Smaller fires illuminate the shanty town of navvies from Ireland and the Black Country who live in shacks and tents in the mud. There is winding gear on the hilltops. The shallow coal is already gone, buildings sag down the hillsides with the ground dug out from under them. There are people everywhere in the valley bottom, tiny swarming black figures, ants on a burning log.

. . .

The Quakers is the old Quaker Burial Ground halfway to Burnt Village. They built their factories here in the valley, built the village for their workers to live in. It's where people go to drink when they've got nowhere else left. Saturday teatimes Mark Fala heads up there to give alms to the destitute. Matchdays are still hard for him. If he ever loses it again it will be a matchday. But he feels calm today. Liam has started, he knows that. He listened to the radio quietly for a while this afternoon. He pictures Ally standing naked in the showers, talking at Liam, 'You are not a footballer, son, do you hear me? You are a fucking warrior, a fucking gladiator. You go out in that second half and dominate that cunt, you understand me, son?'

For ages after Mark and Liam would put that voice on, try to get that wild look in their eyes. They would laugh about it, but the truth was they believed it too. That talk did the trick as well, Mark remembers, an away game at Port Vale or somewhere. Some old cunt playing for one last contract, to pay his mortgage, and Liam giving it all back to him, kicking lumps off him, taking an elbow and giving one back, grinning at the bloke and then taking the ball off him, shutting him up, dominating him. That was Liam: a fucking gladiator. He can see the floodlight pylons from here as he climbs the lane past the last houses and gets the feeling that sometimes comes, that he could be there right now, sitting in that dressing room, unlacing his boots, joking with Liam, or sat staring at the tiles, beaten. He doesn't know today's score. Burton Albion. They've started the season well, Irontown haven't. It doesn't matter. In the wheel of the days, there's always another match coming. Until there isn't. Even then, look at Ally, at Archie Hill, old Ted Groves who does the kit. Mark could've stayed for ever. He knows he has to shut out these thoughts. He'll have a can with the others in the Quakers if it's calm there, you can never predict. He doesn't drink that much these days, though, barely at all, contrary to what people think. Nothing compared with what he did. Let them think it, it suits him, means people leave him alone. If ever reporters come and bang on the door, track him down for some story of one of England's great lost football talents, he pretends to be so pissed as not to be able to speak. They can write what they want.

He puts a foot on the low wall. You have to be careful here. He is usually fine, it's usually just drink in here, the lifers.

Crackheads and the like don't climb the hill, not this late in the year. The drinkers enjoy a sunset, appreciate the autumn colours. Gravestones lean at angles against the wall. Drummer Pete salutes him, his belly bare and red and a can of cider resting on it.

'All right, Mark. Here he is look. Told yer he'd be here.'

A couple lie sleeping up the slope from where Pete reclines. A bloke called Jigsaw pisses loudly against the far wall. Stevie from Oxton stands a little way from Pete, his face to the sun, the last wisp of a roll-up tucked in the corner of his mouth. Mark pulls a couple of the Superkings from the pack in his pocket and presses them into his cracked hand. Stevie smiles at him, his eyes not quite there, whispers a thanks. When he's had a big session his voice goes.

Mark passes Pete a couple of cans, lays the bottle of sherry down on the tough grass. The ground here is uneven, the drinkers lie in little hollows where the graves subside.

'Cheers, Mark. Good to see yer. You are a saint.'

He cracks open a can himself, takes a sip, lights a cigarette.

'Not many here today,' Mark says.

'Some of 'em gone down the Assembly Rooms, there's a way in round the back.' Pete shrugs. 'We'll have to head indoors soon.'

'We could head down the caves again, or the old shaft at Black Park.' Stevie talks into the golden light and no one answers.

Mark enjoys the quiet, pulls long on the cigarette until his head buzzes. He has the odd one in the week, then a couple on a Saturday night. He is a man of moderation.

Tomorrow he will rise early as always. He will make the same walk up the hill, past the burial ground. He has often gone past and seen the shapes of bodies huddled against the stone walls. Pete and Jigsaw and Stevie sleep up here as late into the year as they can, come down with the first frost. If you're only drinking, you can go on a long time.

He will walk the hill to the cemetery and the crem, has to climb the gate sometimes when he's very early, clean his parents' graves with a roll of toilet paper, flowers if he can, walk round to the rose garden and sit for a while near Sonia's plaque. His weeks follow a careful pattern.

When Mark looks past Jigsaw, holding a fresh can out for him as he stumbles up the hill, he sees there are others, huddled by the bottom wall. He makes out Bobby Ahmed's wild hair. Dee Dee's nephew gone awry. He is not a boy for a nice steady drink on a late summer's afternoon. Mark has a screwdriver in his back pocket, not that it would do any good against Bobby. Mark is not a fucking warrior. Bobby was a kick-boxing champ until he went off the rails.

'Bobby Ahmed,' Mark says.

'Fucking headcase,' Pete says. 'It's all right, he won't come over if we're all here. Won't start nothing, anyway.'

Mark is dubious.

'Who's that with him?'

'Fuck knows.'

The figure beside Bobby crouches, wears a hood. He raises his hand and it looks as if Bobby will pull him up but instead he just takes whatever he has been passed and sticks it in his pocket. So Bobby's on the hard stuff now then, he reckons. So many different ways to kill the pain. There is something in the shape the figure makes against the wall that causes Mark to pause.

Jigsaw opens his can, tilts it towards the two men in a gesture of cheers.

'Leave it, Jig, fuck's sake,' Pete says, 'leave 'em to it, let's have a bit of peace.'

The hooded figure stands, climbs the wall, and heads along the path which runs down below the village and arcs back towards the Anvil Yards, an ancient drover's track that winds down to the old market where the rivers meet, through the ruins of Lysaght's and Watkins Cylinder Works. Mark takes that way home some-times, along the canal. He will not do so tonight. He looks at the shape of the man running away.

Bobby Ahmed strides towards them. There is a sudden charge to the air. Mark tenses, remains half hidden behind Stevie. He is not a fucking gladiator.

Bobby nods at each in turn. 'All right, gents. Give us a can, eh.'

'Here you go, Bobby, cheers.' Mark holds a drink out towards him. Bobby takes it, looks at each of them in turn.

He clinks his can against Jigsaw's, looks at Mark.

'What you up to Bobby?' Jigsaw says. Bobby sucks his teeth, this is not a question he likes. Pete says 'fucking hell,' under his breath, still lying back on the grass, a hand over his eyes against the low sun.

'You should think about what you're up to yourselves, boys, you should.' His eyes stay on Mark. 'Get yourselves indoors, maybe. Storm coming, I reckon. Storm coming.'

'We'll get ourselves in then Bobby, cheers.'

He turns and strides to go over the wall and the direction from which Mark came.

'Storm coming,' he says again.

'Fucking headcase,' Pete says when Bobby is at a safe distance.

'He might have just meant the weather,' Jigsaw says to no one in particular.

Mark sits down, lights another cigarette, plans a route home which means he won't run into Bobby. He will not go anywhere for a while. When it starts to rain the world is safer. He thinks of the shape of the running man.

. . .

Corineus took his axe to the King's throat, son of Brutus or not he would have his way. He had wrestled giants, would not be denied.

'You must marry my daughter,' Corineus said in the blade's gleaming light.

So Gwendolen became queen, bore Locrinus a son. Corineus was pleased, watched his grandson play in the reflection of his polished axe as his own days grew short, dreamed of killing giants and of the Trojan sun he would never see again. But Locrinus loved another, Estrildis, the most beautiful woman of the islands. He hid her in caves and in shadowy clearings and loved her there out of view of the world. With Estrildis, Locrinus had a daughter, Habren, hidden away in the dark woods and as beautiful as her mother.

When Corineus died, Locrinus abandoned Gwendolen,

took Estrildis as his new queen. But Gwendolen sought out the wild men of the south and west, brought an army to Locrinus' lands. They fought a war along muddy riverbanks and Gwendolen fired an iron arrow across the water into Locrinus' heart.

Gwendolen had Estrildis and Habren bound tight with chain at their ankles and wrists and then cast down the river to the sea, watched as their hair twisted in the current and slid under the brown water, saw the willow trees bow their heads, set the crown on her own head.

.   .   .

Gary Newbon: When Mark Fala puts the ball down on the spot you go over and say something to him. Can you remember what you said?

Liam Corwen: I know what I said. Listen, he'd been messing around when he took penalties since, well since I'd ever known him. In training, anyway. In matches he'd usually just stick it in the corner, but I knew he had it on his mind. We used to watch the same videos over and over as kids. They'd been his dad's. They'd not long bought a video when he died so we only had a few tapes, George Best and whatnot, over and over again. That chipped penalty was on one of them. Panenka, for Czechoslovakia, you know? Mark always loved that sort of thing. I knew what was on his mind. I just said to him, 'Don't f—in' chip it.'

Gary Newbon: And what did he say to that?

Liam Corwen: Nothing. I think I might have made his mind up for him, to be honest. Maybe. I wish I hadn't said it now. He sort of waved me away, the way he always knew best, you know? The more I think of it now, it all had to do with his dad, all of it, of course it did. His mum as well, of course. Maybe that was worse, I don't know. He never talked about it.

Gary Newbon: His parents were dead?

Liam Corwen: Died when he was a kid. You know the story. What's that saying? The straw that broke the camel's back or whatever, the penalty, that is. He saw his dad get killed, he was there for some reason, at the works the day it happened. Jesus. His mother couldn't cope with it all after, not really. I mean, who would? It hit us all bad when she went, to be honest, so god knows how it must have affected him. Like I say, he never talked about it.

Gary Newbon: Something I've noticed.

Liam Corwen: What?

Gary Newbon: You always refer to him in the past tense. As if Mark Fala is also . . .

Liam Corwen: He's dead to me, to a good many others as well. It was his choice. I think he died when he last kicked a football, the day of that penalty miss. He's dead to us.

Gary Newbon: You never see him now? You've never been in contact since he stopped playing?

Liam Corwen: I saw him at another funeral not long

after. A friend of ours who died on the day of
the game, the play-off. You know all this. There
was enough of it in the papers. He don't want the
contact. He wants to be left alone. There are days
I don't blame him. Can we stop talking about this
now?

He should never have agreed to the documentary in the first
place, thought it would disappear, but they still show it every
now and again, late at night after the football highlights. It's on
Youtube, anyway. He has tried not to read the comments. He
agreed to take part when he was in Finland, thought he was rid
of the place, never coming back. As he asks to stop the interview
and puts his hand to his face, they play footage of that goal against
Stockport as Liam says these last words, the one they always seem
to show, the one Mark scored on his eighteenth birthday. Wayne
Coombs wins a header under his own bar at a corner and the
ball goes up in the air and drops near the edge of the box. Mark
nips in front of their midfielder who is watching the ball, about
to hit it, and heads it over him, runs the other side of him and
takes it on his thigh, bounces it once, twice, three times on his
right leg as he runs, with a player having two kicks at him, they
called it the M'bou, Mark and Liam, after the Cameroon player
who ran with it down the line against Argentina in the Miracle
in Milan. Liam has it tattooed on his left ankle, he has Benjamin
Massing taking out Claudio Caniggia in the same match on his
right. Sometimes he thinks the tattoos are just some kind of
coded message to Mark. That he'll see a photo of Liam, his body
adorned, and the world will make sense.

And the Stockport fullback tries the Massing trick, throws his whole body at Mark, who lets the ball drop to his left foot, still midway inside his own half, and Mark twists and the bloke goes hurtling past him and crashes into his own player instead, and now Mark takes off. He runs straight up the middle of the pitch with the ball at his feet, defenders surging back and clipping his heels and falling away, they cannot catch him, running full pelt, he looks like a boy on a beach, and then twenty yards out or so, he gets it away from his feet for the first time, looks like he's miscontrolled it, and there's another defender sliding in from his right now, but he's got his head up and he clips the ball, no back lift, over the sliding challenge and over the keeper too, and the ball arcs perfectly into the net and he wheels away. You can see Liam on the edge of the screen, he was on the bench that day and Ally had got him warming up, he runs on the narrow track between the East Stand and the pitch, arms aloft towards the Greenfield End, going crazy. People always forget they lost that game 3-2, won the league though, and that's what mattered.

· · ·

He is the eagle. There is low, hard autumn sun for the derby. The stadium is a bowl of light, rightly named, the white-shirted crowd shine. When Eusébio rises to meet the ball he sees his shadow ripple across the pitch and he is the eagle, of course. He hears this in Guttmann's voice, but Guttmann has been gone two years now, yet his voice lingers on, whispering doubts, except not in Eusébio. For a moment he is not sure that this voice has not arrived with the ringing in the ears he got from the clatter of the Sporting keeper as he beat him to the ball's bounce off the hard surface and zigzagged his legs to clip it past the brim of the keeper's hat and have it bounce away from the direction he'd run and into the corner of the net. He takes the ball down and arches his back, head up, his eyes in their matchday squint, eagle eyes. The keepers wear hats like workers at the docks. Torres. Where is Torres? His arms reach, swim him through the light and past defenders, propel him, wings. He looks for Torres and races his own shadow across the grass.

. . .

She finds a length of broken iron pipe. Rust bubbles foam down one side. Goldie '89 is painted in an unidentifiable media (correction fluid?). The G and o are formed in thick sweeps, the lettering fades until the '89 appears in thin scratched strokes. It gives the impression of a boy in a hurry, a careless boy. The hairs rise on Alina's neck.

She takes the pipe from the outside wall of Lisbon House, an abandoned block of flats near where they used to all hang about. It's up the road from Stevedore House, where the Falas had lived, where that photo she loves had been taken. It's there she was headed for, to see if she could get onto the roof, when she stops to take a look around Lisbon House. Then she sees the lettering on the pipe, the kind of thing she'd been searching for all along. She stands and looks at it for a long time, prises it free with the iron cutters she bought from the place in Lascar that sells stolen bikes and the equipment with which to steal them.

It's the sort of place her dad would've appreciated from what she can tell.

She keeps it in a box with some other stuff at the back of Tony's studio. If her mum sees it, she might get the pipe wrapped around her head.

. . .

Saturday teatime Mark likes to turn the telly on, sometimes he can face *Final Score*, sometimes not. The telly was a bit of company, his mum used to say. Not enough for her, it turned out. He likes quizzes. Right now a couple from Leicester are being shown around houses in Tenerife. They don't seem very happy with the situation, red-faced and looking as though they are being short-changed against a hard blue sky. He presses the tea bag to the side of the cup, adds a sugar and watches it spread and dissolve like a galaxy flaring and dying millions of miles away. He has his routines. The apartment is close to a water park. The Corwens all went to Tenerife one year not long after Christmas, during the season, of course. Liam missed a week of school and a Mercian Cup game. Freddie Rogers, their old coach at Lascar Boys Club got in a mood about it, tried to drop Liam for the next game, but then Joey Corwen got involved. Mark remembers watching from the minibus window as Liam's dad pushed his bronzed head into Freddie's bobble hat, 'You leave him out then I'll take him up to Cowton Sports, don't you worry about that, you ungrateful cunt.'

It was always a bit like that, like Liam was doing them a favour.

He started next match, of course, and all the others. Freddie was a good coach though, a bit soft with them maybe, still lived in the same house with gnomes in the front yard, roses and canes of runner beans in the summer, rode his mobility scooter up to the row of shops at the Ironport.

'Yer fit?' Freddie asks him if he sees him, same as he used to greet him as a fourteen-year-old out on the old Heath junior pitches.

'I am, Fred. You?'

'What's it look like? I see your mate's up to no good again.'

There had been letters about Liam and the Wolves supporters in the *Chronicle*. Ally has promised an investigation. Liam can do whatever he likes, just as he always has.

'What, Liam? I don't see him no more Fred, you know that.'

'No, that other one. Him who robbed the shop, got that girl killed.'

'What?'

'That one. I seen him in the Bull Ring the other day, up to no good, most likely, I thought.'

'No Fred, no, he ain't ever coming back round here, must've been somebody else.'

But as he says it he thinks of a crouching man, a running man. 'There's a storm coming,' is what Bobby Ahmed said.

Flies rise past the window. They are demolishing some old outhouses down near the docks wall, buildings gone the shape of cardboard boxes left in the rain. There is something in the afternoon paper about progress being made on the redevelopment plans, architect's drawings.

'I'll believe it when I see it,' is what Freddie Rogers mutters, on his way back from the new Ukrainian shop, when he sees these pictures of landscaped gardens between flats and offices with shiny windows, no men on mobility scooters or clutching oxygen masks or even straggling along with sticks and walking frames in these drawings, uniform couples and families, none of them old, or poor, not one too black, or too white for that matter, not one shuffling along with one shoe on and a football boot on the other foot, not one sprawled with a can on that neatly trimmed grass, no one sitting with their shirt off having a smoke, or dragging their kids and stepkids along with bags of shopping hanging off the pushchair with a dodgy wheel, and none of them reflected in any of the glass, these vampires.

When they knock the buildings down the flies come this way on the wind, rats scatter in all directions.

'What are you thinking?' asks the young woman in the summer dress on television, who looks not unlike one of those figures in the drawing, of the couple from Leicester who look not unlike some of the people not present in the picture. Perhaps that's where they'll all get moved to, Tenerife.

'What are you thinking?'

They stare at palm trees and lizard-backed mountains. If they don't like the place they shouldn't move. That life is very long, is what Mark thinks. He sips his tea, still too hot, like he does every afternoon. He waits for it to cool, for the couple to make up their mind and his afternoon quiz to start. You need routines. People always say life's too short. He thinks they're wrong. A fly taps the window glass. There are creatures that only live for a day, for a few hours. They have no memories, no sense of themselves at all, or if they do it's all present, all happening right now, an endlessly running moment, so that in a sense they live for ever, like the way they say fish think, which he does not fully believe. The couple from Leicester say they expected more wow factor. Outside the flies rise.

. . .

A list of the proposed redevelopments of the Greenfield Ironworks and the surrounding areas of the Anvil Yards since British Steel finally ended production in 1984:

A shopping centre.

A J.R.R. Tolkien-inspired theme park (this in the days before Middle-Earth was outsourced to New Zealand. There was a story that a trip Tolkien made to the Iron Towns, west from Birmingham or Oxford, inspired his vision of Mordor. But travel the lanes that weave across the Heath, or go on the back roads through Far Valley or the Welsh Ridge and you could just as easily be in The Shire).

A site for the World Student Games and/or Commonwealth Games.

Another shopping centre.

A King Arthur-inspired theme park (a 1960s New Age paperback linked the valley with the journeys of the Knights of the Round Table. There was a plan to use one of the Lascar docks as the lake, from which the sword would emerge every afternoon).

A Japanese car plant (before the Japanese economy went the way of the Iron Towns).

A new home for the BBC.

A mega-casino and attendant hotel development. (Quickly nicknamed Ironvegas, this idea is unique in that part of it was actually built. The hotel in which Liam currently lives is the only building that was completed before permission was halted and the money ran out. The project revived the idea of using a dock as the lake, for a giant lap-dancing venue called Guinevere's. A topless lady of the lake was set to emerge each evening.)

Another shopping centre.

Arcadia: an eco-development which meant emptying out anything that was left and letting nature take its course, introducing deer, eagles, even wolves in one version of the plan. Chernobyl-chic.

An airport and giant freight terminal. (In one set of plans called London Iron Town. The developers tried the old Eusébio trick.)

A privately run complex of super-prisons.

A Chinese-owned steelworks with surrounding factories supplying the People's Army (in spite of terrible feng-shui, it was the absence of any skilled workers that put an end to this plan. The whole thing has now gone on so long that there are plenty of people who were in their teens when the Anvil Yards began to rust, now approaching retirement age, who have never worked).

There are arguments about who owns the land, contamination, decontamination, compensation, what to do with the businesses that simply refuse to die, not to mention the people who live there and refuse to move, viewed by developers in the way that divers look at molluscs on the hulk of the *Titanic*. Then there is the issue with UNESCO placing the Greenfield Ironworks, the Samson Foundry, the Watkins Cylinder Factory, Lysaght's, the East Stand and half the docks on their World Heritage Sites list. Soldiers in blue helmets, Bengali, Armenian, Dutch, might arrive to halt any dynamiting.

. . .

Mark Fala did not go to school that morning. There were days when his mum said not to bother, he helped carry her shopping bags or took wet clothes up to the washing line on the roof. Or he would spend the whole day on the uneven wasteland that doubled as Wembley, Anfield, the Azteca, and drill his tennis ball against the flats' end wall and take the rebound anywhere on his body, on the full, and drop the ball dead to do the same thing all over again.

That morning she asks him to take two empty pop bottles back for the deposit, and to drop his dad's sandwiches at work for him. He has left them sitting in the foil in which she wrapped them last night next to the sink, distracted by something out of the window in the blue dawn light.

His dad hauls a chain, backlit by a furnace which burns some-where deep in the works. He sees him, sees Mark standing there outside in the yard, his foot on his ball, an empty pop bottle in each hand, a thin plastic bag holding the sandwiches hangs from his wrist. They both smile. His dad goes to raise an arm. Mark thinks it is to motion him to the gates, or wave, or tell him to wait, when something happens to the chain.

His dad jumps backwards and then the bucket that swings above the moulds, that his dad is set to pour, wobbles and spills.

Here is the molten metal, so white hot that it burns a shape into Mark's eyes that he is not sure he ever really blinks away. And it pours, liquid and heavy, not into the mould, but onto Antony Fala. The movements are slapstick, innocent, a broken chain, a spilled bucket, a fall-guy. Mark sees his dad crumple, his body withers, the way a match does if you leave it alight and wait for it to burn your fingertips. There are screams, shouts. Men run. A bell starts to ring over the clanging sounds from elsewhere in the factory. Mark remembers later that there was a magpie chuckling, hopping across a pile of scrap metal in the yard. The magpie flies away as the men run through the gates. When he thinks of this later, he believes that it is his dad's soul leaving his body and jumping into that of the bird. He puts silver foil pellets on his window ledge to see if the magpies will come.

'The boy, look, the boy.'

'What?'

'His boy, Fala's boy, in the yard.'

'Oh, Jesus.'

'Come here, son, come here.'

'Get him away from here.'

This is Mark Fala, eleven years old. High clouds move over the Anvil Yards. Mark stands with his foot on his ball, a bottle in either hand, the sandwiches his dad will never eat hanging from his wrist and he looks past the running, shouting men and sees the blackened shape on the floor. The empty mould sits on the stopped conveyor, a broken chain swings back and forth above it. Mark does not remember anything about what comes next, days, weeks. He kicks his ball against the end wall.

. . .

'I found a johnny in the toilets this morning, Dee Dee.'

'What?'

'Has it been that long that you've forgot what one is? A condom, a johnny, in the bogs.'

Dee Dee pauses to consider this.

'Used?'

'I wouldn't say otherwise, would I?'

'I wouldn't have thought they'd got that much life in them.'

Dee Dee is suddenly pleased by this news, that she might be running somewhere that inspires enough passion for a quickie in a toilet cubicle. She thinks for a minute about who was drinking in the lounge last night.

'Which toilets?' she asks. Roni holds her mug of tea in both hands. Her pyjamaed legs are folded beneath her.

'The ladies,' she says, 'in the bar.'

'In the bar?' Dee Dee says.

'In the bar, behind the cistern. I fetched it out with the mop.'

'The only people we had in the bar last night was Manjit Kohli and them from the bakery.'

The bakery is the last factory open in the Anvil Yards, sliced bread on an industrial scale, Sikh men backlit by yellow sodium at all hours of the day and night.

Roni shrugs.

'Life in the old dogs yet, Dee Dee.'

'Am yer having me on?'

'I swear to god. Behind the tank in one of the ladies cubicles.

Disgusting, really, they could put it in the bin.'

'Well,' Dee Dee says, pauses for effect, doesn't look at Roni, 'I had it in the bogs here once.'

Roni spits a mouthful of tea onto the yard, swears. 'What? Who with?'

'Who with? Who'd yer think? Liam. Who else would it have been? Who with?!'

'I don't know what to say.'

'In the lounge, mind. We had standards. I did, anyway.'

. . .

He rises from the French mud, where he lay bootless.

Leônidas rises, this mud man, as if a ghost of the middle passage torn from the seabed, and then skips and dances with the ball through the hacking legs. Defenders move like magnets repelled.

This European dream of Brazilian football is born in Strasbourg. Men think of that goal, some of them in their motley workers' caps, as they trudge away from the river, as their trains slowly pick up speed, heading south and west, when they evacuate the city, empty it completely, when the Germans come across the Rhine. Another iron town, with its factories and cranes and its port so many miles inland.

Wenger grew up there, in a pub stained brown with tobacco smoke, in a town stained grey from chimney smoke. Liam tells himself the pub was called the King of Sparta. He doesn't even know if pubs have names in France.

Leônidas's footsteps, which barely mark the ground, become

those of Vava and Didi and Garrincha and Pelé and Jahrinio and Zico and Eder and Socrates and Ronaldinho, a whole string of little Juninhos, and Ronaldo and Neymar and on and on into the future.

I am the resurrection and I am the life, runs the text in the shape of Leônidas's dash for the goal, which winds along Liam's spine towards Ronaldo as Christ the Redeemer.

'Biblical quotations,' says the journalist, a woman in her twenties, into her recorder, her dark hair cut into a harsh fringe. She looks at him and her fingers almost brush his flesh.

'Nah, The Stone Roses,' he says, then wishes he hadn't and had just held her stare. The words were Tony's idea. The words do not mean anything, but the swaying run through the mud, the goal that brings the sun out in Strasbourg, the one that Leônidas scores without a boot on his foot, to make it Brazil 5, Poland 4, they win 6-5, that is real. He wonders if the boots remain buried. Some corner of a foreign field.

Except he watched it later, after the tattoo, some bleached-out newsreel resurrected on the internet, and the mud isn't there, not really, and the sun shines and it is so, well, deflating, and lacks all of the grandeur that they have invested in it, words or not, this dark figure rising from European mud etched halfway up his back.

'And what does it mean?' she asks him, and he is struck that no one English would ever ask this kind of question with this earnestness, no one he has ever met, anyway.

'Leônidas was the King of Sparta,' he says, 'leader of the three hundred, hero of Thermopylae.' And she nods but looks confused, not sure if he is serious, or if this is just one big English joke, and this time he holds her gaze, smiling, with a kind of half-mocking look. Of course it isn't serious. Of course it is. He knows she is staying in the hotel. He cannot play golf, has no share prices to check, just the afternoons to fill stuck inside the room's four walls, inside his own head.

.   .   .

And if you're the Baggies,
or the Wolves,
or them sheep shagging bastards,
then you ain't no friend of mine.
All together now,
My old man . . .

They do not sing about us, these other clubs, Liam thinks from the dugout, his feet up on the breeze block, concentrating on the pock marks the players' studs have made and the sheen of mud and the white line in front of him as the lights become stronger. He will not get on today. The game drifts along rudderless. Needles of rain come suddenly in the lights. He hears the clatter of seats behind him as people stand to leave before the end. He cannot understand this, begins to lift his head and turn to glare at the punters behind, but what's the point? He wears a snood. Dee Dee and Sonia had them once, luminous green and orange. His is Eton Blue. He sees Sonia's eyes waiting for him through the rain. They saw each other once at a bus shelter on the Heath, like a mossy cave with the rain beating on it, down by the Goat Wood where the witches meet.

And those other clubs do not sing about the Iron Towns, do not even consider them worth acknowledging, not even Wrexham he doesn't think, not even Newport, unless you count 'Stand up if you hate England.'

'We need some new songs,' he says.

Shaunie McLaughlin nods his head, now neither of them are starting. Ally's got a lad in on loan from Cheltenham Town, looks half-decent.

'New songs,' Shaunie repeats and nods like this is wisdom of great import. Ally must have told him to listen to everything Liam says. That's all the kid needs, Liam thinks, wipes his nose on his snood.

. . .

Caller: I mean, you lot all talk about how Liam
    Corwen is a great player, a great servant to
    this club. Listen, when he got in the team we was
    fifteenth in the old second division or whatever
    it was called then. He's played for twenty years
    and in that time we've had relegations, all them
    money worries and nothing but trouble. Them
    years he was away, we had the Trophy final, we
    had the play-offs again. They was the best years
    of the last twenty. Then he come back. What's he
    come back for? He's on the biggest contract, the
    highest wages. Bleeding the club dry, that's what
    people like him am doing. That Julius Williams,
    Devon Samuels, the same. Listen, my old man worked
    on the railways. They used to have a name for

folks who'd bring bad luck, straight from the Old
Testament. He's a Jonah, Liam Corwen. Throw him
overboard now, before it's too late.

Dave 'Iron' Willis: Graham, Graham, you cannot
be seriously saying that the problems faced by
Irontown Football Club are caused by Liam Corwen?
He's a club legend. The guy bleeds Eton Blue.

Caller: Legend? I've told yer what he is. And it's
not just him to blame, no. I'll tell yer what,
though. He is plain bad luck.

Joey turns the radio off and sits in the car outside the shops. They used to say pay no attention to the table until October was out. They might win a few and be in the play-off places come the new year. He knows this will not happen.

They are a cancer, these phone-ins. Joey does not use the term lightly. Liam wasn't even getting a game. Maybe if Ally picked him for more than one game out of three, if Ally picked the same back four two games running, in fact where was Ally in all this moaning? That bloke could swim through honey, nothing stuck to him.

Cancer the crab, he thinks of pincers taking hold, of never letting go. It's why the disease is so named, pub quiz knowledge. He thinks of young doctors, consultants, peering at pictures of Liz's insides between rounds of golf or skiing trips, or whatever they do, these men from a different world, their hands on your wife, cutting your wife, laying her down on their cold slabs.

They would pore over the shapes and patterns that come from Liz's insides like maps of some strange empire, discuss strategy, absentee generals. Not for too long, though, had tee-off times to meet and the like. Mr Ali is not here on Friday afternoons. Dr Roberts isn't in until tomorrow. The arms, pincers, tentacles stretch and writhe inside her body. Some terrible, invisible war raging. And then thank you doctor, thank you doctor, thank you . . .

The nurses were better, the porters. At least they spoke to you like you were another human being, like if you saw them in the street or at the football or whatever they'd smile and say hello.

Liz wants to move and who can blame her. She'd wanted to go when the kids were young. He hadn't wanted to move Liam, already showing a bit of promise, hadn't thought the whole place would close down, just showed what he knew. They say they stay for his old man now, so Liz can do his ironing, clean the house, take his meals round. But Joey knows it's really him they stay for. He tells himself he'll look at those brochures she put out, houses in Bridgnorth and Brecon, retirement villages on the Algarve and Costa Dorada, anywhere, anywhere but here.

'Cup of tea, love?'

'Yes please.'

What else to say?

Now it's over, she's better. They don't say better, but she's clear, and there's nothing to say to each other at all. If Liam visited once in those months without being reminded, without still just sitting himself down and his tea done for him, then Joey was being kind.

Cup of tea, love, cup of tea, love, cup of tea . . .

. . .

These noises would destroy most men, that's what Goldie tells himself these first few weeks. He'd adjusted to prison noises over time, the breathing of other men close by, shouts down tiled corridors, a low, constant hum of strip-lights. The twitches and pain in your temples at the sharp movements or sudden sounds of other men who might do you real damage, given half a chance. With time, with the days, that sense eases, but only somewhat. If he thinks about it all, perhaps that feeling has always been with him, way before prison days, that knowledge of the harm you might inflict, that might be done to you, always there, the steady hum at the temples, the sound of windowless rooms and boys' shouts down tiled corridors.

Noises and the dark fill his mind. The first night he hears an owl hoot and imagines the rustle of wings. There are bars at the window. The desk drawers are stuffed full of reams of typed paper, fading text and digits in purple and grey. The figures make an indentation on the paper, each one a little hammer blow. Rats splash in the narrow canal under the window. The men left the place as if everyone would be back in work tomorrow, thirty years and more now. No one is coming back.

He has five hundred pounds in dirty notes done up in red elastic bands that the postmen use and little plastic change bags. Some of it from the back of Nadine's underwear drawer; some from the biscuit tin in the cupboard in her mum's kitchen, first places anyone would look. It was money to go away with. They were going to book something for the bank holiday week,

Nadine, her mum and the girls. That has passed now. Summer is over. He was tired of trying to look after another man's kids and not doing very well at it. He has not done a good job of anything since climbing through those skylights into warehouses stuffed full with treasure all those years ago.

'Here comes Spider-Man,' Stan Ahmed had said to him, clapped him on his back, so hard as to knock him over, just to let him know who was boss. He thought the name might stick but it never did.

This morning he sits on a step in a doorway that opens onto the canal towpath. The gap between the tall buildings makes a ravine that the water runs through, iron rings and hooks jut from the brickwork, rust stains trailing from them. He is safe here, he thinks. No one comes this far into the works, not even people up to no good. He looks at the blue swirl of the lion's mane on the signs which warn of security guards and dogs. They walk the perimeters from a Portakabin office over by the Ironport, sometimes they drive around the buildings in small white vans. The roads are subsiding, potholed, soon they'll need diggers, caterpillar tracks, bulldozers. One day they'll flatten the place but not yet. This will do for now.

When he stands his trousers fall down over his arse. He was always skinny, now his hips jut out and his jeans hang from them. When he came out the second time, after he'd gone back in for robbing and whatnot, like what was he expected to do now, to keep going, put food in his empty belly while they expected him to carry on in one scheme or the other, cleaning the kitchens at the college, chopping onions and taking scraps out to the bins, giving him a knife. He remembers the shock of seeing soft-faced white boys on the bus with their trousers falling down to show their pants. Everyone wants to be a bad boy now.

He is safe as he can be here, he thinks. No one comes this far into the world of cobwebs and typed paper and telephone dials, back through time and space. The money will run out. His trousers will fall down. Winter will come. He thought phoning Dee Dee would spur him on, make him do something. It got him here. He used to dream about Dee Dee and Sonia together, wanking as quiet as he could under scratchy blankets, still does sometimes. He wishes he hadn't phoned now, let them all know. He'd like to see Liam, he thinks, to see Mark. There are days he thinks he'd like to meet them with a knife, they just cut him off, not one message or card or anything like that. Something will come to him, he thinks, something is out there waiting for him.

. . .

'Hey,' a voice calls from the dark entrance to the old Assembly Rooms, a figure leans forward off the cardboard that patterns the steps. Mark has got too casual. He steps off the pavement into the gutter, rests his boot's worn-down studs on the high kerb, doesn't want to run or look too startled, his heart going.

A hand reaches out at him from the gloom.

'Hey, geezer, all right?'

It's Bobby Ahmed grinning at him, not quite looking at him. Still, Bobby must be the only person in the whole of the Iron Towns not to call Mark by name. It irritates him for a moment.

Geezer. No one says that within a hundred miles radius, more.

They came to see Bobby fight here when he was a kid, no more than a little boy really, before he switched to kick-boxing and steroids and weed, and whatever else he is doing now, boys boxing against clubs from the Welsh valleys or the Black Country. *Iron Towns, Iron Towns, Iron Towns* would echo from the back of the hall. He went to one once with the team where there were blokes eating steaks watching kids batter each other's heads in. *Kill him, Bobby,* they would shout.

'Penny for the guy, blood?'

Bobby's open hand reaches out to him, cracked and dirty. Mark thinks he must have slept on the steps, it's not much after first light, a thick dew on the world, cold first thing in a morning now but the sun still shines in the afternoons. Bobby's mum and dad live in a mansion somewhere up by the Heathside, he must still have his bedroom there. Just go home, Bobby, he wants to say.

It was a mistake to stand down the kerb like this with Bobby standing over him, no one else around, this the turning that the bread lorries use for the bakery and be careful not to step back and get flattened, Mark thinks, and somewhere wonders at his own capacity for survival. But then there's Bobby's soft face and the way he doesn't really look at him. The idea that he really would hand some money over to him, although he's done it in the past, of course.

'Where's your guy?'

'What?'

'You ain't got no guy, Bobby.'

He sees that Bobby is surprised that he uses his name, wonders if he can actually see anything, looking like a blind beggar, some roadside penitent from a painting of centuries past, dressed in a ragged Nike track suit.

'You can't ask for money with no guy, mate.'

Bobby giggles like a little boy. Mark feels a stab of pity and then disgust. He has a handful of change in his pocket. He is going to the back hatch at the bakery to buy a warm misshaped loaf, teacakes if they've got any.

'It's trick or treat they go for now, Bobby, any road. You should try that instead, mate.'

Bobby nods and smiles, his shoulders tremble with mirth and he laughs again. The punch comes quick, so fast that Mark is out on the wet pavement before he even realises he has been hit. Bobby had nothing in his hand, he will think later, when he tries to convince himself he's been hit by a brick, by some gargoyle tumbling off one of the ruins, but no, it's Bobby's fist all right, hard and fast and the last ability to leave him.

Mark covers up in the gutter, waits for more blows. Instead there's an iron grip on his shoulder and lips that brush his ear.

'I am the fucking guy,' Bobby says, steps over him, hasn't even bothered to pick up the change that jangles from Mark's pocket.

He lies on the wet stones for a bit, his head getting bigger and then smaller, the street rising and falling. The running man was Goldie, a thought that comes with the throb in his head, like a vision across the years.

A bread van slows as it goes past him, the sound of the tyres on the tarmac like that of a tide coming in, going out, he moves so they don't think he's dead, and the van doesn't stop.

. . .

Stanley Matthews, Duncan Edwards, Billy Wright. Men from Hanley and Dudley and Ironbridge. Princes of Mercia, like Offa, like Kenelm. They run together around the Highbury pitch at England training, conscious of the photographer's gaze. They match each other's stride. Legs built on cobbles, by racing up slag heaps and terraces. Stanley Matthews runs on Blackpool sands. It's one reason why he plays until he's fifty. Duncan Edwards wears a jumper to build up a sweat, the two older men wear shirts open at the neck, day-trippers at the seaside. Older men: Matthews is forty-two, in his last year with the England team. There's a happiness and confidence and determination in their look.

Billy Wright's dad worked in a foundry, big Duncan's too. Matthews's was a barber and pro boxer; his own son plays tennis, wins the Boys championship at Wimbledon just five years hence, they say he's the new Fred Perry. But this photo offers nothing of what is to come. Look at the big young man in the middle of the three. Ten months after the picture is taken he is dead, twenty-one. Later, Duncan Edwards's dad leaves his foundry job, works at the cemetery where his son is buried, tends the flowers and the verges and the graves.

. . .

Liam sometimes went to watch the Villa on his own, midweek or on a Sunday, when they hadn't got a game. This in the years when it went wrong for them, Irontown, for him, with the team struggling, with Mark gone, no chance of an England call ever coming again, just ridicule, in fact, because Taylor had been sacked and everyone said the players he'd picked had been no good. And the big money and the TV came now and they'd missed out on it all thanks to a fluffed penalty, a loss of heart, loss of nerve. When he played away from home now Liam was singled out with braying donkey noises, even though he held that defence together, and that's what Ally whispered in his ear, and Ally kept him going. It was a kind of big man syndrome, everyone wanting to have a pop at him. His dad kept quiet, like he thought he had it coming. Maybe he did.

'If they're making a noise, son, you're doing something right. They are scared of you, terrified. You just carry on as you are,' Ally would stand naked in the middle of the dressing room, telling them that Liam is the best defender he's ever worked with.

Sometimes their opponents – places like Peterborough and Doncaster – would sing 'Where's Mark Fala gone?' to the tune of 'Where's your caravan?' but it never really took off, and the Iron Towns support would drown it out with his name, over and over, like he'd gone nowhere at all. It was Liam they really liked to taunt, sensing a wound, sensing blood.

He'd pull a cap down tight, bury his face in an old scarf, lose himself in the crowd round Villa Park, in the red brick and the rain. There was a cup match he went away to, Sheffield United, Bramall Lane in the snow, when Yorke chipped a penalty just like Mark had tried.

You needed an iron will to do it, to carry it off.

Yorke runs up as if to strike it, does not shorten his stride, but instead digs his foot underneath it, like a pitching wedge or something and hits it with back-spin, almost too hard, so it dips just under the cross bar and into the net and he runs off to the side of the goal, laughing.

Back then people fixated on Yorke's smile, like it was all a joke, which it was of course, but they'd patronise him and say he played with a smile on his face, like none of it mattered, like you didn't need an iron will to pull that off, to come from where he had come from and end up where he did, that's what Liam thought. Everyone missed the point. He might have had a happy smile but he had balls of fucking iron.

Then they ended up with Liverpool in the semi-final. Liam went to that too. They got undone by Robbie Fowler, who flitted in and out of the Villa area like he wore an invisible cloak. It was at Old Trafford, that semi-final, in the time before they played them all at Wembley. He wouldn't have gone to Wembley, was glad when they pulled the place down. He stood and looked at the Busby Babes' stopped clock before the match. He wished he had Mark to talk to, Dee Dee as well, too late now. Most clocks keep ticking.

. . .

He can hear horses' hooves. It must be a Friday, Goldie thinks, and is caught somewhere between now and then, because it is Friday, and there really is the sound of horses' hooves echoing through the estate.

They used to call the Pengwern the Lost Valley or The

Island. There was a little iron bridge that went over the cut, the Navvy they used to call it, the Chain Navigation, and led into Lysaght's, where the men had worked, and apart from the road that ran down from Lowtown, that was the only way on and off the place without a coracle. The gate at the bridge was rusted shut now, of course. There was the gasworks on one side, towers of scrap and the river itself on the other, so the Peng had always been a little world to itself.

They used to ride pony traps all around the estate on Friday afternoons. The ponies came off the back field next to the river. The traps were customised, seats from old cars, rigs from the fairground, all from the scrapyards that petered out into the back field. All the kids who never bothered with school used to meet down the stables early afternoon and sort out who was riding with who, a kind of rough democracy, common owner-ship to it all. A mate of his called Tommy Knock used to take him out. Goldie was scared of horses. This was in the days before he started to hang around with Liam and Mark, Dee Dee and Sonia, before he got into all that stuff with the Ahmeds. He should've just stayed here, he thinks, not for the first time in his life, looks at the grass that grows out of the gutter, up the middle of the road in places. There were people when he was growing up who'd never even been into Hightown. He wasn't sure his mum ever had. He could've stayed here, headed out in the dark for ware-houses packed with treasure, ridden around in a carriage like a prince on a Friday afternoon.

It looks the same, the houses anyway, more or less. There are grilles here up at the windows and doors at the end house where the Sadlers used to live, a family where it was the women who used to go to prison, forward thinking, thieving even when everyone else was still trudging over the bridge to start their shift. Nana Sadler was an old flame of Stan Ahmed's, would fence stuff down at the row of garages. They called her the Black Cat, perhaps because of her ability to get away with things, but also because of her luck at the bingo, at the horses. She'd been a bookie's runner as a girl, left from the pubs and the factory gates to take messages to the Carter boys who waited at the Hightown station. There is nothing left of the Sadlers. He wonders what is behind the green metal shutters. With eyes half-closed they look like windows on a doll's house, or on postcards of happy places in the mountains in countries far from here. There is the odd blue brick among the red.

The hooves get louder, closer, there is a whooping shout from somewhere and then a flashing movement from the end of the street and a young brown horse comes trotting down the middle of the road and he sees the trap make a clean arc around the bend behind it. He steps onto the pavement and tugs at his hood and when he looks again, swears to god that it is Tommy Knock's freckled face above that of the horse. Red freckles on Tommy, white freckles on the horse's face, a mop of red hair on both. Tommy holds the reins three-quarters taut in his hands. A young girl sits next to him, leaning back and laughing, pale faced, with black hair tied up on her head, wearing clothes too thin for the weather.

And then they are gone, and he listens to the sound bouncing off the Sadlers' empty house and he puts his hands on the low wall and takes a gulp of air to steady himself.

He will have had kids, Tommy, of course he will have. He probably still lives down there on Stream Crescent, out the other end of the road, past the shops or whatever is left of them, past Goldie's old house. Where would he have gone? The towers of scrap are all still there. It was Tommy's son, must have been.

His legs will not move as he wants them to, will not go one step more in the direction he wants to go. He listens to the hooves as they fade and the boy drives the trap on the old circuit, Goldie can tell from the sounds, down to the road that runs parallel with the cut, where you could really get a speed up before having to slow into the corner, unless you wanted to end up in the drink. In summer, they'd have races after tea as the sky turned a darker blue. Lads would come to race cars there on Sunday nights. There is just a faint clip-clop now in the distance, that far corner, and Goldie turns his back and walks up the road back towards the Lowtown turning. He'll come back another time, another day, when he feels a bit better, a bit more up to it.

He has not seen his mother since she used to get the early morning bus to Birmingham, visiting orders in her handbag, wearing her best clothes and trying not to catch anyone's eye, but all that faded, and they have not spoken since he moved in with Nadine, wrote the address carefully in a Christmas card that he sent her much too late. Strange, how they'd got through the hardest part, she could've just disowned him, never spoken to him again, but she didn't, then everything faded away after he'd been released, like she thought he should still be inside. Maybe that had been easier for her. A few days won't make any differ-ence now.

. . .

In the photograph Tony has laid out on the desk for him, there is a man running, telephone wires stretched above him. Abundant green leaves explode at the roadside. In the foreground another man, shirtless, wearing a beret, turns and smiles, a rifle held down at his side. He seems to look back at the man in mid-stride who stares nowhere in particular, down the road and out of shot. But it is not the running man at whom he smiles but the severed head that sits in the road like an unkicked football, eyes half-open, a snail's trail of blood behind it.

'Fucking hell,' Liam says. He realises the shock is in not seeing the head at first. Or that you see it – it is right there in the middle of the picture, it is what is being photographed – but don't reg-ister it. And that is what the running man does too. The longer that Liam looks at the picture the more he believes that the run-ning man has not seen the head. It is the man in the foreground who makes us see it, grinning back at it. The other man runs down the road, towards something, away from something, both, maybe that isn't important. This is just another picture from some unknown African war. Liam wonders briefly about the men, the boys who straggle in a line by the tree. That everyone in this picture is now dead. Another image forms, another photo he must have seen once or something half-registered from the telly. It is one of the men today, maybe the man that grins and holds his gun down, older but not that much, another roadside. The man rides a wobbly bicycle, rings a bell. An icebox is balanced on the handlebars and leaks across his shorts. In the box he keeps cold beers, bottles of pop, river fish, whatever he can buy and sell. Sometimes at night he dreams that he opens the icebox and finds a severed head.

'Just think about the shape of the figures,' Tony says. Liam shuffles the cuttings and sketchbook pages on the desk. Running men across all of them. The door bell rings and Tony steps away to pull back the curtain which separates this small space at the back of the shop, which he insists on calling his studio, which has the table at which they sit and an old green velour comfy chair that Liam thinks used to be in Dee Dee's nana's front room and a rattling fridge which leaks water against the back door. The door and window are barred and look out onto the yard. A bag of rubbish has burst across the uneven concrete, chicken bones and batter, and Liam thinks of the foxes, how there are so many more of them each year and how only that morning he'd seen one sitting out on the path that ran along the old railway line under the hotel window and how the colour of the path with no rain is the same as that in the picture. He wonders what the fox might do, confronted with a head on the path in the Anvil Yards. How it might accept it, unquestioning, circle it and lap at the bloody trail or whether it would become spooked by the heavy lidded eyes and hide.

More men running. This time Liam recognises the face in the picture a while before he realises who it is, half-listening to the muffled voices at the front of the shop. The young man's face is almost hidden behind the bulk of an older man, bearded and fierce, who leads the run.

'Run so I can throw a goal net over you all,' was a line Freddie Rogers used to use when he had them training at Lascar Boys. Liam uses it himself, now, when he sometimes trains the kids or leads a warm-up. It is how these men run, how the camera has caught them, beads of sweat and a gob of spit glint in the sunlight, their feet arch or leave the ground completely as they run slightly askance to the white touchline. Behind them the spindle and mesh of a half-finished football stand rises. There is a distant worker in a yellow hard-hat. Beyond that are mountains, with snow on top although these players shine with sweat and water bottles dot the pitch.

Luis. It is Luis, Liam is sure. The slender black boy, half-hidden behind the bearded man. He pulls the picture closer to him. It has been torn hastily from a magazine and the desk lamp catches the page's gloss.

. . . *a team of nomads that have so far played matches across Central Asia. They take their ground with them, the club erects a temporary stadium the week before a match in a feat of impressive engineering, dismantles it after the game and moves on. The club have played local sides in front of thousands in the middle of the Gobi Desert, on the Mongolian plains and in the shadow of banks of . . .*

The threat of bans from FIFA dooes not seem to have bothered these trans-national mercenaries. The club employs players from several African countries, Brazil and Eastern Europe. 'It's the future of football,' says the club founder and president Yusuf Khan, a petrochemical bil-

lionaire with influence in several Central Asian states, in his strangely
Midlands-inflected English (learned in spells at Business School
in Oxford and, oddly, Birmingham, he says). 'Certainly the future
of football here.' His ambition is to play one of the great European
clubs somewhere out in the Gobi Desert. To paraphrase what Kevin
Costner's character is told in Field of Dreams, *'If you build it, they*
will come.'

There is a crash from the front of the shop, glass breaking, a shout. Liam jumps, spills tea across the pictures and bends to get under the rows of pictures hanging low from the washing lines. Not for the first time he is too big for a room, so that by the time he has struggled around the chair and got to the doorway, the shop's front door is swinging shut.

'What's going on?' Liam asks and Tony waves him away from the broken glass. A display case is smashed.

'I'll get a brush. Watch that glass is still hanging.' Tony reaches up to bolt the door and says 'Fuckin' Bobby.'

There is blood on the glass still in the case, a foam of spit where Bobby had gobbed past Tony's ear, more blood spots on the chequered lino floor.

'What, your Bobby? What's he done that for?'

'He ain't our Bobby no more. He wants me to do his face. I've told him no faces. He only comes in when he's drunk or off his head on summat else. Do me face, he says to me. I've told him not to bother me with his crap and I get this.'

'You better watch that blood, Tone.'

'Eh? Oh. I'll get some gloves on, stand back.'

As they work they remember Bobby as young boy, big and round faced, a cheeky boy whose big crazy hair the grown-ups would ruffle and give him a pound for an ice cream. Liam watched him up close at the gym a couple of times, so quick, and with something in him, jagged and clever. He watched him fight a boy from up in Cowton, quite fancied before he got in with Bobby, at the Hightown Town Hall, how Bobby sliced down all the angles so the boy was cornered, big punches to the body and angled kicks to the head. Bobby left the boy standing for his own amusement, a cat with an injured bird. The ref stepped in and the crowd booed.

'Kill him, Bobby, kill him.' He remembers a voice from some-where at the back of the room. It was Gracie, Bobby's own mother. Liam knew the plea in that voice; how people look at you and want you to do what they can't, feel you've betrayed them if you can't do it either. He is glad his own mother has stopped coming to watch him. She is not speaking to him since he didn't turn up for that Sunday roast. He needs to find a way to make amends, feels he's been trying to do that to people one way or another half of his life. He'll send her some flowers or something.

He sweeps up the pieces of glass from the floor, fills the bucket for the mop and Tony removes the big jagged edges from the display case, broken heart designs and pictures of sailors' girls beneath.

'We used to look after him Tuesday nights upstairs at the pub, me and Dee Dee. For years, really, when he was a little kid, two, three.'

'Tuesday nights was when they went to the bingo,' Tony says.

'That's right.'

'Where was I?'

'What?'

'I wonder where I was, if you babysat Bobby.'

'I don't know. You're, what, seven years older than him. Maybe yer mum never went. Maybe Natalie or somebody had yer.'

'That's my point, though. Nobody can remember, even me. But we can all remember where Bobby was.'

Liam is not sure where this is going.

'What yer saying, Tone? Who'd yer rather be? Yerself or Bobby? Look at the state he's in.'

'Killed by love, eh, all that attention.'

'He ain't dead, though, is he? Maybe he'll sort himself out.'

With this Tony makes a sort of noise in his throat, like he won't even grace that with an answer. Bobby is only going in one direction. He has cleared the glass from the case, wrapped it in a towel.

'I'll make another cup of tea.'

'What's he want, any road?'

'What?'

'On his face?'

'Eh, oh, tonight it was a spider and a web he wanted. Round his bad eye down onto his cheek, had it all planned out.'

'Man of tradition, see. Couldn't yer just do it for him?'

The same noise from Tony.

'I'll phone Lionel tomorrow. He'll know someone who can do it cheap, I hope. The son smashes it and the dad patches it up, eh?'

'I don't know. Lionel's done his fair share of smashing things up, I reckon.'

Liam pulls a couple of notes from his wallet.

'Here, have this towards it.'

Tony goes to wave it away.

'Go on,' Liam says, 'put it on me account.'

. . .

The leaves sweep down Meeting House Lane with the gusts that come now, bonfire weather, great pyres going up on the wasteground at Cowton and by the Peng scrapyards, kids dressed as witches and spiders roaming the streets and demanding money and sweets. There's the sound of fireworks every night, whistles in the dark, the crack of bangers up the hillsides, barking dogs. It makes it sounds like there's life, but there's no one in the pub. Dee Dee is scared to look at the books, pays Roni out of petty cash, then her own purse, prays there's enough in the bank for Paul. God knows what she's going to do for the Christmas boxes. At least Lionel hasn't invoiced for the cameras.

Mark stands at the hatch, shifts from foot to foot, in need of his overcoat today, although he's worn it all summer anyway.

'My god Mark what have you done to yer face? Who's done that to you?'

He is shocked by her shock, has spent a week or more living with it, staring into the mirror at an eye that would not open, bathing it in warm salt water, something remembered, he thinks, from his mum. It had been swollen tight at first, then slowly turned purple until a jaundiced yellow spread across that half of his face and the eye opened a crack. There's a lump still on his cheek, which he wondered if he'd broken, but there's not much pain, a numbness to it, a tingling in the morning. He thought of walking to A&E at the Bethel, the colour of the leaves changing over the Heath. He's OK as long as he remembers to chew up the side and he doesn't eat so much anyway. He has reduced his life. But he's been staring in the mirror and thinking about how stupid he's been and then trying to tell himself how lucky as well, could have been much worse, the white of his eye has begun to show again, criss-crossed with blood, much worse, in an attempt to ward off demons.

He nearly says he walked into a door. He remembers how Sonia turned up with a black eye once and no one did anything about it, Goldie with scratch marks all down his face, mind. She'd been dancing with some boy from the posh houses up by the Heath. They split up for a few weeks, Dee Dee indignant about it, warning Goldie to steer clear.

'Admit it, though, she was asking for it,' Liam had said to him while they sat waiting for the minibus to training, he remembers it now, same time of year and the pitches strewn with big yellow leaves old Ted got them to rake up down at the training ground, and he hadn't said anything at all, just put his back into the work.

'Fell off the pavement,' he says, a variation on a theme, 'when I run into your Bobby the other day.'

'And he did that to yer?!'

Mark shrugs, 'You should see what he looks like, eh.'

He turns to her, with his good eye and his half-closed one.

She can't remember the last time she'd seen his face, not properly, not without him looking down at the ground, shuffling about, eyes always somewhere else. She knows he hasn't seen a doctor, decides not to even bother with that line.

'Fucking hell, Mark.' Tears come quickly to her eyes and she leans through the hatch. He is just a step too far away, the counter a bit too wide and she is left on tiptoe with one arm rubbing his shoulder and her hair falling out of its clip between them. They both smile at the position they are in.

'Do you want to come in Mark? Do you want a cup of tea? Something to eat?' He has never been in the pub, never been in a room with her since a couple of times when he came to see her when she first took Alina, when she and Liam still lived together and he knew Liam was at training, and he knew Liam was leaving her, the first year he stopped playing and the club were trying to persuade him to come back, threatening all sorts on the one hand, trying to get him in the Bethel on the other.

'I don't need a psychiatrist, Dee Dee, I don't need doctors, nothing, I just need to stop playing football,' is what he said to her, looking out of the leaded windows onto the hills, like they'd trespassed into some other country, which they had in a way, he supposed. He spent a lot of time trying to sneak back, to get home, that's what he thinks. He had needed a psychiatrist, needed some help at least, they were right on that score.

'No Dee Dee, thanks, you're all right. I'll let you know if I need anything.'

She is crying, trying not to, sniffs, feels the anger rising at the same time.

'Hang on there a minute. I'll get you something.'

He nearly says that he thinks he saw Goldie, but the certainty left him when the headache eased, why should he worry her over nothing, a phantom, a ghost? He tries to forget what Freddie Rogers said to him. He has scared her enough with his face, with the ghost of her cousin, too many ghosts all still alive, trick or treat, he thinks, and what is he?

She expects him to disappear, but there he is standing in a pattern of leaves in the autumn light, an autumn pattern across his face. She gives him a bottle of whisky and two packs of Co-Codamol. She worries afterwards that he'll take them all in one go.

. . .

Bladud was a leper, cured by the waters of the willow streams, and a good king too. He could speak to the dead as well as to the living, to Maddan, his father, Gwendolen, his mother, and Corineus his father's father. He lit fires that burned his whole life, that heated the baths that he built to wash away the evils of the world.

He had a son named Leir. To entertain him, Bladud had red kite feathers collected from the fields, stitched them into a great set of wings, did not heed the dead voices in his ear, and launched himself from the highest treetop.

The boy laughed to see that his father could fly and Bladud swooped through the clouds and flew for a while without a care, saw the green island, the white island, spread out beneath him, and then tumbled and fell, as men must do, and was dashed into pieces on the city that grew beneath him.

'The boy, look, the boy.'

'What?'

'Bladud's boy there in the yard.'

A magpie hopped across the stones and strewn body and called something to Leir that he could not understand, spent his whole life wondering, and he watched as it flew over the ruins, over the island, and on out of sight.

. . .

On the coach journey up to Hartlepool, a six-pointer in the December gloom, Liam watches the man commonly agreed to be the world's second best footballer chase a ball across a field in Stockholm. Sometimes he watches all three goals and waits until Ronaldo disappears under a pile of gambolling teammates, under the whole of Portugal, laughing and cheering and crying with joy. Sometimes he pauses it after the second goal, the real killer punch, the young man stood off by the near-post where he finished his run, his hair still perfectly in place, banging his chest, bellowing, and then opens the images Greta has sent that week, in an email with no heading or text at all, just attachments, pictures and video of their little boy, one swift exit left from Greta's bottom half in a long skirt and barefoot in one of the clips which he has now played twenty times or more. He touches the screen. When did we start stroking these things? He can't remember. Jari ran his hands across the old television set at his grandad's in an effort to find a cartoon. There he is, running with the mud between his toes. These films from the last weeks at the lake house before they boarded it up for winter. They had been back at the house in town for weeks now, darkness settling in.

When it gets too much he turns back to Ronaldo. Liam is conscious of telling himself that it is too much, aware somehow outside himself of playing the role of the heartbroken, absent father, feels his throat tighten. This is no state, he tells himself, at the same time aware that he tells himself, this is no state to be in, as if he could choose something else, some other way of being Liam Corwen, iron man from the Iron Towns, football man, tough and classy defender, heartbroken absent dad, failed husband. Ronaldo accelerates over the halfway line, after the ball, with all the movements of a man who knows what is coming, what is written, as though he has scored this goal a hundred thousand times before, knows he will outpace these chasing defenders even with the ball at his feet, knows how the keeper will come towards the near-post and how he will hit it low and hard across him into the far corner, none of his showmanship here, until the ball sits softly in the net, and he turns to the side of the goal and waits for the world to catch up.

'I am here!' is what Ronaldo shouts, bangs his chest, 'I am here! I am here!'

Liam has started six matches in a row now. Unprecedented in these later years, he tells himself in a voice that is not his own, some highlights-reel voice-over. Everything hurts. He cannot get his hip comfortable on this seat, shifts himself again, these long coach rides are a problem themselves, past Wakefield, Doncaster, Beverley, in the English rain.

'Unbelievable,' Devon has moved down the aisle, stands and looks at the screen, 'He ain't human.'

Liam shakes his head, eyes wide, in a kind of mock-awe that he really means.

'Think of all the things they might try to stop him.'

'Force him wide . . .'

'There is no stopping him.'

'. . . get bodies between him and the goal, that's all, bodies.'

'They can try and kick him if they catch him, look, but he's six foot odd, built like a cruiserweight.'

'Bodies, that's all it is, all you've got. Sit deep is all you can do. Chasing the game, Sweden are fucked.'

Their voices sound strange to Liam, amphibian, muffled by the coach seats and drowned in the sound of spray. There is the odd thumping beat from the other players' headphones up and down the coach. It strikes him that the build-up to games has become quieter and quieter over the years. The young lads barely say anything. And it wasn't just their age, even Ally, Archie Hill, spoke in calm, measured tones these days, most of the time, that is. Liam prefers a bit of sound and fury. When he first got in the team they still had headcases like Wayne Coombs in the side who would shout 'Who wants it? Who fucking wants it?' and stare unfocussed into your eyes and carry that on right into the tunnel. They had Kevin Burns playing Iron Maiden on one of those twin-tape decks. And the thing was, these were better players than the ones they had now would ever hope to be. When Liam first got in the first team squad there was a card school up the back of the coach that preferred these long trips to the north-east to get the pot built up. He and Mark would pass mix-tapes back and forth – not Iron Maiden – and listen to their Walkmans, sometimes a headphone each, the way Dee Dee and Sonia did. They'd never do that anywhere other than the sanctuary of the coach. Liam glances backwards now and sees Kyran stroke his phone, not attached to him by wire, but a pair of goldie-looking headphones sat like a crown on his head.

The coaches have not changed, the sort that would take them to Weston or Rhyl or Alton Towers when they were kids, the kind with ashtrays that pulled out from the headrest in front, with plastic covers on the seats or else plastic fake-leather that his grandad would organise from the Miners' Welfare to take them each October, a real adventure, over land and sea, to Longchamp and the Prix de l'Arc de Triomphe, sick bags and rare cigar smoke, tots of whisky in hip flasks. He thought the Arc was the race, not the monument. Dee Dee caught him out with it and laughed. They went to Paris for a weekend once. He fancies a drink right now, which is not a great sign three hours before kick-off. He read that McGrath played pissed a few times, Tony Adams too. Had decent games. He is not them.

They are sealed inside this coach. The young lads are sealed inside their headphones, all of them locked inside their own heads. They wait quietly in rooms. His hotel room. The dressing room. Until out they spill when that bell goes, spat out onto the scrap of green, silent no more, hidden no more, exposed. He used to dream recurrently of playing naked.

Devon walks back up the coach aisle. He is playing well. Devon is keeping him in the team, truth be told, but he doesn't care. They work well together, fit each other, though neither of them is getting any quicker. Devon moves soft on his feet for a big man, he treads like an astronaut negotiating a space station corridor, uncertain of the gravity. There are signs for Scarborough and Darlington. There are ferries to Norway up here somewhere. He imagines continuing. He could hitch lifts through the forests, the tundra, cross borders, ride into Lapinlahti in the snow, look up at a lighted window, a man come home.

'I am here!' Ronaldo shouts, 'I am here!' and it seems to Liam, at least right now at this moment, heading through rainy England, half a continent distant from his wife and son – that it is maybe all most of us ever, ever want to say.

'I am here! I am here!'

. . .

Goldie's old man had twenty kids. A bloke told him that once in the back room of The Magpie, an old pub with sagging walls that sat just outside the Greenfield East Gates. He's sure the pub has gone now, the man too, who he remembers toothless, his lips puckered over a barley wine and half a mild. Those men have gone, he thinks to himself, twenty years gone by and more, because he was a kid when he heard that, tilting the pool table in the back room to get a free game when no one was looking, Tuesday, Wednesday afternoons when he should've been at school. Men in daytime pubs knew him, knew who he was and where he came from. The bloke that day must have assumed he never saw his dad, never knew him, but he was wrong on that score. He would come by and stay a few days every year when he was a kid, must have stopped when he was nine or ten or so. He took him fishing a couple of times, right up onto the Welsh Ridge one time to an old run-down farm, 'To see a man about a dog,' he had said, and it was true that dogs had barked all through the yard and in pens out against the hill, and for ages Goldie thought he was getting a dog and it was years later that he heard it as a saying, and understood, too late by then to do anything about it, too late always to catch on to things. His old man had grown up on farms, worked on them, and on the roads, when they built the motorways, was never at home in the towns. It's strange to think he might still be alive, but Goldie guesses he would've heard somehow if he'd died, maybe not, people slipped through the cracks, into the shadows. He never had twenty kids anyway, but a few, here and there.

But it's true he has half-brothers, half-sisters somewhere, twenty years older than him, some of them, older, in their sixties, dying off themselves now, most likely. His own flesh and blood. He used to think he should try and get in touch with them, track them down like you see on the telly. When he was with Nadine, she'd pointed a bus driver out to him, on the number 7, similar age, lighter skinned than Nadine, but the same cheekbones high up his face.

'That's my brother,' she'd said.

'What? Your brother don't work on the buses.'

'Half, half-brother. Me dad's babby with that Denise, who-ever, fat Irish cow. Lives in Erdington, don't speak to us.' She'd given the finger to the bus as it sat in traffic. The driver wore dark glasses and sat looking at the lights. Nadine had stepped out into the road and Goldie could picture her hammering on the bus doors with her hard little fists, mouthing off, spitting up the window as the bus edged along, people looking and then looking away, but he was saved from this by the lights going green and the bus pulling across the junction.

'He's normally on the 11,' she'd said, and then they must've got distracted because he can't ever remember talking about it again. No idea what his name was. But then, he didn't know the names of his relations either. Ann had a son, Michael, who everyone knew as Snowball because he had a patch of white hair big as a fist above his right ear, even from when he was a little kid. He was killed that year there was the big feud between the Oxo and Cowton, kicked to death in a back field. Snowball had run with the Bullet Krew, before they were even called that, just young kids messing about. They only became the Bullet Krew after Goldie went inside. He'd hear stories. The Bullet Krew only came after everything fell apart with the Ahmeds. Not that Stan Ahmed ever had anything to do with Cowton or the Oxo. 'Leave 'em to it,' he'd say, 'Scottish Jamaican cunts. There's no one you can speak to up there. They'm all nine years old, running round with razors.' Which had some truth in it. No hierarchy. The Ahmeds were a family, a clan, and they'd only come to the fore with Stan and his brothers, taken over from the Carter family, the ones they said had stolen the FA Cup in Birmingham and buried it somewhere on the Heath and got the Anvil Yards cursed by a gypsy because of it, who'd ruled the roost since way back in the days of the Peaky Blinders and the Iron Towns Sloggers fighting it out at the Heath races. The gangs had come down from Glasgow in the thirties as well but they ran out steam after the war when Oxton and Cowton went up.

Funny thing was, everything had reversed now, from what Goldie heard. The Bullet Krew had old men his age sitting up there, looking down the valley. When everything collapsed they'd taken over. All the drugs came in and out of Cowton. Lowtown, the Ironport and the Anvil Yards, were just full of empty buildings with holes kicked through them and kids running wild. But now there were real Somalis and Bengalis in Lascar again and power was going to come back down the valley. It would come to whoever was most desperate and then seep away from them like blood running down a drain. It was a whole secret history, he thought to himself, the kind that never gets written down or anything like that, or if it does, they just get it all wrong. Because the Ahmeds grew rich and lazy and moved away, other groups moved in. You cannot have a vacuum. Nothing stands still. Because the works closed everyone started killing themselves in as many ways you could think of, and some you couldn't. It was cause and effect.

The gangs were the opposite of the works, the opposite of working for a living. Thousands and thousands of people poured through those gates when the works were open, banging metal, crawling through mine tunnels under the hills, all for nothing if you asked him, all for lungs full of black dust and a few days at the seaside. A handful sat in back rooms with people like Stan Ahmed. It was a way of setting yourself apart. And they'd been right, of course, because nobody worked now, and everyone was on the hustle, on the make, and desperate too. They were pioneers. The gangs had always know that working was a waste of time. Everyone was a gangster now.

And here he was, a gang of one, just like his old man, like

everyone else these days. But without as many kids, he laughed to himself. Just one, he thinks to himself, one little girl. A man should have a daughter.

.   .   .

'He is here! He is fucking here!' Devon grabs Liam's head and pulls it into his chest. Liam sits, slumped forward, in his shorts, with his socks rolled down and shin pads untaped, pushes his matted hair into Devon and kisses him as Devon pulls away to point at Liam again.

'He is here! He is here!' Devon bangs his own chest now and moves towards the showers. Liam wants him to stay here, to savour the moment, everyone grinning, laughing, Ally talking thirty to the dozen to someone. There has been some talk of him taking an ice bath after a game, Devon and Julius too, the over-thirties, but steam curls through this dressing room now, pipes hiss, mud splatters the floor. The classified results plays from somewhere, patrician English voice, like every Saturday teatime he has ever known. They are announced as a late result.

He scored when time was up. A late, late free kick down the left, Kyran somehow skipping along the heavy pitch. He didn't even want to go up for it. They were lucky to get the point, luckier still with a clean sheet after getting the runaround for ninety-odd minutes, a chasing, he wasn't sure he could move. But there was Archie waving him up there from the touchline.

He got fouled, thought he was blocked off, stumbled at the back post and then there was the ball, a shit free kick which had barely risen off the ground, through a thicket of players who all missed it, body after body in front of him until there it was, and because he was tumbling, falling, he headed it, not eighteen inches off the ground, down into the wet turf, and it skidded inside the post at some pace and he saw it go in and heard the whistle and nestled his face into the soft pitch as they all leapt on top of him. Pandemonium. He saw a pair of black brogues come running past, a bloke had leapt the hoarding and onto the pitch in the rain, trailing an Irontown flag. In the melee, he could hear Devon shouting, 'He is here! He is here!'

When he got to his feet, groggy, he hadn't realised the ref had blown for time, and walked with his fist clenched and raised towards the hundred or so Irontown supporters behind the goal, all going crazy in the rain, up and down the old terrace, the Baa Baa boys starting a conga, the bloke who'd run on the pitch, old enough to know better and red-faced drunk, clinging to an orange-coated steward.

Big Archie hauls him up, slaps him on the back, tells him to speak to the radio. He doesn't want to leave the dressing-room warmth, steps on the toes of his socks to pull them off so to walk barefoot across the wet floor, mud between his toes. He pulls on a too small T-shirt that someone else has sweated in to dip his head out of the door and speak to Dave Willis who grins at him with crooked teeth, thrusts what looks to be his phone up at Liam. He is aware of steam coming off him.

'We can hear, Liam, how much you all enjoyed that victory.'

It is true. The commotion inside comes through the thin walls. Devon still going on. 'Stop that fucking swearing, but,' he hears Ally say and hope it isn't picked up, some fuck-up to take the edge off the warm glow. Dave Willis and his crooked grin.

'Well, last-minute winner, last touch, I think. Away from home. Clean sheet as well, rode our luck a bit, maybe, but we deserve some. Delighted.'

'Relief as well, I guess. Had you not scored, the way the results have gone would have put you in the bottom two tonight. As it is, eighteenth. The only way is up?'

'Of course. Listen. We know we're better than the table suggests. So do the people who turn up every week. With this group of players we know we can achieve more. I'm just delighted for everyone tonight, the supporters who come up here to stand in the rain, it's a long way, everyone.'

'Liam,' Dave Willis leans forward, puts his hand on his shoulder. When Liam left for Finland Dave wrote a piece in the *Chronicle* which said end of a chapter long unfulfilled, basically saying what a disappointment Liam had turned out to be. Still spoke to him like they were good mates, seemed quite a nice bloke really, always cheerful, asked Liam if he fancied doing a book with him, to which Liam had said no, he didn't believe in books. 'I know it's a team game but a word on your defensive partner, Devon Samuels. He's playing well for an old-stager.'

There it is, a barb about his age. He is six years older than Devon.

'Immense, a rock. He's great to play with, reads the game so well.'

'And you must be delighted with your goal.'

'Well, yeah, of course. I was shocked it come to me really.

Shocked to be up there. I thought I'd been fouled, got summat on it, yer know. Not bad for an old-stager, I suppose.' He smiles now, pleased with himself. Dave doesn't.

'Well said, Liam. You're still breathing heavy, what a battle today. We'll let you get back in the dressing room and have a well-earned sit down.'

Dave presses something on the phone, looks grey in the tunnel strip-lights.

'Well played, Liam,' he says in his everyday voice, a lower pitch than for the radio. Liam says thanks but he is already halfway back through the door.

And last in the showers until the water cools, same as it's been all these years. The shouts and the bangs die down but the feeling remains.

Julius flashes his phone at him as they board the coach, he feels his own phone beep in the pocket of his blazer, under the Irontown badge. He sees his name, Corwen 90+6 mins. A goal in the time beyond time. You just never know. He settles into his seat, lets his phone ring away in his pocket, closes his eyes, holds on to this feeling of early Saturday night. Ally says they're stopping for a fish supper on the way home. Old school, old school. Kyran asks if they do chicken. They move through the English dark. Wet snow falls gently on fast tarmac and metal.

. . .

In a small room in the museum in Dudley are Duncan Edwards's things, caps, shirts, medals and cups. A screen plays flickering images of the '57 cup final on a loop, a strange choice in many ways, it's his last appearance at Wembley. Peter McParland flattens Ray Wood, smashes his cheek and wins the game for the Villa, a curse on them ever since in the cup. They say it was the only time Big Duncan lost his temper on the pitch.

This shrine is in a small room in a building of red Victorian brick, the relics are neighbours to dinosaur footprints and paintings of furnaces long since put out. The caps used to be held in a glass case in the foyer of Dudley Baths. You could look at them and sip a hot chocolate from the machine, the smell of chlorine and shouts of kids everywhere. This place is a quieter tomb. On a shelf there is a coffee set, Ottoman style, stamped 'Red Star Belgrade', never used.

.   .   .

. . . will complete the draw for the Third Round of the FA Cup.

They are the first team out of the hat. Here in the hotel where the players are gathered to watch the draw, not everyone is sitting down or even listening yet. Liam leans towards the screen and concentrates, sees the hands swirl the balls in the glass bowl. They are the same balls they used to use at the bingo. He remembers sitting with a bottle of vimto or dandelion & burdock if he went to the Miners' Welfare when his nan was alive, the clack of the bingo balls and the tray they'd be placed in when drawn.

. . . Irontown . . .

He has only ever played in the Third Round twice, the years they were in the second division, first division, Championship, whatever you want to call it, it had the same name for a hundred years and now they change it every five minutes. The year they lost the play-off final, they got beaten by Crewe in a replay, extra-time. Their cup record had been terrible since the twenties, apart from that one run in the fifty-seven and a couple of seasons when Ally first took over. Liam made his debut in a First Round match when he was sixteen, Ally threw him on wide on the left, the only time he ever played there apart from his seconds with England, getting beaten by Leigh Railwaymen's Institute, non-leaguers. He remembers them all sat in the dressing room with their heads down afterwards, Ally standing in the middle of them all, naked, telling them all what a waste of space they were apart from Liam, exempt from all blame, and the older blokes looking at him under their eyebrows and him thinking that he was in for a kicking if he joined first team training again. And he was, but he kicked them back.

There are voices shushing each other in the seats behind. It had been his idea to get people together, players who live close enough, a few families and hangers-on, Sunday night out, there are sausage rolls on plates on a side table, they sit in one of the conference rooms in the hotel with sofas and chairs laid out in front of the telly. Amir thought it was a good idea, would bring a bit of cash in at the bar. The camera pans to Ally, who has been invited to the draw, they're making a big deal of it, trying to revive the cup, which is dying, like all things.

 . . . *will play* . . .

He knows, wills it, as he watches the hand retrieve the ball, that it's a big one.

'Come on,' he hears himself say.

It used to be Monday dinnertimes. He remembers hopping over the school wall and across the garage roofs to get to Mark's where his mum let them listen to it on the radio, in the kitchen, and she made them cheese on toast. There were those years when they got to the quarter-finals, lost to Liverpool, then to Everton, and nothing since.

. . . Number twenty-six . . . Manchester United . . .

They are on their feet. Liam has his fists clenched above his head, someone is banging him on the back, there are whoops and cheers around the room, people lifting their heads from the carvery table and their meal deals to ask what all the fuss is about, the sound of thirty ring tones all going at once.

They'll switch it, Liam thinks, as he goes to each player in turn, clasps their hand and then pulls them into a bear hug, like he willed that ball out of the pot. They'll switch it for the money and we'll get to play at Old Trafford, either that or we'll have the telly here. He can see Steve Stringer at the back of the room, talking on the phone, a smile in his grey face for once, heading out into the corridor. Liam puts his thumb up to him. This season, you just never knew, what with the Hartlepool game and now this, win a couple more and their game in hand and they were mid-table, fringe of the play-offs, some kind of miracle against United, some kind of backs to the wall draw in the mud and then a replay, cannot even dare to dream of a win, and the telly again, you just never knew. He looks around at the shining eyes. There is life yet, is what he thinks. He'll be marking Van Persie. Fucking hell.

Ally is talking on the telly, too noisy to hear him. They must have finished the rest of the draw. He hears a voice say, 'Possibly the tie of the round, certainly the most drenched in cup folklore is Irontown versus Manchester United, a repeat of a famous tie played there by the Busby Babes nearly sixty years ago ...'

Dave Willis, by the plate of sausage rolls, is talking into his phone with another one clamped to his ear.

Liam sees Amir, asks for some champagne, when he looks back at him, says, 'Well, that cheap fizz you put out for the weddings,' and Amir grins and says he'll find some good stuff and put it on Liam's room.

He sits down with a bottle of beer in a chair next to Devon and the Irish lads and Kyran who cannot stop saying, 'Man United, man, Man United, man,' over and over, where they have settled in the lounge bar. They've put the big screen on in here now and switched Sky Sports on and they've got Ted Groves on the phone, Ted, who is standing with Steve Stringer near the bar, Steve holding the phone to Ted's ear, who is being interviewed about the game in '57, a match that Liam knows his dad was at too, as a kid, down the front of the Greenfield End, the record crowd, fifty-six thousand and Liam thinks of old records books, sat poring over numbers and results and memorising whole lists of matches and scorers and attendances like some kind of cat-echism. He thinks of Mark, wonders if he is sitting there in that same kitchen now, listening to it on the radio with his toast. It's possible. One day he'll go round there and just bang on the door. Maybe he'll take him a ticket round for this match.

All things are possible, he thinks.

. . .

Like Bonnie and Clyde or something is how they took off. Goldie had bought these magazines for ages, years, still never got the full collection, which concentrated on a particular criminal or crime. Bonnie and Clyde were one of the editions. Then there were those kids in that film *Badlands*, which Dee Dee made them watch, and Liam took the piss out of all the way through. He remembered thinking that if he was going on a killing spree then Liam Corwen might well end up first in line and that was sort of how the events of that afternoon started. He'd talked about it so much since, that the language he used, even in his head, was touched with other people's view of the world, therapists and the prison chaplain and social workers and the like. It wasn't even his story, not any more.

After Mark had missed the penalty, after they had shown Liam lying on the pitch, his face pressed into the grass, after they showed them both crying, and the commentator said, 'You have to feel for these Irontown boys. They have given everything,' the whole pub swooning over them, Sonia looking at Liam lying there on the grass and going to hug Dee Dee, he had to do something.

They'd always had this thing between them, egging each other on.

'I don't believe you've got it in you, Goldie, I don't,' Sonia would say, that kind of thing. Well, he called her bluff this time.

'Goldie, you're not OK to drive,' Dee Dee said, came out to the street, her make-up all run across her face with the tears. Goldie imagined Liam's big homecoming that night.

'He's all right, Dee Dee, honest,' Sonia had jumped in, and she was pissed, an unlit cigarette hanging out of her mouth, did not even smoke. Alina was sitting there in the back of the car, always a calm baby, assured. God knows who she got that from.

So they headed off across the Heath and they didn't even say anything to each other, perhaps they must have talked about it before, he had certainly described the place to her, he was sure now, but there was something making him think that Stan Ahmed would not be very pleased if he found out, still, he didn't need to find out, and this was Sonia's voice in his head now.

Just on the last stretch of Anvil Yards, past the South Gate at Greenfields and almost at the turn in the road near where Lionel's car yard was, there was a paper shop, a paki shop as they would call it and then have Dee Dee go 'Eh, eh, none of that,' and have Liam stare at them, anyway, there was a shop on its own just before the road turned towards the Heath, always this old woman just sitting there on her own behind the till. Goldie and Sonia had worked it up into some story that the place made a fortune. It was a shithole. There was nothing on the shelves. No one went in there, no people to go in, Greenfields had been shut ten years by then and the South Gate was rusted shut.

He pulled up in front of the shop, there were parking spaces out in front, no one around. They never said anything to each other, knew what they were going to do from previous conversations. There was a baseball bat, well rounders bat, that he kept in the car and he knew that would do, picked it up from between his feet and opened the car door, intending to leave it open, so he could jump back in and make their getaway.

Then Sonia jumped out of the car as well. 'Let me do it, Goldie,' she said, grinning drunk, had dropped the cigarette. So they left both doors open. Alina was sat in her car seat in the back, listening to that Prince tape they always played. He would swear now that they were only in there for what twenty seconds, thirty maybe.

He walked in with the bat and, sure enough, it was the old woman behind the till, pointing the bat at her head and she was up off her seat and back against the wall without a sound, something like a whimper, maybe. It was Sonia who pulled the till drawer out, found a some fifty pound notes hidden under there, so maybe there was something in the idea the place wasn't quite right. They thought they'd hit the big time, one big massive rush, and out of the shop they went, laughing and shouting, so fucking easy, and into the car, and he remembers swinging out so hard into the road that they almost ended up in a hedge then and that would have saved Sonia's life and that was something he often thought about because he was no way in control of the car and it was just luck, plain luck, that they didn't crash then. The other thing was that at the trial they said that it was all Goldie, that Sonia had not even been in the shop, that it was Goldie who had ripped open the till drawer and found those fifties, although they never mentioned the fifties either, said all they robbed was fourteen pound ninety, which was what they took in change and threw it onto the back seat next to Alina and it went rolling around the car floor.

The woman only spoke Tamil. The shop was Sri Lankan. His solicitor said it must have been misinterpreted, the business of

Sonia and the till, Sonia wanting to do it in the first place, leaving her daughter in the car while she robbed the shop. In court it was just him. His solicitor shrugged.

Sonia took the money and it was Sonia who was laughing as they drove away, her legs kicking the dashboard, and then screaming at him to get away, to drive faster, when they heard the siren, Alina crying in the back now, 'Oh God, Goldie, Oh God,' Sonia said over and over then. She'd even done up her seat belt. This bad girl. If she'd left that off she might even still be here and the whole world different, that's what he thinks.

.   .   .

Liam never answers his phone, never has, and with the way it was ringing for two days after the cup draw, he thinks that if people want to find him they know where he is, so the message is a couple of days old at least, maybe more than that. A mortgage advisor keeps ringing him and he assumed it was another of their calls. They want to know if he's thought about leverage options, whatever they are. He could rent the place out, he supposes, but he could ask Devon about that kind of thing. When he hears her voice he stops, stands at the window, looks across the Anvil Yards towards the pub, realises he's doing that as she speaks.

'Hello Liam, it's Dee Dee, I'm sorry for ringing you and I know you're probably busy,' she has been smoking, he can tell from the huskiness in her voice, smoking or drinking or crying or something, no good for her asthma, or her singing, but then, she didn't sing any more. He wonders if someone is dead. 'You're probably not going to want to hear this either. I saw Mark today. You should see the state of his face, someone's set about him. His face is a right state. Look, I think he's doing OK generally. But I just wondered, I don't know, if you could check on him or something.'

There's a pause, the sound of Dee Dee listening to her own voice, her own silence.

'Anyway, I hope you're OK. I hope the results get better soon, they're not very happy in the pub, maybe they'll drink more. Listen, I'm rambling, and there is something else, Liam. There is something else. If you could call me back that would be great.'

He is leaning against the window glass. He can see the cranes just about, the top of the flats, but he can't make out which block is which from this distance, across time and space. From the hotel roof he'd be able to see the pub. He has thought a few times that he should ask Amir if he could change rooms every now and again, get a different view. He leaves his head against the glass, breathes onto it.

Her voice, he always loved her voice, singing, talking, whatever. She used to read poems out loud, lyrics, half-singing, half-talking. There is something else, she said. There is something else.

. . .

He is dressed as Father Christmas when Greta phones him, the day before they are meant to arrive, to say they aren't coming. It was all arranged, they would get here on the 20th and stay until the 29th. He had it all written down on a pad of hotel stationery. Ally told him not to worry about Boxing Day, to be ready for Shrewsbury on the 21st, for York on the following Saturday, to keep himself fit for United. Things are on the up. His mum has got the rooms ready at the house, made Jari's bed for him, although Liam knows that the boy would sleep with them, although maybe not, so much will have changed in six months, the seventh or so of his son's whole life that he has just missed, and he tries not to think about it. Probably not with both of them in the same bed either, more like in the summer when Liam slept in a chair at the side of the bed with Greta and Jari in it, and he would hold the boy's foot or hand, apart from that one night they went for a meal in Heathside and things had felt good, but then they'd argued afterwards about something which he now can't remember at all.

'You can't do this to me, Greta, to us.'

'It is too much, Liam. I am sorry, I am sorry. I should have said something earlier. It is too much for Jari. He is settled and happy. He is looking forward to Christmas here.'

'Without his dad.'

'You are not here, Liam.'

'It's not right.'

'We did not leave anywhere. We belong here.'

He hadn't asked her about coming back to England, had just assumed that was what they'd do. They weren't really living together when he agreed to come home, things had already gone wrong. He couldn't work her out. He tries not to think of his beautiful son. She is right that they belong there. He thinks of the cold hitting his face when they got out of the car at the shops near the lake once, the wind coming across the frozen water and the dark forest beyond it, straight from the Arctic, winds from places from storybooks, from Lapland, from Siberia; or the procession to the church that time, Jari strapped to him and under his coat, the baby's face poking out from under a fur-lined hood, the crunch of snow under their boots, the line of candles, Greta holding his arm.

'What about all his stuff that's here, his presents and things? It's too late for the post.'

'He does not need plastic robots, Liam. He needs a father.'

He is dressed as Father Christmas and sits on the edge of the bed he slept in as a boy. He wonders how he might tell his parents. They want to see their grandson. Just say it straight out, he supposes. They aren't coming. He guesses Greta will never come here now. Part of him can't blame her. He never told her he was coming back.

He has seen the way she watched the streets as they drove through the Iron Towns, a place she could not believe existed. England was a disappointment to her, she had thought of it as a land of kings and queens, country cottages and hedgerows and winding lanes. And it is that. But what she saw was the rust and the people, his people, shuffling up the Anvil Yards pavements.

She'd visited Russia as a student during the days of the collapse, she'd say the names of the towns to him, show him photos, Baikalsk and Vydrino, and a place called Asbest, named for asbestos, the worst place on earth she'd said, and then shown him photos from her dissertation, and there was something in the look in people's faces, he wanted to tell her that he knew them, these people. The worst place on earth, she said. But that couldn't be true. They joked about it in his parents' kitchen one time, one of the few visits. It was the Jubilee. Spitfires had flown up the valley. There was Union Jack bunting strung up and down the street. She held up a jar of instant coffee and a carton of sterilised milk.

'But the war is over, Liam. What's more, you won.'

'There's always a war,' is all he said, joking, not sure what that meant, like something his grandad would mutter, but certain there was something hard and true underneath it all.

He sits on the edge of the bed with the phone in his hands. A horn sounds from outside. Devon is collecting him. He and some of the others are taking presents to the children's ward at the Bethel. He opens the window, shouts, 'Hang on a minute,' goes downstairs and takes a couple of black bin bags from the kitchen drawer, pushes Jari's presents into them, heads outside and motions to Devon to open the boot. He wonders if he might even look at flights to Helsinki, there is time still for that, just. He has always been a man for the grand gesture.

.   .   .

The same routine every morning. She opens the bar doors dead on eleven. It used to be that a straggle of old men would be waiting out on the pavement, hats on, their morning shopping done and a bag of potatoes or sausages wrapped in paper in their hands. Those men had gone now, but you still got the odd early morning drinker. She can remember weekday mornings with men stood shoulder to shoulder in the bar, the days of the old livestock market, or at the shift-change at Greenfields. Not much this morning except hard shadows in low winter sun. There is a swirl of grit across the road they put down with the meagre snow, the bottom of Meeting House Lane is a brown puddle, the shape of the buildings murky on its surface. She likes these mornings best of all, quiet with the sun as it angles across the road. She latches the door open to air the bar, considers a cigarette on the step, queen of all she surveys. It isn't cold, winter still not here, not really, in spite of the snow flurry. Instead, she heads back behind the bar and through the darkened lounge to the doors. She doesn't know why she still opens up so early. Perhaps hopeful of some stray Christmas shoppers, men on the roads finishing up for the holidays maybe, a few up from the bakery. Court was sitting today, so it's possible she'd get a few of them in from there.

The lock makes a solid click as it slides back with the key, and it's as she does this, and moves her hand up towards the bolt, that maybe a shape catches the corner of her eye that she remembers an old man, a tramp of the old sort with a piece of rope tied round his middle holding his clothes together that used to come to the hatch for her nana to give him tobacco and papers and a bottle of something. He had a great beard, grey and white, tobacco stained, and he'd take off his hat, a battered version of the ones the men wore to market, and scratch at the skin peeling from his head. They had a name for him. She can't remember it. A stray line comes into her head, *My many-coated man*. The rest of that stays at the edge of her memory, something just out of reach.

'Got something for me dog, Dee Dee?' she thinks of Mark.

And then of Goldie. 'Yer dad's here Goldie.' She remembers Sonia, after some argument they'd had, saying it in reference to the old tramp at the off sales hatch, but no, it couldn't have been him, because he was a memory from years before that, when Dee Dee toddled about behind her nana through the daytime pub and her mum and dad were still here. With the same meaning, though, one of the ragged old men in the bar. 'Yer dad's here Goldie.' Sonia said it with a smirk, she had that streak in her, Sonia, and they must have had a row. Goldie didn't see his dad, it was said to hurt him, to dig into him. His face would flinch with pain but it was a kind of habit. They'd have a row about nothing in particular, the way she looked at some bloke, or where he'd been the night before, both jealous like that, needing to cling to one another, to someone. They were an accident waiting to happen, the old saying. Then the accident happened.

And there he is in front of her. She turns back from the lounge doors, touches the frosted glass in the window and then stands in mid-step. He is there in front of her, sitting on one of the heavy wrought iron chairs, the shape of him part reflected in the hammered copper table at which he sits. There he is from across the years.

'All right, Dee Dee,' he says.

All right?

All right?

All right?

She feels everything fall away from her. And she thinks of that idea of your life flashing before your eyes and has never believed it, never believed in any of that stuff, she has seen people die, but that is what happens now, even as she thinks that all that stuff is rubbish. She sees herself toddling after her nana and hears the sound of glasses and singing and voices in the bar, the glamour of blue smoke and pub chandeliers, the warm press of drinking, dancing crowds, tiny rooms off hospital wards, where she was told she'd have to say goodbye to her daddy, to her mum.

She sees him as she first saw him, as she first saw Liam and Mark, all the swagger and laughter and dead certainty that life owed them all something. It owed them something, all right. A kick in the guts for being so sure of themselves. And then another and another. More than that. He has crawled from the wreckage of his life and everyone else's. She wants this to stop, to turn back to the doors and he will not be there, sitting with two coats on, her own many-coated man. His face wears the years. He is dirty. There is a smell coming off him. She sees the knife on the table top.

'Get me a drink please, Dee Dee,' he says in that voice that was always a bit too soft, a country lilt or lisp that did not match his hard, sharp edges, leans back on the chair like a king restored to his throne.

.   .   .

Liam sits on the tram, pulls stray white strands of beard from his chin. There were a couple of kids on the ward who might not make it to Christmas Day. He'd watched Kyran sit at one boy's bedside, holding his hand, reading him a story. He'd underestimated Kyran, just a young lad himself, growing a beard now which somehow made him look even younger, a boy who'd gone to the Ironport school, same as Liam, grew up on Cowton, this latest great hope of the Iron Towns. He held the boy's hand, who lay very still in the bed, just his eyes watching Kyran as he read a story about Rudolph lost in the snow on Christmas Eve, trying to get back home so that he could pull the sleigh. When he finished the story the boy's eyes started to close. Kyran leaned over and kissed the top of his head. Liam thought he might not hold it together, watched the nurses coming past with tinsel in their hair, and the kids in their dressing gowns, smiles on their faces, Kyran walking towards him now, and told himself he better had.

'Ho, Ho, Ho,' he boomed down the ward, felt the ripple of excitement, felt his own son's toys in the sack over his shoulder.

Outside in the car, after Liam had changed in the toilets and stuffed his Santa suit into one of the torn bin bags, Kyran sat in the passenger seat with his head against the glove compartment. Devon had his hand on the lad's back. Liam motioned to Devon that he had somewhere to get to, headed towards the tram stop.

. . .

The boy Merlin tells of times to come, times that have gone, of better days, and days of rage. He says the streams and valleys will boil with blood, tells of a red dragon and a white in endless struggle. That lion cubs will become fishes, that silver will flow from cows' hooves, that the hills will be hollowed and their black insides burned. He tells of kings that will come and go, of war and plague and famine, of how Arthur will die on a riverbank, his insides leaking into the mud, and how they will set him off downstream in a coracle, to his island of apple blossom, to sleep and wait. He tells of life enduring, in the rocks and the trees, of people biding time out in lost valleys, of dispersing and re-forming, of things changed, transformed, but enduring still, of death by fire and death by water. All things come again, he says.

. . .

There is the deep tick of the clock. It hangs high in the lounge. Someone comes from the museum to wind it every third week, then Dee Dee gets up on the stepladder when they've gone to push it forward a few more minutes.

Anvil Yards, England, it says, and it is too loud for this empty room, for her head, and she needs to think. She pours him a brandy, gets him a little bottle of coke, remembers he and Sonia drank that for a while when they came back from the holiday they had in Majorca, when her uncle had given Goldie a load of money for god knows what, and she hadn't wanted to ask.

'Do you want ice?' she says.

'Yes please, Dee Dee,' he says, 'and get one for yourself,' and he smiles faintly and she feels her legs go a bit, and says, 'Fuckin' hell, Goldie,' but she pours the drink just the same, and does herself a glass of water from the tap, and thinks that if she had any sense at all she'd have had a panic button fitted, or something, Lionel had even mentioned it. From here at the bar she hears a footstep on the loose floorboards upstairs, prays for a moment that maybe

Tyrone has stayed over, something she was expecting to happen soon enough, but she can tell from the movement that it is Alina and her legs go again, just a bit. Nowhere to go but back here, to the table that Roni has rubbed a shine into. *Nowhere to run to baby, nowhere to hide.* She thinks to herself that this is how people go, with old songs playing through their heads, and what they might do on Tuesday, and what they might do in twenty years' time, and how there are always thoughts of a happy ending right up until the end and maybe even beyond, because there is the knife on the table and what else has he come back for after all these years other than damage, more damage.

'I wanna see her, Dee Dee.'

'You can't.'

'I stayed away, Dee Dee, I kept away.'

'And now you're back,' she says.

'And now I'm back.'

When he reaches for the drink she thinks he's going for the knife and her heart stops, she can feel it actually stop, and he takes the bottle and pours some coke into the brandy and it fizzes and the ice cracks and she is back in the world again and her heart thumps and the clock ticks. It is a proper brandy glass, fresh ice. She has wet herself, she can feel it under her, not too much, and she shifts in the chair with a small puddle to sit in, glad to be still breathing, a crackle to her breath like that of the ice.

'Fuckin' hell, Goldie,' she says again and he lifts the glass towards his lips and she can see that his hand shakes, and it gives her a bit of hope.

'Cheers,' he says.

. . .

Liam watches the pub doors from the tram shelter, and then from under the sign at Tony's shop, a flickering arrow that says 'tattoos', and Liam stood under it thinks it would make a great photo if they do any more magazine stuff. There is no one on the street, not a soul. The winter has not been cold but he shivers now, looks at the pub doors and then at his watch, a few minutes past already and the pub not open.

It was a ritual, opening up, he used to help Dee Dee with her nana, when he and Dee Dee were first together. After the cleaning and whatever needed doing in the cellar, the walk down to the post office for change, or the counting of tomato juice bottles and the like in their green crates, the filling of the ice machine, the placing out of beer towels and mats and ashtrays, in those days, a last dust over of the tables. All this in the same order, depending on which day of the week, like on a Thursday, for instance, the shifting of empty barrels and unbolting the cellar hatch and waiting for the drays.

There was a ritual to observe, all through the day, from half-seven when you let the cleaners in, to a last check of the locks at half-eleven, a nip of something warm from the shelf and the kettle on. He remembers that Dee Dee's nana would set the clock to the one at the Lowtown market and then push it a couple of minutes forward. When the market one rusted to a standstill, she'd phone the speaking clock and do the same thing using that. These same things each morning, every morning.

It's not like Dee Dee to be late, he thinks, but then wonders really how many times he's seen her in these years. Since they split up, perhaps only a dozen times, if that, twenty years gone by. To have someone in your head, there and not there, all those years, that's how they all live, he supposes.

He can see a light on in the lounge, thinks of the old chandeliers and flock wallpaper and wood and brass, and then realises the bar might be open. Perhaps they only open the bar in the daytime now, it's not like they've got any punters, god knows how the place stays open.

So he crosses the road and walks towards the pub and he swears he can see someone at the bar, people sat at a table, through the frosted glass of the only window with the curtains half-drawn back.

. . .

He wears the years on his face, the pain, she can see that. Something, maybe that she can see the lad she once used to flirt with and then deny, and she thought she has hated all these years, makes her pause.

'She's my daughter, Dee Dee, and I kept away.'

Because he did. And why did he have to anyway? She could've written to him, sent him photos of Alina growing up. There was nothing from the courts about not doing that. She managed to get some message to him inside, though, through her uncles, Stan was still here then, maybe she never had any choice. Don't come near, don't come back to the Iron Towns ever again, or you're a dead man.

She sees his face now and the years on it, the face of a man with just the thoughts of what he has done, and she thinks that a few words of comfort would not have gone amiss. A visit might have taken something out of his eyes, something that she sees now, a shadow across them.

And maybe for Alina, to have known her dad, at least a bit, and not just through old photographs or worse, through newspaper clippings that she knows she has pored over at the Hightown library. He pulled her out of the river, after all.

Dee Dee does not speak. His hand does not move towards the knife.

'I saved her, Dee Dee. I pulled her out that car, out of the water.'

And something inside her, like the weather shifting, because she wants to say, but you put her in there in the first place, and you left Sonia in there, and she knows deep inside herself, like the way she feels when she opens the cellar door and sees the wooden steps drop into the dark, that there will always be a part of her, hidden and unspoken even to herself almost all of the time, that wishes he'd done the opposite and it appals her, scares her, the layers beneath. So all she says is, 'I know Goldie, I know.'

She jokes to Alina that she wears the years on her hips, and here they are on his face, and on Mark's face, she thinks, these coats they have wrapped themselves in, these lost boys. It's a secret joke to herself, a solace, that Alina really is her daughter and that she wears her on her hips, like all mothers. She gave up so much. Maybe it is on all their faces, in all their eyes. She doesn't look in the mirror so often these days.

And she sees his eyes change now, like the way they see the light across the valley here in summer and things that are there are suddenly gone and the hills appear out of the haze, and his face does look lighter, just for a moment, as if a terrible weight has shifted and eased and then settled again as his eyes fix back to their stare.

She moves her hand onto the table and touches his. There are scars on his fingers, knife cuts and scabs. He is cold. He does not know what to do now and neither does she and she feels calmer for a moment, can hear her own breathing with just the trace of a rattle in it, because she can see it is no longer in him, perhaps never was, not really, an unlucky boy is all, out of his depth.

They could have stood up in that water, something that stuck with her from what the papers wrote afterwards. He'd only taken the car to show off, jealous of Liam and Mark, is what Dee Dee thinks, she was sure at the time, some inkling. Liam hadn't let Dee Dee go to the match, he was a big one for luck back then, all superstitions and ritual to be followed. She never went to away games so she wouldn't go to Wembley. His parents went, of course. So she helped out here in the pub where they set a screen up in the lounge and then there was some problem with it and Lionel rigged up a bedsheet on the wall on which to project the match, right there under the ticking clock. Then when Mark missed that penalty and then the goal went in at the other end, Goldie was off, stamping around, he'd never even liked football, but he was angry now, and the next thing they got was the phone call.

'I want to see her, Dee Dee.'

'I understand,' is what she says, and then, 'Not like this though, Goldie, eh?' and gestures towards him, at his dirty clothes and his exhausted face, this many-coated man.

'No,' he says, 'no.'

. . .

The bar door is ajar, Liam opens it, smells the mopped tiles and the traces of beer underneath. He steps inside and for a moment, just stands there because this is harder than he imagined. There's something else, Liam, she'd said. He is wearing a roll-neck jumper because she hates his tattoos, he knows this, she always said to him, don't get any more now, after those first few, and then after that she had no say anyway. He thinks he can hear voices in the other room.

'Hello?' he says. 'Hello, Dee Dee?'

They used to come and sit here in the cool of the bar sometimes, with all the old timers, the clack of dominoes and the telly playing quietly off to the side, sit and hold hands and look at the smoke coil up towards the ceiling. He hears a commotion, the thump of a chair going over and a little cry, like a whimper or something and he can tell it's Dee Dee's voice but no sound he ever heard from her, not even when they would ride out to that clearing in the woods or when they bought that house up the hill and would wander through those rooms naked, a curse on that place he is sure now, and he thinks that he is disturbing something here, and does not want to see her, does not want to see her like that, as if you might find her with a boyfriend at this time of the morning with the door open, and as he thinks this he walks through the open hatch at the bar and off the tiles and onto the lino with the swirls where someone has mopped, still drying, and he sees them in a mirror etched with a picture of the old Chain brewery, two figures standing facing each other. Her hair has never changed. He loved her hair and her voice and he sees her shape in the mirror and this other figure half turned to him that he doesn't know, with an old coat on and the smell and he thinks for a minute that it is Mark, but then thinks it can't be, and something in his head is not making sense, which is when he sees the knife.

He shouts, is not sure what, into the mirror, and then again as he turns through the doorway into the lounge. There is still the bar between them and he sees the man's hand go for the table and hears Dee Dee scream and run towards the hatch.

And he tries to vault the bar, his hands firm on it, but there are too many matches locked in his knees for that, too great a distance run, and it's more of a scramble, this, kicks a tray of drying glasses, which smash, and he comes over the bar towards the man with the knife in his hand head first, not with his feet, as he thought to, and sees the blade and thinks, this is it, and that he should've grabbed a glass, too late.

Goldie –

. . .

He is not dead, not dead, but changed.

At low tide the men on the cliff-top sleep in their tents. The giants and parts of giants lie strewn across the rocks and shingle down to the foam of the receding sea. Gogmagog, what's left of him, severed head and a severed arm pulling it along, drags himself across a ribbon of rough sand, assembles limbs on the rocks as the rain comes down, a spray comes in. He pieces together arms and legs from his comrades and his own head like a crown atop them, and scuttles along the cliff-base like a monstrous crab.

Up the wet rock he goes in the rain, a sea fret coming in to hide him, just the shape of legs working through the mist. The creature moves through the grey morning, through the green island, the white island, looks for a quiet hollow hill in which to rest, to wait.

· · ·

– it is Goldie, the way he moves in this big coat like the way he used to dance that Liam always envied, even now his movement smooth across the floor and the knife is going away from him and not towards him. Goldie turns and gets to the lounge doors, rattles the bolt, and Liam has his hands up to grab him, is coming at him, but there is the knife held out in front of Goldie, and Liam stops, and in that moment of indecision Goldie has the door open, flings it open so the patterned glass shatters at Liam's feet, and he is away down the road and Liam starts after him and is through the door and onto the pavement and would catch him no problem but for Dee Dee's screams. So with Goldie halfway down the road he turns back to see her hanging onto the bar as if it's a raft.

There's something else, she had said to him, there's something else.

. . .

Oh I wish I was you Billy Meredith
I wish I was you, I envy you, indeed I do.

When he lifts the cup they sing his name. You cannot see the crowd's end, they fill the square and the streets beyond, the gaps between the grand brick buildings. They lean from windows, edge along tree branches in the far distance, throw their caps in the air and cheer and sing. He lifts the cup and they sing his name.

Oh I wish I was you
Indeed I do
Indeed I do.

And he lifts the cup and thinks but you are me. I am you and you are me. They have come from their factories and mills and docks and he has come from the deep black underground and into the light.

He would feed the ponies in the mine, feel their wet noses on his hand, the clink of chains, crawl down those tunnels and dream of the green fields above, the path of the ball across it, the arc of it across a bright sky. Those crosses he hit to Sandy Turnbull, the goal in the final, how he let it run across his body to strike it, to whip his foot through it with the force of all his dreams, all that came from the blackness, from his brothers too, of course, but the force of it, the whip of it so no one would stop it, that came from the very depths. And when it went in, and when he lifts the cup now, it's like that moment you see the daylight when you're coming from deep below, that surge inside yourself. It's the same for them, he can see that, his dark eyes like there is still coal dust on them, star dust.

Oh I wish I was you Billy Meredith
I wish I was you, I envy you, indeed I do.

And I am you and you are me, he thinks, *though there be many members yet there is one bod*y, Corinthians, he remembers the preacher on a Sunday, the green hill, and they cheer as he raises the cup.

. . .

Steve Stringer hears footsteps come out of Chain Street and along under the grandstand, sees a figure running, his overcoat flapping open, what he thinks could be a knife in his hand. He hears the man breathing, heavy, running full pelt, the slap of the soles of his shoes offers percussion to the echoing steps. Steve gets just a glimpse and he is gone. He stays here, rests his cup of tea on the scaffolding pole, looks up and down the street for a pursuer. He sees nothing but a fox nosing around at some bins at the far end of the street. It is quiet. This place, he thinks, shakes his head, thinks of the curse for a moment and wonders if he should contact anyone about the running man, maybe not, probably not a knife anyway, he couldn't be sure, and why break this new sense of optimism? This is the first month he can remember for years when he hasn't been talking to the bank about how to pay the wages. The posters are in a pile in the corner of his office, to be pasted up on the corrugated iron at the Greenfield End later today. He'd checked the design of those from 1957, gone for the same look:

Football Association Challenge Cup
3rd Round Tie,
Sunday January 5th 2pm ko
Irontown FC v. Manchester United

There are banners that say *SOLD OUT* to paste up over them and add to the effect. The phone rings in his office, unusual these days, people usually call his mobile. Might be the FA themselves, he thinks, as he looks up and down the empty street.

'Discrepancy?' he says, when he hears out the voice on the other end of the line, thinks he can hear steps again in the street below, not so much worried as a sense of unease rising within him, 'What do you mean, a discrepancy?'

.   .   .

He has his arms around her at the bar and she sobs into his chest. He kisses the top of her head, not sure what to do.

'It's OK,' he says, 'it's OK. He's not going to hurt you.'

She has her arms against his chest and it feels good to hold her like this, and he knows he should not be thinking of this right now, looks at the upturned table and chair and the threadbare carpet, hears the ticking clock, feels the palms of her hands on his chest and she pushes him away.

'What you come in like that for?' she says. 'You could've just phoned. I was talking to him,' she says. 'Why didn't you just phone back?' She hits him in the chest with the flat of her hands, 'Like any normal person,' she says, and thumps him again and starts to sob.

He hugs her to him again and she shakes as she cries.

'I'm sorry,' he says. 'He had a knife, Dee Dee, he had a knife. Jesus, what did you want me to do?' but softly, quietly into her hair, like he is telling her a story in the middle of the night because she has woken from a bad dream.

They stay like this, at the edge of the bar. In the mirror that reflects into the other room Liam sees a man come in wearing an ill-fitting suit. He stands at the bar for a while. Then he rings the little bell but they stand there and don't say anything. The man cannot see them in the mirror. Liam sees the man go to speak and then shake his head and turn and leave.

Then they sit and look at each other over the righted table, each with a cup of tea. Dee Dee has poured them each a brandy, she says, 'For the shock,' with the intention of making a joke, but knows she just sounds like her nana, who would often reach for a glass after closing, shock or no. 'Goldie never finished his,' she says, again in a voice completely neutral, drained of all colour, and Liam doesn't reply.

He tells her to ring the police and she says no and he doesn't know what else to say.

She has put the bolts back on but is conscious she wants them open again soon, to act like nothing at all has happened. While the kettle was on she hurried upstairs, changed her clothes as quick as she could, heard water running in the bathroom, and stood at the door,

'All right, love?' she called, then a moment of surging panic when there was no reply, her hand flat against the locked door, until she heard Alina's quiet singing and smiled. She wore her headphones in the bath, could never hold a tune.

The room is quiet and cold with the air coming through the door's broken window.

'So nothing before? Just the phone call. No contact, no turning up like that before?'

'Nothing between when he phoned and now. I mean, that's five months, I thought it was just talk, a mistake, you know, tried to put it out of my mind.'

'You need to phone the police, Dee Dee.'

'Maybe,' she says.

'Maybe Lionel or somebody . . .' he starts, but his words tail off.

Alina comes from upstairs, moves behind the bar, looks confused, her hair up in a towel.

'What's going on?'

'Just a bit of trouble, love.'

'Bobby again?' she says.

'No. No one we know.'

'Better phone Lionel,' Alina nods towards the broken glass, looks at Liam.

'Liam was just passing, love,' Dee Dee says. Alina nods at him as with the broken glass, moves back towards the stairs as quietly as she arrived.

'Bobby?' Liam looks at her.

Dee Dee nods, 'In here kicking up a fuss a while ago. He's in a bad way.'

'He did the same at Tony's,' Liam says. He needs to go. Seeing the girl has made him uneasy.

Dee Dee asks him about Greta and Jari and he's surprised she remembers their names. He tells her about not seeing them over Christmas, that he thinks that means a change, an ending. She just nods.

'That must be hard,' she says to him and he can't tell if her voice has changed or not. 'I'd phoned you about Mark,' she says. 'You could go and see him, Liam. It wouldn't kill you.'

'Has he said he wants to see me?'

'It'd be good for him, Liam. Might be good for you both.'

'No,' he says, 'he doesn't want to see me.'

When he stands up to leave it's awkward.

'Thanks, Liam, thanks,' she manages to say, although there's something about it that doesn't ring true to him, he's just saved her life and she wants to talk to him about Mark. They hug at the door with the broken glass. He goes to kiss her and she puts the palms of her hands on his chest again and pushes him away.

'It's a bit late for that, Liam, don't you think?' is all she says.

. . .

Billy Meredith sits in his good suit at the FA Tribunal. It's a much better cut, more expensive cloth, than the ones worn by the men who accuse him, these petty men, these rich men who know nothing and yet think they own the world. When they accuse him of those things, as if he'd have fixed those matches in the way they said, in full sight of everyone, he wishes he had the toothpick, so he could play it along his lips and show them what he thought of them. He would stroll down the wing chewing on it sometimes, and the crowd would laugh and sing his name.

Oh I wish I was you Billy Meredith
I wish I was you, I envy you, indeed I do.

It is a game, nothing more, and people should remember that. He shows how he feels instead with the look in his dark eyes. He knows all about contempt, how to give it and receive it. He knows they can see what he thinks of them, these rich men, these men who think they have the power, think they can buy the world. The people do not sing their names.

These men want to treat them like the pit ponies, stabled in the dark underground, and he wants to see the stars in the night sky, the sun on the fields. These ways of thinking are irreconcilable. It's what one of them says. And he has seen all this before. At Black Park as a boy, and at all the mines and factories and mills beyond. The whole country is a robbers' den. Well, the tables can be overturned. The world does not have to be the way it is.

They ban him and he comes back stronger, looks at them with his dark eyes and doesn't blink. (Cantona, years later, points at the three Federation officials, 'Idiot! Idiot! Idiot!', leaves France and starts out on a road that leads to Old Trafford.)

And when he lifts the cup again, for United this time, not City, the colours of the shirt matter little to these men and, it's true, that is the difference between them and the crowds.

The people sing his name over and over.

It is their own names they sing.

. . .

Christmas night. Liam sits on the bed that had been his as a child. His mum and dad have never altered his room, all these years. His sisters used to share the bigger bedroom and now that's made up as a spare room, but this room has stayed the same, as if some kind of shrine.

He has brought a bottle of beer upstairs with him, it's been too hard trying not to drink, been trying to hide it all day. He wonders if there's a way to get back to the hotel, gives that idea up, will sleep in this narrow bed, with his legs sticking out of the end like they always have since he was fourteen or so, and his dad will take him to the match tomorrow.

'I thought I'd told you to stay at home, son?' Ally said to him this morning, down at the Heath after he'd watched Jari wave at him on the computer screen, saying, 'Merry Christmas, Daddy' in English, looking happy, a few thousand miles away.

'They're not here, Ally. They never came. She wants to keep

him over there,' was what he said to him, nothing more, and trained on Christmas morning like they always had, ran around the field like a kid. Everyone else quick to get off and back home and Liam was last away, doing a proper warm-down.

'You OK, son?' Ally said to him, the last two in the showers and he'd just nodded.

'It must be hard,' and Liam nodded again and Ally went to say something more and then didn't, patted his shoulder as they came out into the damp car park with their wet hair.

He looks at the pictures on the walls, all taken from the football magazines he and Mark would pore over. Baresi, Maldini, Paul McGrath, Des Walker. There's an Italia '90 wall chart, filled in meticulously up until the semi-finals, then nothing, as if he didn't fill in the score Gazza's tears might cry their way back into his head. He used to look at these pictures and imagine himself as these men, in the way that all boys do with their heroes he supposes, but then he somehow stepped into the pages of the magazines, was somehow out there on the pitch, like he walked out of the real world at some point and now couldn't find a way back, became his own tattoo. There are pictures of these men on his walls, pictures of them on his body.

He should not be playing tomorrow. He could still have gone to Finland. God knows what to do about Dee Dee; Goldie's resurrection.

He reaches to the shelf, takes down one of his old football annuals to flip through, to distract himself. He remembers this one. *Ally Barr's All Time Anvil Yards XI*. The players must have played at the Anvil Yards at least once: *Lev Yashin, Djalma Santos,*

*Luigi Allemandi, John Charles, Billy Wright, Duncan Edwards, Billy
Meredith, Steve Bloomer, Eusébio, Alfredo di Stéfano, George Best.* He
and Mark would pick their own teams, riding in his dad's car on
the way to games, or in the back of the minibus, students of the
game. On the back leaf of the book is some writing in pencil.

DAD: Banks, Santos (D), Santos(N), Moore, Beckenbauer,
   Jairzinho, Edwards, Charlton (R), Pelé, Greaves, Best.
MARK: Schumacher, Josimar, Bossis, Olsen, Koeman, Laudrup,
   Baggio, Socrates, Van Basten, Maradona, Gullit.
LIAM: Shilton, Kaltz, Maldini, Baresi, McGrath, Matthäus,
   Gascoigne, Baggio, Dalglish, Maradona, Barnes.

If only everything could be contained by eleven names on a
team-sheet, by the white lines around a pitch. He has lived his life
as if it could, and look at the mess it's brought.

He hears his mum say downstairs, 'Where's our Liam?' in a
voice that could not sound more tired or disappointed, hears his
sisters and the kids getting ready to leave so Gary and Martin can
have a drink at home. He wonders how they manage to keep
their lives in such order. And she could be a bit more sympathetic, his mum, with him stuck here and exiled from his own
family. He exiled himself, all right. But he treads carefully around
his mum, kept his distance when she was ill. He can see in the
look in her eyes, the mess she thinks he's made of things.

And Dee Dee. He saved her life, for god's sake, from a maniac
with a knife, because that is all Goldie is now, perhaps all he ever
was, not that she seemed very grateful. He wants that to be dif-

ferent. On the phone it had sounded like she needed him. He might go and see Lionel, tell him about Goldie, considers the police but thinks Lionel might know what to do. He wishes he did, that's for sure. He tries to think about the United match, the excitement building, and a quiet dread in his stomach that they might run riot, end up with eight, nine, ten, imagine. He should leave off the drink, that's for sure. He lies back on the bed and thinks of lifting the cup, the same dreams he had in this room as a kid, to stop himself thinking of anything else.

. . .

A man in a room dreaming dreams, bloated and reaching for the drink. He tells that joke so often, the one where he is in bed with Miss World and a couple of bottles of champagne, or is it one bottle and two Miss Worlds, and the waiter bringing room service, the fall guy, with his thinning hair and an odd button on his uniform sewn on by his wife, with his grey face and Manchester accent and season ticket for the Stretford End and pale blue eyes, who says, 'Oh George, where did it all go wrong?'

And they laugh their brittle laughs, on the television chat shows and in after-dinner smoke-filled rooms, but he understands as he says it, even as they laugh with him that these people are from a world that is not his.

Where did it all go wrong, George?

Whole iron towns warped with rust and time and pain.

. . .

Liam remembers the story that they picked Yorke off the beach, that he'd been a crab fisherman, would haul his lines up and down and do tricks with the ball for the tourists. There were Union flags that flapped in the harbour, under the Caribbean sun, people in yachts waiting for crab meat and cocktails and black people to fetch and carry for them, it was how they'd built an empire. Taylor could spot a player, in spite of what they said when he managed England, signed John Barnes from a London park pitch, so there was at least something to the story.

Then he did it again, like he'd perfected it this time, and it's unusual, because when you've done it once, why would you try it again, because at some point you'll mess it up.

At home against Arsenal, this, a full house at Villa Park, and he runs up with more purpose than the one before, like he's about to blast it into the corner, and this time opens his foot as he strikes it, might have toppled backwards as he hit it, balls of iron, so it hovers in the air, a couple of feet off the ground, and Seaman sits down, tries to get up, crumples, and the ball lands in the goal, and in Liam's head at least, stops dead. Sits there like a full stop at the end of a story.

Liam imagines watching this with Mark.

'You should've just done that,' he says to him.

'I should've just smashed it,' is what Mark – the Mark in his head – says back.

. . .

Jeff Stelling: And another goal at the Anvil Yards. Dave Willis is there for us.

Dave 'Iron' Willis: A third for Accrington Stanley.
Francis Jeffers, the original fox in the box,
strikes again. Very little seasonal cheer at the
Anvil Yards for the second year running for Liam
Corwen, sent off for a foul on Jeffers, who in
all honesty was giving the big man a runaround,
definitely getting the upper hand in the battle of
the former England internationals, and the red card
might have put Corwen out of his misery. That's the
tenth sending off of his career, incidentally. Looks
like Irontown will be in the relegation places
for the new year. They need to liven up their act
for the visit of Manchester United in the cup,
a wonderful distraction from the reality of the
league table, that's for sure . . .

. . .

He can tell something's up when he gets to training, thinks
for a moment that it's just the six-nil to Accrington, a feeling
of doom all around. The sending off was a joke, he barely
touched him. There's been an intensity in the last few weeks
since the cup draw, but with a few wins as well, and the sense,
if nothing more than that, that they might start to climb the
table, but the wheels fell off the wagon with the Boxing Day
match and there's something even about the way the cars
are parked haphazardly in the car park, as he walks across it
from the bus turnaround and up the wooden steps into the
prefab that moonlights as the canteen and gym and sometime
meeting room, that doesn't add up at all. Half a dozen of them

sit on plastic chairs not looking at each other.

'You heard?' Devon asks him.

'Who's dead?'

'We've been thrown out of the cup. Ally's been sacked.'

And he is halfway across the room, to the connecting doors that lead to the dressing rooms, before this registers.

'What?'

'He fucked up the paperwork for that First Round game. That kid we'd got in from Cheltenham, he'd played in the qualifiers for some non-league side, fucking August they start them games, never thought to say though, the kid must have forgot, not realised.'

'Thrown out the cup for that?'

'Ineligible player. It's in the rules.'

'He was shit an' all!'

Liam can't tell who says this but still replies, 'But better than you.'

'He probably forgot. He was a good player. Prick.' Kyran says towards the floor and the unidentified voice.

Liam stands in the doorway, 'No one's dead,' he says, 'no one died.' He does not know why he says this. The players look at the floor. He thinks of Boris Becker that time, another picture from his bedroom wall, summer distractions, when Becker lost for the first time at Wimbledon, 'I did not lose a war. No one died.'

No one ever gets sacked here. No one has made a decision for twenty years. Dorothea sits there drooling in the Atlantic sun, from what he understands, refuses to sell up, refuses to do anything, holds all the shares, the last in the dynasty. Steve Stringer fills out bits of paper, writes cheques and invoices, talks to the bank and the league.

'Who's sacked him?'

No one answers.

'Archie says there's a meeting in a bit, to wait here.'

'Where else we gonna go?'

'Archie didn't fucking sack him,'

'Archie's in charge for now.'

'Who said that?'

'Archie.'

'Better get changed anyway, lads,' is all Liam says, punches the wall in the dressing room when he gets in there, doesn't notice Julius sitting there in the corner until he's already done it and his knuckles are bleeding, staring into space, thinks, this whole place is fucking cursed.

'Archie said to go home,' Julius says, sitting there, staring into space with a towel wrapped around him, 'Have the day off. There'll be a meeting tomorrow.'

. . .

He pulled her out, saved her. Even the judge had mentioned it when he sentenced him. He pulled her out. There was the shock of hitting the water. It came in through the open window and he felt the shock of it, cold, as it hit his leg and the lurch of the car with the water entering so they went nose first into it and it felt like Alina was in a seat above them as well as behind them, at the angle now, but all of them sinking. The log flume at Alton

Towers, that's what he thought of, shocked by the water. Sonia's head had gone forward and thumped into the dashboard, she turned to him with her nose bleeding and they look at each other. He swears he can see the look on her face when he shuts his eyes. The back half of the car dropped into the water. Alina was quiet, had been crying, was quiet now, with the shock of the impact he guesses, and the car filling up, going under, the sound of the water sloshing up the sides of the culvert and then come running in through the car windows. She tries to hit him, scratches at his face, his eyes. Both of them still in their seats, water up to their waists. They would find his skin under her nails in the post-mortem. He grabs her wrists and she won't calm down. He can hear the siren. Alina begins to scream. The windscreen gives way with the brown water, there was a crack in it he knew he should've seen to. The glass and water hit him. He twists and reaches to the baby seat, has to pull himself with the water filling the car. They are jammed tight against the bank on Sonia's side. This is what kills her, when she's underwater she tries the door handle but it won't open. Goldie pulls Alina to him, through the gap between the headrests the sound of water pouring in. A splinter in his brain says they are going to die. He pulls him to her, ducks under the water, pushes her from him through the window now because the car is full of water, they are underwater now, and from somewhere, somewhere, some old action film or something he thinks later when he talks of it, and talks and talks, in counselling, and it is not all bullshit, it has not all wrecked his head, his mind is the shape of the crumpled car all right, but he knows, he understands that with the car full of water they can come out through the window, it shows his speed of thought, he thinks, and he saves his daughter's life that way, pushes her out and away from him through the window, has to take a hand off her to get himself through the gap wriggling and swallowing some of it, so that he's choking when he gets his head out, holding Alina away from him half on the steep grass bank that rises from the concrete and if the grass had not been so steep he might have been able to lay Alina down and go back and get Sonia, her belt still fastened, and it is here, still choking and holding Alina and not thinking she is dead, never thinking that until some minutes later, when he sees the policewoman walking away from him with the baby in her arms looking down at her and talking into her radio.

'Jesus, Rita, there's a babby.' He hears a man's voice, the policeman, and the sound of their boots on the lane. Sonia struggling, the water only just above her head, not quite filling the car, the water not that deep, she could've stood up in it.

She didn't stand up in it. He remembers looking at the water sloshing against steep banks and then back again towards the car roof that was still above the water, at an angle, sloping forward, and the water going more and more still. There was no movement at all. He looked at the banks, still thinking he'd see Sonia, not thinking anything, looking back at the still water and the still car.

'There's someone in the car,' he says to them.

That's what they talked about after, in the court, how calm he'd said this. He was trying not to panic.

. . .

Scotland against England is serious business. It is 5 April, 1902, and at Ibrox they have to walk past dead bodies to get back onto the pitch. There are arms and legs at angles they would never be in life. There are men behind the men in charge, always, men in suits in the dressing rooms who tell them to get back out there. They say if they don't play on there'll be more dead. They say this time and again through the years.

Steve Bloomer is captain that day, the first time, and he leads his men past the bodies and back out onto the pitch. It bothers him that he should have said no, respect the dead. They ferry people to hospital on makeshift stretchers as the match goes on. There is a black hole in the stand where the wood gave way; men of iron towns, laid out by the side of the Ibrox pitch. It will happen again, at regular intervals in the century ahead. The authorities decide to replay the match at Villa Park in the end. They give the gate receipts to the families, at least.

When he looks at great tides of people he always sees that black hole. There are people absent from every crowd.

. . .

Ally looks relieved, is what he looks. Jesus, Liam thinks. How terrible can managing this club be if you don't feel too bad about passing up a game against Man United, putting the final nail in the place's coffin with this last mess-up. Ally won't work again.

With the money and attention from the United match they would have had a chance. Without it, now, out of the cup, near the bottom of the league, struggling to pay the players, there is very little hope. The cup draw was a miracle. To ask for another seems to be stretching the bounds of reality. Although with this club you never know . . .

Dave Willis did a piece on Midlands Today last night. They found the most dilapidated corner of the car park to film in, both the factory wall and the Chain End looking like they might fall into the canal at any moment. There were kids jumping around in the background, giving the fingers, one of them was even wearing a United bobble hat. There are no kids in the Anvil Yards any more, god knows where they had come from, maybe the people from the telly had brought them with them.

Ally looks like a man who has slept sound in his bed all night. Fifty years in football, he's had, just over, signed for Celtic at fifteen, has managed Irontown for more than twenty of the last thirty years. When he became player-manager in 1984 the club was one place in the league better off than it is now, except what Ally will tell you is that he has never taken the club down. He would win promotion, leave for somewhere else with a bit of glamour, more money, then come back when Irontown had been relegated again. That was the pattern. Hail, hail.

He is thanking everyone. Last night in an interview he said he'd be off to Portugal for a bit of sunshine and golf, was looking forward to spending time with the grandkids.

'I've done nothing wrong,' he said, 'I'll sleep soundly in ma bed.'

Dave Willis tried to press him, wasn't it the manager's responsibility to check these things?

'It's the club's,' Ally said. 'We acted in good faith.' Then he was off, the camera lingered on the Mercedes come from Lionel Ahmed's garage which Liam guessed Lionel would be calling to get back. The club say they've sacked him, Ally says it's mutual.

He could speak to Lionel about Dee Dee. About the situation. What else to call it? The situation, the emergency, the trouble. He might have been describing the Iron Towns themselves, he knows. Thirty years of it, three hundred nearly, just times when you might not have noticed. Lionel might know what to do. He thinks of going to the police. She might thank him in the end. She might not.

They've got the heating on full blast for once, everyone crammed in the canteen, the carpet threadbare, there are framed photos of old players and matches on the walls, there's one of Ally on Archie Hill's shoulders with the Welsh Cup, from the days when Midlands sides could enter, Ally wrote to UEFA to try to allow them into Europe. Liam feels like his eyes might close. He is not a man who sleeps easy in his bed, any bed, any more. Ally is thanking Ted Groves, really hamming it up now. Ted and Ally have got tears in their eyes. Liam puts his head in his hands. He hears a camera whirring.

They've revived talk of the curse with this latest catastrophe, especially because it involves the cup. There are two versions that Liam knows of, probably more if you asked around. One is that when the team arrived back on the train from the old Crystal Palace after the last final they won, to be greeted by great crowds at Hightown Station, men in caps hanging from the castle walls, the Crusader stone, the trees at the arboretum, James Greenfield took the cup in his new car, his latest toy, the first to be seen on Iron Towns roads, and drove across the Heath. His driver slowed for an old gypsy woman, picking flowers at the roadside. It was a hot day and she called out to them to ask for a drink of water. They slowed and Greenfield laughed and told her to go and get a drink from the brook. She pointed at the cup, sitting next to him on the seat, and told him that it would never be seen in the Iron Towns again.

The other story involves the cup when it was stolen from Birmingham, when the Villa put it on display in a jewellers' shop. There was a rumour the Carter family took it, melted it down for coins in an Anvil Yards furnace. Another version has them burying it out on the Heath and forgetting where they left it, like that Saxon gold they say is somewhere, piles of coins stamped 'Offa Rex'. This forgetfulness has always seemed unlikely to Liam, from what he understands of the Carters, the Greenfields, the Ahmeds, well, some of them, and from what he understands of Saxon chieftains, for that matter. People who make money keep it, most of them, anyhow.

All football grounds have curses on them, it's just some of these curses work better than others, that's what he thinks, really. They could undo the curse by playing well.

Ally says Liam's name and eyes turn towards him. Ally is telling them all to pull together. Through the window Liam can see Steve Stringer on the phone. No one has made a decision at this club for years. Old Dorothea is almost a hundred, no family left. From the way that Steve is pacing up and down and the bags under his eyes, it seems to Liam that he's taken a stand about this and now regrets it. Who's going to want to come here? Big Archie has been named as caretaker, but he's not a manager. There's a rumour going round that they've asked Wayne Coombs, just been sacked by a club in Malta, back at his ex-wife's in Calon. That's all they fucking need. Liam moves to put his head back in his hands, realises it might not look good. Ally says his name again, talks about fighting spirit, the embodiment of the club.

Liam clenches his fist and nods his head to murmurs of support. Julius pats him hard on the back.

Steve Stringer is nuts letting Ally talk like this. Ted Groves is crying.

And then he's done. 'This club will go on,' he says, and they're already clapping, on their feet. 'and maybe we'll meet again, you never know, Happy New Year, everyone, Happy New Year,' and he's gone.

Out the door he goes and towards his car, ignores Steve who moves towards him and then gets the message, so hangs back and maybe he's even pretending to be on the phone, no one is going to want to talk to him except Dave Willis for the latest gossip. Liam can see brake lights from the cars out on the Heath road, they shine blurred through the dirty window and damp January air, through the leafless trees and then move around the corner and out of sight, it's where he came off the road, keep going half a mile and it's where Goldie drove into the river, there's a turn-off for the clearing where they used to go in summer, up there on the hill is where the people took that German parachutist and killed him and stuffed his body down an old mine shaft that no one still is meant to talk about, and there's the Goat Wood, where the witches still go on full-moon nights and the solstice, and it's already getting dark.

. . .

It starts to rain.

They missed the floods before Christmas, just a postponement against Torquay to show for them, as the weather skirted the Iron Towns, but now it comes hard and Liz and Joey watch the rain gutter down the steep Black Park hill.

'It's coming now,' Joey says, his nose almost touches the steering wheel. White water froths up out of the drains, comes in a wave down the kerbs, a pink child's wellington boot tumbles over and over.

'What was he thinking?' Liz says.

'Nothing, nothing.'

The light is falling, either that or the rain is coming even harder now, picked out in the streetlights. 'That's not true. Himself, of course, thinking of himself, as usual.'

Liz sighs.

'You warm enough, love?' he asks. He has the window open a crack to stop the windscreen steaming up.

'I'm OK.'

Eli is missing, out when he should be in, not for the first time. They have told him not to try the hill on his own any more, certainly not just with his stick. He refuses a walking frame, laughs when they suggest a scooter. All talk of him moving has long since gone. They'll have to carry him out, as the saying goes, unless the houses fall down or wash away first. It is possible.

The water has gathered at the bottom of the hill, meeting other water in brown swirls, a lagoon, cars pull in, hazard lights blink in the water.

'Well, I can't go through that,' Joey says. On the radio an excited woman's voice plays at low volume.

'There's boxes of stuff just floating along the road. What's this? Saris and communion dresses and flat caps,' she says.

The Lowtown Bull Ring is flooded. The radio says to avoid the area if possible.

'I've avoided it for twenty years,' Liz says, pleased with her joke.

A bus ploughs into the flood, headlights on full beam, sends up a plume of water. It is not a designated stop but the bus creeps carefully along the kerb, opens its doors. The driver leans half out of his cab. Sure enough, there on the platform is Eli. In the rain's din they can see but not hear the conversation, but can imagine, they get the gist.

'Don't get out in this, mate. Wait till it knocks off a bit.'

'I'm all right, what's the matter with yer? I'm all right.'

Eli teeters on the bus steps. A young woman's arm stretches out to help him. Joey jumps from the car, headfirst into the deluge, grits his teeth. There's his dad ankle-deep, the water rushing over his smart brown shoes, spreading up his trouser legs, neatly creased by Liz.

'What am yer doing?' Eli says. 'What yer playing at?'

'What do yer think?' Joey says and takes his elbow, half expects to feel it in his ribs.

The last time he did this was in the riots. Well, he did it all the time, but the last time he put himself in danger that they knew of.

'He puts himself in danger every time he inches down them stairs in his carpet slippers.' Liz says.

'Yer couldn't even get a stair-lift in here. Yer couldn't fit one,' Eli'd say right to the face of the occupational therapist come from social services, moving his teeth in agitation so the bottom set nearly came flying out, some girl young enough to be his great-grandaughter telling him otherwise about the lift, come to visit him at home and assess his needs, as they put it. Joey and Liz would smile and apologise with their eyes.

At least the riots were in the summer. He'd got the bus out towards the flyover to go and have a look at the trouble himself, a bonfire burning in the Tesco car park at four in the afternoon. Young lads tried to nick trainers at the shopping village. Joey could never get to the bottom of whether Eli had gone to tell them all to go home or whether he thought the revolution had come at last.

'Not even any proper trouble, just some young lads setting fires and the police watching 'em do it,' was Eli's only comment afterwards.

That night, some of the Bullet Krew attempted to burn down the police station, set squat and flat just off the Wrexham Road on the rise between Oxton and Cowton, but the flames didn't take, it was a night of soft drifting rain coming out of Wales, the last night. The men went home, the boys got their new shoes, people too tired to riot any more.

. . .

Dee Dee stands in her boots, the water darkens her jeans. A couple of empty barrels bob in the water and make hollow sounds on the cellar walls. The rain beats on the iron doors which rattle and threaten to fold in on themselves with the weight of the water. She tells herself not to breathe in, does anyway, concentrates for any smell of shit in the water. She needs Roni to descend. All she can smell is dead leaves, mulch, the usual damp cellar wall smell. She should be worried about the beer spoiling, she knows that, is not sure of the insurance procedures. This could mean the end, but the actual fact of the water sweeping through the Anvil Yards streets exhilarates her. She thinks of the language of survival, keeping your head above water, going under, holed below the water line, and the like. She imagines the door at the top of the steps swung shut, the water at her chin, her mouth, nose, ears. The temptation to let go, her hair floating in the water.

'Mum, what you doing? Come on.'

The door is open and the lights on. Alina stands at the top of the stairs with that rope in her hands, coiled round her slim body.

Alina floats down the river towards her. The child saves the parent in the end, she thinks, wishes for a moment she still tried to write songs.

. . .

The rain comes through the whole building. There is glass in the skylights and he is afraid they might give way with the force of the rain but it comes in everywhere else anyway. He's got a candle lit, eats a cold tin of beans with an old carpet wrapped round him. Goldie would never have thought he could've coped with something like this. The one time they went camping at school he walked back from the Heath himself, wanted his own bed, his mum. He wishes he had never left his room, imagines himself there now, the water washing time backwards.

There's a glow that comes from the motorway flyover that enters at the far end of the building. He can see the rain guttering down in the orange light, holds his hand to the candle and shivers, the fire escape stairs at the far end of the building dissolve in the rain. They were only held together by rust, he sees them peel off the wall and crumble and disappear without even making a sound. He wonders if it's the end of the world.

. . .

'Death by fire, death by water, death by fire, death by water,' Mark Fala stands at the window, rocks back and forth, looks out into the storm. Half the lights are out up the hill, so he is left with the sounds. He knows that when they found her there was mud and brick dust under her fingernails where she'd tried to claw herself out, stones in her pinafore dress, clothes her own mother wore.

The inquest was inconclusive. She might have slipped down the bank in the rain. It was possible. He almost went in himself a couple of times, when he used to go down there just to sit and think about things. He went there a lot during that last season, thought a lot about packing it all in right there. Not just the football, everything. You could see the back of his dad's old works from the bank, no one ever mentioned that at the inquest and he didn't feel any urgent need to say.

He told himself she didn't mean it. It was one thing to wish yourself dead. It was another thing to actually go ahead and do it. She wouldn't have left him. That was what everyone said. But then, they hadn't been there in the dark nights, had they? They hadn't heard her crying, or not crying, other noises, just shuffling from room to room in a small flat she said she wouldn't leave, even though he was earning the money then. Ally had got them with money coming in hand over fist. The older players loved it. What use was it to him? He used to ask sometimes, and they took it as some quirk or other, but he knew there was something wrong with him. They'd have put up with anything as long as he kept performing, as long as they kept winning.

He'd beckon with his hands for the ball, had never been one for saying much on the pitch, never one for saying that much anywhere, really.

'Give it to Mark, give it to him. Hit Mark's feet. Release him. Just fucking give it to him!' Liam's monologue coming from the other end of the pitch. At first the older players didn't want to be spoken to like that, not by Liam, big and cocky and decent player as he was, but still just a kid, and then they looked at Mark, and knew that he was right.

He'd always known. He'd chased around the flat as soon as he could walk with a little ball at his feet that the dog had chewed. His dad always liked to keep a dog. They had two scrappy puppies once that his dad called Jackie and Bobby. And he'd have the ball at his feet when they went down the shops and would play one-twos off the kerb before he even knew what a one-two was. His dad had been a good player, his mum's dad too. His mum had been a great one for dancing. His balance he got from her. She'd always had great balance, something else he was glad no one ever mentioned at the inquest. The bank was steep and it could be slippery in the rain, but still, it was hard to see her floundering about like that. She always walked with her head up. Not two pennies to rub together, as they used to say, not a pot to piss in, except maybe the last few months, years, with the pay-out for his dad's accident and the money Mark had started to get paid. He got offered adverts, a boot deal. Those other clubs came in for him. Everyone was mad to go to Italy then. Imagine, him on the same pitch as Van Basten, as Baggio. What was strange was that it almost happened, like with the Torino thing. There was talk of Lazio too. He was meant to get an agent. Liam's dad looked after it all for a while. A lot of good the money did her, anyway.

It suited everyone to think it was another accident, there was the mud under his mum's fingernails. She always kept her hands nice. He could sit now and conjure up the smell of the cream she used to use on them, there was probably some in the back of a drawer somewhere. He'd never thrown her things out. It suited them all, meant the priest could come round and sort out the funeral without any complications. Very good for everyone, they could all feel a bit better about themselves.

She couldn't swim. That was why she chose that way, he supposed. It was a while before they found her. Just under the surface, face down, bobbing against the wooden planks that held off the bank there, her skirt billowing out behind her. The police had taken a picture. He hadn't seen her until the hospital. Her body was all swollen up because of the water, three times the size she'd been in life. He'd been worried she'd got too thin. He'd got his build from her as well.

He knew well before he missed that penalty that he was going to walk away. In fact, missing it almost made him think he'd go back, even just for the start of the season, if only to shut everyone up.

What he thinks is that she changed her mind. That itself was unusual. Something else he got from her was that he knew his own mind, never had any doubts. That's why packing it in was a question of when and not if. He tried to drink himself to death. He thought that might be a solution, but it was harder than you might think. His heart wasn't in it maybe, he had never been that much of a drinker, would get drunk and pass out. You had to really give yourself over to it, like Stevie and Jigsaw and the others at the Quakers. You could admire their determination in a way. He wasn't joking. To achieve anything, you had to put some effort in, even if it was just leaving. He thinks she changed her mind, thought that what she wanted was to leave and then realised too late that she wanted to live, if only for him. In dreams she would come to him and ask for forgiveness and he would say it's OK, it's OK, Mum, don't cry. Maybe she just wanted to be with his dad, but he wasn't sure that any of them believed in that stuff, not really. You didn't go anywhere. You just stayed here in the Iron Towns.

He can't swim. It occurs to him that one day he might do the same as she did, but he doubts it now. He's come through dark days, hours, minutes, sometimes the world just reduced to nothing, but he has started to not feel so bad. He wonders if it is simply the fact of getting older. He couldn't play football now even if he wanted to. He can't drive. He has not had a girlfriend for twenty years, even back then just someone to hold hands with. He wasn't like Liam, like Goldie. He used to look at Sonia and imagine, dream about what it might be like. She had all sorts under her fingernails too, she had clawed for life too, but then Sonia had never wanted to die.

The wind changes and the rain drills against the window. When it comes at a certain angle, a wind out of the north-west, from out of the far mountains, the water gets in and patters the floor in his mother's room, sometimes the bed cover. He'll go and get some old sheets from the cupboard. Everything is still here. He thinks of it as her room. There's still some stuff of his dad's in the back of the wardrobe. His funeral suit, for one thing. Didn't need it, after all. He is not sure what clothes he was buried in. There was a kid who died, one of the ones they'd visit down at the children's ward at the Bethel, buried with one of Mark's shirts. The grave wasn't far from Sonia's plaque, just outside the garden of remembrance. Mark thought about it every time he went up there. When the wind blows from the other way, it brings his name on it. The way they still sing it. They need some new songs, is what he thinks.

· · ·

With the game off, Liam sits and drinks in the hotel bar with Devon and Julius. The car parks are under water, both at the ground and the hotel. Devon and Julius are shipwrecked.

'So if the ball went over the stand, right, you had to scamper down these steps and open this door, like a hobbit door, right. There was three of 'em. One level with each penalty spot and another at halfway.'

'Scampering, that's a great word, scampering.' Julius grins at his bottle of beer.

'And each door opens onto the riverbank, right, except there ain't much bank just there. You know you could only get into the East Stand at either end of the ground, it's one of the reasons they closed it, right.'

'Health and safety considerations,' Devon says.

'Exactly. Anyway, you'd open this door and have to watch your step, what with studs on the concrete, to not end up in the drink, and then you'd put your head out and, I swear to God, there'd come this old bloke in a bobble hat rowing a little boat, a coracle it's called, this kind of boat, and he'd fish the ball out with a net and row it over to you to take back. I can't think of his name.'

'Someone needs to scamper to the bar.'

'I can't think of his name. This bloke was ancient, all bent over, thick glasses on, three coats in winter. Looked like he slept in the boat, but, get this, his old man had done the same job before him, right, before they even built the stand and there was just a bank and a wall down that side, so what, the twenties or summat, the same boat, a coracle.' He is losing them, their eyes glaze, fix on their drinks, with this story of his days as a ballboy, on the results of games that have made it through the weather. They toast and drink whenever they hear Irontown mentioned. 'Archie Hill stuck it in the river six times one afternoon, I swear.'

'Archie Hill is a cock,' says Julius.

Archie had dropped him, named the team yesterday, decided to try Kyran up front, and then the rain came.

'I am the curse,' is what Julius had said when he'd had a couple of drinks. 'Archie better believe it.'

Liam can see a man reflected in a mirrored column. He stands near the reception desk, looks uncomfortable, checks a heavy-looking watch, dark blue suit and – this is what has caught Liam's attention – dark glasses. It is pouring with rain in the English Midlands.

'Is that one of the Portuguese?' Liam nods towards the mirror and looks at the other two. When he looks back there is no one there.

'What Portuguese? I'll have another.' Julius rarely drinks, is feeling it.

'Remember,' Liam starts, 'that kid, start of the season, Luis . . .' Then, 'You heard about that club that takes their ground with them, erects a whole stadium? They build the stadium the week of the game out in the desert, out where they don't have football, like Mongolia and places, play their match, then that's it they're away and the ground goes with them, on to the next place.'

'What you on about? Who do they play?'

'You two need to slow down a bit,' Devon says, 'I'll get a round in.'

'They travel round like nomads and that. Wanderers. That's where the team name Wanderers comes from, teams that didn't used to have a home ground.' He says this to no one in particular, sometimes has conversations he thinks he might have with Jari in the future in his head, out loud too now, it seems. If Jari can speak English by then, if Liam can speak Finnish or Swedish or Russian or German or whatever else he might learn.

Liam stands and walks towards the mirror, walks around the column with his drink in his hand, no one there, shakes his head, and walks back to their seats. He'd been sure.

Devon comes back with the drinks on a tray, motions to the TV screen. On the news they show Eusébio's coffin, carried high through weeping streets, into the stadium, out onto the pitch. It is pelting with rain in Lisbon.

. . .

It rained whenever Caesar came.

The shield Nennius used was forged on Manawydan's stone. It swallowed Caesar's sword the first time he came, and Nennius took the sword and cut the invaders down so that the valley filled with blood.

Caesar sailed up the river but the people were ready. They set great iron spikes beneath the still waters. Caesar's ships were drowned and the valley filled with water.

Then Caesar came a third time and the people ran and hid, and the valley filled with ghosts.

There is always a war. Invaders come and go, settle and remain, become the people that live among the valleys and the stones, wait things out, hollow out the hills and burn their black insides. There is always a war, always a fire that burns within, without, and the rivers only ever run with blood.

Arthur died on the muddy, muddy banks.

There was no boat to carry him.

. . .

He needs three or four attempts to get the card in the door lock and then even when he opens it he misses the doorway and walks into the frame. A bump rises on his forehead and he puts his fingers to it to check for blood and this sobers him enough to realise how drunk he is. He giggles and unzips himself and pisses loud and long in the toilet bowl in the dark with the doors open to the corridor, sings 'Oh it's a grand old team to play for,' loudly, and then stops and puts the card in the slot to operate the lights and puts his cock away and zips up carefully and only then closes the door as quietly as he can and then slumps against it and sits down and wonders if he has left a can of beer in the fridge.

He was probably this far gone the night they pulled him up for drink-driving. He had not been playing, had been out with a heel injury and then not back in the side for a couple of months or more, but he kept plugging away in training and got a chance when they played Shrewsbury on a Friday night, live on telly, and he came on with them one-down and getting murdered, only for them to come back and win 3-1 with Liam getting the second himself from a corner.

They'd had a drink in the hotel that night, celebrated, Ally included, with a couple of them with rooms booked because of the late finish. Liam had already been too drunk to drive when he left them and drove back to his house on the hill. He was still trying to live there on his own then and not doing very well at it. So when he got in he turned every light on and got a bottle of wine from cupboard, he'd had intentions at one point of a cellar, and drank that looking out into the dark from the living room, still restless. That was when he went back out for another drive, to see what was happening, Friday night and all that, put some old stuff that he used to listen to with Dee Dee on the stereo as he drove, went back down the hill towards the Anvil Yards with the vague intention of returning to the hotel bar, telling Ally he deserved a start next match.

He drove around, sobering up, he thought, when he saw the young kids queueing to get into a club under the arches in Lowtown that he did not know the name of, did not know existed. And something, in the music and thoughts of the night's match and hating the transition between being surrounded by the crowd and laughter and noise and being on his own in his own silent house and bed, made him keep driving. He thought he might go and bang on Mark's door, go and visit him, had these grand visions of a reconciliation, arms round each other crying, he was crying as he was driving now, of course, but when he got down near the flats he couldn't work out how to drive into them, he had never gone there with a car and Goldie had always parked out here on the main road and he was not stupid or drunk enough to be leaving an almost new BMW parked half-way across the pavement in the Anvil Yards, so he did a couple of circuits, couldn't see any lights on in Stevedore House anyway, and drove off, leaving the big reconciliation for another night. It had been twenty years since they last spoke, after all.

Still, that wasn't enough though, and after driving down to see if the Salamander was still serving, which of course it wasn't as it was after two o'clock by this point, and looking forlornly at the lights on in the upstairs of the pub, even thinking he saw a shape, Dee Dee, pass behind the net curtains, he headed out towards the Heath, past the big cut-out of himself advertising the entrance to Lionel Ahmed's car yard and the reason he was driving a BMW in the first place, just over the hump-backed bridge where he began to list towards the left-hand verge and drove along half in the hedge for thirty yards or so before fully leaving the road. He stayed in the car for a while, might even have slept for a few moments, so peaceful it was here at the Heath's edge in the dead of night. The driver's door was jammed against a branch in the hedgerow and so he was halfway out of the sun-roof, and struggling with this, stiffening up with driving after a match, when a police car came round the corner on its way back to the Lowtown station for a shift-change.

He could have killed someone. The following day his head was full of this. Or he could've killed himself, which at the time felt much the lesser of the evils, he was only a few turns in the road from where Goldie had crashed with Sonia and Alina. In fact, where he was headed in the car at that hour was the clearing in the Goat Wood, to sleep in his car under the trees and think of better days. And he could've gone to prison, something that only really dawned on him on the day of his trial and he couldn't stop his legs shaking when he stood up in court and had to listen to himself described in ways that he did not want to listen to at all. It was a stupid thing to have done, OK but these fuckers in their wigs and with their accents which came from nowhere near the Iron Towns had no right to pass any judgement. Well, there was a judgement, of course, banned for three years, an alcohol awareness course, a speed awareness course, a few hundred hours of community service.

'You'll have to stop your drinking now Liam. You could've killed somebody.' His mum's voice that night as he sat in their front room still in his court suit, still in the dock from what he could tell, with his sisters looking at him through the breakfast hatch and his old man not looking at him at all but his lips disappearing in that grim smile he used to get just before he'd blow, drop the nut on someone if he had to. As if the drinking was the problem, really. In court, his barrister had talked about the stress of Liam's estrangement from his wife and young child. It wasn't a word he would have used, but it made sense. His own wife and son becoming strangers to him, the same with everyone he had ever known.

'You'll have to smarten up your act, love,' his mum repeated phrases she used to say to him when he was a kid. He smiled at this, a man in his thirties crumpled in the soft armchair in his parents' front room.

'All their furniture is too big for the house,' is something Greta had said to him, and it was true, he'd never noticed before, but it was.

Strangers all of them, to each other, to themselves.

. . .

Liam has only ever seen the girl, what, half a dozen times. No more than a few minutes each time. Less than that usually, like when she stood behind the bar the other day and then was gone, like the Portuguese, who are not even Portuguese, in the bar downstairs.

It unnerves him every time, though. He lies on the bed, half-clothed, too pissed to undress. This is what hotels are for, he thinks, is not unhappy right now this moment, but knows he must be pissed to be thinking of it like this.

He thinks of last things, does this sometimes to try to get to sleep, a variation on running through League Cup winners, or trying to remember every player he has ever played with. He thinks of the things that when he dies will go as well, locked inside his head, things that he knows or remembers and, if he lives long enough, will be the last to know.

Such as coal scuttles, the one at his nan and grandad's, the one that still sits in a bucket by his grandad's back door, and dial telephones and houses with no phone at all, like Goldie's all the time they knew him, and Mark's for a good while too, no washing machine; spin dryers; no telly in the daytime or after midnight, black and white, turned on early to warm it up for your programme; copying machines that you got asked to wind the handle of if you were a good boy in class, the print a fading purple; the half-time scores being put up on an old wooden scoreboard under the East Stand, letters of the alphabet that correspond to the day's fixtures; the man in the coracle to fish out any balls that went in the river, and what was his name?

The smell of piss and the sheen of the tiles in the outside toi-lets; clean, evenly hung net curtains as a sign of something, what?, important to your mum, your position in the world; changes of shift and the men coming up or down the valley like a tide, lines of cars in the rain, a procession huddled along the pave-ments; seeing Concorde at the air show, a flickering white splin-ter through the clouds.

They are locked in his head, these last things.

There's the shape of Mark Fala as he sends a volley off the factory wall, then another, then another, always the same poised follow-through, dead still for an instant, like Zidane when he hit that volley at Hampden, like a kid exaggerating a footballer's movements, someone taking the piss, but then you see his face and you know he's for real, the real thing, and the ball hits the same spot time and again. Dee Dee pushing her hair from her face, kneeling over him in that single-bed with the tight white sheets on the top floor of the pub. Sonia, not looking at him, looking at the road, sunshine, then shadow from the trees, then sun again, goading him he tells himself, they shouldn't even be in the car together, have already gone too far.

'I don't believe you want to Liam, I think you're all talk, full of it.'

Last, last things.

. . .

Hengist said he'd bring peace but Hengist brought war. But first he brought his daughter, the most beautiful woman on the island since Elstridis was drowned. Vortigern, the new king, saw her and wanted her, believing in the power of kings.

'What will you offer for my daughter?' Hengist asked.

And Vortigern thought, and he bargained, but what he said and what he thought were different things.

'I will give you the island and everything in it,' is what Hengist heard.

And they burned Vortigern in his tower in the end.

. . .

Liam takes the page from one of the broadsheets that has been left open on the table he sits at for breakfast. Before looking at the paper, he watches the geese that waddle across the car park leaving a trail of green shit. Amir sends cleaners out to scrub the tarmac. The geese used to stay the other side of the water, but Liam reckons they've got scared by the foxes and whatever else is there in the ruins. They aren't stupid, he thinks to himself, as he concentrates on his egg and ignores the newspaper. He likes to watch them fly in formation from out of his window. If only his own back four could maintain some of their awareness of each other.

He doesn't like these newspapers, the accent they are written in, so that they make football sound like something that is theirs and not his own. Ours, theirs, he knew he sounded like his grandad, this reduction to us and them. He looks across to the Anvil Yards. The workers have disappeared. Us and them was how football worked, as well. But the workers have not disappeared, of course, just become invisible most of the time, because here come the cleaners with buckets of soapy water to scrub away the shit so the mobile phone salespeople and the like, workers themselves of course, but god knows how that was work, although more work than chasing a ball across a field maybe, have a nice clean car park to drive on to. One of the cleaners, a woman, older than the two young men with her, wearing a turban above her green uniform shoos the geese with a broom, doesn't speak. One of the geese spreads its wings, hisses, but its heart isn't in the fight and the geese file away towards the canal towpath. Liam knows this woman, nods to her in the foyer and the corridor, where she trails a small vehicle stacked with all sorts of cleaning materials behind her, more a headdress than a turban, and she nods back, doesn't speak. She is African, he supposes, realises that he could not guess one thing about her, what country she is from, who she has at home, how she ended up here. Silence, even in his own head.

He looks at a column on the right-hand side of the page, sees the same picture he'd seen at Tony's, cropped so you could see Luis's face as he runs in the heat in front of some half-built stadium.

A tug of war between Europe's top clubs is underway for football's next big thing. Luis Fonseca Andrade, who hails from Cape Verde but is yet to represent the Blue Sharks at senior level, and who was apparently plucked from the relative obscurity of the Sporting Lisbon B team at the start of the season to sparkle for the nomadic central Asian club Petrosat Tajik Star, plaything of the mysterious gas tycoon Yusuf Khan. Petrosat are not recognised by FIFA or any Asian football federation and any move clubs make for the player will be complicated by this, and by the thorny issue of third party ownership. The player's contracts are managed by Luisito Holdings, registered in the Cayman Islands with investors from three different continents, according to the company website.

None of this seems to be deterring scouts from the Premier League and La Liga heading for the central Asian states (Petrosat are trans-national, with no home ground, one of the many sticking points with FIFA) to watch the slight, tricky, left-footed number 10 (at least that is what he looks like in grainy internet footage) dubbed inevitably 'the new Messi'. If, indeed, the player is actually real. In the virtual world of football gaming, he is already priced in the hundred million euros bracket and yet, 'This player is a sprite, a ghost,' a Sporting Lisbon source suggested yesterday, intimating that a player called Luis Fonseca Andrade had never appeared for any of the club's teams.

As if the player's background and the stories swirling around him were not exotic enough, he began the season, playing in a hastily arranged friendly for League 2 Irontown at their historic Anvil Yards ground, or at least someone with that name did. If even some of the rumours are true, he might be starting next season at Old Trafford or Camp Nou, unless, of course, the player's existence is some sort of elaborate hoax.

The boy is real, that is all he can think. Imagine your whole existence being doubted. Liam thinks of the way he turned and hit the ball in the friendly, the way the boy moved across the defenders, not that any of the Irontown team were going to pick him out with a pass. The real thing, maybe. He pictures men leaving modest flats on the edge of iron towns the world over, and flying on planes to places they would never have believed existed, seekers of something, searching out boys to run through other men's dreams, men looking for lost sons. Maybe that is what he will do when he has finished playing. Wander the earth in search of the one, he thinks. He'll buy a ticket to Finland first.

His only training this morning is to be some stretching and a massage. Archie wants him fit for the weekend, wants him to stay fit, no question of whether he is in or out of the team now.

The woman sloshes soap suds across the tarmac, finishes the mopping. The two boys wait alongside her, and their lives he can well imagine, waiting for the early morning bus from Cowton or the Peng, their mums and grandads telling them they're lucky to have any job at all, and them hating it, hating it, scraping the shit left by other people's shoes, by fucking birds for god's sake, and thinking there must be something else than this, knowing other lads who don't work, fuck that, who get by. They drift back towards the building. They disappear into their headphones and computer games, dream of gold training shoes and Luis Fonseca Andrade. He is suddenly pleased that Jari is two thousand miles away, not here, far from here.

. . .

Because he was the eagle for a long time.

That run angled behind the fullback, the piece of a puzzle falling into place, and Eusébio knows what's going to happen before it does, but then so does everyone by that point, the crowd hoarse now, hushed from cheering the North Koreans into a three-nil lead, these men who've come from nowhere.

And now the English crowds cheer him.

He whips his whole body around the ball, through it, so he hits it across the keeper, right footed, into the far corner, but he knows twenty yards or so before he gets there what will happen.

He moves flat footed almost, this way and that, but those feet barely touch the ground, they kiss it and keep moving, that's the secret, part of it. Don't stay in the same place for too long.

. . .

Liam watches the hooded figure out of the window for a while. He or she – he thinks that the slight frame inside the baggy sweatshirt suggests a thin girl. Something also in her movements, graceful in spite of her clothing, careful, that a man or boy would surely do more clumsily or with more self-conscious bravado – reaches high up the fence panel balancing against a wet trunk and branch, turns the screwdriver methodically. She reaches up and grips the mesh and lifts the panel to drop it against the fence's lower half. She – he has convinced himself now and is already building the picture of a lonely girl living out her days somewhere in these last Anvil Yards streets, maybe a neighbour of Mark Fala himself – has a red scarf wrapped high up her face so just a strip of her eyes shows. He cannot see these from this distance. He remembers the phrase indeterminate ethnicity. There are some binoculars up at his mum and dad's. He should get them, get a chair here at the window, stay in his room.

She jumps inside the fence, a spray can bounces at her hip, attached to her with coiled plastic. She lets it swing as she walks alongside the railway track into the Anvil Yards, looks up and down the track. There will be no train now, for sure, only that long, rumbling goods train that comes through some time after midnight, carrying god knows what to where.

He sees now where she is headed. The bridge that spans the canal and train track at the Greenfield End is not one of Victorian iron. It is poured concrete, and a blank wall reflects in the still water. You might get a glimpse from the road. From the top deck of the buses that rattle past Dee Dee's front room you could get a good look. He feels the sensation of buses and lorries making the rooms above the pub rattle, wonders if he will ever see those rooms again.

She moves quickly, he does not know who she thinks will want to catch her, doesn't know that anyone will care, takes the paint from her hip. He wants a fresco. Diego Rivera in the Anvil Yards. He wants to see some picture emerge that makes him think, yes, of course, this is what it all means, for his life to be changed by this moment. Instead, he gets a quickly scrawled hieroglyph. The girl loses all grace and care in the act, reaches too high up the concrete.

Bobo.

Bobo, of course, perhaps that is what it all means. Tag names mean nothing very much, he knows that, refer only to themselves. I am here, he thinks again. The girl is finished already, has put the cap on the can's nozzle, returned it to her sweatshirt pocket, regained some sense of control. She hurries back along the track. He looks again at the way she moves, on tiptoe and alive, thinks she could've easily climbed the fence quicker than removing the panel. Maybe there is some ritual to it. It only counts with a set of rusting screws to hold like worry beads as you spray your imagined name. He wonders if the name has come to her from Bobby Ahmed. He used to hate it if you ever reminded him, even when he was still a young boy, missing teeth that would still grow back, a shadow across his face that used to seem comical, touching, then, 'Bobby, he would say. Me name's Bobby.'

Before he went to Finland, Liam had a spell of watching mid-week Celtic games, if there was no Irontown match, at the supporters club in Cowton. He wasn't a member but he'd been taken up there in years gone past with Mark by Mark's dad, and they recognised him on the door anyway. The big man who looked after the place would nod to him and he'd follow the same ritual each time he went, sit on his own with his pint of Guinness, off to the side of the screen opposite the bar, on a plastic garden chair, under the green curtains. Not so close to the electric fire which they turned on full force on winter nights.

'Well up, Bobo.' The voices of the older men would come, those still with Glaswegian accents, fifty years in the south most of them, in their suit jackets with pullovers and ties underneath in muted browns and greys and greens that their wives picked for them from the stalls at the Lowtown Bull Ring.

Bobo Baldé was the Celtic centre back. Liam watched him, admired him, knew there was something shared in their movements. He had a faint hope in those days – receding by the game – that Celtic might come in for him. Not that he'd have said no to anyone by that point, was desperate to get out, the club in a shambles, could not really stomach making the break to go down the road to Hereford or somewhere like it. You'd think it might feel strange in the old men's mouths, this name come from Guinea by way of Marseille, but it didn't at all. And when he skewed a pass that year, stuck it high into the crowd when the ball was on, Larsson somewhere up ahead and spinning into a channel, and this was a weakness in Baldé's game perhaps, and one Liam knew all too well, the old men would admonish him. 'Oh, Bobo,' and fill the syllables with daft affection, like for an errant grandson who knew no better and never would but would be loved always the same.

Liam loved that purred familiarity. He thought back then that it was what he heard himself on a Saturday. Maybe he did, back then.

'That's it, Liam, well up, Liam, go on, Liam, our kid, well in, son.'

When he lost concentration he could hear individual voices, 'Oh Liam, what yer done that for?' When he stuck it onto the roof of the East Stand, the Greenfield End gave an ironic cheer. Even in exasperation, there was a warmth that came through. Then that faded, or he listened in a different way, something, 'That is fucking shite, Corwen', 'How did this bloke get an England cap? Jesus!', the club on the slide again, 'You ain't fit to wear the shirt.' But he wanted to say that even when he played badly he was better than them. That was why they were paying money to watch him. He tried his best, he told himself, even when he didn't. They pay their money, they can say what they like, was what Ally Barr said, but Ally had already gone when Liam left for Finland, coaching in Dubai until they asked him back for a third spell when the club hit rock bottom. There was the year they had four managers, finished bottom of the league, relegated by Easter. Those last few matches, Liam tried to avoid the Main Stand touchline, would sprint as far away as he could to warm up, at least still get a few cheers from the Greenfield End, wouldn't cover his fullback on that side, funny that none of them noticed, these experts who thought they knew it all because they'd paid for a seat. It got bad. He gave them the V-sign late that season when he scored a consolation after they'd booed him, getting a real mauling against Rotherham. His mum stopped going some time that season, couldn't bear to hear it. 'I should think about coaching, Liam, think about what you'll do when you stop play-ing,' she'd said, dishing out some carrots one Sunday afternoon. Everyone was an expert.

'Finland?' she said. 'What's in Finland? Do they even play football?'

So he did it, he left. That was the hard part, made easier by the angry chorus at the end, the boos in his ears, like he could've done anything about it, saved the club, saved the towns on his own. They still sung Mark Fala's name. Still, today. They'd all had too much faith. It was the year Liam started to believe in the curse. And then he was out of there, free, told himself he was never coming back, and then what had he done?

Greta told him she wanted him out, no reason at all as far as he could see, a break she said, the same week as Ally Barr phoned him, asked him if he'd consider it. A whim, nothing more, she wanted him out, she wanted space, here was some space. 'I need you here, son,' Ally said and that was that. They all stood and clapped when he led them out that first day of the season, all sang his name. He felt vindicated, missed Greta and Jari, kidded himself they'd be with him soon, paced the rooms of his empty house.

. . .

Dee Dee lets the water rise so that the bubbles come up over the bath. Steam fills the room. She slips off her dressing gown and thinks of a lovely silk one that she will buy one day, that she could look for, mention to Alina for her birthday. The water is almost too hot to bear, just as she likes it, and she stretches out so the bubbles come up to her mouth almost, lets the back of her neck rest against the porcelain rim.

She closes her eyes and tries to think of good things, thinks of herself on a beach far from here, no one she knows within hundreds of miles, but her mind drifts towards it like it often does when she stops and tries to relax. She should have told Goldie when he was sat there stinking in the bar. Mali, they were thinking of calling the baby Mali for a while. Rearrange the letters, Goldie, she should've said. You work that out, although you were never the quickest on the uptake. You think about your knives and your anger and who that might be aimed at and you leave Alina alone because she's nothing to do with you, you think about that, you think about what that might mean.

What else might she have said to him? It could have killed him to hear it. All those years she'd been scared he'd come back and then when she saw him, she pitied him, she really did. She knows she'll see him again, come like Mark to the off sales hatch or like that morning to sit in the half-light with his knife in front of him, dressed in rags.

She thinks of Sonia's face, when she said it, when Dee Dee asked her about names.

'We're thinking of Mali,' she said, a kind of innocent look on her face, looking Dee Dee in the eye and smiling.

If she hadn't died, Dee Dee thinks, one of them might have killed her anyway. She shuts her eyes, pushes it all away from her. Too late to stir all this up now. Alina walks past the bathroom door humming something out of tune. She seems happy. Tyrone seems a nice lad. Dee Dee sits and feels the water slowly cool, senses her daughter as she moves through the upstairs rooms.

. . .

When Liam tries to buy the ticket his bank card is refused. There was a message at reception that he phone Amir urgently. He knows it's about the room bill, so he avoids him as best he can. If he asks him to leave he'll have to sleep back at his mum and dad's or ask if he can use Devon's spare room, something. He is not sleeping in his own house ever again. He pictures it full of cobwebs and rats, the thing crumbling into the hillside, which he knows cannot be true as his mum still goes to clean every week, and his dad had been round to look at the damp-proofing. Maybe he could give it to them, to one of his sisters, another grand gesture before he goes. If he goes.

There's a credit card in his wallet that he doesn't have the pin number for, a flight from Heathrow the day after the end of the season. It might take another day to get to the lake house without his own car, doesn't matter. He thinks of unshuttering the lake house, spiders' webs in there to be cleaned out, and the golden light off the lake, the sun through the trees.

This week Greta sent him a video of Jari singing, performing something he has learned at nursery. He looks older, taller, strange words tumbling from his mouth and Liam feels him against him, the boy in his arms from this distance. He tells himself he will get this all over with and be a better man.

He gets a taxi to the car yard, cannot think of a bus that goes anywhere near, feels like he is running out of people to give him lifts. Lionel's office is on the first floor above the showroom, there are cars parked in rows so that you can see them as you drive past. The giant cut-out, Liam twenty foot tall and arms folded, has disappeared since his driving ban. Liam wonders what Lionel has done with it, knows he won't try to find out, scared Lionel has burned him in a back field.

'That ban nearly finished, son? You in for another car.' Lionel sits behind his desk, half-looking at his computer screen. Someone is talking about interest payments in the adjacent office, Liam can hear tools clanking downstairs.

'Morning, Lionel,' he says. 'No, I'm off the road for a while yet.'

'I was gonna say you could have your gaffer's. He'd done a few miles in it, mind you.'

'Ex-gaffer.'

'Ex,' Lionel says, motions for Liam to sit down, then stands up himself, 'I'm surprised he brought that motor back. Gone to Portugal, has he?' and doesn't wait for a reply. 'I don't know, they go to these places, Portugal, Spain, wherever, in the sun, think it'll make them happy, solve their problems. Gracie keeps pestering me about a cruise, Barbados, Miami, Jesus. I say, it's fine, a bit of sun, but you've still got yourself with you, you don't leave yourself behind. All them problems am still the same in the sun. I told our Stan that. He had to leave, I know he did, but still, you can't escape your own self, kid.'

Liam thinks he might be pissed, has second thoughts about talking to him for a moment. He turns in the chair to where Lionel now stands at the window, looking out over the rows of cars, the green hills beyond, small white clouds at the rusted edge of the Iron Towns and a field of four-by-fours and glittering cars worth more than houses in the space below them. These cars were like the sun, he thought, it was still you sitting inside them, they carried you and all your problems with you.

'No, I haven't come about a car,' he says, straight in, he supposes, 'it's about Dee Dee, really. Goldie's come back, went to the pub.'

Lionel turns from the window, goes and shuts the door and then sits back down at his desk. He doesn't say anything for a while.

'You know, I thought it was strange when she asked for them cameras to be fitted,' he says, shakes his head and smiles, 'you know what Dee Dee's like, how stubborn she can be.'

Liam nods.

'When?'

'A good few weeks ago now. Christmas. I wasn't sure what to do. He phoned her a while back, last summer, told her he was coming, threatening, you know.'

'Ex-wives, ex-gaffers,' Lionel says, 'ex-brothers, ex-sons, daughters. I don't know. Any idea what he's up to, where he's staying?'

'He looked in a bad way,' Liam says, remembers he thought it best not to say he'd actually seen him. 'That's what Dee Dee told me, said he had a knife. Homeless, maybe, you know. I don't know if his mum still lives on the Peng or what.'

'She went years ago, son. Got together with a bloke I used to know. Things turned out all right for her. They went to live somewhere near Malaga, I think.' Lionel smiles at this.

'He wants to see Alina.'

'Of course he does, it's only natural, son. Man wants to see his children.' Lionel looks at Liam now, for the first time that morning it seems, Liam looks away, 'Wonder he never come back earlier, really. He knows where they are.'

'You told him you'd kill him.'

Lionel nods. 'We warned him, that's all. We thought that was for the best, give Dee Dee a bit of time and space. We thought of telling you we'd kill you if you didn't stay with her, look after the girl. Then we thought she might be better off without you.'

He says these words very quietly and Liam finds it hard to follow and there's a delay before the shock of what Lionel is saying to him registers, so he sits there and nods his head and feels the colour drain from his face. It strikes him later that Lionel might have been joking.

'Don't worry. I'll sort it,' Lionel says. Liam goes to speak and

Lionel puts his hand up to quieten him, rises from the desk at the same time, 'Don't worry any more about it. We'll smoke him out. The problem will go away.'

'Come on,' Lionel motions down the interior stairs, 'have a look at what you might get when your ban's finished.'

Outside, under the awning, a rainbow forms where they spray the cars clean. Liam sees a figure move quickly around a black jeep, all limbs like a spider, a cloth in each hand, with which he works on the metal. Something in the movement, the way the boy, the man, turns on the balls of his feet makes Liam pause. It's Bobby.

'How's he doing?' Liam says, tries to disguise the shock of seeing him here.

'He's OK. I've got him working down here now, as you can see. I can keep my eye on him. He's doing OK.'

Liam raises his hand to the figure through the window. Bobby moves gracefully with long strides between the cars, stops to peer through the water-splashed glass, grins when he sees Liam, looks like the kid he once was, puts his thumb up to him.

'He's doing OK,' Lionel says again and motions with his head towards the showroom floor. It is quiet. Liam looks at his own reflection in the shiny machines, cars to drive away from everyone he has ever known, to drive past ruins, through hedgerows, to park up in quiet clearings, to drive into the waters of shallow rivers.

．　．　．

Hampden Park, again, April 1956, one hundred and thirty-three thousand people there, Scotland winning until the very last minute. Big Duncan Edwards never gives in. See him now, driving up the pitch out of his own half with the ball at his feet and his head up, looking at Johnny Haynes, as if he is operating in a different time and space to everyone else, as if he has all afternoon, and then he strikes the ball and Haynes is in, and he strokes the ball into the corner and England have equalised. The goal means all four countries share the Home Nations trophy – an unusual enough event – but that is not really the point. When the ball goes in, Duncan gives a little skip, might look strange on a big man, but is the kind of foot movement you see with great boxers, like a kind of Ali shuffle, so balanced and alive, he is a great dancer in fact, and now comes a clenched fist. Sometimes we get the faintest glimmer of who we might truly be.

. . .

'But what is it, all this stuff?'

It's a map, is what Alina wants to say to him, a map of the Anvil Yards and of her own life. She has not thought about it in this way before, but Tyrone is the first person who has asked her what she is doing here. No one has ever known what she is doing before other than a few scraps of film she has put on the internet, a few photos of the huge Greenfield mills with tree branches coming through the roofs and the sun on the gravestones on the far hill in the distance, comments from a lonely girl in Gary, Indiana, from a Japanese man who sent details of the Nowa Huta steelworks in Kraków and posted photos of the workers' broad, sad faces at shift-change, an industrial glow in the sky beyond endless chimneys and blocks of flats, and she was flattered to get any kind of reaction at all but she knew that it was not the places themselves that she wanted to capture. It wasn't about sunsets, it wasn't even about steelworks, not for her, not really.

It was a map, of that she is now convinced. That was why the rope had been important to her. The thread had been something with which to find your way through the labyrinth, to wind yourself up towards the light, to escape the monster. The rope had gone nowhere very fast, another failed piece of work, but it had led her to Tyrone. It was good to feel these separate pieces – the photos of graves and empty buildings, the names she'd tagged on crumbling walls to be glimpsed from passing cars, Bobo and Goldie and Sonia, the artefacts of rusted chain, the apple blossom that blew through giant empty buildings and that no one saw – as part of a whole piece of work, a body, her body. Maybe the work was her own life. The rope had led her to Tyrone, had not had to go anywhere else.

Her own life and everyone else's, and the map spiralled out of the Anvil Yards and out across the Heath and up the hillsides because there was the turn in the road where the car skidded off and there is the river, not even a river, not really, a culvert with steep concrete sides and there is the car within it, there is the dockside where her great-grandad, not really her great-grandad at all, hauled boxes from barges and dreamed of the Bay of Bengal, here are the lanes that pattern the valleys like spiders' webs and maybe give rise to those stories, and here the rows of empty terraces where the people have gone, and tunnels that wind through the hills, and here is the tent of a homeless man, she guesses, empty pill bottles and drink cans scattered around on the banks of the canal, on the land where the navvies pitched their tents in the mud to cut channels between the rivers. And there are the graves and the ash, marked like her mum's, and unmarked like the cholera pits and the body-shaped hollows where the men drank themselves stupid at the Quakers for want of anything else to do and no one seemed to care. And there are the lives, she thought, there are the lives. It is a map of her own life and of innumerable others, to show her the way, to show her who she is.

'It's a kind of map,' she says, takes a deep breath.

· · ·

A couple of postponements and the cup matches, which feel a long time in the past now, mean they have three games in hand. Trouble with this kind of thing is that you have to win them. They are bottom of the league now, games running out, games coming twice a week, with a back four with a combined age of one hundred and thirty-four and when did you ever hear anything given as a combined age, when and where in life would that ever be useful? But that is what the *Chronicle* write about the Irontown defence, like they've even got anybody else to stick in there really, and Liam clips the line out of the paper and puts it in his wash bag to use as a kind of charm, a curse. He is going to play for ever.

But what Liam knows is that he has not played two games a week like this for years, he can barely move now, on the pitch or off, but here he is tonight, under the floodlights, heading everything that comes near him. They defend deep, deep, deep, hanging on for a point, the clock ticking down, ticking down, a point takes them off the bottom and that's a start. Archie has not won a match in charge yet and spring is here. You can feel it in the blood-warm earth beneath the pitch. No one has been paid. Supporters' club members collect change in buckets outside the turnstiles in order to pay for the electricity for the floodlights.

Last minute, a nothing ball towards the box and they get a shout of 'Keeper's ball,' that echoes up the empty East Stand. This is their seventh goalkeeper of the season, must be some kind of record. They can't get any more, have been banned from loan deals by the league because they can't pay anybody anything, administration beckons, a points deduction and then it will be all over. Tommy Starr this lad's name is.

'Fuckin' Freddie Starr, more like,' a voice comes to Joey, who sits biting his nails in the stand.

But he's kept a clean sheet tonight and they're heading off the bottom except now, as Tommy shouts, he realises he's misjudged it, is underneath it, and the ball goes over his outstretched hands, and all in one go, Liam has realised this too, and this man who can barely move, who has headed every ball that has come into the box that night is getting back, getting back, stretching, and he gets his toe to the ball just as it hits the sandy goalmouth, as it is about to bounce inside the post, and is able to flick it wide and continues his run full into the post itself and the whole goal frame shakes and he lies crumpled on the floor.

Liam stays down even though he is not hurt, thinks he can

probably eke this out to run down the clock, realises they will
still have to defend the corner, so may as well have a breather. He
could go to sleep right here curled around the post. Devon has
his hand on his shoulder.

'You all right, skipper? Stay down, stay down if you're hurt,'
all in one breath. 'Give him some space, eh?' Devon says above
him. They are clapping, proper applause, people on their feet,
even in the stand.

*If Irontown do go down, it will not be through lack of effort on the part
of Liam Corwen. He has been a colossus tonight . . .* goes Dave Willis's
radio voice across the warm night.

'I bet Archie enjoyed that,' Les Martin taps Joey on the shoulder, and Joey nods, but doesn't take his eyes of Liam, not able to
tell if he is really hurt, the goal frame is still wobbling, something
in Joey's chest and stomach tightens as he claps his hands louder,
they should carry him off on a shield, his son, the way he's playing for them, what he's doing, keeping them up with the strength
of his will. Another hand thumps Joey on the back from behind.
Devon puts his thumbs up to the Greenfield End to signal Liam
is OK. They sing *One Liam Corwen, there's only one Liam Corwen*
and then *Irontowns, Irontowns, Irontowns.*

But Archie Hill has not enjoyed tonight one bit. In fact Archie
did not even see this clearance, there are men wearing luminous
jackets running with a stretcher down the touchline, Tyrone running from the other direction with the defibrillator that he prays
to God they don't ask him to use, because Archie is lying on his
back with the soles of his shoes facing towards the pitch and his
heart has stopped.

. . .

On the way to the camp Steve Bloomer remembers another train ride years before, how they had changed stations in Birmingham with all their things in a hand cart. Had he really ridden on board like a visiting maharajah?

They had been nailers, his family. Across the river in Cradley Heath they made chain. They'd moved up to Dudley, his mum and dad, come back for his dad to work in the foundry, a puddler. It was a steep hill in the mud and the houses ran in, were falling down.

In Derby the houses were new and the factories lined the railway lines and gleamed in the sun. There was always the sound of metal and the beautiful arc of a ball, these two certainties.

The men work hard to improve the conditions in which they are kept. The winter mud, the threat of dysentery is kept at bay, they sleep in the dry, rooms more sound, perhaps, drier certainly, than the houses they'd flitted from all those years ago, houses that sagged with the water. They organise themselves. They play football, cricket all through the summer to the bemusement of the Germans, write the scores in heavy ledgers.

All his life he's been around hard men, tough men, in Cradley and Derby and Middlesbrough, and now here in Ruhleben, in Spandau. He moves between them. Run into the spaces between them and someone will pass the ball there. There are things that are more simple than they appear.

The war goes on and on, sun and rain and snow. They play

whole league seasons, test matches. He scores a double hundred one afternoon. His eye is good, has never left him. Often it's best to sit and watch and wait, he thinks, move through the gaps when you can.

. . .

They got him going on the side of the pitch. They said his heart was stopped and they brought him back to life. He lies with his head on the pillow now with his pyjama top open and pads with wires coming from them stuck onto his chest, a big man with grey skin. Liam watches his body rise and fall gently as they talk, like it will stop if Liam loses concentration.

Just a few minutes, is what the nurses said. It's family visiting only in this hot private room off the ward. Archie's wife, Anne, had gripped Liam's hand at the door when they came in. He heard her say to his dad that she told Archie not to take the job on, let someone else do it, he'd done enough for them over the years, a few weeks in charge and it had almost killed him.

Liam is wearing his club blazer in case there are any photographers about. The crest catches his eye as he moves his arm. He tells Archie that Steve Stringer called him in this morning, after he and Devon had taken training. That he is in charge for these last few games. Tells Archie not to worry, that his job is to get better, to rest. Archie tries to nod his head from the pillow. He's in a bad way.

Liam waited for Archie's autograph once, as a kid, by the Players' Entrance in the rain. Archie was wearing his club blazer, his hair was slicked in a side parting. Liam had never stood next to such a big man, a strong man. Where they sat, the crowd would groan when Archie put a clearance over the stand, the Greenfield End cheered, Liam loved it. He told Archie he played at the back, just like him,

'Remember,' Archie said, as he signed his looping autograph, 'just keep things simple back there. That's the most important thing, the first thing you need to do.'

He still said it sometimes. It was the last thing he'd said before he sent them out the other night.

Keeping things simple is easier said than done, that's for sure, Liam thinks, sighs.

He holds Archie's hand, is surprised by how soft it is. His dad stands behind him, puts his hand on his shoulder, which is his signal that's it's time.

'All right, Archie,' Joey says, 'you take it easy.'

Liam keeps hold of his hand as he gets up from the plastic chair. He can feel his hip, his thigh, there's a bruise that's spread up his leg from where he crashed into the post, from Socrates all the way up to Yashin. He doesn't think he'll be able to play on Saturday. He tries not to limp in the hospital, thinks it looks like he's taking the piss.

'He's in a bad way, Dad, eh?'

'He didn't look very well, son, no.'

They are barely speaking, him and his dad, they sit in the car with the radio on while his dad drives him around. He asks Devon to drive him when he can, gets on the bus, the tram, the drivers and conductors nod to him, ask him when results will improve. He wants to avoid talking to them about Archie, about the side he is going to pick now he's in charge. His mum has barely said a word to him since Christmas.

They parked on the far car park, the one near the old Bethel, which was the workhouse and is now the psychiatric hospital. He sees that lad Tyrone coming down the path, an old woman bent over a walking frame with him. Tyrone the hero, Liam thinks, probably does hospital visiting in his spare time, he got that thing on Archie's chest with the St John's ambulance people, saved his life, everyone said.

Tyrone has the woman's arm and she has both hands on the frame, stares at the path. A blackbird flits past. They can hear the traffic on the flyover.

'Come on, Mum,' he hears Tyrone say, 'you're doing really well.'

He is aware that they have slowed their pace to look at the woman attempt an incline, not get anywhere very fast, 'You're doing great,' they hear him say.

At the car his dad asks him if he fancies a pint and he nearly says no, I've got a team to pick, but says, 'Yeah, that would be nice,' and they talk about that time they played Liverpool in the League Cup and Ian Rush kept fouling big Archie, clipping his heels, when the midfield slipped the ball through. Archie got more and more angry but couldn't get anywhere near Rush or Dalglish.

Liam goes back to their house for his tea, asks his dad to pull in so he can pick up some flowers from the Lowtown Bull Ring on the way, tries not to look at the back of the *Chronicle* while they eat. They have printed a kind of doomsday clock above the Anvil Yards, set at five to midnight.

. . .

He moves like a breaking wave, a sense of deep power locked within. Eusébio is broader now, at twenty-six, stronger. Bang the ball in at his chest, his back to goal, and watch him hold the defenders at bay.

He receives the ball in space, side-on to goal, and the couple of strides he takes give him the start he needs. Nobby Stiles hurtles at him, as he does all night, as he had done two years before in the World Cup, a fierce little dog yapping at the tide, but this time Eusébio is gone. He strides past him, over him, lengthening his stride with the ball, until he slows for an instant. Sadler backpedals and keeps going, skittering, as Eusébio pauses. Space opens out around him, even as the United players converge. He looks up, strikes it. The bones of his foot which whip through the ball are called the cuboid, the lateral cuneiform, the metatarsals. They will one day become relics. The ball veers and rises and crashes down and back off the crossbar. Béla Guttmann's curse and the ghosts of Munich fall like dew on the Wembley night.

His free-kicks come back off the United wall, Stiles clatters his ankles again and again. When he glides through the United defence he can't quite get purchase on a left-foot shot on the run. And then the ball falls into his path and he thumps it, the soles of both feet off the ground, and Stepney, the United keeper, clutches it to his chest in mid-air. Eusébio stands and looks and applauds. Then George Best cuts through the Benfica lines, like an elf skipping between summer foxgloves. Eusébio feels heavier. Tides come in and they go out. Time moves one way.

. . .

He sees the news on the ticker on Sports 24, the channel he now leaves on permanently in the room with the sound down low even when he is sleeping. It helps him sleep in fact, the shadows the images make on the wall and the low murmur of voices. He sometimes turns over in the middle of the night to see pictures of luge tobogganing and cliff diving and ultra-distance marathons through a desert somewhere. His body aches and his eyes close.

Real Madrid confirm the signing of Luis Fonseca Andrade from Petrosat Tajik Star for an undisclosed fee. Move to be completed at the end of the season.

He jumps to his feet and laughs, paces up and down the room. He phones Devon but it goes straight to voicemail, starts to blabber on about it, feels embarrassed, not even sure he should be phoning him and talking like this now he's the gaffer, although Devon is his mate, his number two now. 'Real Madrid,' he says, 'just you think about that.'

And with the news they play a clip that someone must have sent in from the dust bowl in the summer, filmed on a phone from the back of the stand, he thinks he can even make out the shape of his dad's head, Liam's hacked clearance wobbles through the air and Luis takes it on his thigh and spins and hits it off the outside of the post and into the hoardings and you see a few people's heads cock like when you try to decide if a car is backfiring or the shooting has begun.

He sits on the edge of the bed. He's got players' names written on a cut-up cereal packet, a tea tray that represents the pitch.

It will be very, very simple. Move Kyran inside and play him off Julius. Hit balls in to Julius and hope it sticks, hit passes into Kyran's feet and let him run at people. If it doesn't work, he can push him out wide again. If it doesn't work he can yank Julius off, stick Shaunie McLaughlin up front to clatter people. Keep it simple, like Archie said. These people have all played with Real Madrid's latest signing. He laughs to himself, the world is beyond all reasoning.

. . .

The Arms Park, 16 March 1896. Billy Meredith looks on from the wing, cannot get the ball, has not touched it, there's an hour gone and not a mark on his kit. To think they fancied their chances in this one, had given Ireland a lesson at the Racecourse Ground. It just shows you how long you get to stay on your perch. He watches the pale arrow on the other side, this young lad Bloomer score one goal after the other. He can't understand why Charlie Parry doesn't kick him, maybe because he just can't get near him, he's like smoke, like a ghost. Nine now, is it? The kid has scored five, half a dozen maybe. Billy thinks the ref blows early, puts them out of their misery.

. . .

Ally looks at the sea below as the taxi climbs the mountainside, up, up out of the city. He's been to the Ronaldo museum to kill some time, enjoyed the photos, enjoyed the chutzpah of a man who opens a museum of himself, wonders idly what he'd put in his own. Ally thinks of what George Best said about Ronaldo, about the passing on of a flame, cannot think for a moment how much he would have seen of him before he died. Ally had been at the funeral, never such a well of emotion had he seen, such love. They said Ronaldo's daddy had been a drinker too. A drinker and a dreamer no doubt, Ally thinks, can afford to let his thoughts drift, to be sentimental. He can afford most things now, of course. He touches the paper of the contracts in the briefcase, his percentage from Luis, money from the Tajiks, from Madrid, all those years of watching and waiting for some kind of break like this. He is a man behind the men now, looks down at the breaking waves through his dark glasses, enjoys the feel of wearing a suit in the hot sun, business to attend to. He thinks of running across cinders in the Finnieston gloom.

Dorothea spends her afternoons on the nursing home terrace, a mirador that overlooks the cliffs. There are ships out on the water that she can't see. Her head lolls over to one side, ninety-nine years old and counting. Her mother's second husband owned a wine exporters, a last crumbling vestige of empire, that's how she ended up here. She was the last baby born at the Greenfield Estate by the Heath. The big house burned down after an air raid late in the war, but everyone always said it had been done for the insurance. They had run out of money even then. Her lawyer and a nurse sit with her in the shade. They all drink lemonade and then a glass of the wine.

She doesn't speak, just nods as they complete the formalities, she signs with a faint spider's leg crawl. Ally has bought plenty of players before but never a whole club. Not that he's really buying this one. She's pretty much giving it him to pass on the debt. But the debt will disappear with the money promised in the briefcase and Iron Towns – he's putting back the s, that's first on the agenda – will rise again, from wherever they find themselves.

'To the Iron Towns,' he says as he raises his glass, sips the warming liquid in the hot afternoon. 'There is one question I have for Dorothea,' he says to the lawyer, a young man with his hair slicked back, he's been warned not to fluster her, to just get the deed done. The lawyer looks not unlike Ronaldo himself, the boy from down the mountain.

'What is it?'

'Why she never sold before. Could maybe have got big money. Was it her love of the club?'

Her voice comes strong out of her tiny frame. Up until now, he has not thought she was entirely with it, assumed the lawyer was offloading the club now for tax reasons.

'No one ever asked, all these years,' she says, and she laughs a hacking laugh, and they all join in. Ally shakes his head, all the stories of the Greenfields' legendary stubbornness, theories of why they wouldn't sell. Money talks, people said. No one even offered. He wonders if she is joking. She raises her hand. The nurse leans forward, sensing something wrong, but the voice goes on.

'No, I lie,' she says, 'Lionel Ahmed asked once, after he forced his brother out. I told him I wouldn't sell to a crook.' And she laughs again and they all join in and Ally turns his face to the sun.

. . .

At full-time they turn to each other to check the scores from Torquay and Northampton and Bristol Rovers and Wycombe. They have been terrible again, another three-nothing, the crowd too tired to even boo them off. There are hurried conversations and confirmations about the results elsewhere. Still third from bottom, win on Saturday and they still stay up.

'There must be some bad teams in this league if we're still in with a shout,' Les Martin says as the players trudge off. Liam stands at the side of the pitch and applauds the Greenfield End even though there are fingers that jab out of the crowd towards him, some others clapping, fans arguing among themselves.

'We can do it,' Joey mutters, although as he says it, he knows he doesn't believe it.

'Fucked anyway, because of the money. It's been nice knowing you, Joey, eh? Cowton Sports for us next year.'

Les taps his arm.

He thinks the bloke is honestly trying to be nice.

. . .

Dave 'Iron' Willis: Liam, you still believe?

Liam Corwen: A thousand per cent. I opened that dressing-room door and said anyone who doesn't think we can do it should walk through it, go home now. No one did. I'll say the same to the supporters, don't bother next week if you can't get behind us.

He had done nothing of the sort, of course, he'd got back through the door from the ref's office to help Devon pull Tommy Starr off Shaunie McLaughlin. Afterwards, Devon told him he was worried that Tommy would break his hands on Shaunie's head. They haven't got another keeper. He says otherwise he'd have left him to it.

.   .   .

People are queueing all the way down Chain Street. They did the same for the United match that never came, and here they are again. Steve Stringer himself is at the booth, as they've got no one else in the office to sell tickets any more. Liam gets out of Devon's car and the others follow. This is his idea, the first, the only one he's had in the couple of weeks he's been in charge. Well, that and playing Kyran inside and further forward, and the kid has barely had a kick.

'Thanks for coming down here,' he says to an old bloke five or six places back in the line.

'I want me head examined,' is all the man says but Liam smiles and holds out his hand to shake and he nods to Devon and the others all do the same. A kid in school uniform wants his picture taken with Kyran, there are all manner of things being brought out for them to autograph. He should've phoned Dave Willis, told him what they were doing, dismissed that as too cynical, realises right now that there is no such thing.

'Will you sign this Liam,' he looks up to see Fraser Parks from the fanzine, the young lad who looks fifty if he's a day, hold out a photo of the '93 side, sees his own younger self looking out from the picture, sees Mark standing there next to him, looking nervous just for a team photograph. 'It's not for me,' he says, 'it's to raffle for the children's ward at the Bethel.' That's right, Liam thinks, he does the hospital radio, as well, this lad. Saints, all of them.

'Could do with some of them players on Saturday,' is what Liam says.

'Think we'll do it, Liam?' he asks.

'Course we will,' he says, and he can see in the lad's eyes that he really wants to know, that he really wants it to be true, standing here, selling his home-made magazines with it threatening rain on a Tuesday morning when he should be at work, if he had any work to get to.

'That's great,' he says, 'that's great.'

And maybe it's the tiredness, or the way he says this, like Liam has got any more idea than him of how things will turn out, or the way the line straggles along the broken pavement, mobility scooters and walking sticks and kids bunking school and blokes who look like his dad, his granddad, among them, that makes something shift inside him. Some reversal he thinks. All his life he's had it the other way round, but it's they who are the saints, this ragged line, and those like it, past, present, future.

It is the players who are the pilgrims.

. . .

'What do you mean, a different direction? What does that even mean?'

They sit in Tony's studio and look at the brick walls of the yard outside. They sit side by side at the desk for lack of space but also to look at Tony's sketchbook. Liam looks at Tony's reflection in the glass, Tony's face turned towards his.

'How do you want me to talk about it?' Liam says. 'I want to think about what we're heading towards, about how this will finish.'

'What do you mean, finish? There's loads to do yet, you've said yourself. Groups, we talked about. Are we still going more for groups? That's what I want to know.'

There are sketches of the Lisbon Lions, Billy McNeill on a white wall holding the cup aloft, of Brazilians, Pelé strok- ing the ball into Carlos Alberto's path, of Romáro and Bebeto rocking the baby. There are team photos clipped from old magazines. For months Tony has been looking at groupings, of teammates. This is the work's new phase. They have gone down different routes before, a whole season with Tony sketch- ing famous stadiums only for them to decide it was figures, people they wanted all along.

'Football is a team game. We need to show people together, with their mates,' is what Liam says to him, a change of direction from the big portraits they'd started with, but now he'd thought one step further, about where this was headed. They had never talked about an ending before.

'This is a group,' Liam gestures to the scrap of paper in front of him, pen in hand. 'It's one big group. This is the whole point of it, Tone. Do you get it? It's what we've been working towards.'

'This is a mess.'

'The crowd, the people.'

'I ain't fucking Lowry. What do we want with all these stick men?'

Liam wishes he hadn't tried to draw it. Jari could do better with those giant crayons Greta let him scribble on the floor with. He wanted crowds, the people. He wanted the great crowd to cover the rest of his body, so the players were subsumed into the mass, so they disappeared, so he disappeared too.

'The crowd are what makes them who they are. Don't you see it?'

'I see it, but this is too clever for its own good. It looks shit.'

'Without the crowd they ain't nobody. With no one looking. Football is the people's game.'

'What happened to Pirlo? I've been drawing his fucking miserable face all winter.'

Liam is glad of a bit of levity. Tony doesn't really think he is serious, that's why he's smiling now.

'Pirlo's still playing. He's gonna go on and on like Stanley Matthews. He's missed the boat. There's a cut-off date. They can't still be playing after I finish.'

Tony takes a sip of his green tea and Liam continues talking to the reflection in the window, 'It's an idea, Tone, I want you to think about it. I want it to end when I stop playing, I want it to be complete.'

'It would be like rubbing it out. Years of work, years to come.'

'Just think about it. OK?' Liam pushes his chair back, exhausted suddenly. He honestly thought Tony would think it a good idea. He doesn't even like football, for god's sake. He stands up and looks to go. Tony is still sitting, looking at the sketchbooks laid out on the desk, shaking his head.

'I think this is your problem, Liam, you never see things through.'

'What's that meant to mean? I'm talking about seeing it through, this is seeing it through, this is an idea for an ending.'

He wants to get out of this small room now, does not know why he has even brought this up, thought this visit would be a nice distraction from trying to pick a team for Saturday.

'I just don't think you've got the bottle to stick with things,' Tony says, his back to Liam now, and the way his face appears in the glass, the way he says this, Liam thinks of Dee Dee, some family resemblance, the kind of thing she said to him when she decided to take on Alina.

'You never see anything through, just leave people to pick up after you.'

This was not true. He'd given the biggest part of twenty years to Irontown, he'd come back here for god's sake, stuck by Ally, the club. It wasn't him who left Dee Dee, not really, she chose the girl, he hadn't left Greta and Jari.

'You get too far into things and then get scared and want to pack them in and leave other people to deal with it.'

'Fucking hell, Tone, I'm going, mate. It's only a few pictures. And they'm my tattoos. Jesus.' He clenches and unclenches his fist. There were times when he'd have gone for him. Picked him up by the throat and had him up against the wall. He wishes he'd never mentioned the crowd. It was a great idea, though, how the players would disappear back into the crowd from which they came, it was beautiful, it was what he was going to do at the end of the season, become invisible, start afresh, again. He knows deep down that Tony has a point. It isn't even Tony speaking, Liam thinks, not really. It's Dee Dee.

He turns and moves into the front of the shop. He expects Tony to follow him or say something else but there's nothing. The bell rattles as he opens the door, surprisingly bright outside after the gloom of the studio and the yard. It occurs to him that this might be the end. They can stay on his body as they are, men running through the world, through other men's heads.

. . .

The body of a man found near the Quaker Burial Grounds Burnt Village, has been identified as that of Stephen Williams, 37, of no fixed address. Mr Williams came from a well-known Oxton family and his death has shocked the community.

His sister, Anne Fraser, 33, also of Oxton, told the Chronicle *'This has been the hardest week of my family's lives. We are all devastated. Stevie was a great brother and son. He battled with drink and depression for many years so maybe he is at some sort of peace now but I can't believe we won't see his face again.'*

Iron Town council have received numerous complaints about street drinking and antisocial behaviour in the Quaker Burial Ground area.

'They come up here, sitting around all day and making a nuisance for decent people,' said a local resident who did not wish to be named. 'I've seen a man using a neighbour's front garden as a toilet in the middle of the day. If you say anything you just get abuse. Nothing gets done.'

West Mercia police issued a statement yesterday to the effect that Mr Williams's death was not suspicious, although an inquest will be heard at a date yet to be fixed. It is assumed he died of an alcohol related illness.

Tributes to the dead man have been left along the north wall of the Burial Ground, these include flowers, cards and bottles.

Liz has one last glance at the paper and steps out into the sunshine, Joey is in the car, already looking at his watch again, sighing. He'll have to wait. She knew the Williams family when she was growing up, the Prentices too, the boy's mother, Maggie Prentice as she was, grew up on Red Lion Street, near where the pie shop was on the way to the Bull Ring. Liz had been born on Silver Street. It was named for the brook that ran behind the houses, under some of them, and out into the Chain, right near the bottom end of Lowtown. They'd knocked most of the houses down in the sixties, moved the families out to Cowton and Oxton. The water would rise into the houses in bad weather, in the summer everything smelled of mud and they were rotten with damp. She remembers being sent to peg the washing out as a girl and the mud squeezing up between her toes, being scared of the frogs that lived along the bank and that her brothers used to torture. The smells that came from the factories settled there in the valley, sank into your clothes. People look into the past one-eyed, she thinks, only remember the good parts. She is glad they've torn the place down. At the Heritage Museum they rebuilt one of the terraces, *industrial age slum dwelling, typical of those through Lowtown and the Anvil Yards and still inhabited into the late 1960s,* she'd read on the information card, was shocked to see the word slum at first, her mother kept their curtains nice, the place as spotless as she could, but later thought, why not call it what it was?

She used to look at the hills, at the estates laid out halfway up and the leaded bay windows of Salop and Calon and think that was where she was headed, Maggie Prentice as well, she knew. They kept their ankle socks as white as they could, out of the mud, dreamed of net curtains and broad avenues. And that was what she got, after a fashion. Her dreams had come true. They'd done OK and she'd been lucky with Joey and the girls. And Liam, well, Liam was Liam, was all she'd begun to think now. Tell a boy, a man, how good he is at something, all stand round and clap him on, and watch what happens. He always thought he could do anything, he didn't need grown men egging him on.

Still, she wasn't Maggie Prentice, sitting there in Oxton still, in a house every bit as dilapidated as the kind they grew up in, just in a different way, grieving her lost boy. She remembers seeing her once in the street with a boy who must have been Stephen alongside her, gap-toothed and laughing and helping her with her shopping bags up the hill. She remembered thinking even then that she'd have her work cut out to get Liam to do that, the girls maybe, said as much to Maggie, gave Stephen some change for an ice-cream. There are many ways of being poor, she thinks, has never quite shaken it off, has never got quite far enough up the hill.

She will do a card for Maggie, she thinks, look for when the funeral is, although doubts she'll go, has always wanted to keep her distance, not get dragged back, which is how she's come to think about the football. She hopes they lose and get put out of their misery and she is only going because Eli passed up his ticket, he has not seen them win in the flesh this season and thinks himself a Jonah and so will listen to it on the radio instead as some kind of sacrifice. These boys with their rituals and magic spells. She wishes they would all grow up.

The weather today would suit a wedding better than a funeral, and she guesses that someone will be getting married somewhere today, blossom in the air like confetti, that not everything is concentrated on the Anvil Yards, and she silently wishes them well, while Joey glares at his watch and sighs again and, she can see, wants to sound the horn at her but considers that might make her go even more slowly. There is all the time in the world.

. . .

Cadwallader looks back across the wave-tops, sees the white cliffs fade in the sea spray, sighs. The island is undone, emptied with war and plague and famine. The hills are full of skulls, the rivers run with blood.

Voices come on the wind, faint across the sound of the sea and between the boat's creaking. They say that none of them are dead, not one, that they will come again, from their caves and wooded valleys, that they will take new forms.

. . .

Ally sits in the car for a few seconds before he turns off the engine, the paint that says 'Owner' on the wall above the space has faded so it's almost just a memory. He considers the gateman's wide eyes when he wound the window down, takes a deep breath, reaches into the back for his suit jacket and opens the door.

'Who's parked there?' Steve Stringer asks from his perch high up the stand. 'You know to keep that clear. You can never tell, today might be the day someone turns up.'

In the room along the corridor, the directors and dignitaries, even the mayor is here in a great gold chain, munch on sandwiches and sip their drinks, like the Heath golf club has relocated for the afternoon for the funeral of an old acquaintance they'd all thought had gone years ago.

There's the crackle of a walkie-talkie, words he can't hear. There's a voice behind him that says, 'You're not going to like this, but listen . . .'

. . .

Watching from where they sit is not made any easier by looking at the Morecambe fans dressed as red-and-white shrimps or wearing great sun hats and generally laughing and enjoying themselves no end, beach balls bobbing away above the Chain terracing, nothing to play for, an end of season fancy-dress party with the added bonus of being a part of football history, the last club to play at the Anvil Yards. There were fans swapping scarves outside the Chain End when they came past. They start to sing *We'll meet again*, which Joey thinks is unlikely. The only thing he can hope is that the Morecambe players are already on holiday as well, but he knows things never work like that. They'll probably play like world-beaters.

He keeps his eyes fixed on Liam, who he swears is hiding a limp, and groans inside as he calls the players into a huddle in front of the Greenfield End. These things just look daft. It's noisy, a breeze comes over the East Stand. Liz puts her hand on his.

When the ref whistles Liam sends Devon up for the toss while he speaks to Tommy Starr, holding the keeper's head in his hands, looking him in the eye. He's probably scaring the kid half to death, Joey thinks, just leave him be.

The noise builds, and he needs the toilet but tries not to move, doesn't want Liz have to get up, nods to Les Martin who leans across after he's made a show of giving Liz a kiss and grins and says, 'Thought you'd decided to give it a miss,' and Joey can't even raise a smile.

'Hey,' Les says now, 'have you seen who's here?' and he nods his head over the directors' box barrier.

Joey glances, aware they are about to kick-off and feeling that if he keeps his eyes on Liam then nothing will go wrong, and sees the glint of the chain and assumes Les means the mayor. The box is full for the first time this season, in years, Joey reckons, all come to put the last nail in the coffin.

That's when he sees Ally, sitting there in his blue suit and dark glasses, relaxed as can be. He swears he's got a toothpick in the corner of his mouth.

'He's got some nerve,' is what he says, drowned by the anxious high-pitched keening that greets the kick-off, too nervous, if you ask Joey, that will transmit to the players and whatever happened to the Irontown roar? That was deeper, came from the depths, and they said sounded like a furnace when a door is opened onto it. This was fear. It was what they'd sounded like for years, all of them, Joey thinks, but they all had reasons to be afraid and the fires were all out long ago.

Morecambe play a ball over the top almost straight away and Liam has the back line pressing up the pitch already, too far up, and the ball lands in space behind them and a red-shirted player simply glides in and onto the pass and Joey looks across at the linesman whose flag is down by his knees as he runs parallel with the forward. The keeper is out too, this lad Starr, who extends his yellow arms to make himself look big, and their player thumps it, hits it true. And Tommy Starr tumbles to his left and he saves it, and Joey is on his feet, shouting, 'What a save!' and they are all up with their necks craned to see the ball crash back off Tommy's leaping frame and into Liam's face as he chases the forward and then, everything slows down, as Devon and Liam both stretch their legs and both run after after the ball, and Joey remembers a man on holiday once when he was a kid, chasing a white handkerchief that had blown off his head across the broad green bank of the Great Orme, Joey was scared the man would chase it over the cliff into the sea, and there are Liam and Devon across the goalmouth sand and into the back of the net in a bundle with the ball.

Silence.

Some fucker with a radio on.

Calamity at the Anvil Yards. An own goal after what can only have been, what, twenty seconds of the match . . .

. . .

Goldie sees him across the empty factory spaces, his shoulders rolling, his hair wild. He has to think for a moment where he has seen him before, then remembers it's the kid he sold those diazepam tablets to all those months ago, the bottle he'd found in the coat, who he asked about the Ahmeds and the boy had said, 'Know em? I am one, sunshine.'

He comes towards him now, from a hundred yards away he sees him, from out of the shadow of the building opposite, looking all around him, puts his hand to his eyes to shield the sun and looks now at Goldie's building, he kicks at the clumps of grass that grow from the cracked, bleached concrete, not intentionally, but a man in a hurry. Goldie doesn't move, watches the kid approach, stays in the shadows.

The crowd noise stops, all of a sudden, just like someone flicked a switch. Then comes louder again, with *Iron Towns, Iron Towns, Iron Towns* coming across the water against the breeze and echoing off the brick. Goldie has taken to walking down to the edge of the market when they pack up, picking up scraps of all kinds, has seen Liam's face on the back of the paper every night for a week. That fucker doesn't age, in his club blazer, with his gelled hair, and all the rest of them, look at them, look at him. Goldie stares down at his body, pink scars across it, his ribs showing and the jut of his hip-bone above his trousers. He's hoisted them up with a length of wire casing he found out by the docks wall where they've started taking buildings down. He still does not know what he is going to do, story of his life, he supposes.

When he looks up the boy is much nearer, bigger. He wonders if he can see him, he walks with such purpose, sees that he is holding something up the sleeve of his hooded top, holds a jerrycan in his other hand, liquid sloshing from the top, which he guesses must be petrol, perhaps he has run out of petrol, and he watches from the broken-down wall where he sits, has plans to watch the light change on the abandoned buildings, until he realises the boy is very near, his shadow walking with him, and so Goldie ducks back in through the open factory doorway and up the concrete steps.

. . .

The pub is empty. Paul queued all Tuesday morning, came back telling her what a genuine bloke he thought Liam was, that he could understand what she must have seen in him. 'Is that right, Paul?' is all she said, in as even a tone as she could manage. No sign even of Mark today and she has bolted the off sales hatch shut. Alina is working on the stall. Tyrone is bringing a Chinese with him when he finishes his shift at the ground. They might wait to eat with her after closing time, sit upstairs at the kitchen table near to midnight, she told Tony to head round when he's locked up the shop. They'll sit like a family with the windows open and the telly on, talking and only half-listening to each other, and she will want the moment to last for ever.

She lets the radio commentary bleed quietly from the kitchen into the bar. They are losing. She thinks of Liam, sees him moving, running across the roof at the flats, Mark, Goldie too, a long time ago, like they could never fall, like they could fly. She stands under the chandelier, looks at the ticking clock, sings quietly to herself, breaks off every now and then, hopes for an answering call.

. . .

Bobby pulls the knife from his sleeve. It's wrapped in newspaper. He has watched the buildings, knows he's been sleeping in this one, that there's an office on an upstairs floor where there's even a bed. He's been coming over here for years, first on training runs, then when he was off his head, as if he's the full ticket now, he thinks to himself, almost laughs. He tears the newspaper into strips to use as firelighters. Try and smoke him out, is what his old man said, see what you can do. He'll show him, he thinks, he'll show him.

If he sets the fire on this stair he can chase him up and out, down the iron staircase that runs down the back wall, trap him on this side of the canal, although it's wide enough to try to jump it there, he supposes, will take that risk. There's that new rope that someone has brought down here. He plans to tie him up, secure him to one of the iron rings that are worked into the brick, text his dad who is over at the football. He can do what he likes with him then. Bobby doesn't want to know. He never has. When he's done this he reckons his dad will give him a car, some cash, something. Half a chance and he's out of here, he tells himself, they'll never hear from him again. He's tried all sorts of ways of escaping apart from the most obvious, just to leave, to disappear.

He hears something on the stairs above, puts the strips down in among the rubbish that has already swirled with the breeze in the bottom of the stairwell, sloshes some petrol on the pile, there are pipes running out of the wall here and down through the floor, and he pauses for a moment, and then there's another noise above him and he hurries and fumbles with the lighter in his pocket.

. . .

There are fires that have burned all their lives. It's what Mark thinks as he drags the little boat down the bank. He can smell burning from somewhere, he is sure. He can see there's a hole in the bottom of the boat and wonders if he risks drowning and thinks of all the ways to go maybe that would be best. They could all wonder whether he'd meant it or not. But you can stand up in this water and it's only a few yards across. God knows how old the coracle is. It was tied up with fraying rope under the bridge, the one with the graffiti. Frank Hughes must have left it there on his last afternoon, thinking he'd be back for it. Frank's dad had been the boatman before, possibly his dad before that, to fish the balls from the river when they kicked them in there, right back before there even was a stand, just an earth bank where the crowd would assemble after the factory whistle.

When they were ballboys here, Mark and Liam loved to get the East Stand duty, run up and down the empty, splintered wood and have the match played out to themselves. When someone stuck it over the low stand and they heard the ball bouncing across the iron roof they would race each other to the little door at the back which opened out over the water. Frank would be there, paddling slowly after it, wherever it had landed. In his last years he shared the river and the banks with swans, geese; before that the water had been dead, bubbles would rise to its brown surface and pop.

It's the door Mark paddles towards, water sloshing in the bottom of the boat as it knocks against the back of the stand, no more than a hatch really. He thought he would have to force it but the splintered wood pushes open into the gloom and he remembers the smell of the place, pulls himself up and forward and through the hatch like a cat. He does not tie the boat up, let it sink, let it sail down the river to the sea, he thinks, knows it will drift to the bank, stay half submerged, a perch for herons. To get home he might walk across the pitch. Why not? He never really said goodbye. There it is, a strip of green in the sun, the players flicker across it in their red shirts, their Eton Blue shirts, a song starts up again at the Greenfield End. He hears his own name, they want to conjure him up like a spirit, cannot see him, perhaps never did, not who he was, saw who they wanted to see. One-nil down already. Well, he is here again. He thinks of how he used to run across that pitch like his feet didn't touch the ground and sits at the back of the stand where the light makes a pattern through the missing slats. He is not quite alone. The fox sits, alert, upright, down near the Chain End. He has not seen her all winter, since she had her cubs, if it's the same one, there's so many now, her nose in the air. She turns her head towards Mark and then bolts away into the dark. There's a gasp from the crowd as a pass goes awry and the players in red steam forward and there's Liam, who clatters it up onto the roof of the stand and Mark hears the familiar bounce and roll of the ball above him, how he would groan when they did that when he was playing, and gesture to the defenders to knock it into his feet. The crowd cheer Liam who claps his hands, shakes his fist, until a new ball is found and they go again in endless to and fro.

. . .

Bobby waits, crouched on the stained concrete, a coil of smoke comes slowly up the stairwell. He waits for movement, for any sound from the man, knows it must come with the smoke, hears the cries and songs come from the Anvil Yards. He thinks for a moment about how wrong your life must have gone, to be living here in the ruins, in the shadows, getting so thin, becoming invisible. But not so hard to imagine. He hears the crowd cry again, a surge, and he thinks of those fights in the Assembly Rooms and up at the Casino. 'Kill him, Bobby, kill him.' He can sense the man's movements above him, it's like he hunts himself.

. . .

Liam has never known a half go so quick. At least they have kept it at one-nil. They are still in it, that's what he wants to say to them, when they've got their breath, had a drink, resists the urge to say anything too soon. He looks round for Archie at some point, who always checks he's OK at half-time, remembers, thinks of his grey face in the hospital bed. He cannot recall what he said to them before kick-off, or on the pitch in the huddle when he let Devon talk and it was too loud anyway. He is aware of the requirement for some grand speech, although he has never seen them work, the words have never mattered, just goes round the room and looks in their faces, tells them if they are patient it will come, moves Kyran back out wide where he might get some space. He asks Ted Groves to tell Shaunie to get warmed up after the hour, if it's still one-nil. There's nothing doing from the other matches, no favours anywhere, they need to win. He'll throw Shaunie on up front and just sling balls in at him and Julius. He has never claimed to be a tactical genius.

At the mouth of the tunnel is a man talking into a microphone. Liam does not recognise him. He has the newspaper from a couple of weeks ago in his hand, waves it towards the camera.

'Rumours swirling around the ground about a new owner and a dramatic late buyout but the fact remains that as it stands Irontown Football Club – founder members of the Football League – are on their way out of the league and most likely out of business. It's about to strike midnight at the Anvil Yards!!'

It hits him now that this is probably it, his last game, and he bounces on his toes to get the blood running. Kyran sprints past him, late out of the tunnel after getting his ankle taped up. He turns in the middle of the pitch and flicks the ball up, drills it hard towards the reporter. The balls strikes the newspaper and it flies out of his hand. The crowd nearby cheers. The reporter just grins. They've got no shame, these people, Liam thinks, claps his hands. The crowd sing *Iron Towns, Iron Towns, Iron Towns* . . .

'Was trying to get him in the balls,' he hears Kyran shout, who runs on the spot now and pumps his knees high.

. . .

Goldie moves as quietly as he can along the old walkway that looks down on what was the factory floor. A couple of apple trees grow where he guesses they must have ripped out some machine or other, ripped up the concrete too. Blossom foams on their branches and he can smell it when the breeze comes through the open windows. He will pick the apples when the autumn comes, thinks he could stay here for ever, eke out less and less, waste away slowly and disappear.

He thinks of calling out, saying hello. It might be a trick of his imagination that the boy came in here at all, probably on a short cut to fill his car with petrol, or more likely off to set light to something somewhere, it doesn't have to be here. He smells smoke and not blossom, is sure of it, crouches at the top of the stairs, should've tried the door at the end of the walkway, just gone down the rusty fire escape, he thinks, too late, instead waits here with a knife in his hand, looking at the turn in the stairs.

. . .

'You've heard then,' Ally stands at the door to Steve Stringer's office and Steve nods, looks at the desk and the closed computer on it, the folders and old copies of football yearbooks on the shelves, at Chain Street down below, empty. There's an old framed photo of the team with the FA Cup at Hightown Station, the last time they won it, when they brought it back from Crystal Palace on the train, a hundred years gone by and more. He thinks he could take that with him, imagines the bare patch of wall it will leave behind. They hear the shouts when the players emerge back onto the pitch.

Steve waits for the words to come, thinks he might not even stay for the second half, will drive home, and his wife's head will jerk up when he comes through the door at this odd hour, she hates football but will have the commentary on all the same, and he'll tell her that there is no job for him any more, that he is finished, washed up, a familiar old Iron Towns tradition.

'You better get ready to get on the phone, son. When that ban gets lifted we're gonna need to get some new players in for next season, I don't care what league we're in, a lot of that shower have got to go.'

Steve looks at himself in Ally's sunglasses. Ally pats him on the arm.

'Come on,' Ally says to him, as they hear the whistle blow, 'let's get settled for the second half. You look like you've seen a ghost.'

. . .

And the boy comes up and round the last step with a knife too in his hand, with Goldie crouched there before him, and there's a twitch and a flicker in both of their faces that they might just both turn and run, but where would they even go now? And Goldie springs at him with a sound coming from within him that he cannot fathom. The boy drops the knife, it clatters onto the steps, but his hands are quick and he hits Goldie once, twice, three times and Goldie can see that these are his fists but can't quite believe it, thinks they are lumps of iron, and it's as if the boy is above him now like some great, breaking wave, but he still has the knife in his hand held tight, tight, and the boy goes to kick him and some instinct means he throws his arm at him, feels the knife go in hard, hit something which must be a bone. There was a plan he and Liam made once that they'd go to Spain, to the bull running when the football season ended, but they never did because Liam was always so full of shit.

Goldie knows it's bad straight away, the boy falls backwards, cracks his head on the step, but it's the blood that's the thing, such a spurt of it already, and Goldie saw this once in the dinner queue, inside, when a bloke got stabbed in the neck with one of those plastic shanks people used to make in the workshops, an old Irish fellow it was, who was in for fiddling his pension and got involved in some other kind of scam, only just survived, pints and pint of blood, and Goldie lands on top of him with his momentum and he can see from the boy's eyes straight away that it's no good. It's true that he's an Ahmed, he looks just like Dee Dee, just here, with the colour draining from him, blood every-where, the smell of smoke and apple blossom all around.

.   .   .

Joey stands and stares at the empty urinal. They've kicked off. He'll tell Liz she's right, been right all along. His old man won't live for ever, although he'll try his best to. They should start looking at what they could get, maybe see about Spain, Portugal, wherever. She's always wanted to leave and she's right, she's right. The girls can come and visit with the children, a bit of sun will do them good. He'll tell her when they get back tonight, whatever the result. Liam can't play for ever, either. He has to look to see if he's actually had a piss or not.

When he gets to the top of the walkway he sees Kyran move, a bit of space at last, and for a second, just a second, it's Mark Fala skipping in from that wing, inside the fullback, running at the centre-half now and inviting a challenge. He hits a shot, a cross more like, but Julius does not move, and it clips the defender with the keeper already moving to his left, and the ball takes a lazy, lovely arc from the deflection and drops into the net, and they've had a bit of luck at last, the first for a hundred years or more from what Joey can tell, and he goes running down the steps past the directors' box with his arms aloft, his flies undone, his tie flailing.

. . .

Bobby lies on the factory steps, huddled, with his hands in his lap and a pool of blood forming fast, too fast, underneath him, spreading and running onto the step below and then the one below that, too fast. Goldie sees a plume of blood that must have sprayed against the wall as the knife hit, a whole wall freckled with blood and he sees it now on his own hands, feels the punches still on his stinging face and head, and he wants to run, and he wants to hold the boy's head and tell him everything will be OK and there is blood pumping away down the step and it cannot go that fast, you cannot lose it at that speed and think anything is going to be all right and Goldie wonders how he got here, cradling the head of a boy he has just stabbed on these dirty steps and he just wants to start over, if he could just start again, he would never leave his room, he would lie on his bed and wait to hear the sound of horses' hooves.

. . .

They used to call what is now the East Stand 'The Bank' and what is now the Greenfield End 'The Hill'. The miners would come down the valley and stand on The Hill, those from the port would stand on The Bank, the workers from Greenfields would fill the space in between, so many more of them, and they would all stand as one, but always these differences between them, delineations. They fought among themselves when the miners went out on strike and the factories back to work, although people pretended differently now, if they talked of those days at all. Divide and rule has always been the way to control these islands. Today people bicker over houses and cars and phones. They killed that boy for his trainers. They swam out of drowned Welsh valleys and walked shoeless from Black Country slums. There is the faintest cloud of smoke above the Anvil Yards, as if the fires have started up again.

. . .

He can see that the boy is dead, but thinks at the same time, no, and imagines him getting to his feet and prepares himself for another assault but the boy does not move and Goldie can feel his heart beating in his chest and a feeling of dread, a different dread to the one that says to be ready for the boy to get to his feet because he will not, because he is dead, the same one he felt before on that riverbank, looking back at the car with his baby girl in his arms and thinking where's Sonia? Where is Sonia? As if he didn't really know, so that he knew she was in the car and under the water and didn't all at the same time. It is exactly that, because there is the boy lying dead on the concrete steps and Goldie still stands ready with a knife in his hands and looks for the boy to get to his feet.

. . .

The ball bounces towards Tommy Starr and Liam looks at the line, sluggish to move up, the end of the season, the end of time itself he can see, as the ref motions towards the linesman and has the whistle in his mouth. Tommy pumps the ball forward, comes after it, comes to join the party, there was that keeper who scored on the last day to keep Carlisle up, Jimmy Glass, he drives a cab somewhere down south now, the crowd noise has gone up a notch to a kind of slowed-down high-pitch shriek.

Liam jumps and he wins it, he feels it, just the faintest of touches, exactly like when he played for England. They always say he never touched the ball, but he did, just like that, with the lightest of touches as he jumped for a header that took the ball away from his marker. He gets clattered, all arms and legs as he hits the ground and he wants to shout for a foul but can't get the words out as the air is knocked from him.

The ball hits the turf, bounces into the area, and there is Kyran, one last burst, clear of his man and onto the ball. Liam is still on the floor when Kyran pulls back his left foot, Liam sees him there, frozen, both feet off the ground, his head down, thousands of people behind him in a full-throated roar as if he is leaping into the crowd. And he sees the trip, the defender gets back, Kyran lands in a heap, and Liam is back on his feet now, shouting, 'Penalty! Penalty!' along with everyone else in the Anvil Yards, and for a second he thinks the ref is blowing for time but, no, he points with great deliberation towards the spot.

There's a penalty at the Anvil Yards . . . he can hear a radio playing behind the goal, there would always be men when he was a kid with a transistor held to their ear. They would relay scores from other matches, relevant or important or not, a litany of names and numbers, a spell to protect you from the world. *Penalty at the Anvil Yards* . . . he hears, as it plays out into empty bedrooms and rose-filled gardens and across the burning yards themselves, from out of Eli's kitchen window and up over the hill, into Archie Hill's hospital room at the Bethel, from the laptop by Stan Ahmed's bed in his hospital room in Marbella as he slips in and out of the world, their chests rise and fall to its sound, across a patio that overlooks the Atlantic waves, Dorothea's head nodding asleep, into empty rooms in houses up the hill, in the Salamander, where Dee Dee sings.

. . .

They recede into the crowd, not completely, of course, but enough to see them as one of many, a whole people, hundreds of thousands for every one of them, who would walk the factory streets to watch them play. Those who moved to the percussion of clanging metal, of great booms across docks and rivers, of bells and sirens and whistles, along black paths and across green fields, through all the iron towns of the world.

Di Stéfano sits on a cushion in the Bernabeau, George Best sits in the corner of the pub, Eusébio watches the eagle as it soars against the hard blue light and into the shadowed rafters. Billy Meredith stands at the bar of the Stretford Road Hotel, talks with the men that come and go about City, about United, sips orange juice. Steve Bloomer walks on Cromer pier, sees boys fishing for crabs off the sides, looks into the grey northern waters, shoulder to shoulder with men who once cheered his name.

And the crowds recede like an ebbing tide, the iron towns rust, and you might think them all ghosts if you think of them at all, but do not be mistaken, they will not die, they take new forms.

. . .

He can smell petrol that comes off the boy, he is sure now, and there is a curl of smoke that comes up the steps. He should run, needs to run, he understands that. Smoke comes up the steps, a curl of it at first but then a thicker rope of it, as if he could grab hold of it and haul himself to safety and he does put his hand to it, drops the knife which clatters off down the steps and he thinks that this is another mistake because his prints are on the knife.

He does not wear a glove. You see kids now on the back of buses, they wear a golf glove like they're off to play the Sunday medal but everyone knows what it's meant to show and they haven't killed anyone, these boys, they haven't hurt anyone, you can see it in their eyes most of them, but that's what we're left with, he thinks. Everyone wants to be a bad man. He goes to follow the knife but as he turns a corner of the stairs the heat and smoke rise and hit his face like the way Nadine slapped him once, just out of nowhere, while they stood in the kitchen trying to do the dishes.

He turns back and the blood runs through under him, pools on an uneven step and he has to step over the boy who lies at a strange angle, feels something in his stomach and stumbles across the wide floor where they had fought, not even a fight, not really, over in seconds, what the football commentators say is a coming together. There is blood on his hand, a handprint on the concrete, his own blood, must have cut himself as he stabbed him. He is crouched, looks at his own palm print there on the floor and then looks up and tries to rise, sees the smoke above him drifting in the murky light that comes through the skylights. Clumps of moss look like black clouds.

There is something he is aware of now, as he moves away from the heat and starts to run towards the far wall. He remembers the way the stairs just melted in the rain during the storm. He gets to the wall and cannot even see the door that would lead there with the smoke all around him now, filling this great space. It is very hot. He hears a pop from the fire below and a surge in the heat. From beyond the murky skylights he thinks he can hear the shouts of the crowd.

He remembers the way the staircase peeled off the building, nothing but rust, disintegrated in the rain. He can fall or he can burn, he thinks, like some great truth revealed, as if that was always the only choice open to him and he looks up towards the light but there is just thick black smoke now, and the heat, and the sound of the flames getting nearer and he understands there is no way out, probably never was.

. . .

We are here.

We come as the creatures from the edges of your dreams, as the griffin and the salamander. We are the ash that will fall on your towns, the pattern of the smoke in the brick, the spores that you will breathe in. We are the iron roar that you thought you'd silenced. We sing of better days. Better days to come.

. . .

Liam picks up the ball and puts it on the penalty spot, thinks he sees it move in the breeze which comes stronger now, warm, places it again. He rubs his hands on the turf either side of the ball. The pitch held up well in the end, he thinks, remembers suddenly a story Dee Dee made him read once, a kid winning a prison race who loses on purpose, throws himself down on the floor when he is miles ahead, because he can, because he won't win for the people in power. Liam grins now. He said to Dee Dee, 'Why didn't he just keep running?' and she shook her head and said he didn't understand.

He smells burning. The crowd are still going nuts behind the goal. He cannot ever remember the ground this packed, he sees bodies, arms and legs and heads jumping, writhing, and a great roar coming from them. This is louder now, like something restored, like the days of the old iron roar that he could not even remember if he tried.

There are players still in the box, god knows what anyone is arguing about, as clear a penalty as you might ever see. One of the defenders tries to say something to Liam, he is smiling, it's like he's asking him when the next bus is due, where he's going on his holidays, but Liam cannot hear him and walks close to him to show he is not backing down from anything, his guard will not slip now. Kyran is on his feet he can see, just to the side of the pitch and he tries to beckon him on and looks at the ref but the ref is already pacing out to the side of the ball with the whistle in his mouth, ushers the keeper towards his line and a hush settles. These things are over so quickly, these moments, to be replayed again and again, on television screens and in memories, locked in people's heads.

Liam turns and looks at the ball and looks at the goal, not at the keeper, at the net either side of him. The faces in the Greenfield End merge into one. There is the blur of orange stewards' jackets in front of the hoardings. Everything is still now. The breeze comes again.

Liam takes a breath and then another, moves his hand in front of his face. Is this snow? A shower of white flakes falls through the spring sunshine. Ash. Something is burning. He glances for a moment at the old East Stand, checks the thing isn't in flames. There's a pattern at the back of the stand where there are holes in the concrete and the light shines through like all the stars in the sky, he thinks he can see the shape of a man at the back of the stand, there is a plume of smoke off in the distance somewhere over the Anvil Yards. They had a match in the Pengwern once where there was a burning car in the next field, they played on through the smoke. There are fires that have burned all their lives.

It is silent, all those people and not a murmur, and the referee blows his whistle into the falling ash and the breeze. Liam takes another breath, empties his mind completely of everything other than the only thing he has ever really understood, the shape of a ball struck across a green field.

He knows what to do.

.   .   .

The fire burned all night. They said there were oil tanks underground that everyone had forgotten about. Old gas cylinders exploded like the sound of gunfire up the valley and there was the deep rumble of walls and ceilings collapsing. Alina thought of the apple trees, of the foxes that would flee from the blaze and streak up the hillsides in the dark, as she dozed in her nana's old chair by the window. Her mum made endless cups of tea. The foxes' tails were alight, spreading fire and mayhem as they ran. She felt strangely calm, shocked maybe, she thought to herself. Her mum looked much the same. Dee Dee stood at the off sales hatch or on the lounge steps with her head craned out to watch the fire-fighters move the cordon nearer and nearer to the pub and then stop not fifty yards or so down the road, a high tide of flame lapping at their doors.

The police used the lounge to co-ordinate things. They had a pub at each corner of the Anvil Yards, kept radioing people in The Magpie three miles distant on a back road into the Heath, which was where the smoke was being blown. Dee Dee hoisted cans of pop from the cellar with Tyrone, bought cups and the kettle down from upstairs. No one slept much and their eyes felt gritty in the morning from the lack of sleep and the smoke that had got into everything. The bulk of the smoke hung as a huge black cloud above the Anvil Yards and drifted slowly to the east.

. . .

Sunday morning Alina and Tyrone drove up above the smoke, to the head of the valley where the road dips and runs into the Sheep Folds and the Iron Towns disappear, set a blanket out some way from the roadside with pastries and the flask of coffee that Alina made that morning while listening to the radio, fire crews from as far afield as North Wales and Birmingham is what they said, that the blaze was contained, it would continue to burn but was under control, and a miracle that there had been no injuries.

When they swung the car out of Meeting House Lane they saw the road block and fire-fighters standing on the other side of the temporary fencing, recognised it from when it was erected on the roadside for when the carnival parade came through the Lowtown Bull Ring. She was shocked at the man standing half in uniform with his arm resting on the top of a police car, his face blackened, like someone made up for a film. The smell was everywhere here. They delivered a last crate of lemonade from the car boot and the fire-fighter grinned through his blackened face as they hoisted the cans over the low fence. She looked at Tyrone for any trace of jealousy and he did look at her and smile but she couldn't work out what the look meant and couldn't decide whether she wanted him jealous or not. Perhaps better not, she thought. She wondered how long the burnt smell would take to leave or if it ever would.

They'd said no casualties but she knew they couldn't be sure. The place was vast, so was the fire, and it would burn for days, maybe weeks they said, but the blaze was under control, the phrase they kept repeating on the radio and TV, so strange to see her own street there on the television screen, all the drama of breaking news. Well, it was broken now. They said no casualties, but there were people living in there, she was certain, she knew it, that tent under the old bridge for one thing, all the drink bottles and rags, and that sense of being watched sometimes, that there were eyes on you in all that space. They meant none of the officials, the fire-fighters and so on. They'd evacuated some flats, some of the houses round and about. They meant those people, but there were others she was sure that no one would account for, and there were people who refused to be evacuated, of course there were, always was. They'd put camp beds in the hall of her old junior school.

Through the Bull Ring there was a sudden shower of ash, soft white flakes fell onto the windscreen and Tyrone put the wipers on with some water and turned it all into a grey, silty wash that meant he had to put his head through the open window in order to see to drive.

There were people out on the hillsides at Cowton, leaning over the walkways and balconies. The sounds of the helicopters now, from the fire brigade, and one that was filming for the TV news. Where they stopped they were above the high-rises, right on the valley-ridge, on the road that ran back down into Black Park. They were above the smoke even, which twisted in the sky as a giant dark plume, the sun coming through it now, and a strange light everywhere.

They spread the picnic blanket out a little way from the car on the sheep-bitten grass. From this distance there were no people and it struck her that this was Greenfield's view, that from the painting, that she had maybe found it at last when she wasn't looking, the lines of the rivers in the valley below, before they entered the smoke, the castle hidden just round the hillside, like the third panel of a triptych, she thought, after the last fire. They'd got the camera with them. Tyrone looked at his phone to see if a picture he'd sent had got on the news.

'We should've taken that fireman,' he said, 'people love that stuff. I reckon he'd blacked his face up on purpose.'

So just the smallest bit of jealousy then, the best sort, she felt, and she squeezed his arm.

It was warm, not just from the fire, but from the sun cutting through the billowing smoke, strange colours at its edge, mauve and purple, chemical smoke.

'But how do they know it's safe? No one remembers what was

left in there,' said a voice on the radio this morning after various reassurances about safety and the size of the exclusion cordon.

She phoned her mum to check she was OK. They ate their pastries. There were birds floating on the air that came from the valley. She waited for one to swoop on some unsuspecting prey but they stayed high up and almost out of sight. Tyrone leaned back, one arm around her waist, his other hand holding the newspaper folded open at a picture of Liam with his shirt off on the pitch at full-time just as he disappeared into the crowd. There were a crowd of bodies on his body, a crowd of bodies all around him. They looked like smoke, all of them, the grey swirls on his flesh and the way the people moved towards him, to swallow him, like the way the smoke moved now and swallowed the hillside graves and half of Burnt Village and then drifted over the hill into the rest of England. When they opened the roads she would have to go and clean her mum's plaque. She wondered if the roses would bloom with the colours of the smoke this year, or whether that took ages to happen, generations, evolution, thought of creatures with blackened bodies that lived among soot and ash, and the people in the bottom of the valley in the second painting.

The road was narrow here, a farmer's track really. It ran over the hill and the shape of it, a sudden incline like a breaking wave, made her wonder what was on the other side, even though she knew full well. More roads, more hills. Tyrone saw her looking that way, had finished leafing through the paper.

'We could carry on,' he said, nodding at the brow of the hill. 'Just keep going.'

It was tempting, to choose this moment to leave. Then she looked back at the black smoke in the valley, the charred buildings beneath, a snow of ash falling again on the Iron Towns, charred lives, she thought, my own and everyone that has ever lived here.

'No,' she said. 'No. Let's go home.'

Acknowledgements

Many thanks to Hannah Westland, Nick Sheerin, and all at Serpent's Tail who helped this novel happen. Likewise to Sam Copeland at Rogers, Coleridge and White, and to Alan Mahar for his ongoing encouragement. And thank you, of course, to my family, for all their support.

Black Country

An essay in response to the EU referendum
By Anthony Cartwright

Geology is destiny.

The Black Country is porous, like its limestone, and hard as Rowley rag, the dolerite in its quarries. For a time this was the most heavily industrialised few square miles on the planet, and yet, as its name suggests, it has never been fully urban. Its hills mark the watershed between the rivers Severn and Trent, the *wrosne* of Old English, a word that translates as 'the link'. The Black Country's borders are ill-defined, corresponding roughly to the old South Staffordshire coalfield (which incorporates enclaves of Worcestershire and Shropshire). It is in the English midlands, to the west of Birmingham, but not of it. On that, at least, we can all agree.

When I ring my dad on the day of the referendum he tells me that he has seen people queuing off the Rowley Road to vote. The hills fall away south below the line of voters, past the blackened brick of the air shaft that comes from the tunnel bored through the land below, past the shell of Cobb's Engine House which used to pump water from the nearby mines into the canal, past Clent and Walton and the woods that once belonged to King Offa and Saint Kenelm, webbed with lanes where they say Harry Ca Nab, the leader of the devil's hunt, still sometimes rides on his wild bull. He will surely be out tonight; Lord of Misrule. Those queuing can see all the way to Malvern, always blue in the distance, under the Severn Jacks, soft clouds that come from the west. This is an old country, layered, like the coal and limestone and ancient seabed buried within it.

England.

England.

My great-great-grandad settled his family here, in a hollow of the hill near the tunnel mouth, in one of the cottages covered by the engine house's shadow in the late afternoons. Llewellyn Williams: grandad Williams, remembering the sun's glitter on the River Dee fading in a soft rain come from Wales. My dad's uncle Sam told us how he could hear the thud of the engine as it pumped through the dark nights and shook the land around it.

The family moved on some time after, down the hill again into Cradley Heath, eventually to the chainyard where my dad was born years later, the same year as the NHS. They banged chain: men, women, children. Almost all the world's chain, the cables and anchors of Empire, came from five towns visible from this hillside. A study in 1897 called the chainmakers 'the white slaves of England', making reference to an outbreak of typhoid in the notorious Anvil Yard a decade before. These were skilled workers kept in squalor, holding their heads high and proud. When the women led a strike in 1910 to secure the country's first ever minimum wage and won, John Galsworthy called them 'the chief guardians of the inherent dignity of man'.

The flags will be out soon for 14 July, Black Country Day. Red, white and black tricolours, links of chain emblazoned across them. The flag of the Black Country is a recent invention, created this century by a schoolgirl called Gracie Sheppard for a competition. The region was 'Black by day, red by night', according to Elihu Burritt, Abraham Lincoln's consul to the industrial midlands and the man credited with first using the term Black Country. The pattern of the flag is shaped like the Red House Cone in Wordsley, where they used to blow glass. So much of the Black Country is in the past tense.

14 July 1712 was the day Thomas Newcomen fired up the world's first working steam engine to pump water from the Earl of Dudley's mines. This is the machine that James Watt later adapted, and which shapes the world we live in today, for better or worse. Newcomen had come to the Black Country from elsewhere, like so many of the others that came afterwards, from Devon in his case. It was one of his engines that pumped in Cobb's Engine House. Henry Ford bought the engine in the 1920s, took it to Detroit as a holy relic. Cobb was the farmer whose fields they undermined. Anyone trying to understand what has happened to England, what happened on 23 June's referendum, and in the many years before, might do well to visit the silent engine house ruin in its green field with black crows, and ponder.

I remember a class trip once, a walk down through the fields and along the canal. This was in 1983, '84, possibly later, one of the lowest years in any case, Thatcher's malice doing more to undermine us all than cutting coal and limestone ever did. There were kids inside the ruin that afternoon. I say kids, they were young men and women in their twenties with bags of glue in their hands, with shaved heads, one holding a bottle of something. I remember the teacher veering us away. But the young people smiled and waved at us and looked so utterly lost, as if they were their own ghosts. I think of them and wonder if any of them were queueing to vote in the line my dad told me about, men and women in their fifties now, if they made it this far, if they are still here, looking out across English hills and waiting.

Last summer we brought my son here, a boy named for a Welsh king over the mountains, dressed in his England shirt, to feed the ducks and climb through the engine house's vacant window. The grass has grown over the slag heaps that we would sometimes run up at football practice. The whole place is a nature reserve, Bumble Hole, so named for an old clay pit filled with water, and it has the soft feel of the English countryside, lichen on the stones of the ruin, faint lettering like runes.

'No one's queued to vote round here since the days of Attlee,' my dad says.

And it's true. In the local elections in May the Labour Party managed to lose overall control of Dudley Council by defeats in two wards on a 30 per cent turnout, one by 3 votes, the other by 13.

'There were some who queued for Powell,' is what I might have said. And that is also true, not so far from here. Enoch Powell's constituency was five miles north-west from us in Wolverhampton; his anti-immigration rivers of blood speech was made in Birmingham; he was born eight miles to the east. 'As I look ahead I am filled with foreboding, like the Roman, I seem to see "the river Tiber foaming with much blood".'

The River Tame is our Tiber. It is 'A tired and sad little river,' says a poem by Ian Henery.

> 'That's forgotten its ancient name ...
> Realigned, under motorways,
> By Wolverhampton, by Dudley,
> Miserable in its canals.'

People never called him Powell, always Enoch. As in, 'Enoch was right', words that you sometimes still hear whispered in Black Country pubs. I used to think about the rivers of blood when I worked in the Three Crowns at the top of Dudley High Street in my late teens, in between the clack of the dominoes played in the tiled bar by white, black and Asian men, with barely a raised voice between them. I wondered if we mocked Powell's curse with our actions, or whether his words will come to mock us.

I consider this and look out across North London, because, of course – like the writer in the Victoria Wood sketch who bemoans the destruction of 'My north, my north!' and confesses he lives in Chiswick – I moved long ago. I would not be writing this from a kitchen table in Dudley. The distance from here to there is far too great. And that social divide is one of our country's main problems.

The gulf between us was something the referendum exposed rather than created, although the histrionics of the reaction to the vote seem to be widening the division still further. That the vote was somehow, on one level, turned by the political and media classes into a referendum between middle-class entitlement and working-class self-respect, with the EU as collateral damage, was a huge, miscalculated gamble, something we should reflect on with a great deal of horror.

Perhaps the ground beneath our feet was never that secure. The Dudley cricket ground disappeared down a hole one day in the eighties, collapsed into old mine workings, undone by old wounds, some kind of metaphor for the state we are in, how a gulf opens up, swallows the world you thought you knew.

Further up the hill from the engine house is where I grew up. Most days on the way to school I would walk up or down Cawney Bank, where you look across at Dudley Castle, the brick softened in the rain and by the years; hard to think of it as once a fortress of an occupying power, Norman blood no doubt now in us all. Lubetkin's pavilions dot the hill below the castle: Dudley Zoo. When it opened, in 1937, it was one of the biggest tourist attractions in England. Lubetkin, a Jewish Georgian from Russia via Dessau, built a shining city on a hill in the English midlands.

I filmed an interview on Cawney Bank last year, looking over to the castle and the zoo, in praise of the Black Country, of our voices, our accent, in the face of our obsolescence. Through a window in the nearby flats I could see my nan. She'd grown up in streets below the castle, demolished in the years they built the zoo, and I could see the families who lived there, part of my own, Roman Catholic, Villa-supporting, in an area where you followed the Albion or Wolves, who had been blown in from who knows where with the clanging of metal, a travelling people, come to settle and work beneath the fortress walls, then scattered over the nearby hills. Just like all those come later, via Peshawar and Muzaffarabad and Kingston and Bridgetown. Our people came to tend the fires of a revolution, drive the buses, keep the hospitals healing. Our people of the green hill.

There were pleasure gardens here once, way back in the eighteenth century. You climbed the ladder and looked through a telescope, all the way through Worcestershire and Gloucestershire, to the Bristol Channel. They say you could see Lundy Island on a clear day. Ours is a country of hills, of long views. We, so far inland, are obsessed with the sea, which fossilised its creatures in our rocks.

The council tried to revive the idea earlier this year, to sell the views back to the people. A giant Ferris wheel stood in Stone Street, where we used to wait for the bus to Wolverhampton, or came gambolling drunk or rolling and fighting out of the Saracen's Head and onto the slabs on a Saturday night.

The town was ridiculed. The national newspapers and TV enjoyed the idea no end. Unaware of the history, people who had never even visited Dudley queued up to sneer about views they had never seen. But the idea worked. The people of Dudley queued up to get on the wheel, it was full every day for a month, raising money for the air ambulance (because ours is a country that funds ambulance services with fairground rides).

After the circus came the clowns. Farage came on his big purple bus and waved his passport around in the market place. He missed a trick that day, bemoaning the word European on British citizens' documents, he never talked about England, English passports; Black Country passports in red, white and black. It was only recently I was told that to describe yourself as English – not British – was to belie your working-class roots. I am English, bizarrely proud of this fact. I was there that day, sat on the 140 bus in the sunshine on Rowley Road in fact, when a woman got on, laughing. 'Quick! The UKIP's coming!' she told the driver, and we made our escape.

Then came the vote. More than two to one voted in favour of Leave across the Black Country, with over double the turnout of the local elections held just a month before. The West Midlands as a whole returned a 59 per cent leave vote, the highest of all the country's regions. If those liberal middle classes scorned us before, they surely do so now. Us, them, and which side are you on? I have often buried the question of whether you can be a Blackcountryman and a Londoner too. I always tried to persuade myself I could be both.

But consider that we live in a country where a section of society might impoverish people, *a people* (and this is where we might choose to go down a long, dark tunnel), and then blame them for their impoverishment, mock them for any attempt to either change or ease that impoverishment. And when they rise up, in their polite, English way after all, and queue past the ruins of their culture in order to put an X in a box that says either/or, them/us, make-your-mind-up time, and they tell you that they have had enough, that something has to give, that they will not go along with you because look where you have led them to already, you blame them for that as well.

'Are you still here?' says a man in a distant parliament, and that is the question read by some on the midlands ballot paper. Jean-Claude Juncker breaks off from a speech in his mother tongue to ask this question in plain English. Another grey man replies, and how this ex-public school, City of London trader from Kent installed himself as some kind of spokesman for the English and Welsh industrial working classes is yet one more mystery in a country where all reason left with the coal. A man of greater wit might have chosen to reply in another language of these islands.

> *'Ry'n ni yma o hyd,*
> *er gwaetha pawb a phopeth'*

is what he might have replied.

from the song Yma o Hyd, a hymn to Welsh nationalism, like the Black Country flag, more modern than it seems, a song that harks back to the departure of the Romans and through the years, to those of the destruction wrought by Thatcher.

And there's a sense, I think, that what that X in the box translates as is seventeen and a half million voices that say, *we're still here.* Because what is clear is that for a long time too many people have felt that they have been 'jamming a key in a changed lock', like the character in Black Country poet Liz Berry's poem, desperate in the snow on a Christmas Eve. People talk of the vote to leave as a catastrophe, and they might be right, but what we must surely, finally, acknowledge is that for some places in our country the catastrophe has been going on for forty years or more and counting, counting.

The River Tame, the canals, do not foam with blood. But the ground has shifted, as it does so often in the Black Country, our hills hollowed out so many years ago now, forever subsiding, but still here, still here, and we must look at each other honestly, across whatever gaps are opening between us, and step away together from the abyss, try to find some firmer ground.

Topics for Reading Group Discussions

1   From early on in the novel, it is clear that the characters in *Iron Towns* are all somehow marked by the events of twenty years ago. How do Liam, Dee Dee, Mark and Goldie differ in the way they deal with their pasts?

2   Football plays a large role in *Iron Towns*. What does it mean to Liam? And what does it mean to the other characters?

3   *Iron Towns* is set in a fictional valley in the post-industrial midlands. How has the region's past affected the people still living in the valley today? More generally, what does the novel have to say about the effect of the geography and history of a place on the people who live there?

4   'We are iron men, from the Iron Towns', sing the supporters of Irontowns FC. How closely is football related to regional identity in *Iron Towns*? Is it a strictly local and tribal relationship, or is there a greater, more international dimension to it?

5   Liam's mother, Liz, remarks that 'People look into the past one-eyed ... only remember the good parts.' How true is this in the Iron Towns? And can nostalgia ever be useful?

6   Liam's football tattoos are referred to by the tattoo artist Tony as 'the work'. What is Liam's intention with these scenes? How do they relate to the events of the novel?

7   As the novel proceeds, early British and Roman myths start to

appear. What effect do these have on our understanding of the story, and of the Iron Towns themselves? How do the characters of these myths relate to the characters in the novel?

8   We see the events of the novel through the eyes of many characters, but Sonia remains a slightly enigmatic figure. How important a figure is Sonia in the novel? Does her remaining a mystery bring to mind other secrets buried in the novel?

9   Bobby and Goldie are threatening presences throughout *Iron Towns*. What do they represent? And how similar are they really?

10   So much of the novel is about the effects of the past on the present, but does Alina's story differ? How does Dee Dee think of her?

11   What does the ending of *Iron Towns* suggest about the future of the characters, and of the valley?

*'The forces that shape people's lives are distant and mysterious.
There's a way that football provides an antidote to that.'*

An interview with Anthony Cartwright

One of the most striking things about Iron Towns *is its sense of place. That's
something that comes through in your previous novels too, but where* The Afterglow,
Heartland *and* How I Killed Margaret Thatcher *were all set in your hometown
of Dudley,* Iron Towns *is set in a fictional cluster of post-industrial towns nestled
in a valley somewhere between Birmingham and Wrexham. Could you tell us a bit
about the Iron Towns and how they came into existence?*

The Iron Towns themselves seemed to be with me a while before I wrote
the novel. I wanted to broaden the canvas of my work, for it to feel like
an expansion of what had come before. You're right to say that the Iron
Towns are a re-imagining of the West Midlands, somewhere west of the
actual Black Country, with their own culture and identity. There is a lot of
the history and geography of the place that I know, have written, that isn't
in the novel.

I've always been interested in this kind of world-creation. My aim with
the Iron Towns was definitely to create an alternative, but plausible, reality.
This meant building up layers of history and myth, especially movements
of people, from the arrival of the Britons as refugees from Troy, to Scottish
families moving south in the 1930s for jobs in the steelworks. So, for example, the valley of Pengwern, which was the last British-speaking – what we
now would call Welsh-speaking – area of England after the Anglo-Saxons
came, exists in the novel as the Pengwern estate. The estate itself, some of
its geography anyway, was inspired by an area called The Lost City, a real
place in Tipton.

I thought a lot about how a writer like Jim Crace creates realistic, but completely invented, versions of England (and elsewhere) in his work, and how Kevin Barry re-imagines the west of Ireland in *City of Bohane*. There was a long arc of history I was after too, back to before there even was an England, and, of course, following industrialisation and its decline. What became the Iron Towns – because there was coal and iron ore near the surface of the hills and steep river valleys – were equally cursed and blessed to be at the heart of the Industrial Revolution.

The characters in Iron Towns *are seemingly cut off from that past – the Britons have disappeared, the witches are gone from the Heath, the steelworks have closed – but, despite appearances, that history is still alive for them, particularly for the two main characters, Liam and Dee Dee . . .*

The idea that history lives within the characters, within us, is really important to me. Much of the work has gone, that's for sure, but I'm not certain about the witches. Where I grew up in Dudley, you could see out to the Clent Hills from our house. The area around there has a reputation for witchcraft. I would spend ages doing keep ups with my football in our back garden and look out to the hills and sometimes think about the witches, or Saint Kenelm, or the 'Who Put Bella in the Wych Elm?' story, or Harry ca Nab, the Devil's huntsman, and so on. I'm fascinated by the way places can exist physically, definably, and also exist in a different way in an imaginative sense.

I think the process of industrialisation, and later deindustrialisation, created huge upheaval, a sense of discontinuity to so many people and parts of the country. It's my intention for there to be a lot of blurred identities in Iron Towns. English, Welsh, Scottish, Irish, of course, but also the story of Mark Fala's family being descended from Spanish sailors washed ashore during the time of the Armada, or Dee Dee's Bengali great-grandad. It strikes me that much of industrial working class identity is deeply rooted in place, and in the work, of course, but go back out of living memory, a few generations, and things get hazy. Where do we come from? Where do we belong? These are questions Liam and Dee Dee ask themselves in the novel, even though they are very much of the Iron Towns.

Liam's identity has a particularly interesting tension, in that he's very much 'of the Iron Towns', but his own idea of himself is bound up in a more recent, more international mythology: he's a journeyman footballer whose body is covered in tattoos of the great footballers of the past . . .

Liam's project – a history of football tattooed across his body – has taken on a life of its own by the time we meet him in the novel. I don't think he started out with such a grand idea. In fact, he started with a small image of Jari Litmanen in his Ajax kit, when he left to play in Finland. (It is no surprise that Liam is drawn to players who never quite lived up to their potential – they remind him of Mark Fala, Liam's childhood friend and the iconic, lost Iron Towns player and great young hope of English football who quit the game before he turned twenty.) Football itself has given Liam the sense of continuity that no longer exists in other areas of life in the towns. The mines have long gone, the steelworks closed in the eighties, the Anvil Yards are empty. He has a difficult relationship with his family and the fans. Football binds him to his people in a sense, and they to him.

As I think about this, I'm struck as to the strange way that football has become so central to mainstream culture when it is so much a product of industrial working class life. Pretty much every other area of that life has been marginalised or destroyed over the last forty years or so.

But back to the tattoos. There's a romance to Liam's choices that he can't express anywhere else in his life. There is a sense of some kind of flame being passed between the players, and maybe what he comes to think is that it can be passed between us all. There's a sequence near the start of the novel which begins at the 1962 European Cup Final, moves from Alfredo Di Stéfano to Eusébio to Johan Cruyff (who was a ball-boy at this match). The point is a kind of pattern – of young men transcending circumstances, borders, ordinary football allegiances, even politics, to attain a state of grace. I think this is what Liam is seeking.

And he still hopes for that moment of grace, of transcendence, even though he's playing in the lower tiers of English football for Irontown FC – we're not talking about a European giant like Real Madrid, Benfica, or Ajax here. Yet this fictional club has its own rich history and folklore, which you've woven into the great 150-year tapestry of English football history.

There is certainly something I wanted to get across about football's rich culture. Also, how interconnected the football world is. I wrote these parts with real love. The distance between a boy kicking a ball against a factory wall and then running out at Real Madrid's Bernabéu stadium isn't so great as we might imagine. Or at least, there is a clear and familiar route of how someone might make that journey. That's a real contrast to most of modern life. In the Iron Towns, hard work has been rewarded with rust and dereliction. That is true of many places in this country. The forces that shape people's lives are distant and mysterious. There's a way that football provides an antidote to that.

The story of the club in Iron Towns is bound up with the history of English football, with its roots deep in Victorian industry. Some of the inspiration for the origins of Irontown FC come from those of the club I support, Aston Villa. So the cricket club looking for winter training, religious non-conformism, the Scottish influence, and, of course, the great factory crowds – it's all there in the origins of the Villa. Of course, I've borrowed heavily from elsewhere too. The cult brown shirts are straight from 1970s Coventry! And Irontown FC is a much more modest club than Villa. The point is, though, that the clubs developed from certain ways of life, culture in a specific time and place, and then became a way of life in themselves.

If there is a deeper point, then it's that the impoverishment that Irontown FC, and the Iron Towns in general, now face cannot erase the grandeur and ambition of those former times (again, I could be writing about the Villa, or the Wolves for that matter, and also about much of industrial Britain). If you have had it once, it can come back. That's one belief. There is an idea in the novel of recurrence, of triumph and disaster in a kind of cycle. I think there is an attitude in a lot of the characters of endurance, of waiting the bad times out. I think Dee Dee and Mark are good examples of that attitude in their own ways, the characters most conscious of it, anyway.

That idea of 'waiting the bad times out' seems fundamental to being a football supporter. Unlikely league victories and improbable relegation escapes almost take on the form of a traditional religious miracle when you look at it like that. And it's not just football – Dee Dee's adoptive daughter Alina seems to be seeking a kind miraculous manifestation of the past in the strange artwork she's creating in the abandoned factories.

Alina's art is a kind of magical thinking, in a way. Maybe Liam's tattoos are as well. Alina sees the Iron Towns as they are, but also how they have been. I am really interested in the overlaying of past and present, of personal memory with recorded history, of the emotional repercussions to the process of history, which is perhaps what Alina's art is about. I also see Alina's work as a response to a kind of catastrophe that has befallen the Iron Towns. Her work is a manifestation of grief, in some form. And to go back to the idea of witchcraft, or of the supernatural at least, I wonder how much of her art is an attempt to somehow conjure into life a world that is dead, or has never been. In a way all the characters in the novel are waiting for that miracle. And, like the lost FA Cup buried out on the Heath in the novel, there are miracles still to be uncovered. The idea that there remains a capacity for joy, and that there are always better days to come, is hopefully buried somewhere in *Iron Towns*.

PENGUIN BOOKS

COLD COMFORT FARM

Stella Dorothea Gibbons, novelist, poet and short-story writer, was born in London in 1902. She went to the North London Collegiate School and studied journalism at University College, London. She then worked for ten years on various papers, including the *Evening Standard*.

Her first publication was a book of poems *The Mountain Beast* (1930) and her first novel *Cold Comfort Farm* (1932) won the Femina Vie Heureuse Prize for 1933. Amongst her other novels are *Miss Linsey and Pa* (1936), *Nightingale Wood* (1938), *Westwood* (1946), *Conference at Cold Comfort Farm* (1949), *The Shadow of a Sorcerer* (1955), *The Snow Woman* (1969), and *The Woods in Winter* (1970). Her short stories include *Christmas at Cold Comfort Farm* (1959) and *Beside the Pearly Water* (1954). Her *Collected Poems* appeared in 1950.

In 1933 she married the actor and singer Allan Webb, who died in 1959. They had one daughter. Stella Gibbons died in 1989.

Cold Comfort Farm

STELLA GIBBONS

PENGUIN BOOKS

Let other pens dwell on guilty misery

MANSFIELD PARK

PENGUIN BOOKS

Published by the Penguin Group
Penguin Books Ltd, 27 Wrights Lane, London W8 5TZ, England
Penguin Books USA Inc., 375 Hudson Street, New York, New York 10014, USA
Penguin Books Australia Ltd, Ringwood, Victoria, Australia
Penguin Books Canada Ltd, 10 Alcorn Avenue, Toronto, Ontario, Canada M4V 3B2
Penguin Books (NZ) Ltd, 182–190 Wairau Road, Auckland 10, New Zealand

Penguin Books Ltd, Registered Offices: Harmondsworth, Middlesex, England

First published 1932
Published in Penguin Books 1938
30

Copyright 1932 by Stella Gibbons
All rights reserved

Penguin Film and TV tie-in edition first published 1994

Printed in England by Clays Ltd, St Ives plc

To
Allan and Ina

NOTE

The action of the story takes
place in the near future.

FOREWORD

TO ANTHONY POOKWORTHY, ESQ.,
A.B.S., L.L.R.

My dear Tony,

    It is with something more than the natural deference of a tyro at the loveliest, most arduous and perverse of the arts in the presence of a master-craftsman that I lay this book before you. You know (none better) the joys of the clean hearth and the rigour of the game. But perhaps I may be permitted to take this opportunity of explaining to you, a little more fully than I have hitherto hinted, something of the disabilities under which I had laboured to produce the pages now open beneath your hand.

    As you know, I have spent some ten years of my creative life in the meaningless and vulgar bustle of newspaper offices. God alone knows what the effect has been on my output of pure literature. I dare not think too much about it — even now. There are some things (like first love and one's reviews) at which a woman in her middle years does not care to look too closely.

    The effect of these locust years on my style (if I may lay claim to that lovely quality in the presence of a writer whose grave and lucid prose has permanently enriched our literature) has been perhaps even more serious.

    The life of the journalist is poor, nasty, brutish and short. So is his style. You, who are so adept at the lovely polishing of every grave and lucent phrase, will realize the magnitude of the task which confronted me when I found, after spending ten years as a journalist, learning to say exactly what I meant in short sentences, that I must learn, if I was to achieve literature and favourable reviews, to write as though I were not quite sure about what I meant but was jolly well going to say something all the same in sentences as long as possible.

Far be it from me to pretend that the following pages achieve what first burned in my mind with pure lambency ten years ago. Which of us does? But the thing's done! Ecco! E finito! And such as it is, and for what it is worth, it is yours.

You see, Tony, I have a debt to pay. Your books have been something more to me, in the last ten years, than books. They have been springs of refreshment, loafings for the soul, eyes in the dark. They have given me (in the midst of the vulgar and meaningless bustle of newspaper offices) joy. It is just possible that it was not quite the kind of joy you intended them to give, for which of us is infallible? But it was joy all right.

I must confess, too, that I have more than once hesitated before the thought of trying to repay some fraction of my debt to you by offering you a book that was meant to be ... funny.

For your own books are not ... funny. They are records of intense spiritual struggles, staged in the wild setting of mere, berg or fen. Your characters are ageless and elemental things, tossed like straws on the seas of passion. You paint Nature at her rawest, in man and in landscapes. The only beauty that lights your pages is the grave peace of fulfilled passion, and the ripe humour that lies over your minor characters like a mellow light. You can paint everyday domestic tragedies (are not the entire first hundred pages of The Fulfilment of Martin Hoare *a masterly analysis of a bilious attack?) as vividly as you paint soul cataclysms. Shall I ever forget Mattie Elginbrod? I shall not. Your books are more like thunderstorms than books. I can only say, in all simplicity, 'Thank you, Tony.'*

But funny ... No.

However, I am sure you are big enough, in every sense of the word, to forgive my book its imperfections.

And it is only because I have in mind all those thousands of persons, not unlike myself, who work in the vulgar and meaningless bustle of offices, shops and homes, and who are not always sure whether a sentence is Literature or whether

8

it is just sheer flapdoodle, that I have adopted the method perfected by the late Herr Baedeker, and firmly marked what I consider the finer passages with one, two or three stars. In such a manner did the good man deal with cathedrals, hotels and paintings by men of genius. There seems no reason why it should not be applied to passages in novels.

It ought to help the reviewers, too.

Talking of men of genius, what a constellation burns in our midst at the moment! Even to a tyro as unpractised as myself, who has spent the best creative years of her life in the vulgar and meaningless bustle of newspaper offices, there is some consolation, some sudden exaltation into a serener and more ardent air, in subscribing herself,

Ever, my dear Tony,

Your grateful debtor,

Stella Gibbons

Watford.
Lyons' Corner House.
Boulogne-sur-Mer.
January 1931–February 1932.

CHAPTER I

THE education bestowed on Flora Poste by her parents had been expensive, athletic and prolonged; and when they died within a few weeks of one another during the annual epidemic of the influenza or Spanish Plague which occurred in her twentieth year, she was discovered to possess every art and grace save that of earning her own living.

Her father had always been spoken of as a wealthy man, but on his death his executors were disconcerted to find him a poor one. After death duties had been paid and the demands of creditors satisfied, his child was left with an income of one hundred pounds a year, and no property.

Flora inherited, however, from her father a strong will and from her mother a slender ankle. The one had not been impaired by always having her own way nor the other by the violent athletic sports in which she had been compelled to take part, but she realized that neither was adequate as an equipment for earning her keep.

She decided, therefore, to stay with a friend, a Mrs Smiling, at her house in Lambeth until she could decide where to bestow herself and her hundred pounds a year.

The death of her parents did not cause Flora much grief, for she had barely known them. They were addicted to travel, and spent only a month or so of each year in England. Flora, from her tenth year, had passed her school holidays at the house of Mrs Smiling's mother; and when Mrs Smiling married, Flora spent them at her friend's house instead. It was therefore with the feelings of one who returns home that she entered the precincts of Lambeth upon a gloomy afternoon in February, a fortnight after her father's funeral.

Mrs Smiling was fortunate in that she had inherited house property in Lambeth before the rents in that district soared to ludicrous heights, following the tide of fashion as it swung away from Mayfair to the other side of the river, and the stone parapets bordering the Thames became, as a consequence, the sauntering ground of Argentinian women and their bull-terriers. Her husband (she was a widow) had owned three houses in Lambeth which he had bequeathed to her. One, in Mouse Place, was the pleasantest of the three, and faced with its shell fanlight the changing Thames; here Mrs Smiling lived, while of the other two, one had been pulled down and a garage perpetrated upon its site, and the third, which was too small and inconvenient for any other purpose, had been made into the Old Diplomacy Club.

The white porcelain geraniums which hung in baskets from the little iron balconies of 1, Mouse Place, did much to cheer Flora's spirits as her taxi stopped before its door.

Turning from the taxi to the house, she saw that the door had already been opened by Mrs Smiling's butler, Sneller, who was looking down upon her with dim approval. He was, she reflected, almost *rudely* like a tortoise; and she was glad her friend kept none as pets or they might have suspected mockery.

Mrs Smiling was awaiting her in the drawing-room overlooking the river. She was a small Irishwoman of twenty-six years, with a fair complexion, large grey eyes and a little crooked nose. She had two interests in life. One was the imposing of reason and moderation into the bosoms of some fifteen gentlemen of birth and fortune who were madly in love with her, and who had flown to such remote places as Jhonsong La Lake M'Luba-M'Luba and the Kwanhattons because of her refusal to marry them. She wrote to them all once a week, and they (as her friends knew to their cost, for she was ever reading aloud long, boring bits from their letters) wrote to her.

These gentlemen, because of the hard work they did in savage foreign parts and of their devotion to Mrs Smiling, were known collectively as 'Mary's Pioneers-O', a quotation from the spirited poem by Walt Whitman.

Mrs Smiling's second interest was her collection of brassières, and her search for a perfect one. She was reputed to have the largest and finest collection of these garments in the world. It was hoped that on her death it would be left to the nation.

She was an authority on the cut, fit, colour, construction and proper functioning of brassières; and her friends had learned that her interest, even in moments of extreme emotional or physical distress, could be aroused and her composure restored by the hasty utterance of the phrase:

'I saw a brassière to-day, Mary, that would have interested you...'

Mrs Smiling's character was firm and her tastes civilized. Her method of dealing with wayward human nature when it insisted on obtruding its grossness upon her scheme of life was short and effective; she pretended things were not so: and usually, after a time, they were not. Christian Science is perhaps a larger organization, but seldom so successful.

'Of *course*, if you *encourage* people to think they're messy, they *will* be messy,' was one of Mrs Smiling's favourite maxims. Another was, '*Nonsense*, Flora. You *imagine* things.'

Yet Mrs Smiling herself was not without the softer graces of imagination.

'Well, darling,' said Mrs Smiling – and Flora, who was tall, bent and kissed her cheek – 'will you have tea or a cocktail?'

Flora said that she would have tea. She folded her gloves and put her coat over the back of a chair, and took the tea and a cinnamon wafer.

'Was the funeral awful?' inquired Mrs Smiling. She knew that Mr Poste, that large man who had been serious about games and contemptuous of the arts, was not regretted by his child. Nor was Mrs Poste, who had wished people to live beautiful lives and yet be ladies and gentlemen.

Flora replied that it had been horrid. She added that she was bound to say all the older relatives seemed to have enjoyed it no end.

'Did any of them ask you to go and live with them? I meant to warn you about that. Relatives are always wanting you to go and live with them,' said Mrs Smiling.

13

'No. Remember, Mary, I have only a hundred pounds a year now; and I cannot play Bridge.'

'Bridge? What is that?' inquired Mrs Smiling, glancing vaguely out of the window at the river. 'What curious ways people have of passing their time, to be sure. I think you are very fortunate, darling, to have got through all those dreadful years at school and college, where you had to play all those games, without getting to like them yourself. How did you manage it?'

Flora considered.

'Well – first of all, I used to stand quite still and stare at the trees and not think about anything. There were usually some trees about, for most games, you know, are played at in the open air, and even in the winter the trees are still there. But I found that people *would* bump into me, so I had to give up standing still, and run like the others. I always ran after the ball because, after all, Mary, the ball *is* important in a game, isn't it? until I found they didn't like me doing that, because I never got near it or hit it or did whatever you are supposed to do to it.

'So then I ran *away* from it instead, but they didn't seem to like that either, because apparently people in the audience wondered what I was doing out on the edge of a field all by myself, and running away from the ball whenever I saw it coming near me.

'And then a whole lot of them got at me one day after one of the games was over, and told me I was *no good*. And the Games Mistress seemed quite worried and asked me if I really didn't *care* about lacrosse (that was the name of the game), and I said no, I was afraid I didn't, really; and she said it was a pity, because my father was so "keen", and what *did* I care about?

'So I said, well, I was not quite sure, but on the whole I thought I liked having everything very tidy and calm all round me, and not being bothered to do things, and laughing at the kind of joke other people didn't think at all funny, and going for country walks, and not being asked to express *opinions* about things (like love, and isn't so-and-so *peculiar*?). So then she said, oh, well, didn't I think I could try to be a little less slack, because of Father, and I said no, I was afraid I couldn't; and after that she left me alone. But all the others still said I was *no good*.'

Mrs Smiling nodded her approval, but she told Flora that she talked too much. She added:

'Now about this going to live with someone. Of course, you can stay here as long as you like, darling; but I suppose you will want to take up some kind of work some time, won't you, and earn enough to have a flat of your own?'

'What kind of work?' asked Flora, sitting upright and graceful in her chair.

'Well – organizing work, like I used to do.' (For Mrs Smiling had been an organizer for the L.C.C. before she married 'Diamond' Tod Smiling, the racketeer.) 'Do not ask me what that is, exactly, for I've forgotten. It is so long since I did any. But I am sure you could do it. Or you might do journalism. Or book-keeping. Or bee-keeping.'

Flora shook her head.

'I'm afraid I couldn't do any of those things, Mary.'

'Well . . . what then, darling? Now, Flora, don't be *feeble*. You know perfectly well that you will be *miserable* if you haven't got a job, when all your friends have. Besides, a hundred pounds a year won't even keep you in stockings and fans. What will you live on?'

'My relatives,' replied Flora.

Mrs Smiling gave her a shocked glance of inquiry, for, though civilized in her tastes, she was a strong-minded and moral woman.

'Yes, Mary,' repeated Flora firmly, 'I am only nineteen, but I have already observed that whereas there still lingers some absurd prejudice against living on one's friends, no limits are set, either by society or by one's own conscience, to the amount one may impose upon one's relatives.

'Now I am peculiarly (I think if you could see some of them you would agree that that is the word) rich in relatives, on both sides of the family. There is a bachelor cousin of Father's in Scotland. There is a sister of Mother's at

Worthing (as though that were not enough, she breeds dogs). A female cousin of Mother's lives in Kensington. And there are also some distant cousins, connections of Mother's, I believe, who live in Sussex . . .'

'Sussex . . .' mused Mrs Smiling. 'I don't much like the sound of that. Do they live on a decaying farm?'

'I am afraid they do,' confessed Flora, reluctantly. 'However, I need not try them unless everything else fails. I propose to send a letter to the relatives I have mentioned, explaining the situation and asking them if they are willing to give me a home in exchange for my beautiful eyes and a hundred pounds a year.'

'Flora, how *insane*!' cried Mrs Smiling; 'you must be *mad*. Why, you would *die* after the first week. You know that neither of us have ever been able to *abide* relatives. You must stay here with me, and learn typing and shorthand, and then you can be somebody's secretary and have a nice little flat of your own, and we can have lovely parties . . .'

'Mary, you know I hate parties. My idea of hell is a very large party in a cold room, where everybody has to play hockey properly. But you put me off what I was going to say. When I have found a relative who is willing to have me, I shall take him or her in hand, and alter his or her character and mode of living to suit my own taste. Then, when it pleases me, I shall marry.'

'Who, pray?' demanded Mrs Smiling, rudely; she was much perturbed.

'Somebody whom I shall choose. I have definite ideas about marriage, as you know. I have always liked the sound of the phrase "a marriage has been arranged". And so it should be arranged! Is it not the most important step a mortal creature can take? I prefer the idea of arrangement to that other statement that marriages are made in Heaven.'

Mrs Smiling shuddered at the compelling, the almost Gallic, cynicism of Flora's speech. For Mrs Smiling believed that marriages should arise naturally from the union of two loving natures, and that they should take place in churches, with all the usual paraphernalia and hugaboo; and so had her own marriage arisen and been celebrated.

'But what I wanted to ask you was this,' continued Flora. 'Do you think a circular letter to all these relatives would be a good idea? Would it impress them with my efficiency?'

'No,' returned Mrs Smiling, coldly, 'I do not think it would. It would be *too* putting-off. You must write to them, of course (making it an *entirely* different letter each time, Flora), explaining the situation – that is, if you really are going to be so insane as to go on with the idea.'

'Don't fuss, Mary. I will write the letters to-morrow, before lunch. I would write them to-night, only I think we ought to dine out – don't you? – to celebrate the inauguration of my career as a parasite. I have ten pounds, and I will take you to the New River Club – angelic place!'

'Don't be silly. You know perfectly well we must have some men.'

'Then you can find them. Are any of the Pioneers-O home on leave?'

Mrs Smiling's face assumed that brooding and maternal look which was associated in the minds of her friends with thoughts of the Pioneers-O.

'Bikki is,' she said. (All the Pioneers-O had short, brusque nicknames rather like the cries of strange animals, but this was quite natural, for they all came from places full of strange animals.)

'And your second cousin, Charles Fairford, is in town,' continued Mrs Smiling. 'The tall, serious, dark one.'

'He will do,' said Flora, with approval. 'He has such a funny little nose.'

Accordingly, about twenty minutes to nine that night Mrs Smiling's car drove away from Mouse Place carrying herself and Flora in white dresses, with absurd little wreaths of flowers at the side of their heads; and opposite sat Bikki and Charles, whom Flora had only met half a dozen times before.

Bikki, who had a shocking stammer, talked a great deal, as people with stammers always love to do. He was plain and thirtyish, and home on leave from Kenya. He pleased them by corroborating all the awful rumours they had heard about the place. Charles, who looked well in tails, spoke hardly at all. Occasionally he gave a loud, deep, musical 'Ha Ha!' when amused at anything. He was twenty-three, and was to be a parson. He stared out of the window most of the time, and hardly looked at Flora.

'I don't think Sneller approves of this excursion,' observed Mrs Smiling, as they drove away. 'He looked all dim and concerned. Did you notice?'

'He approves of me, because I look serious,' said Flora. 'A straight nose is a great help if one wishes to look serious.'

'I do not wish to look serious,' said Mrs Smiling, coldly. 'There will be time enough to do that when I have to come and rescue you from some impossible relations living in some ungetatable place because you can't bear it any longer. Have you told Charles about it?'

'Good heavens, no! Charles is a relation. He might think I wanted to go and live with him and Cousin Helen in Hertfordshire, and was angling for an invitation.'

'Well, you could if you liked,' said Charles, turning from his study of the glittering streets gliding past the windows. 'There is a swing in the garden and tobacco flowers in the summer, and probably Mother and I would quite like it if you did.'

'Don't be silly,' said Mrs Smiling. 'Look – here we are. Did you get a table near the river, Bikki?'

Bikki had managed to do that; and when they were seated facing the flowers and lights on their table they could look down through the glass floor at the moving river, and watch it between their slippers, as they danced. Through the glass walls they could see the barges going past, bearing their romantic red and green lights. Outside it had begun to rain, and the glass roof was soon trickling with silver.

In the course of supper Flora told Charles of her plan. He was silent at first; and she thought he was shocked. For though Charles had not a straight nose, it might have been written of him, as Shelley wrote of himself in the Preface to *Julian and Maddalo*, 'Julian is rather serious.'

But at last he said, looking amused:

'Well, if you get very sick of it, wherever you are, phone me and I will come and rescue you in my plane.'

'Have you a plane, Charles? I don't think an embryo parson should have a plane. What breed is it?'

'A Twin Belisha Bat. Its name is Speed Cop II.'

'But, really, Charles, do you think a parson *ought* to have a plane?' continued Flora, who was in a foolish mood.

'What has that to do with it?' said Charles calmly. 'Anyway, you let me know and I will come along.'

Flora promised that she would, for she liked Charles, and then they danced together; and all four sat a long time over coffee; and then it was three o'clock and they thought it time to go home.

Charles put Flora into her green coat, and Bikki put Mrs Smiling into her black one, and soon they were driving home through the rainy streets of Lambeth, where every house had windows alight with rose, orange, or gold, behind which parties were going on, card or musical or merely frivolous; and the lit shop windows displayed a single frock or a Tang horse to the rain.

'There's the Old Diplomacy,' said Mrs Smiling interestedly as they passed that ludicrous box, with baskets of metal flowers tipping off the narrow sills of its windows, and music coming from its upper rooms. 'How glad I am that poor Tod left it to me. It *does* bring in such a lot of money.' For Mrs Smiling, like all people who have been disagreeably poor and have become deliciously rich, had never grown used to her money, and was always mentally turning it over in her hands and positively revelling in the thought of what a lot of it she had. And this delighted all her friends, who looked on with approval, just as they would have looked upon a nice child with a toy.

Charles and Bikki said good night at the door because Mrs Smiling was too afraid of Sneller to ask them in for a last cocktail, and Flora muttered that it was absurd; but all the same she felt rather subdued as the two wandered to bed up the narrow, black-carpeted staircase.

'Tomorrow I will write my letters,' said Flora, yawning, with one hand on the slender white baluster. 'Good night, Mary.'

Mrs Smiling said 'Good night, darling.' She added that to-morrow Flora would have thought better of it.

CHAPTER 2

NEVERTHELESS, Flora wrote her letters the next morning. Mrs Smiling did not help her, because she had gone down into the slums of Mayfair on the track of a new kind of brassière which she had noticed in a Jew-shop while driving past in her car. Besides, she disapproved so heartily of Flora's plan that she would have scorned to assist in the concoction of a single oily sentence.

'I think it's *degrading* of you, Flora,' cried Mrs Smiling at breakfast. 'Do you truly mean that you don't ever want to work at *anything*?'

Her friend replied after some thought:

'Well, when I am fifty-three or so I would like to write a novel as good as *Persuasion*, but with a modern setting, of course. For the next thirty years or so I shall be collecting material for it. If anyone asks me what I work at, I shall say, "Collecting material". No one can object to that. Besides, so I shall be.'

Mrs Smiling drank some coffee in silent disapproval.

'If you ask me,' continued Flora, 'I think I have much in common with Miss Austen. She liked everything to be tidy and pleasant and comfortable about her, and so do I. You see, Mary' – and here Flora began to grow earnest and to wave one finger about – 'unless everything is tidy and pleasant and comfortable all about one, people cannot even begin to enjoy life. I cannot *endure messes*.'

'Oh, neither can I,' cried Mrs Smiling, with fervour. 'If

there is one thing I do detest it is a mess. And I do think *you* are going to be messy, if you go and live with a lot of obscure relations.'

'Well, my mind is made up, so there is no purpose in arguing,' said Flora. 'After all, if I find I cannot abide Scotland or South Kensington or Sussex, I can always come back to London and gracefully give in, and learn to work, as you suggest. But I am not anxious to do that, because I am sure it would be more amusing to go and stay with some of these dire relatives. Besides, there is sure to be a lot of material I can collect for my novel; and perhaps one or two of the relations will have messes or miseries in their domestic circle which I can clear up.'

'You have the most revolting Florence Nightingale complex,' said Mrs Smiling.

'It is not that at all, and well you know it. On the whole I dislike my fellow-beings; I find them so difficult to understand. But I have a tidy mind, and untidy lives irritate me. Also, they are uncivilized.'

The introduction of this word closed, as usual, their argument, for the friends were united in their dislike of what they termed 'uncivilized behaviour': a vague phrase, which was nevertheless defined in their two minds with great precision, to their mutual satisfaction.

Mrs Smiling then went away, her face lit by that remote expression which characterizes the collector when upon the trail of a specimen; and Flora began on her letters.

The oleaginous sentences flowed easily from her pen during the next hour, for she had a great gift of the gab, and took a pride in varying the style in which each letter was written to suit the nature of its recipient.

That addressed to the aunt at Worthing was offensively jolly, yet tempered by a certain inarticulate Public School grief for her bereavement. The one to the bachelor uncle in Scotland was sweetly girlish, and just a wee bit arch; it hinted that she was only a poor little orphan. She wrote to the cousin in South Kensington a distant, dignified epistle, grieved yet business-like.

It was while she was pondering over the best style in which to address the unknown and distant relatives in Sussex that she was struck by the singularity of their address:

> *Mrs Judith Starkadder,*
> *Cold Comfort Farm,*
> *Howling, Sussex.*

But she reminded herself that Sussex, when all was said and done, was not quite like other counties, and that when one observed that these people lived on a *farm* in Sussex, the address was no longer remarkable. For things seemed to go wrong in the country more easily and much more frequently, somehow, than they did in Town, and such a tendency must naturally reflect itself in local nomenclature.

Yet she could not decide in what way to address them, so she ended (for by now it was nearly one o'clock and she was somewhat exhausted) by sending a straightforward letter explaining her position, and requesting an early reply as her plans were so unsettled, and she was anxious to know what would happen to her.

Mrs Smiling returned to Mouse Place at a quarter after the hour, and found her friend sitting back in an arm-chair with her eyes shut and the four letters, ready for the post, lying in her lap. She looked rather green.

'Flora! What is the matter? Do you feel sick? Is it your tummy again?' cried Mrs Smiling, in alarm.

'No. That is, not physically sick. Only rather nauseated by the way I have achieved these letters. Really, Mary' – she sat upright, revived by her own words – 'it is rather frightening to be able to write so revoltingly, yet so successfully. All these letters are works of art, except, perhaps the last. They are positively *oily*.'

'This afternoon,' observed Mrs Smiling, leading the way to lunch, 'I think we will go to a flick. Give Sneller those; he will post them for you.'

'No . . . I think I will post them myself,' said Flora, jealously. 'Did you get the brassière, darling?'

A shadow fell upon Mrs Smiling's face.

'No. It was no use to me. It was just a variation on the "Venus" design made by Waber Brothers in 1938; it had three elastic sections in front, instead of two, as I hoped, and I have it already in my collection. I only saw it from the car as I drove past, you know; I was misled by the way it was folded as it hung in the window. The third section was folded back, so that it looked as though there were only two.'

'And would that have made it more rare?'

'But, *naturally*, Flora. Two-section brassières are *extremely* rare: I intended to buy it – but, of course, it was useless.'

'Never mind, my dove. Look – nice hock. Drink it up and you'll feel more cheerful.'

That afternoon, before they went to the Rhodopis, the great cinema in Westminster, Flora posted her letters.

When the morning of the second day brought no reply to any of the letters, Mrs Smiling expressed the hope that none of the relatives were going to answer. She said:

'And I only pray that if any of them *do* answer, it won't be those people in Sussex. I think the names are awful: *too ageing* and putting-off.'

Flora agreed that the names were certainly not propitious.

'I think if I find that I have any third cousins living at Cold Comfort Farm (young ones, you know, children of Cousin Judith) who are named Seth, or Reuben, I shall decide not to go.'

'Why?'

'Oh, because highly sexed young men living on farms are always called Seth or Reuben, and it would be such a nuisance. And my cousin's name, remember, is Judith. That in itself is most ominous. Her husband is almost certain to be called Amos; and if he *is*, it will be a typical farm, and you know what *they* are like.'

Mrs Smiling said sombrely:

'I hope there will be a bathroom.'

'Nonsense, Mary!' cried Flora, paling. 'Of course there will be a bathroom. Even in Sussex – it would be too much . . .

'Well, we shall see,' said her friend. 'And mind you wire me (if you do hear from them and do decide to go there) if either of your cousins is called Seth or Reuben, or if you want any extra boots or anything. There are sure to be masses of mud.'

Flora said that she would.

Mrs Smiling's hopes were dashed. On the third morning, which was a Friday, four letters came to Mouse Place for Flora, including one in the cheapest kind of yellow envelope, addressed in so barbed and illiterate a hand that the postman had some difficulty in deciphering it. The envelope was also dirty. The postmark was 'Howling'.

'There you are, you see!' said Mrs Smiling, when Flora showed her this treasure at breakfast. 'How revolting!'

'Well, wait now while I read the others and we will save this one till the last. Do be quiet. I want to see what Aunt Gwen has to say.'

Aunt Gwen, after sympathizing with Flora in her sorrow, and reminding her that we must keep a stiff upper lip and play the game ('Always these games!' muttered Flora), said that she would be delighted to have her niece. Flora would be coming into a real 'homey' atmosphere, with plenty of fun. She would not mind giving a hand with the dogs sometimes? The air of Worthing was bracing, and there were some jolly young people living next door. 'Rosedale' was always full of people, and Flora would never have time to be lonely. Peggy, who was so keen on her Guiding, would love to share her bedroom with Flora.

Shuddering slightly, Flora passed the letter to Mrs Smiling; but that upright woman failed her by saying stoutly, after reading it, 'Well, I think it's a very kind letter. You couldn't *ask* for anything kinder. After all, you didn't think any of these people would offer you the kind of home you *want* to live in, did you?'

'I cannot share a bedroom,' said Flora, 'so that disposes of Aunt Gwen. This one is from Mr McKnag, Father's cousin in Perthshire.'

Mr McKnag had been shocked by Flora's letter: so shocked that his old trouble had returned, and he had been in bed with it for the last two days. This explained, and he trusted that it excused, his delay, in replying to her suggestion. He would, of course, be delighted to shelter Flora under his roof for as long as she cared to fold the white wings of her girlhood there ('The old *lamb*!' crowed Flora and Mrs Smiling), but he feared it would be a little dull for Flora, with no company save that of himself – and he was often in bed with his old trouble – his man, Hoots, and the housekeeper, who was elderly and somewhat deaf. The house was seven miles from the nearest village; that, also, might be a disadvantage. On the other hand, if Flora was fond of birds, there was some most interesting bird-life to be observed in the marshes which surrounded the house on three sides. He must end his letter now, he feared, as he felt his old trouble coming on again, and he was hers affectionately.

Flora and Mrs Smiling looked at one another, and shook their heads.

'There you are, you see,' said Mrs Smiling, once more. 'They are all quite hopeless. You had much better stay here with me and learn how to work.'

But Flora was reading the third letter. Her mother's cousin in South Kensington said that she would be very pleased to have Flora, only there was a little difficulty about the *bedroom*. Perhaps Flora would not mind using the large attic, which was now used as a meeting-room for the Orient-Star-in-the-West Society on Tuesdays, and for the Spiritist Investigators' League on Fridays. She hoped that Flora was not a *sceptic*, for manifestations sometimes occurred in the attic, and even a trace of scepticism in the atmosphere of the room spoiled the conditions, and prevented phenomena, the observations of which provided the Society with such valuable evidence in favour of Survival. Would Flora mind if the parrot kept his corner of the attic? He had grown up in it, and at his age the shock of removal to another room might well prove fatal.

'Again, you see, it means sharing a bedroom,' said Flora. 'I do not object to the phenomena, but I do object to the parrot.'

'*Do* open the Howling one,' begged Mrs Smiling, coming round to Flora's side of the table.

The last letter was writen upon cheap lined paper, in a bold but illiterate hand:

Dear Niece,

So you are after your rights at last. Well, I have expected to hear from Robert Poste's child these last twenty years.

Child, my man once did your father a great wrong. If you will come to us I will do my best to atone, but you must never ask me what for. My lips are sealed.

We are not like other folk, maybe, but there have always been Starkadders at Cold Comfort, and we will do our best to welcome Robert Poste's child.

Child, child, if you come to this doomed house, what is to save you? Perhaps you may be able to help us when our hour comes.

Yr. affec. Aunt,

J. STARKADDER

Flora and Mrs Smiling were much excited by this unusual epistle. They agreed that at least it had the negative merit of keeping silence upon the subject of sleeping arrangements.

'And there is nothing about spying on birds in marshes or anything of that kind,' said Mrs Smiling. 'Oh, I do wonder what it was her man did to your father. Did you ever hear him say anything about a Mr Starkadder?'

'Never. The Starkadders are only connected with us by marriage. This Judith is a daughter of Mother's eldest sister, Ada Doom. So, you see, Judith is really my cousin, not my aunt. (I suppose she got muddled, and I'm sure I'm not surprised. The conditions under which she seems to live are probably conducive to muddle.) Well, Aunt Ada Doom was always rather a misery, and Mother couldn't abide her because she really loved the country and wore artistic hats. She ended by marrying a Sussex farmer. I suppose his name was Starkadder. Perhaps the farm belongs to Judith now,

26

and her man was carried off in a tribal raid from a neighbouring village, and he had to take her name. Or perhaps she married a Starkadder. I wonder what has happened to Aunt Ada? She would be quite old now; she was fifteen years or so older than Mother.'

'Did you ever meet her?'

'No, I am happy to say. I have never met any of them. I found their address in a list in Mother's diary; she used to send them cards every Christmas.'

'Well,' said Mrs Smiling, 'it sounds an appalling place, but in a different way from all the others. I mean, it does sound *interesting* and appalling, while the others just sound appalling. If you have really made up your mind to go, and if you will not stay here with me, I think you had best go to Sussex. You will soon grow tired of it, anyhow, and then, when you have tried it out and seen what it is really like to live with relatives, you will be all ready to come sensibly back here and learn how to work.'

Flora thought it wiser to ignore the last part of this speech.

'Yes, I think I will go to Sussex, Mary. I am anxious to see what Cousin Judith means by "rights". Oh, do you think she means some money? Or perhaps a little house? I should like that even better. Anyway, I shall find out when I get there. And when do you think I had better go? To-day is Friday. Suppose I go down on Tuesday, after lunch?'

'Well, surely you needn't go quite so soon. After all, there is no hurry. Probably you will not be there for longer than three days, so what does it matter when you go? You're all eager about it, aren't you?'

'I want my rights,' said Flora. 'Probably they are something too useless, like a lot of used-up mortgages; but if they are mine I am going to have them. Now you go away, Mary, because I am going to write to all these good souls, and that will take time.'

Flora had never been able to understand how railway time-tables worked, and she was too conceited to ask Mrs Smiling or Sneller about trains to Howling. So in her letter she asked her cousin Judith if she would just mention a few trains to Howling, and what time they got in, and who would meet her, and how.

It was true that in novels dealing with agricultural life no one ever did anything so courteous as to meet a train, unless it was with the object of cutting-in under the noses of the other members of the family with some sordid or passionate end in view; but that was no reason why the Starkadders, at least, should not begin to form civilized habits. So she wrote firmly: 'Do let me know what trains there are to Howling, and which ones you will meet,' and sealed her letter with a feeling of satisfaction. Sneller posted it in time for the country collection that evening.

Mrs Smiling and Flora passed their time pleasantly during the next two days.

In the morning they went ice-skating at the Rover Park Ice Club with Charles and Bikki and another of the Pioneers-O whose nickname was Swooth and who came from Tanganyika. Though he and Bikki were extremely jealous of one another, and in consequence suffered horrid torments, Mrs Smiling had them both so well in hand that they did not dare to look miserable, but listened seriously while she told them, each in his turn, as they glided round the rink holding her hands, how distressed she was about yet a third of the Pioneers-O named Goofi, who was on his way to China and from whom she had not heard for ten days.

'I'm afraid the poor child may be worrying,' Mrs Smiling would say, vaguely, which was her way of indicating that Goofi had probably committed suicide, out of the depths of unrequited passion. And Bikki or Swooth, knowing from their own experience that this was indeed probably the case, would respond cheerfully, 'Oh, I shouldn't fret, if I were you, Mary,' and feel happier at the thought of Goofi's sufferings.

In the afternoons the five went flying or to the Zoo or to hear music; and in the evenings they went to parties; that is, Mrs Smiling and the two Pioneers-O went to the parties, where yet more young men fell in love with Mrs Smiling, and Flora, who, as we know, loathed parties, dined quietly with intelligent men: a way of passing the evening which she adored, because then she could show-off a lot and talk about herself.

No letter had come by Monday evening at tea-time; and Flora had thought that her departure would probably have to be postponed until Wednesday. But the last post brought her a limp postcard; and she was reading it at half past ten on her return from one of the showing-off dinners when Mrs Smiling came in, having wearied of a nasty party she had been attending.

'Does it give the times of the trains, my dove?' asked Mrs Smiling. 'It *is* dirty, isn't it? I can't help rather wishing it were possible for the Starkadders to send a clean letter.'

'It says nothing about trains,' replied Flora with reserve. 'So far as I can make out, it appears to be some verses, with which I must confess I am not familiar, from the Old Testament. There is also a repetition of the assurance that there have always been Starkadders at Cold Comfort, though why it should be necessary to impress this upon me I am at a loss to imagine.'

'Oh, do not say it is signed Seth or Reuben,' cried Mrs Smiling, fearfully.

'It is not signed at all. I gather that it is from some member of the family who does not welcome the prospect of my visit. I can distinguish a reference, among other things, to vipers. I must say that I think it would have been more to the point to give a list of the trains; but I suppose it is a little illogical to expect such attention to petty details from a doomed family living in Sussex. Well, Mary, I shall go down to-morrow, after lunch, as I planned. I will wire them in the morning to say I am coming.'

'Shall you fly?'

'No. There is no landing-stage nearer than Brighton. Besides, I must save money. You and Sneller can work out a route for me; you will enjoy fussing over that.'

'Of course, darling,' said Mrs Smiling, who was by now

beginning to feel a little unhappy at the prospect of losing her friend. 'But I wish you would not go.'

Flora put the post card in the fire; her determination remained unmoved.

The next morning Mrs Smiling looked up trains to Howling, while Flora superintended the packing of her trunks by Riante, Mrs Smiling's maid.

Even Mrs Smiling could not find much comfort in the time-table. It seemed to her even more confused than usual. Indeed, since the aerial routes and the well-organized road routes had appropriated three-quarters of the passengers who used to make their journeys by train, the remaining railway companies had fallen into a settled melancholy; an idle and repining despair invaded their literature, and its influence was noticeable even in their time-tables.

There was a train which left London Bridge at half past one for Howling. It was a slow train. It reached Godmere at three o'clock. At Godmere the traveller changed into another train. It was a slow train. It reached Beershorn at six o'clock. At Beershorn this train stopped; and there was no more idle chatter of the arrival and departure of trains. Only the simple sentence 'Howling (see Beershorn)' mocked, in its self-sufficing entity, the traveller.

So Flora decided to go to Beershorn, and try her luck.

'I expect Seth will meet you in a jaunting-car,' said Mrs Smiling, as they sat at an early lunch.

Their spirits were rather low by this time; and to look out of the window at Lambeth, where the gay little houses were washed by pale sunshine, and to think that she was to exchange the company of Mrs Smiling, and flying and showing-off dinners, for the rigours of Cold Comfort and the grossnesses of the Starkadders did not make Flora more cheerful.

She snapped at poor Mrs Smiling.

'One does not have jaunting-cars in England, Mary. Do you never read *anything* but "Haussman-Haffnitz on Brassières"? Jaunting-cars are indigenous to Ireland. If Seth meets me at all, it will be in a wagon or a buggy.'

'Well, I do hope he won't be called Seth,' said Mrs Smiling, earnestly. 'If he *is*, Flora, mind you wire me at once, and about gum-boots, too.'

Flora had risen, for the car was at the door, and was adjusting her hat upon her dark gold hair. 'I will wire, but do not see what good it will do,' she said.

She was feeling downright morbid, and her sensations were unpleasingly complicated by the knowledge that it was entirely due to her own obstinacy that she was setting out at all upon this absurd and disagreeable pilgrimage.

'Oh, but it will, because then I can send things.'

'What things?'

'Oh, proper clothes and cheerful fashion papers.'

'Is Charles coming to the station?' asked Flora, as they took their seats in the car.

'He said he might. Why?'

'Oh – I don't know. He rather amuses me, and I quite like him.'

The journey through Lambeth was unmarked by any incident, save that Flora pointed out to Mrs Smiling that a flower-shop named Orchidaceous, Ltd, had been opened upon the site of the old police-station in Caroline Place.

Then the car drew into London Bridge Yard; and there was Flora's train, and Charles carrying a bunch of flowers and Bikki and Swooth looking pleased because Flora was going away and Mrs Smiling (so they feverishly hoped) would have more time to spend in their company.

'Curious how Love destroys every vestige of that politeness which the human race, in its years of evolution, has so painfully acquired,' reflected Flora, as she leaned out of the carriage window and observed the faces of Bikki and Swooth. 'Shall I tell them that Mig is expected home from Ontario to-morrow? No, I think not. It would be downright sadistic.'

'Good-bye, darling!' cried Mrs Smiling, as the train began to move.

'Good-bye,' said Charles, putting his daffodils, which he had forgotten until that moment, into Flora's hands. 'Don't forget to phone me if it gets too much for you, and I will come and take you away in Speed Cop II.'

'I won't forget, Charles dear. Thank you very much – though I am quite sure I shall find it very amusing and not at all too much for me.'

'Good-bye,' cried Bikki and Swooth, falsely composing their faces into some semblance of regret.

'Good-bye. Don't forget to feed the parrot!' shrieked Flora, who disliked this prolongation of the ceremony of saying farewell, as every civilized traveller must.

'What parrot?' they all shrieked back from the fast-receding platform, just as they were meant to do.

But it was too much trouble to reply. Flora contented herself with muttering, 'Oh, any parrot, bless you all,' and with a final affectionate wave of her hand to Mrs Smiling, she drew back into the carriage and, opening a fashion journal, composed herself for the journey.

CHAPTER 3

**DAWN crept over the Downs like a sinister white animal, followed by the snarling cries of a wind eating its way between the black boughs of the thorns. The wind was the furious voice of this sluggish animal light that was baring the dormers and mullions and scullions of Cold Comfort Farm.

The farm was crouched on a bleak hill-side, whence its fields, fanged with flints, dropped steeply to the village of Howling a mile away. Its stables and out-houses were built in the shape of a rough octangle surrounding the farm-house itself, which was built in the shape of a rough triangle. The left point of the triangle abutted on the farthest point of the octangle, which was formed by the cowsheds, which lay parallel with the big barn. The out-houses were built of rough-cast stone, with thatched roofs, while the farm itself was partly built of local flint, set in cement, and partly of some stone brought at great trouble and enormous expense from Perthshire.

The farm-house was a long, low building, two-storied in parts. Other parts of it were three-storied. Edward the Sixth had originally owned it in the form of a shed in which he housed his swineherds, but he had grown tired of it, and had it rebuilt in Sussex clay. Then he pulled it down. Elizabeth had rebuilt it, with a good many chimneys in one way and another. The Charleses had let it alone; but William and Mary had pulled it down again, and George the First had rebuilt it. George the Second, however, burned it down. George the Third added another wing. George the Fourth pulled it down again.

By the time England began to develop that magnificent blossoming of trade and imperial expansion which fell to her lot under Victoria, there was not much of the original building left, save the tradition that it had always been there. It crouched, like a beast about to spring, under the bulk of Mockuncle Hill. Like ghosts embedded in brick and stone, the architectural variations of each period through which it had passed were mute history. It was known locally as 'The King's Whim'.

The front door of the farm faced a perfectly inaccessible ploughed field at the back of the house; it had been the whim of Red Raleigh Starkadder, in 1835, to have it so; and so the family always used to come in by the back door, which abutted on the general yard facing the cowsheds. A long corridor ran half-way through the house on the second story and then stopped. One could not get into the attics at all. It was all very awkward.

... Growing with the viscous light that was invading the sky, there came the solemn, tortured-snake voice of the sea, two miles away, falling in sharp folds upon the mirror-expanses of the beach.

Under the ominous bowl of the sky a man was ploughing the sloping field immediately below the farm, where the flints shone bone-sharp and white in the growing light. The ice-cascade of the wind leaped over him, as he guided the

33

plough over the flinty runnels. Now and again he called roughly to his team:

'Upidee, Travail! Ho, there, Arsenic! Jug-jug!' But for the most part he worked in silence, and silent were his team. The light showed no more of his face than a grey expanse of flesh, expressionless as the land he ploughed, from which looked out two sluggish eyes.

Every now and again, when he came to the corner of the field and was forced to tilt the scranlet of his plough almost on to its axle to make the turn, he glanced up at the farm where it squatted on the gaunt shoulder of the hill, and something like a possessive gleam shone in his dull eyes. But he only turned his team again, watching the crooked passage of the scranlet through the yeasty earth, and muttered: 'Hola, Arsenic! Belay there, Travail!' while the bitter light waned into full day.

Because of the peculiar formation of the out-houses surrounding the farm, the light was always longer in reaching the yard than the rest of the house. Long after the sunlight was shining through the cobwebs on the uppermost windows of the old house the yard was in damp blue shadow.

It was in shadow now, but sharp gleams sprang from the ranged milk-buckets along the ford-piece outside the cowshed.

Leaving the house by the back door, you came up sharply against a stone wall running right across the yard, and turning abruptly, at right angles, just before it reached the shed where the bull was housed, and running down to the gate leading out into the ragged garden where mallows, dog's-body, and wild turnip were running riot. The bull's shed abutted upon the right corner of the dairy, which faced the cowsheds. The cowsheds faced the house, but the back-door faced the bull's shed. From here a long-roofed barn extended the whole length of the octangle until it reached the front door of the house. Here it took a quick turn, and ended. The dairy was awkwardly placed; it had been a thorn in the side of old Fig Starkadder, the last owner of

34

the farm, who had died three years ago. The dairy over-looked the front door, in face of the extreme point of its triangle which formed the ancient buildings of the farm-house.

From the dairy a wall extended which formed the right-hand boundary of the octangle, joining the bull's shed and the pig-pens at the extreme end of the right point of the triangle. A staircase, put in to make it more difficult, ran parallel with the octangle, half-way round the yard, against the wall which led down to the garden gate.

The spurt and regular ping! of milk against metal came from the reeking interior of the sheds. The bucket was pressed between Adam Lambsbreath's knees, and his head was pressed deep into the flank of Feckless, the big Jersey. His gnarled hands mechanically stroked the teat, while a low crooning, mindless as the Down wind itself, came from his lips.

He was asleep. He had been awake all night, wandering in thought over the indifferent bare shoulders of the Downs after his wild bird, his little flower ...

Elfine. The name, unspoken but sharply musical as a glittering bead shaken from a fountain's tossing necklace, hovered audibly in the rancid air of the shed.

The beasts stood with heads lowered dejectedly against the wooden hoot-pieces of their stalls. Graceless, Pointless, Feckless, and Aimless awaited their turn to be milked. Some-times Aimless ran her dry tongue, with a rasping sound sharp as a file through silk, awkwardly across the bony flank of Feckless, which was still moist with the rain that had fallen upon it through the roof during the night, or Pointless turned her large dull eyes sideways as she swung her head upwards to tear down a mouthful of cobwebs from the wooden runnet above her head. A lowering, moist, steamy light, almost like that which gleams below the eyelids of a man in fever, filled the cowshed.

Suddenly a tortured bellow, a blaring welter of sound that shattered the quiescence of the morning, tore its way across the yard and died away in a croak that was almost a sob. It was Big Business, the bull, wakening to another day, in the clammy darkness of his cell.

The sound woke Adam. He lifted his head from the flank of Feckless and looked around him in bewilderment for a moment; then slowly his eyes, which looked small and wet and lifeless in his primitive face, lost their terror as he realized that he was in the cowshed, that it was half-past six on a winter morning, and that his gnarled fingers were about the task which they had performed at this hour and in this place for the past eighty years or more.

He stood up, sighing, and crossed over to Pointless, who was eating Graceless's tail. Adam, who was linked to all dumb brutes by a chain forged in soil and sweat, took it out of her mouth and put into it, instead, his neckerchief – the last he had. She mumbled it, while he milked her, but stealthily spat it out as soon as he passed on to Aimless, and concealed it under the reeking straw with her hoof. She did not want to hurt the old man's feelings by declining to eat his gift. There was a close bond: a slow, deep, primitive, silent down-dragging link between Adam and all living beasts; they knew each other's simple needs. They lay close to the earth, and something of earth's old fierce simplicities had seeped into their beings.

Suddenly a shadow fell athwart the wooden stanchions of the door. It was no more than a darkening of the pallid paws of the day which were now embracing the shed, but all the cows instinctively stiffened, and Adam's eyes, as he stood up to face the new-comer, were again piteously full of twisted fear.

'Adam,' uttered the woman who stood in the doorway, 'how many pails of milk will there be this morning?'

'I dunnamany,' responded Adam, cringingly; ''tes hard to tell. If so be as our Pointless has got over her indigestion, maybe 'twill be four. If so be as she hain't, maybe three.'

Judith Starkadder made an impatient movement. Her large hands had a quality which made them seem to sketch vast horizons with their slightest gesture. She looked a woman without boundaries as she stood wrapped in a crimson shawl to protect her bitter, magnificent shoulders from the splintery cold of the early air. She seemed fitted for any stage, however enormous.

'Well, get as many buckets as you can,' she said, lifelessly, half-turning away. 'Mrs Starkadder questioned me about the milk yesterday. She has been comparing our output with that from other farms in the district, and she says we are five-sixteenths of a bucket below what our rate should be, considering how many cows we have.'

A strange film passed over Adam's eyes, giving him the lifeless primeval look that a lizard has, basking in the swooning Southern heat. But he said nothing.

'And another thing,' continued Judith, 'you will probably have to drive down into Beershorn to-night to meet a train. Robert Poste's child is coming to stay with us for a while. I expect to hear some time this morning what time she is arriving. I will tell you later about it.'

Adam shrank back against the gangrened flank of Pointless.

'Mun I?' he asked piteously. 'Mun I, Miss Judith? Oh, dunna send me. How can I look into her liddle flower-face, and me knowin' what I know? Oh, Miss Judith, I beg of 'ee not to send me. Besides,' he added, more practically, ' 'tes close on sixty-five years since I put hands to a pair of reins, and I might upset the maidy.'

Judith, who had slowly turned from him while he was speaking, was now half-way across the yard. She turned her head to reply to him with a slow, graceful movement. Her deep voice clanged like a bell in the frosty air:

'No, you must go, Adam. You must forget what you know – as we all must, while she is here. As for the driving, you had best harness Viper to the trap, and drive down into Howling and back six times this afternoon, to get your hand in again.'

'Could not Master Seth go instead o' me?'

Emotion shook the frozen grief of her face. She said low and sharp:

'You remember what happened when he went to meet the new kitchenmaid . . . No. You must go.'

Adam's eyes, like blind pools of water in his primitive face, suddenly grew cunning. He turned back to Aimless and resumed his mechanical stroking of the teat, saying in a sing-song rhythm:

'Ay, then I'll go, Miss Judith. I dunnamany times I've thought as how this day might come . . . And now I mun go to bring Robert Poste's child back to Cold Comfort. Aye, 'tes strange. The seed to the flower, the flower to the fruit, the fruit to the belly. Aye, so 'twill go.'

Judith had crossed the muck and rabble of the yard, and now entered the house by the back door.

In the large kitchen, which occupied most of the middle of the house, a sullen fire burned, the smoke of which wavered up the blackened walls and over the deal table, darkened by age and dirt, which was roughly set for a meal. A snood full of coarse porridge hung over the fire, and standing with one arm resting upon the high mantel, looking moodily down into the heaving contents of the snood, was a tall young man whose riding-boots were splashed with mud to the thigh, and whose coarse linen shirt was open to his waist. The firelight lit up his diaphragm muscles as they heaved slowly in rough rhythm with the porridge.

He looked up as Judith entered, and gave a short, defiant laugh, but said nothing. Judith crossed slowly over until she stood by his side. She was as tall as he. They stood in silence, she staring at him, and he down into the secret crevasses of the porridge.

'Well, mother mine,' he said at last, 'here I am, you see. I said I would be in time for breakfast, and I have kept my word.'

His voice had a low, throaty, animal quality, a sneering warmth that wound a velvet ribbon of sexuality over the outward coarseness of the man.

Judith's breath came in long shudders. She thrust her arms deeper into her shawl. The porridge gave an ominous leering heave; it might almost have been endowed with life, so uncannily did its movements keep pace with the human passions that throbbed above it.

'Cur,' said Judith, levelly, at last. 'Coward! Liar! Libertine! Who were you with last night? Moll at the mill or Violet at the vicarage? Or Ivy, perhaps, at the ironmongery? Seth – my son ...' Her deep, dry voice quivered, but she whipped it back, and her next words flew out at him like a lash.

'Do you want to break my heart?'

'Yes,' said Seth, with an elemental simplicity.

The porridge boiled over.

Judith knelt, and hastily and absently ladled it off the floor back into the snood, biting back her tears. While she was thus engaged, there was a confused blur of voices and boots in the yard outside. The men were coming in to breakfast.

The meal for the men was set on a long trestle at the farther end of the kitchen, as far away from the fire as possible. They came into the room in awkward little clumps, eleven of them. Five were distant cousins of the Starkadders, and two others were half-brothers of Amos, Judith's husband. This left only four men who were not in some way connected with the family; so it will readily be understood that the general feeling among the farm-hands was not exactly one of hilarity. Mark Dolour, one of the four, had been heard to remark: 'Happen it had been another kind o' eleven, us might ha' had a cricket team, wi' me for umpire. As ut is, 'twould be more befittin' if we was to hire oursen out for carrying coffins at sixpence a mile.'

The five half-cousins and the two half-brothers came over to the table, for they took their meals with the family. Amos liked to have his kith about him, though, of course, he never said so or cheered up when they were.

A strong family likeness wavered in and out of the fierce, earth-reddened faces of the seven, like a capricious light. Micah Starkadder, mightiest of the cousins, was a ruined giant of a man, paralysed in one knee and wrist. His nephew, Urk, was a little, red, hard-bitten man with foxy ears. Urk's brother, Ezra, was of the same physical type, but horsy where Urk was foxy. Caraway, a silent man, wind-shaven and lean, with long wandering fingers, had some of Seth's animal grace, and this had been passed on to his son, Harkaway, a young, silent, nervous man given to bursts of fury about very little, when you came to sift matters.

Amos's half-brothers, Luke and Mark, were thickly built and high-featured; gross, silent men with an eye to the bed and the board.

When all were seated two shadows darkened the sharp, cold light pouring in through the door. They were no more than a growing imminence of humanity, but the porridge boiled over again.

Amos Starkadder and his eldest son, Reuben, came into the kitchen.

Amos, who was even larger and more of a wreck than Micah, silently put his pruning-snoot and reaping-hook in a corner by the fender, while Reuben put the scranlet with which he had been ploughing down beside them.

The two men took their places in silence, and after Amos had muttered a long and fervent grace, the meal was eaten in silence. Seth sat moodily tying and untying a green scarf round the magnificent throat he had inherited from Judith; he did not touch his porridge, and Judith only made a pretence of eating hers, playing with her spoon, patting the porridge up and down and idly building castles with the burnt bits. Her eyes burned under their penthouses, sometimes straying towards Seth as he sat sprawling in the lusty pride of casual manhood, with a good many buttons and tapes undone. Then those same eyes, dark as prisoned kingcobras, would slide round until they rested upon the bitter white head and raddled red neck of Amos, her husband, and then, like praying mantises, they would retreat between their lids. Secrecy pouted her full mouth.

Suddenly Amos, looking up from his food, asked abruptly: 'Where's Elfine?'

'She is not up yet. I did not wake her. She hinders more than she helps o' mornings,' replied Judith.

Amos grunted.

"'Tes a godless habit to lie abed of a working day, and the reeking red pits of the Lord's eternal wrathy fires lie in wait for them as do so. Aye' – his blue blazing eyes swivelled round and rested upon Seth, who was stealthily looking at a packet of Parisian art pictures under the table – 'aye, and for those who break the seventh commandment, too. And for those' – the eye rested on Reuben, who was hopefully studying his parent's apoplectic countenance – 'for those as waits for dead men's shoes.'

'Nay, Amos, lad – ' remonstrated Micah, heavily.

'Hold your peace,' thundered Amos; and Micah, though a fierce tremor rushed through his mighty form, held it.

When the meal was done the hands trooped out to get on with the day's work of harvesting the swedes. This harvest was now in full swing; it took a long time and was very difficult to do. The Starkadders, too, rose and went out into the thin rain which had begun to fall. They were engaged in digging a well beside the dairy; it had been started a year ago, but it was taking a long time to do because things kept on going wrong. Once – a terrible day, when Nature seemed to hold her breath, and release it again in a furious gale of wind – Harkaway had fallen into it. Once Urk had pushed Caraway down it. Still, it was nearly finished; and everybody felt that it would not be long now.

In the middle of the morning a wire came from London announcing that the expected visitor would arrive by the six o'clock train.

Judith received it alone. Long after she had read it she stood motionless, the rain driving through the open door against her crimson shawl. Then slowly, with dragging steps, she mounted the staircase which led to the upper part of the house. Over her shoulder she said to old Adam, who had come into the room to do the washing up:

'Robert Poste's child will be here by the six o'clock train at Beershorn. You must leave to meet it at five. I am going up to tell Mrs Starkadder that she is coming to-day.'

Adam did not reply, and Seth, sitting by the fire, was growing tired of looking at his postcards, which were a

41

three-year-old gift from the vicar's son, with whom he occasionally went poaching. He knew them all by now. Meriam, the hired girl, would not be in until after dinner. When she came, she would avoid his eyes, and tremble and weep.

He laughed insolently, triumphantly. Undoing another button of his shirt, he lounged out across the yard to the shed where Big Business, the bull, was imprisoned in darkness.

Laughing softly, Seth struck the door of the shed.

And as though answering the deep call of male to male, the bull uttered a loud tortured bellow that rose undefeated through the dead sky that brooded over the farm.

Seth undid yet another button, and lounged away.

Adam Lambsbreath, alone in the kitchen, stood looking down unseeingly at the dirtied plates, which it was his task to wash, for the hired girl, Meriam, would not be here until after dinner, and when she came she would be all but useless. Her hour was near at hand, as all Howling knew. Was it not February, and the earth a-teem with newing life? A grin twisted Adam's writhen lips. He gathered up the plates one by one and carried them to the pump, which stood in a corner of the kitchen, above a stone sink. Her hour was nigh. And when April like an over-lustful lover leaped upon the lush flanks of the Downs there would be yet another child in the wretched hut down at Nettle Flitch Field, where Meriam housed the fruits of her shame.

'Aye, dog's-fennel or beard's-crow, by their fruits they shall be betrayed,' muttered Adam, shooting a stream of cold water over the coagulated plates. 'Come cloud, come sun, 'tes ay so.'

While he was listlessly dabbing at the crusted edges of the porridge-plates with a thorn twig, a soft step descended the stairs outside the door which closed off the staircase from the kitchen. Someone paused on the threshold.

The step was light as thistledown. If Adam had not had the rush of the running water in his ears too loudly for him to be able to hear any other noise, he might have thought this delicate, hesitant step was the beating of his own blood.

But, suddenly, something like a kingfisher streaked across the kitchen, in a glimmer of green skirts and flying gold hair and the chime of a laugh was followed a second later by the slam of the gate leading through the starveling garden out on to the Downs.

Adam flung round violently on hearing the sound, dropping his thorn twig and breaking two plates.

'Elfine ... my little bird,' he whispered, starting towards the open door.

A brittle silence mocked his whisper; through it wound the rank odours of rattan and barn.

'My pharisee ... my cowdling ...' he whispered, piteously. His eyes had again that look as of waste grey pools, sightless primeval wastes reflecting the wan evening sky in some lonely marsh, as they wandered about the kitchen.

His hands fell slackly against his sides, and he dropped another plate. It broke.

He sighed, and began to move slowly towards the open door, his task forgotten. His eyes were fixed upon the cowshed.

'Aye, the beasts ...' he muttered, dully; 'the dumb beasts never fail a man. They know. Aye, I'd 'a' done better to cowdle our Feckless in my bosom than liddle Elfine. Aye, wild as a marsh-tigget in May, 'tes. And a will never listen to a word from anyone. Well, so 't must be. Sour or sweet, by barn or bye, so 'twill go. Ah, but if he' – the blind grey pools grew suddenly terrible, as though a storm were blowing in across the marsh from the Atlantic wastes – 'if he but harms a hair o' her little goldy head I'll *kill* un.'

So muttering, he crossed the yard and entered the cowshed, where he untied the beasts from their hoot-pieces and drove them across the yard, down the muddy rutted lane that led to Nettle Flitch Field. He was enmeshed in his grief. He did not notice that Graceless's leg had come off and that she was managing as best she could with three.

Left alone, the kitchen fire went out.

43

THE timeless leaden day merged imperceptibly towards eve. After the rude midday meal Adam was bid by Judith to put Viper, the vicious gelding, between the shafts of the buggy and drive backwards and forwards to Howling six times to revive his knowledge of the art of managing a horse. His attempt to stave off this event by having a fit during the rude meal was unfortunately robbed of its full effect by the collapse of Meriam, the hired girl, while in the act of passing a dish of greens to Seth.

Her hour had come upon her rather sooner than was anticipated, and in the ensuing scene Adam's fit, which he had staged in the cowshed out of regard for his personal comfort and safety, passed almost unnoticed except as a sort of Greek chorus to the main drama.

Adam was therefore left without any excuse, and spent the afternoon driving backwards and forwards between Howling and the farm, much to the indignation of the Starkadders, who could see him from their position at the side of the well they were supposed to be getting on with; they thought he was an idle old man, and said as much.

'How shall I know the maidy?' pleaded Adam of Judith, as they stood together while he lit the lantern hanging on the side of the buggy. Its dim flame flowered up slowly under the vast, uncaring bowl of the darkening sky, and hung heavily, like a brooding corpse-light, in the windless dusk. 'Robert Poste was ay like a bullock: a great moitherin' man, ay playin' wi' batses and ballses. Do 'ee think his maid will be like him?'

'There are not so many passengers as all that at Beershorn,' replied Judith, impatiently. 'Wait until everybody has left the station. Robert Poste's child will be the last; she will wait to see if there is anyone to meet her. Be off wi' you,' and she struck the gelding upon his hocks.

The great beast bounded forward into the gloom before

Adam could check him. They were gone. Darkness fell, a clouded bell of dark glass, eclipsing the soggy landscape.

By the time the buggy reached Beershorn, which was a good seven miles from Howling, Adam had forgotten what he was going there for. The reins lay between his knotted fingers, and his face, unseeing, was lifted to the dark sky.

***From the stubborn interwoven strata of his subconscious, thought seeped up into his dim conscious; not as an integral part of that consciousness, but more as an impalpable emanation, a crepuscular addition, from the unsleeping life in the restless trees and fields surrounding him. The country for miles, under the blanket of the dark which brought no peace, was in its annual tortured ferment of spring growth; worm jarred with worm and seed with seed. Frond leapt on root and hare on hare. Beetle and finch-fly were not spared. The trout-sperm in the muddy hollow under Nettle Flitch Weir were agitated, and well they might be. The long screams of the hunting owls tore across the night, scarlet lines on black. In the pauses, every ten minutes, they mated. It seemed chaotic, but it was more methodically arranged than you might think. But Adam's deafness and blindness came from within, as well as without; earthly calm seeped up from his subconscious and met descending calm in his conscious. Twice the buggy was pulled out of hedges by a passing farm-hand, and once narrowly shaved the vicar, driving home from tea at the Hall.

'Where are you, my birdling?' Adam's blind lips asked the unanswering darkness and the loutish shapes of the unbudded trees. 'Did I cowdle thee as a mommet for this?'

He knew that Elfine was out on the Downs, striding on her unsteady colt's legs towards the Hall and the bright, sardonic hands of Richard Hawk-Monitor. Adam's mind played uneasily, in bewildered pain, with the vision of his nursling between those casual fingers ...

But the buggy reached Beershorn at last, and safely: there was only one road, and that led to the station.

Adam pulled Viper up on his haunches just as the great

45

gelding was about to canter through the entrance to the booking-hall, and knotted the reins on the rennet-post near the horse-trough.

Then animation fell from him, a sucked straw. His body sank into the immemorial posture of a man thought-whelmed. He was a tree-trunk; a toad on a stone; a pie-thatched owl on a bough. Humanity left him abruptly.

For some time he brooded, but time conveyed to him nothing of itself. It spun endlessly upon a bright point in space, repeating the names of Elfine and Richard Hawk-Monitor. If time passed (and presumably it did, for a train came in, and its passengers got out, and were driven away) there was no time for Adam.

He was at last roused by an obscure agitation which seemed to be taking place on the floor of the buggy.

The straw which had lain upon the floor for the past twenty-five years was being energetically kicked out into the road by a small foot shod in a stout but shapely shoe. The light of the lantern showed nothing above this save a slender ankle and a green skirt, considerably agitated by the movements of the leg which it covered.

A voice from the darkness above his head was remarking, 'How revolting!'

'Eh ... eh,' muttered Adam, peering blindly up into the vague air beyond the lantern's rays. 'Nay, niver do that, soul. That straw was good enough for Miss Judith's wedding-trip to Brighton, and it must serve. Straw or chaff, leaf or fruit, we mun all come to't.'

'Not while I can prevent myself,' the voice assured him. 'And I can believe *most* things about Sussex and Cold Comfort, but not that Cousin Judith ever went to Brighton. Now, shall we be getting along, if you have finished brooding? My trunk is coming up to the farm by the carrier's van to-morrow. Not' (the voice went on, with a certain tartness) 'that you would be likely to care if it stayed down here until it seeded.'

'Robert Poste's child,' murmured Adam, staring up at the face he could now dimly see beyond the circle of lantern

46

light. 'Eh, but I was sent here to meet 'ee, and I niver saw 'ee.'

'I know,' said Flora.

'Child, child – ' began Adam, his voice rising to a wail.

But Flora thought otherwise. She checked him by asking him if he would prefer her to drive Viper, and this so affronted his male pride that he unhitched the reins from the rennet-post and the buggy drove off without any more delay.

Flora sat with her fur jacket drawn close round her throat against the chill air, nursing her small case containing her night-gown and toilet articles upon her knees. She had not been able to resist the impulse to slip into this small case, at the last moment, her dearly loved copy of the *Pensées* of the Abbé Fausse-Maigre; her other books would come up in her trunk to-morrow, but she had felt she would find it easier to meet the Starkadders in a proper and civilized state of mind if she had her copy of the *Pensées* (surely the wisest book ever compiled for the guidance of a truly civilized person) close at hand.

The Abbé's other and greater work, *The Higher Common Sense*, which had won for him a Doctorate of the University of Paris at the age of twenty-five, was in her trunk.

She thought of the *Pensées* as the buggy left the lights of Beershorn behind and began to mount the road which led to the invisible Downs. Her spirits were somewhat discomposed. She was chilly, and felt soiled (though indeed she did not look it) by the rigours of her journey. The prospect of what she would find at Cold Comfort was not calculated to cheer her spirits. She thought of the Abbé's warning: 'Never confront an enemy at the end of a journey, unless it happens to be his journey,' and was not consoled.

Adam did not say a word to her during the drive. But that was all right, because she did not want him to; he could be coped with later. The drive did not last so long as she had feared, because Viper seemed to be a pretty good horse and went at a smart pace (Flora supposed that the Starkadders had not owned him for long), and in less than an hour the lights of a village appeared in the distance.

'Is that Howling?' asked Flora.

'Aye, Robert Poste's child.'

There did not seem to be anything more to say. She fell into a slightly more comfortable muse, wondering what her rights were, those rights which her Cousin Judith had mentioned in her letter, and who had sent the postcard with the reference to a generation of vipers, and what was the wrong done by Judith's man to her father, Robert Poste.

The buggy now began to climb a hill, leaving Howling behind.

'Are we nearly there?'

'Aye, Robert Poste's child.'

And in another five minutes Viper stopped, of his own will, at a gate which Flora could just see in the obscurity. Adam struck him with the whip. He did not move.

'I think we must be there,' observed Flora.

'Nay, niver say that.'

'But I do say it. Look – if you drive on we shall go slam into a hedge.'

"Tes all one, Robert Poste's child.'

'It may be all right for you, and all one, but it isn't to me. I shall get down.'

So she did; and found her way slowly, through darkness only lit by faint winter starlight, along a villainous muddy path between hedges, which was too narrow for the buggy to enter.

Adam followed her, carrying the lantern, and leaving Viper at the gate.

The buildings of the farm, a shade darker than the sky, could now be distinguished in the gloom, a little distance on, and as Flora and Adam were slowly approaching them a door suddenly opened and a beam of light shone out. Adam gave a joyful cry.

"Tes the cowshed! 'Tes our Feckless openin' the door fer me!' And Flora saw that it was indeed; the door of the shed, which was lit by a lantern, was being anxiously pushed open by the nose of a gaunt cow.

This was not promising.

But immediately a deep voice was heard: 'Is that you, Adam?' and a woman came out of the cowshed, carrying the lantern, which she lifted high above her head to look at the travellers. Flora dimly discerned an unnecessarily red and voluminous shawl on her shoulders, and a tumbling mass of hair.

'Oh, how do you do?' she called. 'You must be my Cousin Judith. I'm so glad to see you. How nice of you to come out in all this cold. Terribly nice of you to have me, too. Isn't it curious we should never have met before?'

She put out her hand, but it was not taken at once. The lantern was lifted higher while Judith steadily looked into her face, in silence. The seconds passed. Flora wondered if her lipstick were the wrong shade. It then occurred to her that there was a less frivolous cause for the silence which had fallen and for the steady regard with which her cousin confronted her. So, Flora mused, must Columbus have felt when the poor Indian fixed his solemn, unwavering gaze upon the great sailor's face. For the first time a Starkadder looked upon a civilized being.

But one could weary even of this; and Flora soon did. She asked Judith if Judith would think her terribly rude if she did not meet the rest of the family that evening. Might she, Flora, just have a morsel of food in her own room?

'It is cold there,' said Judith, draggingly, at last.

'Oh, a fire will soon warm it up,' said Flora, firmly. 'Too nice of you, I do think, to take so much care of me.'

'My sons, Seth and Reuben – ' Judith choked on the words, then recovered, and added in a lower voice, 'My sons are waiting to see their cousin.'

This seemed to Flora, in conjunction with their ominous names, *too* like a cattle show, so she smiled vaguely and said it was so nice of them, but she thought, all the same, she would see them in the morning.

Judith's magnificent shoulders rose and fell in a slow, billowy shrug which agitated her breasts.

'As you will. The chimney, perhaps, smokes – '

'I should think it more than probable,' smiled Flora. 'But

49

we can see to all that to-morrow. Shall we go in now? But first' – she opened her bag and took out a pencil and tore a leaf from a little diary – 'I want Adam to send this wire for me.'

She had her way. Half an hour later she sat beside a smoky fire in her room, pensively eating two boiled eggs. She thought these were safest to ask for; Starkadder bacon, especially if cooked by Adam, might interfere with the long night's rest which she proposed to take, and for which, a short time later, she began to prepare.

She was really too sleepy to notice much of her surroundings, and too bored. She wondered if she had been wise to come. She reflected on the length, the air of neglect and the intricate convolutions of the corridors through which Judith had led her to her bedroom, and decided that if these were typical of the rest of the house, and if Judith and Adam were typical of the people who lived in it, her task would indeed be long and difficult. However, her hand was on the handle of the plough, and she would not turn back, because, if she did, Mrs Smiling would make a particular sort of face, which in another and more old-fashioned woman would have meant: 'I told you so.'

And, indeed, Mrs Smiling, far away in Mouse Place, was at that moment reading with some satisfaction a telegram saying:

'Worst fears realized darling seth and reuben too send gumboots.'

CHAPTER 5

BUT her resolve to sleep late into the next morning was partly frustrated by a shocking row which broke out below her window in what she, muttering sleepily and furiously from her bed, described as the middle of the night.

Male voices were raised in anger, coming up out of the blanket of dead, sullen darkness pierced by the far-off shrilling of cockerels. Flora fancied she knew one of the voices.

'Shame on 'ee, Mus' Reuben, to bite the hand that fed thee as a cowdling. Who should know the wants of the dumb beasts better nor me? 'Tes not for nought I nursed our Pointless when she was three days old and blind as a wren. I know what's in her heart better than I know what's in the heart o' some humans.'

'Be that as it may,' shouted another voice, strange to Flora. 'Graceless has lost a leg! Where is it? Answer me that, ye doithering old man. Who will buy Graceless now when I take her down to Beershorn Market? Who wants a cow wi' only three legs, saving some great old circus man looking round for freakies to put in his show?'

There was a piercing cry of dismay.

'Niver put our Graceless in one o' they circuses! The shame of it would kill me, Mus' Reuben.'

'Aye, and I would, tu, if I could get hold of anyone to buy her, circus or no circus. But no one will. Aye, 'tes all the same. Cold Comfort stock ne'r finds a buyer. Wi' the Queen's Bane blighting our corn, and the King's Evil laying waste the clover, and the Prince's Forfeit bringin' black ruin on the hay, and the sows as barren as come-ask-it – aye, 'tes the same tale iverywhere all over the farm. Wheer's that leg? Answer me that?'

'I don't know, Mus' Reuben. And if I did, I wouldn't tell 'ee. I know what goes on in the hearts of the dumb beasts wi'out spyin' round on them to see where they leaves their legs, from morn till eve. A beast needs solitude, same as a man does. I'd take shame to myself, Mus' Reuben, to watch over them beasts like you do, a-waitin' for dead men's shoes and a-countin' every blade of sporran and mouthful the dumb beasts eat.'

'Aye,' said another voice, meaningly, 'and countin' the very feathers the chickens let fall to see as no one makes off wi' em.'

'Well, and why should I not?' shouted the voice called Mus' Reuben. 'Do I pay 'ee wages, Mark Dolour, to steal the chickens' feathers and carry them off into Beershorn and sell them for good money?'

'I doan't sell the feathers. May I niver set hand to plough again if I do. 'Tes my Nancy. I takes 'em whoam to my Nancy.'

'Oh, ye do, do ye? And for why?'

'Ye know well why,' returned the third voice, sullenly.

'Aye, ye told me a pack o' tales about trimmin' dolls' hats wi' the good chicken feathers. As though there was no other use for them feathers them chickens drop than to trim the hats of a lot of idle, worthless dolls. Now hark ye, Mark Dolour – '

Here Flora found it useless to try to pretend herself back into sleep any longer, so she got crossly out of bed and felt her way across the room to the glimmering grey square which marked the window. She pushed it open a little wider and called down into the darkness:

'I say, *do* you think you would mind not talking quite so loudly, please? I *am* so sleepy, and I should be *so* grateful if you would.'

Silence, emphatic as a thunderclap, followed her request. She felt, half asleep as she was, that it was a flabbergasted silence. She hoped, drowsily, that it would last long enough for her to drift off into sleep again; and it did.

When she again woke it was daylight. She rolled over in bed and dutifully did her morning stretch and looked at her watch. It was half past eight.

Not a sound came up from the yard outside nor from the depths of the old house. Everybody might have died in the night.

'Not a hope of hot water, of course,' thought Flora, wandering round the room in her dressing-gown. However, she rubbed a little of the water in the ewer (yes, there was a ewer) between her palms, and was pleased to find that it was soft water. So she did not mind washing in cold. The regiment of small porcelain jars and pots on her dressing-table would help her to protect her fair skin from any rigours of climate, but it was pleasant to know that the water was her ally.

She dressed in pleasant leisure, studying her room. She decided that she liked it.

It was square, and unusually high, and papered with a bold though faded design of darker red upon crimson. The fireplace was elegant; the grate was basket-shaped, and the mantelpiece was of marble, floridly carved, and yellowed by age and exposure. Upon the mantelpiece itself rested two large shells, whose gentle curves shaded from white to the richest salmon-pink; these were reflected in the large old silvery mirror which hung directly above it.

The other mirror was a long one; it stood in the darkest corner of the room, and was hidden by a cupboard door when the latter was opened. Both mirrors reflected Flora without flattery or malice, and she felt that she could easily learn to rely upon them. Why was it, she wondered, that people seemed to have forgotten how to make mirrors? The old mirrors one found in deserted commercial and family hotels in places like Gravesend, or in the houses of Victorian relatives at Cheltenham, were always superb.

One wall was almost filled by a large mahogany wardrobe. A round table to match stood in the middle of the worn red and yellow carpet, which was covered with a design of big flowers. The bed was high, and made of mahogany; the quilt was a honeycomb, and white.

There were two steel engravings upon the walls, in frames of light yellow wood. One showed the *Grief of Andromache on beholding the Dead Body of Hector*. The other showed the *Captivity of Zenobia, Queen of Palmyra*.

Flora pounced on some books which lay on the broad window-sill: *Macaria, or Altars of Sacrifice*, by A. J. Evans-Wilson; *Home Influence*, by Grace Aguilar; *Did She Love Him?*, by James Grant, and *How She Loved Him*, by Florence Marryat. She put these treasures away in a drawer, promising herself a gloat when she should have time. She liked Victorian novels. They were the only kind of novel you could read while you were eating an apple.

The curtains were magnificent. They were of soiled but regal red brocade, and kept much of the light and air out of the room. Flora looped them back, and decided that to-day they must be washed. Then she went down to breakfast.

She followed a broad corridor, lit by dirty windows hung with soiled lace curtains, until it came to a flight of stairs; and at the foot of the stairs, through an open door, she could see into a room with a stone floor. She paused here for a second, and noticed a tray on which was the remainder of what had obviously been a large breakfast, lying on the floor outside a closed door a little way along the corridor. Good. Someone had breakfasted in their room, and if someone else could, so could she.

A smell of burnt porridge floated up from the depths. This did not seem promising, but she went down the stairs, her low heels clipping firmly on the stone.

At first she thought the kitchen was empty. The fire was almost out, and ash was blowing along the floor, and the table was covered with the intimidating remnants of some kind of a meal in which porridge seemed to have played the chief part. The door leading into the yard was open, and the wind blew sluggishly in. Before she did anything else, Flora went across and crisply shut it.

'Eh!' protested a voice from the back of the kitchen, near the sink. 'Niver do that, Robert Poste's child. I cannot cletter the dishes and watch the dumb beasts in the cowshed both together if ye shut the door. Aye, and there's something else I'm watchin' for, too.'

Flora recognized one of the voices which had disturbed her in the middle of the night. It belonged to old Adam Lambsbreath. He had been listlessly slicing turnips over the sink, and had interrupted his work to make his protest.

'I am sorry,' she replied, firmly, 'but I never could eat breakfast with a draught in the room. You can have it open again as soon as I have finished. *Is* there any breakfast, by the way?'

Adam shuffled forward into the light. His eyes were like

slits of primitive flint in their worn sockets. Flora wondered if he ever washed.

'There's porridge, Robert Poste's child.'

'Is there any bread and butter and some tea? I don't much care for porridge. And have you a piece of clean newspaper I could just put on the corner of this table (a half-sheet will be enough) to protect me from the porridge? It seems to have got tossed about a bit this morning, doesn't it?'

'There's tea i' the jar, yonder, and bread and butter i' the crocket. Ye mun find 'em yourself, Robert Poste's child. I have my task to do and my watch to keep, and I cannot run here and run there to fetch newspapers for a capsy wennet. Besides, we've troubles enough at Cold Comfort wi'out bringing in sich a thing as a clamourin' newspaper to upset us and fritten us.'

'Oh, have you? What troubles?' asked Flora, interestedly, as she busily made fresh tea. It occurred to her that this might be a good opportunity to learn something about the other members of the family. 'Haven't you enough money?'

For she knew that this is what is the matter with nearly everybody over twenty-five.

'There's money enough i' the farm, Robert Poste's child, but 'tes all turned to sourness and ruin. I tell ye' – here Adam advanced near to the interested Flora and thrust his lined and wrinkled face, indelibly etched by the corrosive acids of his dim, monotonous years, almost into hers – 'there's a curse on Cold Comfort.'

'Indeed!' said Flora, withdrawing slightly. 'What sort of a curse? Is that why everything looked so gone to seed and what not?'

'There's no seeds, Robert Poste's child. That's what I'm tellin' ye. The seeds wither as they fall into the ground, and the earth will not nourish 'em. The cows are barren and the sows are farren and the King's Evil and the Queen's Bane and the Prince's Heritage ravages our crops. 'Cos why? 'Cos there's a curse on us, Robert Poste's child.'

'But, look here, couldn't something be done about it? I mean, surely Cousin Amos could get a man down from London or something – (This bread is really not at all bad, you know. Surely you don't bake it here.) – Or perhaps Cousin Amos could sell the farm and buy another one, without any curse on it, in Berkshire or Devonshire?'

Adam shook his head. A curious veil, like the withdrawing of intelligence from the eyes of a tortoise, flickered across his face.

'Nay. There have always been Starkadders at Cold Comfort. 'Tes impossible for any on us to dream o' leavin' here. There's reasons why we can't. Mrs Starkadder, she's sot on us stayin' here. 'Tes her life, 'tes the life in her veins.'

'Cousin Judith, you mean? Well, she doesn't seem very happy here.'

'Nay, Robert Poste's child. I mean the old lady – old Mrs Starkadder.' His voice sunk to a whisper, so that Flora had to bend her tall head to catch the last words.

He glanced upwards, as though indicating that old Mrs Starkadder was in heaven.

'Is she dead, then?' asked Flora, who was prepared to hear anything at Cold Comfort, even that all the family was kept in order by a domineering ghost.

Adam laughed: a strange sound like the whickering snicker of a teazle in anger.

'Nay. She'm alive, right enough. Her hand lies on us like iron, Robert Poste's child. But she never leaves her room, and she never sees no one but Miss Judith. She's never left the farm this last twenty years.'

He stopped suddenly, as though he had said too much. He began to withdraw to his dark corner of the kitchen.

'I mun cletter the dishes now. Leave me be in peace, Robert Poste's child.'

'Oh, all right. But I do wish you would call me Miss Poste. Or even Miss Flora, if you'd rather be all feudal. I do feel that "Robert Poste's child" every time is rather a mouthful, don't you?'

'Leave me in peace; I mun cletter the dishes.'

56

Seeing that he was really bent on doing some work, Flora let him be, and thoughtfully finished her breakfast.

So that was what it was. Mrs Starkadder was the curse of Cold Comfort. Mrs Starkadder was the Dominant Grandmother Theme, which was found in all typical novels of agricultural life (and sometimes in novels of urban life, too). It was, of course, right and proper that Mrs Starkadder should be in possession at Cold Comfort; Flora should have suspected her existence from the beginning. Probably it was Mrs Starkadder, otherwise Aunt Ada Doom, who had sent the postcard with the reference to generations of vipers. Flora was sure that the old lady was Aunt Ada Doom, and none other. It was a most Aunt Ada-ish thing to do, to send a postcard like that. Flora's mother would have said at once, Flora was sure, 'That's typical of Ada.'

If she intended to tidy up life at Cold Comfort, she would find herself opposed at every turn by the influence of Aunt Ada. Flora was sure that this would be so. Persons of Aunt Ada's temperament were not fond of a tidy life. Storms were what they liked; plenty of rows, and doors being slammed, and jaws sticking out, and faces white with fury, and faces brooding in corners, faces making unnecessary fuss at breakfast, and plenty of opportunities for gorgeous emotional wallowings, and partings for ever, and misunderstandings, and interferings, and spyings, and, above all, managing and intriguing. Oh, they *did* enjoy themselves! They were the sort that went trampling all over your pet stamp collection, or whatever it was, and then spent the rest of their lives atoning for it. But you would rather have had your stamp collection.

Flora thought of *The Higher Common Sense*, by the Abbé Fausse-Maigre. This work had been written as a philosophic treatise; it was an attempt, not to explain the Universe, but to reconcile Man to its inexplicability. But, in spite of its impersonal theme, *The Higher Common Sense* provided a guide for civilized persons when confronted with a dilemma of the Aunt Ada type. Without actually laying down rules of conduct, *The Higher Common Sense* outlined a philosophy for the Civilized Being, and the rules of conduct followed automatically. Where *The Higher Common Sense* was silent, the *Pensées* of the same author often gave guidance.

With such guides to follow, it was not possible to get into a mess.

Flora decided that before she tackled Aunt Ada she would refresh her spirit by re-reading part of *The Higher Common Sense*; the famous chapter on 'Preparing the Mind for the Twin Invasion by Prudence and Daring in Dealing with Substances not Included in the Outline'. Probably she would only have time to study a page or two, for it was not easy to read, and part of it was in German and part in Latin. But she thought that the case was sufficiently serious to justify the use of *The Higher Common Sense*. The *Pensées* were all very well to fortify one's spirit against everyday pricks and scourges; Aunt Ada Doom, the crux of life at Cold Comfort, was another matter.

While she was eating the last piece of bread and butter, Flora was thinking that there might be a difficulty about her food while she was at Cold Comfort, for possibly Adam was cook to the family, and eat food prepared by Adam she could not and would not. She would probably have to approach her Cousin Judith, and have what older people love to call a little talk about it.

On the whole, Cold Comfort was not without its promise of mystery and excitement. She had hopes that Aunt Ada Doom would provide both; and she wished that Charles could have been there to enjoy it all with her. Charles dearly loved a gloomy mystery.

Adam, meanwhile, had finished slicing turnips and had gone out into the yard, where a thorn-tree grew, and returned with a long thorn-spiked twig torn from its branches. Flora watched him with interest while he turned the cold water on to the crusted plates, and began picking at the incrustations of porridge with his twig.

She bore it as long as she could, for she could hardly believe her own eyes, and then she said:

'What on earth are you doing?'

'Cletterin' the dishes, Robert Poste's child.'

'But surely you could do it much more easily with a little mop? A nice little mop with a handle? Cousin Judith ought to get you one. Why don't you ask her? It would get the dishes cleaner, and it would be so much quicker, too.'

'I don't want a liddle mop wi' a handle. I've used a thorn twig these fifty years and more, and what was good enough then is good enough now. And I don't want to cletter the dishes more quickly, neither. It passes the time away, and takes me thoughts off my liddle wild bird.'

'But,' suggested the cunning Flora, remembering the conversation which had roused her that morning at dawn, 'if you had a little mop and could wash the dishes more quickly, you could have more time in the cowshed with the dumb beasts.'

Adam stopped his work. This had evidently struck home. He nodded once or twice, without turning round, as though he were pondering it; and Flora hastily followed up her advantage.

'Anyway, I shall buy one for you when I go into Beershorn to-morrow.'

At this moment there came a soft rap at the closed door which led out into the yard; and a second later it was repeated. Adam shuffled across to the door, muttering 'My liddle wennet!' and flung it wide.

A figure which stood outside, wrapped in a long green cloak, rushed across the room and up the stairs so quickly that Flora only had the merest glimpse of it.

She raised her eyebrows. 'Who was that?' she asked, though she was sure that she knew.

'My cowdling – my liddle Elfine,' said Adam, listlessly picking up his thorn twig, which had fallen into the snood of porridge on the hearth.

'Indeed, and does she always charge about like that?' inquired Flora, coldly; she considered her cousin deficient in manners.

'Aye. She's as wild and shy as a pharisee of the woods.

59

Days she'll be away from home, wanderin' on the hills, wi' only the wild birds and the liddle rabbits an' the spyin' maggies for company. Aye, and o' night, too...' His face darkened. 'Aye, she's away then, too, wanderin' far from those that loves her and cowdled her in their bosoms when she was a mommet. She'll break my heart into liddle sippets, so she will.'

'Does she go to school?' asked Flora, looking distastefully in a cupboard for a rag with which to dust her shoes. 'How old is she?'

'Seventeen. Nay, niver talk o' school for my wennet. Why, Robert Poste's child, ye might as soon send the white hawthorn or the yellow daffodowndilly to school as my Elfine. She learns from the skies an' the wild marsh-tiggets, not out o' books.'

'How trying,' observed Flora, who was feeling lonely and rather cross. 'Look here, where is everybody this morning? I want to see Miss Judith before I go out for a walk.'

'Mus' Amos, he's down seein' the well drained for Sairy-Lucy's Polly, we think she's fallen into it; Mus' Reuben, he's down Nettle Flitch, ploughin'; Mus' Seth, he's off a-mollocking somewhere in Howling; Miss Judith, she's upstairs a-layin' out the cards.'

'Well, I shall go up and find her. What does mollocking mean?... No, you need not tell me. I can guess. What time is lunch?'

'The men has their dinner at twelve. We has ours an hour later.'

'Then I'll come in at one. Does – do – are – I mean, who cooks it?'

'Miss Judith, she cooks the dinner. Ah, was ye feared I would cook it, Robert Poste's child? Set yer black heart at rest; I wouldn't set me hand to cook even a runnet of bacon for the Starkadders. I cooks for the men, and that's all.'

Flora had the grace to colour at his accurate reading of her thoughts, and was glad to hurry upstairs out of his accusing presence. But it was a relief about the cooking. At least she would not have to starve during her visit to Cold Comfort.

She had no notion where Judith's bedroom might be, but she found a guide to take her there. As she reached the head of the stairs the tall girl in the green cloak, who had just dashed through the kitchen, came running lightly down the corridor towards her. She stopped, as though shot, at the sight of Flora, and stood poised as though for instant flight. 'Doing the startled bird stunt,' thought Flora, giving her a pleasant smile; or rather, smiling at the hood which half concealed her cousin's face.

'What do you want?' whispered Elfine, stonily.

'Cousin Judith's bedroom,' returned Flora. 'Would you be a lamb and show me the way? It's easy to get lost in a large house when everything is strange to one.'

A pair of large blue eyes looked at her steadily above the green hand-woven hood. Flora pensively noted that they were fine eyes, and that the hood was the wrong green.

She said, persuasively, 'Do forgive me saying so, but I would love to see you in blue. Some shades of green are good, of course, but dull greens are *very* trying, I always think. If I were you, I should try blue – something *really* well cut, of course, and very simple – but *definitely* blue. You try it, and see.'

Elfine made a brusque, boyish movement, and said off-handedly, 'This way.'

She strode along the corridor with a long, swinging step, letting the hood fall back so that Flora could see the back of her unbrushed mane of hair; it might have been a good gold if it had been properly dressed and cared for. It all seemed deplorable to Flora.

'Here,' jerked out Elfine, stopping in front of a closed door.

Flora thanked her so much, and Elfine, after another long stare at her, strode away.

'She will have to be taken in hand at once,' thought Flora. 'Another year, and there will be no doing anything with her; for even if she escapes from this place, she will only go and keep a tea-room in Brighton and go all arty-and-crafty about the feet and waist.'

And sighing a little at the greatness of the task which she had set herself to perform, Flora rapped at Judith's bedroom door, and in reply to a muttered 'Come in', entered.

Two hundred photographs of Seth, aged from six weeks to twenty-four years, decorated the walls of Judith's bedroom. She sat by the window in a soiled red dressing-gown with a dirty pack of cards on the table in front of her. The bed was not made. Her hair hung about her face, a nest of lifeless black snakes.

'Good morning,' said Flora. 'I'm so sorry to interrupt you if you are busy writing letters; I just wanted to know if you would like me to amuse myself and make my own arrangements, or would you like me to come in and see you about this time every morning. Personally, I think it's much easier if a guest wanders round and finds her own ways of passing the time. I am sure you are far too busy to want to bother with looking after me.'

Judith, after a long stare at her younger cousin, flung back her head with its load of snakes. The raw air splintered before the harsh onslaught of her laugh.

'Busy! Busy weaving my own shroud, belike. Nay, do what you please, Robert Poste's child, if so be as you don't break in on my loneliness. Give me time, and I will atone for the wrong my man did to your father. Give ... us ... all ... time ...' – the words came draggingly and unwillingly – 'and we will all atone.'

'I suppose,' suggested Flora courteously, 'you would not care to tell me what the wrong was? I do feel it would make matters a little easier ...'

Judith thrust the words aside with a heavy movement of her hand, like the blind outflinging of a tortured beast.

'Haven't I told you my lips are sealed?'

'Just as you like, of course, Cousin Judith. And there is another thing ...'

Then Flora, as delicately as possible, asked her cousin when and how she should pay to her the first instalment of the hundred pounds a year which Flora had anticipated that she would have to hand over to the Starkadders for her keep.

'Keep it – keep it,' said Judith violently. 'We will never touch a halfpenny of Robert Poste's money. While you are here, you are the guest of Cold Comfort. Every middock you eat is paid for with our sweat. 'Tes as it should be, seeing the way things are.'

Flora privately thanked her cousin for her generosity, but she privately resolved that, as soon as it was possible, she would make the acquaintance of Aunt Ada Doom, and find out if the old lady approved of this prodigal arrangement. Flora felt sure that she would not approve; and Flora herself was irritated by Judith's remark. For, if she lived at Cold Comfort as a guest, it would be unpardonable impertinence were she to interfere with the family's mode of living; but if she were paying her way, she could interfere as much as she pleased. She had observed a similar situation in houses where there were both poor relations and paying guests.

But this was a point which could be settled at some other time; just now there was something more important to discuss. She said:

'By the way, I adore my bedroom, but do you think I could have the curtains washed? I believe they are red; and I should so like to make sure.'

Judith had sunk into a reverie.

'Curtains?' she asked, vacantly, lifting her magnificent head. 'Child, child, it is many years since such trifles broke across the web of my solitude.'

'I'm sure it is; but do you think I might have them washed, all the same? Could Adam do them?'

'Adam? His frail arms have not the strength. Meriam, the hired girl, might have done them, but – '

Her gaze strayed again to the window, past whose open casement a fine rain was blowing.

Flora, who was willing to try anything once, gazed too. Judith was looking at a little hut which stood at the far end of Nettle Flitch Field, and almost abutted upon the sag-pieces which railed in the yard. From this hut came distinct cries of distress in a female voice.

Flora looked at her cousin with inquiring eyebrows. Judith nodded, lowering her eyelids while a slow scarlet wave of blood swept over her breasts and cheeks.

' 'Tes the hired girl in labour,' she whispered.

'What – without a doctor or anything?' asked Flora, in alarm. 'Hadn't we better send Adam down into Howling for one? I mean – in that grim-looking hut and every-thing – '

Judith again made the blind animal gesture of repudia-tion which seemed to thrust a sodden wall of negation be-tween herself and the world of living things. Her face was grey.

'Leave her in peace . . . animals like Meriam are best alone at such times . . . 'Tes not the first time.'

'Too bad,' said Flora, sympathetically.

' 'Tes the fourth time,' whispered Judith, thickly. 'Every year, in the fullness o' summer, when the sukebind hangs heavy from the wains . . . 'tes the same. 'Tes the hand of Nature, and we women cannot escape it.'

('Oh, can't we?' thought Flora, with spirit, but aloud she only made such noises of tut-tutting regret as she felt were appropriate to the occasion.)

'Well, she's out of the question, anyway,' she said, briskly.

'What question?' asked Judith, after a pause.

She had fallen into a trance-like muse. Her face was grey.

'I mean the curtains. She can't wash them if she's just had a baby, can she?'

'She will be about again to-morrow. Such wenches are like the beasts of the field,' said Judith, indifferently.

She seemed bowed under the gnawing weight of a sorrow that had left her too exhausted for anger; but, as she spoke, an asp-like gleam of contempt darted into her over-lidded eyes. She looked quickly across at a photograph of Seth which stood on the table. It showed him in the centre of the Beershorn Wanderers Football Club. His young man's limbs, sleek in their dark male pride, seemed to disdain the covering offered them by the brief shorts and striped jersey. His body might have been naked, like his full, muscled throat, which rose, round and proud as the male organ of a flower, from the neck of his sweater.

'He is a thought too fat, but really very handsome,' mused Flora, following Judith's glance. 'I don't suppose he plays football any more – probably mollocks instead.'

'Aye,' suddenly whispered Judith, 'look at him – the shame of our house. Cursed be the day I brought him forth and the nourishment he drew from my bosom, and the wooing tongue God gave him to bring disgrace upon weak women.'

She stood up and looked out into the drizzling rain.

**The cries from the little hut had stopped. An exhausted silence, brimmed with the enervating weakness which follows a stupendous effort, mounted from the stagnant air in the yard, like a miasma. All the surrounding surface of the countryside – the huddled Downs lost in rain, the wet fields fanged abruptly with flints, the leafless thorns thrust sideways by the eternal pawing of the wind, the lush breeding miles of meadow through which the lifeless river wandered – seemed to be folding inwards upon themselves. Their dumbness said: 'Give up'. There is no answer to the riddle; only that bodies return exhausted, hour by hour, minute by minute, to the all-forgiving and all-comprehending primeval slime.

'Well, Cousin Judith, if you really think she will be about again in a few days, perhaps I might look in at her hut this morning and arrange about the curtains,' said Flora, preparing to go. Judith did not answer at first.

'The fourth time,' she whispered at last. 'Four of them. Love-children. Pah! That animal, and love! And he – '

Here Flora realized that the conversation was not likely to take a turn in which she could join with any benefit, so she went quickly away.

'So they all belong to Seth,' she thought, while putting on her mackintosh in her bedroom. 'Really, it is too bad. I suppose on any other farm one would say that it set a bad example, but of course that does not apply here. I must see, I think, what can be done about Seth . . .'

She picked her way through the mud and rancid straw which carpeted the yard without encountering anyone except a person whom she took from his employment to be Reuben himself. He was feverishly collecting the feathers dropped by the chickens straying about the yard, and comparing them in number with the empty feather-sockets on the bodies of the chickens; this, she supposed, must be a precautionary measure, to prevent any feathers being taken away by Mark Dolour to his daughter Nancy.

Reuben (if it were he) was so engrossed that he did not observe Flora.

CHAPTER 6

FLORA approached the hut in some trepidation. Her practical experience of confinements was non-existent, for such of her friends as were married had not yet any children, and most of them were still too young to think of marriage as anything but a state infinitely remote.

But she had a lively acquaintance with confinements through the works of women novelists, especially those of the unmarried ones. Their descriptions of what was coming to their less fortunate married sisters usually ran to four or five pages of close print, or eight or nine pages of staccato lines containing seven words, and a great many dots arranged in threes.

Another school dismissed confinements with a careful brightness, a 'So-sorry-I'm-late-darling-I've-just-been-having-a-baby-where-shall-we-go-for-supper-afterwards?' sangfroid which Flora, curiously enough, found equally alarming.

She sometimes wondered whether the old-fashioned, though doubtless lazy, method of describing the event in the phrase, 'She was brought to bed of a fine boy,' was not the best way of putting it.

66

A third type of woman novelist combined literature and motherhood by writing a good, serious first novel when they were twenty-six; then marrying and having a baby, and, the confinement over, writing articles for the Press on 'How I Shall Bring Up My Daughter', by Miss Gwenyth Bludgeon, the brilliant young novelist, who gave birth to a daughter this morning. Miss Bludgeon is in private life Mrs Neil McIntish.

Some of Flora's friends had been exceedingly frightened, not to say revolted, by these painstaking descriptions of confinements; and had been compelled to rush off to the Zoo and bribe the keepers to assure them that the lionesses, at least, got through the Greatest Event of Their Lives in decent solitude. It was comforting, too, to watch the lionesses cuffing their fubsy cubs about in the sunlight. The lionesses, at least, did not write articles for the papers on how they would Bring Up their Cubs.

Flora had also learned the degraded art of 'tasting' unread books, and now, whenever her skimming eye lit on a phrase about heavy shapes, or sweat, or howls, or bedposts, she just put the book back on the shelf, unread.

Musing thus, she was relieved when a voice replied: 'Oo's there?' to her tap upon the door of the hut.

'Miss Poste from the farm,' she answered composedly. 'May I come in?'

There was a silence; a startled one, Flora felt. At length the voice called suspiciously:

'What do 'ee want wi' me and mine?'

Flora sighed. It was curious that persons who lived what the novelists called a rich emotional life always seemed to be a bit slow on the uptake. The most ordinary actions became, to such persons, entangled in complicated webs of apprehension and suspicion. She prepared to make a long explanatory statement – but suddenly changed her mind. Why should she explain? Indeed, what was there to explain?

She pushed the door open and walked in.

To her relief, there were no sweat nor howls nor bedposts.

There was only a young woman whom she presumed to be Meriam, the hired girl, sitting over an oil stove and reading what Flora, who had a nice sense of atmosphere, at once identified as *Madame Olga's Dream Book*. Baby there was none, and she was puzzled. But she was too relieved to wonder much what the explanation could be.

The hired girl (who was, of course, rather sullen looking and like a ripe fruit) was staring at her.

'Good morning,' Flora began pleasantly, 'are you feeling better? Mrs Starkadder seems to think you will be about again in a day or two, and if you feel well enough, I want you to wash the curtains in my bedroom. When can you come up to the farm and fetch them?'

The hired girl huddled closer over the oil stove, looking at Flora in what the latter interestedly recognized as the Tortured Dumb Beast manner. When she spoke, her voice was low and drawling:

'Why do ye come here, mockin' me in me shame – and me only out of me trouble yesterday?'

Flora started, and stared a little.

'Yesterday? I thought it was to-day? Surely you – er – didn't I hear? – that is, weren't you crying out, only about ten minutes ago? Mrs Starkadder and I both heard you.'

The beginnings of a sullen smile, rather like a plum in quality, touched the hired girl's sensual lips.

'Aye, I moithered out a bit. I was rememberin' me trouble yesterday. Mrs Starkadder she weren't in the kitchen when me time came on me. How should she know what I bin through, and when I bin through it? Not that I ever say much while it's goin' on. 'Taint so bad as some people make out. Mother says it's because I keeps me spirits up and eats hearty aforehand.'

Flora was pleasantly surprised to hear this, and for a second wondered if the women novelists had been misinformed about confinements. But no; she recollected that they usually left themselves a loophole by occasionally creating a primitive woman, a creature who was as close to the earth as a bloomy greengage and rather like one to look

68

at and talk to, and this greengage creature never had any bother with her confinements, but just took them in her stride, as it were. Evidently, Meriam belonged to the greengage category.

'Indeed,' said Flora, 'I am glad to hear it. When can you take the curtains down? The day after to-morrow?'

'I never said as I'd wash your curtains. Haven't I enough to bear, wi' three children to find food for, and me mother lookin' after a fourth? And who's to know what will happen to me when the sukebind is out in the hedges again and I feels so strange on the long summer evenings – ?'

'Nothing will happen to you, if only you use your intelligence and see that it doesn't,' retorted Flora firmly. 'And if I may sit down on this stool – thank you, no, I will use my handkerchief as a cushion – I will tell you how to see that nothing happens. And never mind about the sukebind for a minute (what *is* this sukebind, anyway?). Listen to me.'

And carefully, in detail, in cool phrases, Flora explained exactly to Meriam how to forestall the disastrous effect of too much sukebind and too many long summer evenings upon the female system.

Meriam listened, with eyes widening and widening.

' 'Tes wickedness! 'Tes flying in the face of Nature!' she burst out fearfully at last.

'Nonsense!' said Flora. 'Nature is all very well in her place, but she must not be allowed to make things untidy. Now remember, Meriam – no more sukebind and summer evenings without some preparations beforehand. As for your children, if you will wash the curtains for me, I will pay you, and that can go towards buying some of whatever it is children have to eat.'

Meriam seemed unconvinced by the argument for coping with sukebind, but she finally agreed to wash the curtains on the next day, much to Flora's satisfaction.

While Flora was making the final arrangements, her glance was wandering thoughtfully round the hut. It was of the variety known as 'miserable', but it was plain to Flora's experienced eyes that, unlikely as this seemed, somebody had been tidying it up. She was sure that the greengage had never even heard of such a process and wondered very much who had been at work.

While she was drawing on her gloves, there came a sharp tap at the door.

' 'Tes mother,' said Meriam, and she called: 'Come in, mother.'

The door then opened and on the threshold, taking in Flora from heels to beret with snapping little black eyes, stood a rusty black shawl with a hat alighting perilously upon the knob of hair which crowned the top of its head.

'Good morning, miss. A nasty day,' snapped the shawl, furling a large umbrella.

Flora was so startled at being addressed in a respectful and normal manner by anyone in Sussex that she almost forgot to answer, but habit is strong, and she recovered her wits sufficiently to agree graciously that the day was, indeed, nasty.

'She comes from up at the farm. She wants me to wash her bedroom curtains – and me with me trouble only a day behind me,' said Meriam.

'Who's "she"? The cat's mother?' snapped the shawl. 'Speak properly to the young lady. You must excuse her, miss; she's more like father's side o' the family. Ah! it was a black day for me when I took up with Agony Beetle and left Sydenham for Sussex (all my people live in Sydenham, miss, and have these forty years). Wash them? Well, I never thought I'd live to hear of anyone up at Cold Comfort wanting a bit of washing done. They might begin on that old Adam of theirs, or whatever he calls himself, and no harm would be done, I'll lay. She'll wash them for you, miss. I'll bring them along myself to-morrow afternoon and put them up for you.'

Flora replied that this would do very well, and it says much for the cumulative effect of the atmosphere of Cold Comfort that she felt almost moved as she spoke the words to one who seemed to possess some of the attributes of an ordinary human being, and who seemed to perceive (however dimly) that curtains must be washed and life generally tidied up before anyone could even begin to think of enjoying it.

She wondered if she should inquire after the welfare of the baby, and had just decided that this might be a little tactless when Mrs Beetle demanded of her daughter:

'Well, ain't you going to ask me 'ow 'e is?'

'I knows. There ain't no need to ask. He'll be doing fine. They allus does,' was the sullen reply.

'Well, you needn't sound as though you wished they wouldn't,' said the shawl, tartly. 'Lord knows, they wasn't very welcome, pore little innercents; but now they *are* 'ere, we may as well bring them up right. And I will, too. It's to me advantage. Come another four years and I can begin makin' use of them.'

'How?' asked Flora, pausing at the door. Was a flaw about to disclose itself in the hitherto admirable character of the shawl?

'Train the four of them up into one of them jazz-bands,' replied Mrs Beetle, promptly. 'I seen in the *News of People* that they earns as much as six pounds a night playin' up West in night-clubs. Well, I thought, here's a jazz-band ready-made to me 'and, as you may say; and it's better still now there's four of them. I've got 'em all under me 'and in one family, so's I can keep an eye on the lot of them while they're learning to play. So that's why I'm bringing them up right, on plenty of milk, and seein' they get to bed early. They'll need all their strength if they 'ave to sit up till the cows come 'ome playin' in them night-clubs.'

Flora was rather shocked, but she felt that, though Mrs Beetle's scheme might be a little *callous*, it was at least *organized*, which was more than could be said of any other life which the four embryo musicians might lead if their upbringing were left to their mother or (a yet darker thought) to Grandfather Agony Beetle himself.

So she went off, after a pleasant farewell to Meriam and mother, and a statement that she would come in some time to see the new baby.

**After she had gone the hut sank into a dim trough of languor, pierced only by the shrill beam shed by the personality of Mrs Beetle, which seemed to gather into one all the tenuous threads of the half-formulated desires of the two women which throbbed about them.

Meriam huddled on her stool, the coarsened lines of her body spreading like some natural growth born of the travail of the endlessly teeming fields. In thick, lewd whispers, she began to tell her mother what Flora had advised her to do. Her voice rose ... fell ... rose ... fell ..., its guttural syllables punctuated by the swish of Mrs Beetle's broom. Once Mrs Beetle flung open a window, muttering that the place was enough to choke a black, but save for this interruption Meriam's voice droned on like the voice of the earth itself.

'Well, you needn't sw-sw-sw-sw about it as though you was talkin' to someone from the Vicarage,' observed Mrs Beetle at the conclusion of her confidences. 'It's no news to me, though I wasn't quite sure 'ow it was done nor 'ow much they cost ... Anyway, we know now; thanks to Miss Interference from the 'ill. And I'll lay she's no better than she ought to be, a bit of a kid like 'er sailing in 'ere as bold as brass and talkin' to you about such things. Still, she does look as if she washed 'erself sometimes, and she ain't painted up like a dog's dinner, like most of them nowadays. Not that I 'old with wot she told you, mind you. It ain't right.'

'Aye,' agreed her daughter, heavily, ' 'tes wickedness. 'Tes flyin' in the face of Nature.'

'That's right.'

A pause, during which Mrs Beetle stood with her broom suspended, looking firmly at the oil stove. Then she added:

'All the same, it might be worth tryin'.'

CHAPTER 7

FLORA's spirits were usually equable, but by lunch-time the next day the combined forces of the unceasing rain, the distressing manner in which the farm-house and its attendant buildings seemed sinking into decay before her eyes, and the appearance and characters of her relatives, had produced in her a feeling of gloom which was as unusual as it was disagreeable.

'This will not do,' she thought, as she looked out on the soaking countryside from her bedroom window, whence she had retreated to arrange some buds and branches which she had picked on her morning walk. 'I am probably hungry; lunch will restore my spirits.'

And yet, on second thoughts, it seemed probable that lunch cooked by a Starkadder and partaken of in solitude would only make her worse.

She had managed yesterday's meals successfully. Judith had provided a cutlet and some junket for her at one o'clock, served beside a smoky fire, in a little parlour with faded green wallpaper, next door to the dairy. Here, too, Flora had partaken of tea and supper. These two meals were served by Mrs Beetle – an agreeable surprise. It appeared that Mrs Beetle came in to the farm and did her daughter's work on those occasions when Meriam was being confined. Flora's arrival had coincided with one of these times, which, as we know, were frequent. Mrs Beetle also came in each day to prepare Aunt Ada Doom's meals.

So Flora had thus far escaped meeting Seth and Reuben or any of the other male Starkadders. Judith, Adam, Mrs Beetle, and an occasional glimpse of Elfine represented her whole knowledge of the inhabitants and servants of the farm.

But she was not satisfied. She wished to meet her young cousins, her Aunt Ada Doom, and Amos. How could she tidy up affairs at Cold Comfort if she did not meet any of the Starkadders? And yet she shrank from boldly entering the kitchen where the family sat at the manger, and introducing herself. Such a move would lower her dignity, and, hence, her future power. It was all very difficult. Perhaps Judith did not actively intend to keep Flora from meeting the rest of the family, but she had so far achieved just this result.

But to-day, Flora had decided, she would meet her cousins, Seth and Reuben. She thought that tea-time would present a good opportunity on which to carry out her intention. If the Starkadders did not partake of tea (and it was probable that they did not) she would prepare it herself, and tell the Starkadders that she intended with their nominal permission to do so every afternoon during her visit.

But this point could be considered later. At the moment, she was going down into Howling to see if there was a pub in which she could lunch. In any other household such a proceeding would be enough to terminate her stay. Here, they probably would not even notice her absence.

At one o'clock, therefore, Flora was in the saloon bar of the Condemn'd Man, the only public-house in Howling, asking Mrs Murther the landlady if she 'did' lunches?

A smile indicating a shuddering thankfulness, as of one who peers into a pit into which others have fallen while she has escaped, passed over the face of Mrs Murther, as she replied that she did not.

'At least, only for two days in August, and not always then,' she added, gladly.

'Couldn't you pretend it is August now?' demanded Flora, who was ravenous.

'No,' replied Mrs Murther, simply.

'Well, if I buy a steak at the butcher's, will you cook it for me?'

Mrs Murther unexpectedly said that she would; and added even more surprisingly that Flora could have some of what they was having themselves, an offer which Flora a little rashly accepted.

What they was having themselves proved to be apple tart and vegetables, so Flora did quite well. She obtained her steak after some little delay with the butcher, who thought she was mad; and it seemed to her that a surprisingly short time elapsed between the purchasing of the steak and her sitting down before it, browned and savoury, in the parlour of the Condemn'd Man.

Nor did the hovering presence of Mrs Murther cast an atmosphere sufficiently dismal to spoil her appetite. Mrs Murther seemed resigned, rather than despairing. Her face and manner suggested the Cockney phrase dear and familiar to Flora in London: 'Oh, well, mustn't grumble', though Flora knew better than to expect to hear it in Howling, where everybody felt that they must grumble, and all the time at that.

'Now I must be off and see to my other gentleman's dinner,' said Mrs Murther, having hovered long enough to see that Flora had all the salt and pepper, bread, forks, and the rest of it that she wanted.

'Have you another gentleman?' asked Flora.

'Yes. Stayin' here. A book-writer,' rejoined Mary Murther.

'He would be,' muttered Flora. 'What's his name?' (for she wondered if she knew him).

'Mybug,' was the improbable answer.

Flora simply did not believe this, but she was too busy eating to start a long and exhausting argument. She decided that Mr Mybug must be a genius. A person who was merely talented would have weakly changed his name by deed-poll.

What a bore it was, she thought. Had she not enough to do at Cold Comfort without there being a genius named Mybug staying a mile away from the farm who would probably fall in love with her? For she knew from experience that intellectuals and geniuses seldom fell for females of their own kidney, who had gone all queer about the shoes and coiffure, but concentrated upon reserved but normal and properly dressed persons like herself, who were both repelled and alarmed (not to say bored) by the purposeful advances of the said geniuses and intellectuals.

'Well – what kind of books does he write?' she asked.

'He's doin' one now about another young fellow who

wrote books, and then his sisters pretended *they* wrote them, and then they all died of consumption, poor young mommets.'

'Ha! A life of Branwell Brontë,' thought Flora. 'I might have known it. There has been increasing discontent among the male intellectuals for some time at the thought that a woman wrote *Wuthering Heights*. I thought one of them would produce something of this kind, sooner or later. Well, I must just avoid him, that's all.'

And she fell to finishing her apple tart a little more quickly than was comfortable, for she was nervous lest Mr Mybug should come in, and fall in love with her.

'Don't you 'urry yourself; 'e's never in afore half past two,' soothed Mrs Murther, reading her thoughts with disconcerting readiness. 'He's up on the Downs in all weathers, and a nice old lot of mud 'e brings into the 'ouse too. Was everything all right? That'll be one and sixpence, please.'

Flora felt better on her return walk to the farm. She decided that she would spend the afternoon arranging her books.

There were sounds of life in the yard as she crossed it. Buckets clattered in the cowshed, and the hoarse bellow of the bull came from his dark shed. ('I don't believe he's ever let out into the fields when the sun's shining,' thought Flora, and made a note to see about him, as well as about the Starkadders.) Belligerent noises came from the henhouse, but nobody was to be seen.

At four o'clock she came downstairs to look for some tea. She did not bother to glance into her little parlour to see if her own tea were on the table. She went straight into the kitchen.

Of course, there were no preparations for tea in the kitchen; she realized, as soon as she saw the ashy fire and the crumbs and fragments of carrot left on the table from dinner, that it was rather optimistic of her to have expected any.

But she was not daunted. She filled the kettle, put some wood on the fire and set the kettle on it, flicked the reminders of dinner off the table with Adam's drying-up towel (which she held in the tongs), and set out a ring of cups and saucers about the dinted pewter teapot. She found a loaf and some butter, but no jam, of course, or anything effeminate of that sort.

Just as the kettle boiled and she darted forward to rescue it, a shadow darkened the door and there stood Reuben, looking at Flora's gallant preparations with an expression of stricken amazement mingled with fury.

'Hullo,' said Flora, getting her blow in first. 'I feel sure you must be Reuben. I'm Flora Poste, your cousin, you know. How do you do? I'm so glad to see somebody has come in for some tea. Do sit down. Do you take milk? (No sugar . . . of course . . . or do you? I do, but most of my friends don't.)'

***The man's big body, etched menacingly against the bleak light that stabbed in from the low windows, did not move. His thoughts swirled like a beck in spate behind the sodden grey furrows of his face. A woman . . . Blast! Blast! Come to wrest away from him the land whose love fermented in his veins, like slow yeast. She-woman. Young, soft-coloured, insolent. His gaze was suddenly edged by a fleshy taint. Break her. Break. Keep and hold and hold fast the land. The land, the iron furrows of frosted earth under the rain-lust, the fecund spears of rain, the swelling, slow burst of seed-sheaths, the slow smell of cows and cry of cows, the trampling bride-path of the bull in his hour. All his, his . . .

'Will you have some bread and butter?' asked Flora, handing him a cup of tea. 'Oh, never mind your boots. Adam can sweep the mud up afterwards. Do come in.'

Defeated, Reuben came in.

He stood at the table facing Flora and blowing heavily on his tea and staring at her. Flora did not mind. It was quite interesting: like having tea with a rhinoceros. Besides, she was rather sorry for him. Amongst all the Starkadders, he looked as though he got the least kick out of life. After

77

all, most of the family got a kick out of something. Amos got one from religion, Judith got one out of Seth, Adam got his from cowdling the dumb beasts, and Elfine got hers from dancing about on the Downs in the fog in a peculiar green dress, while Seth got his from mollocking. But Reuben just didn't seem to get a kick out of anything.

'Is it too hot?' she asked, and handed him the milk, with a smile.

The opaque curve purred softly down into the teak depths of the cup. He went on blowing it, and staring at her. Flora wanted to set him at ease (if he had an ease?), so she composedly went on with her tea, wishing there were some cucumber sandwiches.

After a silence which lasted seven minutes by a covert glance at Flora's watch, a series of visible tremors which passed across the expanse of Reuben's face, and a series of low, preparatory noises which proceeded from his throat, persuaded her that he was about to speak to her. Cautious as a camera-man engaged in shooting a family of fourteen lions, Flora made no sign.

Her control was rewarded. After another minute Reuben brought forth the following sentence:

'I ha' scranleted two hundred furrows come five o'clock down i' the bute.'

It was a difficult remark, Flora felt, to which to reply. Was it a complaint? If so, one might say, 'My dear, how too sickening for you!' But then, it might be a boast, in which case the correct reply would be, 'Attaboy!' or more simply, 'Come, that's capital.' Weakly she fell back on the comparatively safe remark:

'Did you?' in a bright, interested voice.

She saw at once that she had said the wrong thing. Reuben's eyebrows came down and his jaw came out. Horrors! He thought she was doubting his word!

'Aye, I did, tu. Two hundred. Two hundred from Tickle-penny's Corner down to Nettle Flitch. Aye, wi'out hand to aid me. Could you ha' done that?'

'No, indeed,' replied Flora, heartily, and her guardian

78

angel (who must, she afterwards decided, have been doing a spot of overtime) impelled her to add: 'But then, you see, I shouldn't want to.'

This seemingly innocent confession had a surprising effect on Reuben. He banged down his cup and thrust his face forward, peering intently into hers.

'Wouldn't you, then? Ah, but you'd pay a hired man good money to do it for you, I'll lay – wastin' the farm's takin's.'

Flora was now beginning to see what was the matter. He thought she had designs on the farm!

'Indeed I wouldn't,' she retorted promptly. 'I wouldn't care if Ticklepenny's Corner wasn't scranleted at all. I don't want to have anything to do with Nettle Flitch. I'd let' – she smiled pleasantly up to Reuben – 'I'd let you do it all instead.'

But this effort went sour on her, to her dismay.

'Let!' shouted Reuben, thumping the table. 'Let! A mirksy, capsy word to use to a man as has nursed a farm like a sick mommet – and a man as knows every inch of soil and patch o' sukebind i' the place. Let . . . aye, a fine word – '

'I really think we had better get this straight,' interrupted Flora. 'It will make things so much easier. I don't want the farm. Really, I don't. In fact' – she hesitated whether she should tell him that it seemed incredible to her that anyone could possibly want it, but decided that this would be rude as well as unkind – 'well, such an idea never came into my head. I know nothing about farming, and I don't want to. I would much rather leave it to people who do know everything about it, like you. Why, just think what a mess I should make of the sukebind harvest and everything. You must see that I am the last person in the world who would be any use at scranleting. I am sure you will believe me.'

A second series of tremors, of a slightly more complicated type than the first, passed across Reuben's face. He seemed about to speak, but in the end he did not. He slapped down his cup, gave a last stare at Flora, and stumped out of the kitchen.

This was an unsatisfactory end to the interview, which had begun well; but she was not disturbed. It was obvious that, even if he did not believe her, he wanted to; and that was half the battle. He had even been on the verge of believing her when she made that lucky remark about not wanting to scranlet; and only his natural boorishness and his suspicious nature had prevented him. The next time she assured him that she was not after Cold Comfort Farm, Reuben would be convinced that she spoke the truth.

The fire was now burning brightly. Flora lit a candle, which she had brought down from her bedroom, and took up some sewing with which to beguile the time until supper in her own room. She was making a petticoat and decorating it with drawn threadwork.

A little later, as she sat peacefully sewing, Adam came in from the yard. He wore, as a protection from the rain, a hat which had lost – in who knows what dim hintermath of time – the usual attributes of shape, colour, and size, and those more subtle race-memory associations which identify hats as hats, and now resembled some obscure natural growth, some moss or sponge or fungus, which had attached itself to a host.

He was carrying between finger and thumb a bunch of thorn twigs, which Flora presumed that he had just picked from one of the trees in the yard; and he held them ostentatiously in front of him, like a torch.

He glanced spitefully at Flora from under the brim of the hat as he crossed the kitchen, but said nothing to her. As he placed the twigs carefully on a shelf above the sink, he glanced round at her, but she went on sewing, and said never a word. So after rearranging the twigs once or twice, and coughing, he muttered:

'Aye, them'll last me till Michaelmas to cletter the dishes wi' – there's nothing like a thorn twig for cletterin' dishes. Aye, a rope's as good as a halter to a willin' horse. Curses, like rookses, flies home to rest in bosomses and barnses.'

It was clear that he had not forgotten Flora's advice about using a little mop to clean the dishes. As he shuffled away, she thought that she must remember to buy one for him the next time she went into Howling.

Flora had scarcely time to get over this before there sounded a step in the yard outside, and there entered a young man who could only be Seth.

Flora looked up with a cool smile.

'How do you do? Are you Seth? I'm your cousin, Flora Poste. I'm afraid you're too late for any tea . . . unless you would like to make some fresh for yourself.'

He came over to her with the lounging grace of a panther, and leaned against the mantelpiece. Flora saw at once that he was not the kind that could be fobbed off with offers of tea. She was for it.

'What's that you're making?' he asked. Flora knew that he hoped it was a pair of knickers. She composedly shook out the folds of the petticoat and replied that it was an afternoon tea-cloth.

'Aye . . . woman's nonsense,' said Seth, softly. (Flora wondered why he had seen fit to drop his voice by half an octave.) 'Women are all alike — ay fussin' over their fal-lals and bedazin' a man's eyes, when all they really want is man's blood and his heart out of his body and his soul and his pride . . .'

'Really?' said Flora, looking in her work-box for her scissors.

'Aye.' His deep voice had jarring notes which were curiously blended into an animal harmony like the natural cries of stoat or weasel. 'That's all women want – a man's life. Then when they've got him bound up in their fal-lals and bedazin' ways and their softness, and he can't move because of the longin' for them as cries in his man's blood – do you know what they do then?'

'I'm afraid not,' said Flora. 'Would you mind passing me that reel of cotton on the mantelpiece, just by your ear? Thank you so much.' Seth passed it mechanically, and continued.

'They eat him, same as a hen-spider eats a cock-spider. That's what women do – if a man lets 'em.'

'Indeed,' commented Flora.

'Aye – but I said "if" a man lets 'em. Now I – I don't let no women eat me. I eats them instead.'

Flora thought an appreciative silence was the best policy to pursue at this point. She found it difficult, indeed, to reply to him in words, since his conversation, in which she had participated before (at parties in Bloomsbury as well as in drawing-rooms in Cheltenham), was, after all, mainly a kind of jockeying for place, a shifting about of the pieces on the board before the real game began. And if, in her case, one of the players was merely a little bored by it all and was wondering whether she would be able to brew some hot milk before she went to bed that night, there was not much point in playing.

True, in Cheltenham and in Bloomsbury gentlemen did not say in so many words that they ate women in self-defence, but there was no doubt that that was what they meant.

'That shocks you, eh?' said Seth, misinterpreting her silence.

'Yes, I think it's dreadful,' replied Flora, good-naturedly meeting him half-way.

He laughed. It was a cruel sound like the sputter of the stoat as it sinks its feet into the neck of a rabbit.

'Dreadful . . . aye! You're all alike. You're just the same as the rest, for all your London ways. Mealy-mouthed as a school-kid. I'll lay you don't understand half of what I've been saying, do you? . . . Liddle innercent.'

'I am afraid I wasn't listening to all of it,' she replied, 'but I am sure it was very interesting. You must tell me all about your work some time . . . What do you do, now, on the evenings when you aren't – er – eating people?'

'I goes over to Beershorn,' replied Seth, rather sulkily. The dark flame of his male pride was a little suspicious of having its leg pulled.

'To play darts?' Flora knew her A. P. H.

82

'Noa . . . me play that kid's game with a lot of old men? That's a good 'un, that is. No. I goes to the talkies.'

And something in the inflection which Seth gave to the last word of his speech, the lingering, wistful, almost cooing note which invaded his curiously animal voice, caused Flora to put down her sewing in her lap and to glance up at him. Her gaze rested thoughtfully upon his irregular but handsome features.

'The talkies, do you? Do you like them?'

'Better nor anything in the whoal world,' he said, fiercely. 'Better nor my mother nor this farm nor Violet down at the Vicarage, nor anything.'

'Indeed,' mused his cousin, still eyeing his face thoughtfully. 'That's interesting. Very interesting indeed.'

'I've got seventy-four photographs o' Lotta Funchal,' confided Seth, becoming in his discussions of his passion like those monkeys which are described as 'almost human'. 'Aye, an' forty o' Jenny Carrol, and fifty-five o' Laura Vallee, and twenty o' Carline Heavytree, and fifteen of Sigrid Maelstrom. Aye, an' ten o' Panella Baxter. Signed ones.'

Flora nodded, displaying courteous interest, but showing nothing of the plan which had suddenly occurred to her; and Seth, after a suspicious glance at her, suddenly decided that he had been betrayed into talking to a woman about something else than love, and was angry.

So, muttering that he was going off to Beershorn to see 'Sweet Sinners' (he was evidently inflamed by this discussion of his passion), he took himself off.

The rest of the evening passed quietly. Flora supped off an omelette and some coffee, which she prepared in her own sitting-room. After supper she finished the design upon the breast of her petticoat, read a chapter of *Macaria, or Altars of Sacrifice*, and went to bed at ten o'clock.

All this was pleasant enough. And while she was undressing, she reflected that her campaign for the tidying up of Cold Comfort was progressing quite well, when she thought that she had only been there two days. She had made overtures to Reuben. She had instructed Meriam, the hired girl, in the precautionary arts, and she had gotten her bedroom curtains washed (they hung full and crimson in the candle-light). She had discovered the nature of Seth's *grande passion*, and it was not Women, but the Talkies. She had had a plan for making the most of Seth, but she could think that out in detail later. She blew out the candle.

But (she thought, settling her cool forehead against the cold pillow) this habit of passing her evenings in peaceful solitude in her own sitting-room must not make her forget her plan of campaign. It was clear that she must take some of her meals with the Starkadders, and learn to know them.

She sighed: and fell asleep.

CHAPTER 8

SHE found some difficulty during the ensuing week in meet-ing her Cousin Amos, while no one so much as breathed a word about introducing her to Aunt Ada Doom. Each morn-ing, at nine o'clock, Flora watched Mrs Beetle stagger upstairs with a tray laden with sausages, marmalade, por-ridge, a kipper, a fat black pot of strong tea, and what Flora caustically thought of as half a loaf; but when once Mrs Beetle had entered Aunt Ada's bedroom, the door was shut for good. And when Mrs Beetle came out she was not com-municative. Once she observed to Flora, seeing the latter regarding the empty tray which had come out of Mrs Stark-adder's bedroom:

'Yes . . . we're a bit off our feed this morning, as you might say. We've only 'ad two goes of porridge, two soft-boiled eggs, a kipper just on the turn, and 'alf that pot o' jam Adam stole from the Vicarage bazaar larst summer. Still, there's room for it where it goes, 'eaven knows, and we keep 'ealthy enough on it.'

'I have not met my aunt yet,' said Flora.

Mrs Beetle replied sombrely that Flora 'adn't missed

much, and they said no more on the matter. For Flora was
not the type of person who questions servants.

And even if she had been, it was plain to her that Mrs
Beetle was not the type of person who gives away secrets.
Flora gathered that she did not altogether disapprove of old
Mrs Starkadder. She had been heard to say that at least
there was one of 'em at Cold Comfort as knew her own
mind, even if she 'ad seen something narsty in the woodshed
when she was two. Flora had no idea what this last sentence
could possibly mean. Possibly it was a local idiom for going
cuckoo.

In any case, she could not demand to see her aunt if her
aunt did not want to see her; and surely if she had wanted
to see her she would have commanded that Flora be brought
into the Presence. Perhaps old Mrs Starkadder knew that
Flora was out to tidy up the farm, and intended to adopt
a policy of passive resistance. In which case an attempt must
sooner or later be made to invade the enemy's fort. But that
could wait.

Meanwhile, there was Amos.

She learnt from Adam that he preached twice a week to
the Church of the Quivering Brethren, a religious sect which
had its headquarters in Beershorn. It occurred to her that
she might ask to accompany him there one evening, and
begin working on him during the long drive down to the
town.

Accordingly, when Thursday evening came during her
second week at the farm, she approached her cousin as he
entered the kitchen after tea (for he would never partake of
that meal, which he thought finicking) and said resolutely:

'Are you going down into Beershorn to preach to the
Brethren to-night?'

Amos looked at her, as though seeing her for the first, or
perhaps the second time. ***His huge body, rude as a wind-
tortured thorn, was printed darkly against the thin mild
flame of the declining winter sun that throbbed like a sallow
lemon on the westering lip of Mockuncle Hill, and sent
its pale, sharp rays into the kitchen through the open door.

85

The brittle air, on which the fans of the trees were etched like ageing skeletons, seemed thronged by the bright, invisible ghosts of a million dead summers. The cold beat in glassy waves against the eyelids of anybody who happened to be out in it. High up, a few chalky clouds doubtfully wavered in the pale sky that curved over against the rim of the Downs like a vast inverted *pot-de-chambre*. Huddled in the hollow, like an exhausted brute, the frosted roofs of Howling, crisp and purple as broccoli leaves, were like beasts about to spring.

'Aye,' said Amos at last. He was encased in black fustian, which made his legs and arms look like drain-pipes, and he wore a hard little felt hat. Flora supposed that some people would say that he walked in a lurid, smoky hell of his own religious torment. In any case, he was a rude old man.

'They'll all burn in hell,' added Amos in a satisfied voice, 'and' I mun surelie tell them so.'

'Well, may I come too?'

He did not seem surprised. Indeed, she caught in his eye a triumphant light, as though he had been long expecting her to see the error of her ways and come to him and the Brethren for spiritual comfort.

'Aye . . . ye can come . . . ye poor miserable creepin' sinner. Maybe ye think ye'll escape hell fire if ye come along o' me, and bow down and quiver. But I'm tellin' ye no. 'Tes too late. Ye'll burn wi' the rest. There'll be time to say what yer sins have been, but there'll be no time for more.'

'Do I have to say them out aloud?' asked Flora, in some trepidation. It occurred to her that she had heard of a similar custom from friends of hers who were being educated at that great centre of religious life, Oxford.

'Aye, but not to-night. Nay, there'll be too many sayin' their sins aloud to-night; there'll be no time for the Lord to listen to a new sheep like you. And maybe the spirit won't move ye.'

Flora was pretty sure it would not; so she went upstairs to put on her hat and coat.

She did wonder what the Brethren would look like. In novels, persons who turned to religion to obtain the colour and excitement which everyday life did not give them were all grey and thwarted. Probably the Brethren would be all grey and thwarted . . . though it was too true that life as she is lived had a way of being curiously different from life as described by novelists.

The yard was painted in sharp layers of gold light and towering shadows, by the rays of the new-lit-mog's-lantern (this was used especially for carrying round the chicken-house at night to see if there were any stray cats after the hens: hence the name).

Viper, the great gelding, was harnessed to the trap; and Adam, who had been called from the cowshed to get the brute between the shafts, was being swung up and down in the air as he hung on to the reins.

The great beast, nineteen hands high, jerked his head wickedly, and Adam's frail body flew up into the darkness beyond the circle of grave, gold light painted by the mog's-lantern, and was lost to sight.

Then down he came again, a twisted grey moth falling into the light as Viper thrust his head down to snuff the reeking straw about his feet.

'Git up,' said Amos to Flora.

'Is there a rug?' she asked, hanging fire.

'Nay. The sins burnin' in yer marrow will keep yer warm.'

But Flora thought otherwise, and darting into the kitchen, she returned with her leather coat, in the lining of which she had been mending a tiny tear.

Adam whisked past her head as she put her foot on the step, piping in his distress like a very old peewit. His eyes were shut. His grey face was strained into an exalted mask of martyrdom.

'*Do* let go of the reins, Adam,' urged Flora, in some distress. 'He'll hurt you in a minute.'

'Nay . . . 'tes exercisin' our Viper,' said Adam feebly; and then, as Amos struck Viper on the shanks and the brute jerked his head as though he had been shot, Adam was flung out of the circle of light into the thick darkness, and was seen no more.

'There . . . you see!' said Flora reproachfully.

But muttering, 'Aye, let un be for a moithering old fool,' Amos struck the horse again and the gig plunged forward.

Flora quite enjoyed the drive into Beershorn. The coat kept her pleasantly warm, and the cold wind dashing past her cheeks was exhilarating. She could see nothing except the muddy road directly under the swinging mog's-lantern, and the large outlines of the Downs against the starless sky, but the budding hedges smelt fresh, and there was a feeling that spring was coming.

Amos was silent. Indeed, none of the Starkadders had any general conversation; and Flora found this particularly try-ing at meal-times. Meals at the farm were eaten in silence. If anyone spoke at all during the indigestible twenty minutes which served them for dinner or supper, it was to pose some awkward questions which, when answered, led to a blazing row; as, for example: 'Why has not – (whichever member of the family was absent from table) – come in to her food?' or 'Why has not the barranfield been gone over a second time with the pruning snoot?' On the whole, Flora liked it better when they were silent, though it did rather give her the feeling that she was acting in one of the less cheerful German highbrow films.

But now she had Amos to herself; and the opportunity was golden. She began:

'It must be so interesting to preach to the Brethren, Cousin Amos. I quite envy you. Do you prepare your ser-mon beforehand, or do you just make it up as you go along?'

An apparent increase in Amos's looming bulk, after this question had had time to sink in, convinced her in the midst of a disconcerting and ever-lengthening pause that he was swelling with fury. Cautiously she glanced over the side of the trap to see if she could jump out should he attempt to smite her. The ground looked disagreeably muddy and far off; and she was relieved when Amos at last replied in a tolerably well-controlled voice:

'Doan't 'ee speak o' the word o' the Lord in that godless way, as though 'twere one o' they pagan tales in the *Family Herald*. The word is not prepared beforehand; it falls on me mind like the manna fell from heaven into the bellies of the starving Israelites.'

'Really! How interesting. Then you have no idea what you are going to say before you get there?'

'Aye . . . I allus knows 'twill be summat about burnin' . . . or the eternal torment . . . or sinners comin' to judgement. But I doan't know exactly what the words will be until I gets up in me seat and looks round at all their sinful faces, awaitin' all eager for to hear me. Then I knows what I mun say, and I says it.'

'Does anyone else preach, or are you the only one?'

'Oanly me. Deborah Checkbottom, she tried onceways to get up and preach. But 'tweren't no good. Her couldn't.'

'Wouldn't the spirit work or something?'

'Nay, it worked. But I wouldn't have it. I reckoned the Lord's ways is dark and there'd be a mistake, and the spirit that was meant for me had fallen on Deborah. So I just struck her down wi' the gurt old Bible, to let the devil out of her soul.'

'And did it come out?' asked Flora, endeavouring with some effort to maintain the proper spirit of scientific inquiry.

'Aye, he came out. We heard no more o' Deborah's tryin' to preach. Now I preaches alone. No one else gets the word like I do.'

Flora detected a note of complacency and took her opportunity.

'I am looking forward so much to hearing you, Cousin Amos. I suppose you like preaching very much?'

'Nay. 'Tes a fearful torment and a groanin' to me soul's marrow,' corrected Amos. (Like all true artists, thought Flora, he was unwilling to admit that he got no end of a kick out of his job.) 'But 'tes my mission. Aye, I mun tell the Brethren to prepare in time for torment, when the roarin' red flames will lick round their feet like the dogs lickin' Jezebel's blood in the Good Book. I mun tell everybody' – here he moved slightly round in his seat, and Flora presumed that he was fixing her with a meaning stare – 'o' hell fire. Aye, the word burns in me mouth and I mun blow it out on the whoal world like flames.'

'You ought to preach to a larger congregation than the Brethren,' suggested Flora, suddenly struck by a very good idea. 'You mustn't waste yourself on a few miserable sinners in Beershorn, you know. Why don't you go round the country with a Ford van, preaching on market days?'

For she was sure that Amos's religious scruples were likely to be in the way when she began to introduce the changes she desired to bring about at the farm, and if she could get him out of the way on a long preaching tour her task would be simpler.

'I mun till the field nearest my hand before I go into the hedges and by-ways,' retorted Amos austerely. 'Besides, 'twould be exaltin' meself and puffin' meself up if I was to go preachin' all over the country in one o' they Ford vans. 'Twould be thinkin' o' my own glory instead o' the glory o' the Lord.'

Flora was surprised to find him so astute, but reflected that religious maniacs derived considerable comfort from digging into their motives for their actions and discovering discreditable reasons which covered them with good, satisfying sinfulness in which they could wallow to their hearts' content. She thought she heard a note of wistfulness, however, in the words, 'one o' they Ford vans', and gathered that the idea of such a tour tempted him considerably. She returned to the attack:

'But, Cousin Amos, isn't that rather putting your own miserable soul before the glory of the Lord? I mean, what does it matter if you *do* puff yourself up a bit and lose your holy humility if a lot of sinners are converted by your preaching? You must be *prepared*, I think, to sin in order to save others – at least, that is what *I* should be prepared to do if *I* were going round the country preaching from a Ford van. You see what I mean, don't you? By *seeming* to be humble, and dismissing the idea of making this tour, you are *in reality* setting more value on your soul than on the spreading of the word of the Lord.'

She was proud of herself at the conclusion of this speech. It had, she thought, the proper over-subtle flavour, that air of triumphantly pointing out an undetected and perfectly enormous sin lying slap under the sinner's nose which distinguishes all speeches intended to lay bare the workings of the religious mind.

Anyway, it produced the right effect on Amos. After a pause, during which the buggy rapidly passed the houses on the outskirts of the town, he observed in a hoarse, stifled voice:

'Aye, there's truth in what ye say. Maybe it is me duty to seek a wider field. I mun think of it. Aye, 'tes terrible. A sinner never knows how the devil may dress himself up to deceive. 'Twill be a new sin to wrestle with, the sin of carin' whether me soul is puffed up or not. And how can I tell, when I am feelin' puffed up when I preach, whether I'm sinnin' in me pride or whether I'm doin' right by savin' souls and therefore it woan't matter if I *am* puffed up? Aye, and what right have I to puff meself up if I *do* save them? Aye, 'tes a dark and bewilderin' way.'

All this was muttered in so low a voice that Flora could only just hear what he was saying, but she distinguished enough to make her reply firmly:

'Yes, Cousin Amos, it is all very difficult. But I do think, in spite of the difficulties, that you ought to consider seriously the possibility of letting hundreds more people hear your sermons. You have a Call, you know. No one should neglect a Call. Wouldn't you *like* to preach to thousands?'

'Aye, dearly. But 'tes vainglorious to think on't,' he replied wistfully.

'There you go again,' reproved his youthful companion. 'What does it matter if it *is* vainglorious – what does your soul matter compared with the souls of thousands of sinners, who might be saved by your preaching?'

At this moment the trap came to a halt outside a public-house, in a small yard opening off the High Street, and Flora was relieved, for the conversation seemed to have entered one of those vicious circles to which only the death or collapse from exhaustion of one of the participants can put an end.

Amos left Flora to get down from the trap as best she could.

'Hurry up,' he called. 'We mun hasten and leave the devil's house,' glancing back disapprovingly at the warmly-lit windows of the pub, which Flora thought looked rather nice.

'Is the chapel far from here?' she asked, following him down the High Street, where coarse yellow rays from the little shops shone out into the wintry dark.

'Nay – 'tes here.'

They stopped in front of a building which Flora at first took to be an unusually large dog-kennel. The doors were open, and inside could be seen the seats and walls of plain pitch-pine. Some of the Brethren were already seated, and others were hurrying in to take their places.

'We mun wait till the chapel is full,' whispered Amos.

'Why?'

''Tes frittenin' for them to see their preacher among them like any simple soul,' he whispered, standing somewhat in the shadows. 'They fear to have me among them, breathin' warnin's o' hell fire and torment. 'Tes frittenin' in a way, when I stands up on the platform, bellowin', but 'tes not so cruel frittenin' as if I was to stand among them before I begin to preach, like any one of them, sharin' a hymn-book, maybe, or fixin' one of them wi' my eye to read her thoughts.'

'But I thought you wanted to frighten them?'

'Aye, so I do, but in a grand, glorifyin' kind of way. And I doan't want to fritten 'em so much that they won't never come back to hear me preach again.'

Flora, observing the faces of the Brethren as they crowded into the dog-kennel, thought that Amos had probably underestimated the strength of their nerves. Seldom had she seen so healthy and solid-looking an audience.

As an audience, it compared most favourably with audiences she had studied in London; and particularly with an audience seen once – but only once – at a Sunday afternoon meeting of the Cinema Society to which she had, somewhat unwillingly, accompanied a friend who was interested in the progress of the cinema as an art.

That audience had run to beards and magenta shirts and original ways of arranging its neckwear; and not content with the ravages produced in its over-excitable nervous system by the remorseless workings of its critical intelligence, it had sat through a film of Japanese life called 'Yĕs', made by a Norwegian film company in 1915 with Japanese actors, which lasted an hour and three-quarters and contained twelve close-ups of water-lilies lying perfectly still on a scummy pond and four suicides, all done extremely slowly.

All round her (Flora pensively recalled) people were muttering how lovely were its rhythmic patterns and what an exciting quality it had and how abstract was its formal decorative shaping.

But there was one little man sitting next to her, who had not said a word; he had just nursed his hat and eaten sweets out of a paper bag. Something (she supposed) must have linked their auras together, for at the seventh close-up of a large Japanese face dripping with tears, the little man held out to her the bag of sweets, muttering:

'Peppermint creams. Must have something.'

And Flora had taken one thankfully, for she was extremely hungry.

When the lights went up, as at last they did, Flora had observed with pleasure that the little man was properly and conventionally dressed; and, for his part, his gaze had dwelt upon her neat hair and well-cut coat with incredulous joy, as of one who should say: 'Dr Livingstone, I presume?'

He then, under the curious eyes of Flora's highbrow friend, said that his name was Earl P. Neck, of Beverly

Hills, Hollywood; and he gave them his 'cyard' very cere-moniously and asked if they would go and have tea with him? He seemed the nicest little creature, so Flora dis-regarded the raised eyebrows of her friend (who, like all loose-living persons, was extremely conventional) and said that they would like to very much, so off they went.

At tea, Mr Neck and Flora had exchanged views on various films of a frivolous nature which they had seen and enjoyed (for of 'Yes' they could not yet trust themselves to speak), and Mr Neck had told them that he was a guest-producer at the new British studios at Wendover, and would Flora and her friend come and visit the studios some time? It must be soon, said Mr Neck, because he was returning to Hollywood with the annual batch of England's best actors and actresses in the autumn.

Somehow she had never found time to visit Wendover, though she had dined twice with Mr Neck since their first meeting, and they liked each other very much. He had told Flora all about his slim, expensive mistress, Lily, who made boring scenes and took up the time and energy which he would much sooner have spent with his wife, but he had to have Lily, because in Beverly Hills, if you did not have a mistress, people thought you were rather queer, and if, on the other hand, you spent all your time with your wife, and were quite firm about it, and said that you liked your wife, and, anyway, why the hell shouldn't you, the papers came out with repulsive articles headed 'Hollywood Czar's Domestic Bliss', and you had to supply them with pictures of your wife pouring your morning chocolate and watering the ferns.

So there was no way out of it, Mr Neck said.

Anyway, his wife quite understood, and they played a game called 'Dodging Lily', which gave them yet another interest in common.

Now Mr Neck was in America, but he would be flying over to England, so his last letter told Flora, in the late spring.

Flora thought that when he came she would invite him

to spend a day with her in Sussex. There was somebody about whom she wished to talk to him.

She was reminded of Mr Neck, as she stood pensively watching the Brethren going into the chapel, by the spectacle of the Majestic Cinema immediately opposite. It was showing a stupendous drama of sophisticated passion called 'Other Wives' Sins'. Probably Seth was inside, enjoying himself.

The dog-kennel was nearly full.

Somebody was playing a shocking tune on the poor little wheezy organ near the door. Except for this organ, Flora observed, peering over Amos's shoulder, the chapel looked like an ordinary lecture hall, with a little round platform at the end farthest from the door, on which stood a chair.

'Is that where you preach, Cousin Amos?'

'Aye.'

'Does Judith or either of the boys ever come down to hear you preach?' She was making conversation because she was conscious of a growing feeling of dismay at what lay before her, and did not wish to give way to it.

Amos frowned.

'Nay. They struts like Ahab in their pride and their eyes drip fatness, nor do they see the pit digged beneath their feet by the Lord. Aye, 'tes a terrible wicked family I'm cursed wi', and the hand o' the Lord it lies heavy on Cold Comfort, pressin' the bitter wine out o' our souls.'

'Then why don't you sell it and buy another farm on a really *nice* piece of land, if you feel like that about it?'

'Nay ... there have always been Starkadders at Cold Comfort,' he answered, heavily. ''Tes old Mrs Starkadder – Ada Doom as she was, before she married Fig Starkadder. She's sot against us leavin' the farm. She'd never see us go. 'Tes a curse on us. And Reuben sits awaitin' for me to go, so as he can have the farm. But un shall niver have un. Nay, I'll leave it to Adam first.'

Before Flora could convey to him her lively sense of dismay at the prospect indicated in this threat, he moved

95

forward saying, ''Tes nearly full. We mun go in,' and in they went.

Flora took a seat at the end of a row near the exit; she thought it would be as well to sit near the door in case the double effect of Amos's preaching and no ventilation became more than she could bear.

Amos went to a seat almost directly in front of the little platform, and sat down after directing two slow and brooding glances, laden with promise of terrifying eloquence to come, upon the Brethren sitting in the same row.

The dog-kennel was now packed to bursting, and the organ had begun to play something like a tune. Flora found a hymn-book being pressed into her hand by a female on her left.

'It's number two hundred, "Whatever shall we do, O Lord",' said the female, in a loud conversational voice.

Flora had supposed from impressions gathered during her wide reading, that it was customary to speak only in whispers in a building devoted to the act of worship. But she was ready to learn otherwise, so she took the book with a pleasant smile and said, 'Thank you so much'.

The hymn went like this:

> Whatever shall we do, O Lord,
> When Gabriel blows o'er sea and river,
> Fen and desert, mount and ford?
> The earth may burn, but we will quiver.

Flora approved of this hymn, because its words indicated a firmness of purpose, a clear path in the face of a disagreeable possibility, which struck an answering note in her own character. She sang industriously in her pleasing soprano. The singing was conducted by a surly, excessively dirty old man with long, grey hair who stood on the platform and waved what Flora, after the first incredulous shock, decided was a kitchen poker.

'Who is that?' she asked her friend.

''Tes Brother Ambleforth. He leads the quiverin' when we begins to quiver.'

'And why does he conduct the music with a poker?'

'To put us in mind of hell fire,' was the simple answer, and Flora had not the heart to say that as far as she was concerned, at any rate, this purpose was not achieved.

After the hymn, which was sung sitting down, everybody crossed their legs and arranged themselves more comfortably, while Amos rose from his seat with terrifying deliberation, mounted the little platform, and sat down.

For some three minutes he slowly surveyed the Brethren, his face wearing an expression of the most profound loathing and contempt, mingled with a divine sorrow and pity. He did it quite well. Flora had never seen anything to touch it except the face of Sir Henry Wood when pausing to contemplate some late-comers into the stalls at the Queen's Hall just as his baton was raised to conduct the first bar of the 'Eroica'. Her heart warmed to Amos. The man was an artist.

At last he spoke. His voice jarred the silence like a broken bell.

'Ye miserable, crawling worms, are ye here again, then? Have ye come like Nimshi, son of Rehoboam, secretly out of yer doomed houses to hear what's comin' to ye? Have ye come, old and young, sick and well, matrons and virgins (if there is any virgins among ye, which is not likely, the world bein' in the wicked state it is), old men and young lads, to hear me tellin' o' the great crimson lickin' flames o' hell fire?'

A long and effective pause, and a further imitation of Sir Henry. The only sound (and it, with the accompanying smell, was quite enough) was the wickering hissing of the gas flares which lit the hall and cast sharp shadows from their noses across the faces of the Brethren.

Amos went on:

'Aye, ye've come.' He laughed shortly and contemptuously. 'Dozens of ye. Hundreds of ye. Like rats to a granary. Like field-mice when there's harvest home. And what good will it do ye?'

Second pause, and more Sir Henry stuff.

'Nowt. Not the flicker of a whisper of a bit o' good.'

He paused and drew a long breath, then suddenly leaped from his seat and thundered at the top of his voice:

'*Ye're all damned!*'

An expression of lively interest and satisfaction passed over the faces of the Brethren, and there was a general re-arranging of arms and legs, as though they wanted to sit as comfortably as possible while listening to the bad news.

'Damned,' he repeated, his voice sinking to a thrilling and effective whisper. 'Oh, do ye ever stop to think what that word *means* when ye use it every day, so lightly, o' yer wicked lives? No. Ye doan't. Ye never stop to think what anything means, do ye? Well, I'll tell ye. It means endless horrifyin' torment, with yer poor sinful bodies stretched out on hot gridirons in the nethermost fiery pit of hell, and demons mockin' ye while they waves cooling jellies in front of ye, and binds ye down tighter on yer dreadful bed. Aye, an' the air'll be full of the stench of burnt flesh and the screams of your nearest and dearest . . .'

He took a gulp of water, which Flora thought he more than deserved. She was beginning to feel that she could do with a glass of water herself.

Amos's voice now took on a deceptively mild and con-versational note. His protruding eyes ranged slowly over his audience.

'Ye know, doan't ye, what it feels like when ye burn yer hand in takin' a cake out of the oven or wi' a match when ye're lightin' one of they godless cigarettes? Aye. It stings wi' a fearful pain, doan't it? And ye run away to clap a bit o' butter on it to take the pain away. Ah, but' (an impressive pause) '*there'll be no butter in hell!* Yer whoal body will be burnin' and stingin' wi' that unbearable pain, and yer blackened tongues will be stickin' out of yer mouth, and yer cracked lips will try to scream out for a drop of water, but no sound woan't come because yer throat is drier nor the sandy desert and yer eyes will be beatin' like great red-hot balls against yer shrivelled eyelids . . .'

It was at this point that Flora rose quietly and with an

apology to the woman sitting next to her, passed rapidly across the narrow aisle to the door. She opened it, and went out. The details of Amos's description, the close atmosphere and the smell of the gas made the inside of the chapel quite near enough to hell, without listening to Amos's conducted tour of the place thrown in. She felt that she could pass the evening more profitably elsewhere.

But where? The fresh air smelled deliciously sweet. She regained her composure while she stood in the porch putting on her gloves. She wondered if she should drop in to see 'Other Wives' Sins', but thought not; she had heard enough about sin for one evening.

What, then, should she do? She could not return to the farm except with Amos in the buggy, for it was seven miles from Beershorn, and the last bus to Howling left at half past six during the winter months. It was now nearly eight o'clock and she was hungry. She looked crossly up and down the street; most of the shops were shut, but one a few doors from the cinema was open.

It was called Pam's Parlour. It was a tea-shop, and Flora thought it looked pretty grim; there were cakes in its windows all mixed up with depressing little boxes made of white wood and raffia bags and linen bags embroidered with hollyhocks. But where there were cakes there might also be coffee. She crossed the road and went in.

No sooner did she stand inside than she realized that she had gone out of hell fire into an evening of boredom. For someone was seated at one of the tables whom she recognized. She seemed to remember meeting him at a party given by a Mrs Polswett in London. And he could only be Mr Mybug. That was who he looked like, and that, of course, was who he was. There was no one else in the shop. He had a clear field, and she could not escape.

CHAPTER 9

He glanced up at her as she came in and looked pleased. He had some books and papers in front of him and had been busily writing.

By now Flora was really cross. Surely she had endured enough for one evening without having to listen to intelligent conversation! Here was an occasion, she thought, for indulging in that deliberate rudeness which only persons with habitually good manners have the right to commit; she sat down at the table with her back to the supposed Mr Mybug, picked up a menu which had gnomes painted on it, and hoped for the best . . .

A waitress in a long frilly chintz dress which needed ironing had brought her coffee, some plain biscuits, and an orange, which she had dressed with sugar and was now enjoying. The waitress had warned her that we were closed, but as this did not seem to prevent Flora sitting in the shop and enjoying her sugared orange, she did not mind if we were.

She was just beginning on her fourth biscuit when she became conscious of a presence approaching her from behind, and before she could collect her faculties the voice of Mr Mybug said:

'Hullo, Flora Poste. Do you believe that women have souls?' And there he was, standing above her and looking down at her with a bold yet whimsical smile.

Flora was not surprised at being asked this question. She knew that intellectuals, like Mr Kipling's Bi-coloured Python-Rock-Snake, always talked like this. So she replied pleasantly, but from her heart: 'I am afraid I'm not very interested.'

Mr Mybug gave a short laugh. Evidently he was pleased. She spooned out some more orange juice and wondered why.

'Aren't you? Good girl . . . we shall be all right if only you'll be frank with me. As a matter of fact, I'm not very interested in whether they have souls either. Bodies matter

100

more than souls. I say, may I sit down? You do remember me, don't you? We met at the Polswetts in October. Look here, you don't think this is butting in or anything, do you? The Polswetts told me you were staying down here, and I wondered if I should run into you. Do you know Billie Polswett well? She's a charming person, I think . . . so simple and gay, and such a genius for friendship. He's charming, too . . . a bit homo, of course, but quite charming. I say, that orange does look good . . . I think I'll have one, too. I adore eating things with a spoon. May I sit here?'

'Do,' said Flora, seeing that her hour was upon her and that there was no escape.

Mr Mybug sat down and, turning round, beckoned to the waitress, who came and told him that we were closed.

'I say, that sounds vaguely indelicate,' laughed Mr My-bug, glancing round at Flora. 'Well, look here, miss, never mind that. Just bring me an orange and some sugar, will you?'

The waitress went away, and Mr Mybug could once more concentrate upon Flora. He leaned his elbows on the table, sank his chin in his hands, and looked steadily at her. As Flora merely went on eating her orange, he was forced to open the game with, 'Well?' (A gambit which Flora, with a sinking heart, recognized as one used by intellectuals who had decided to fall in love with you.)

'You are writing a book, aren't you?' she said, rather hastily. 'I remember that Mrs Polswett told me you were. Isn't it a life of Branwell Brontë?' (She thought it would be best to utilize the information artlessly conveyed to her by Mrs Murther at the Condemn'd Man, and conceal the fact that she had met Mrs Polswett, a protégée of Mrs Smiling's, only once, and thought her a most trying female.)

'Yes, it's goin' to be dam' good,' said Mr Mybug. 'It's a psychological study, of course, and I've got a lot of new matter, including three letters he wrote to an old aunt in Ireland, Mrs Prunty, during the period when he was work-ing on *Wuthering Heights*.'

He glanced sharply at Flora to see if she would react by a

laugh or a stare of blank amazement, but the gentle, interested expression upon her face did not change, so he had to explain.

'You see, it's obvious that it's his book and not Emily's. No woman could have written that. It's male stuff . . . I've worked out a theory about his drunkenness, too – you see, he wasn't really a drunkard. He was a tremendous genius, a sort of second Chatterton – and his sisters hated him because of his genius.'

'I thought most of the contemporary records agree that his sisters were quite devoted to him,' said Flora, who was only too pleased to keep the conversation impersonal.

'I know . . . I know. But that was only their cunning. You see, they were devoured by jealousy of their brilliant brother, but they were afraid that if they showed it he would go away to London for good, taking his manuscripts with him. And they didn't want him to do that because it would have spoiled their little game.'

'Which little game was that?' asked Flora, trying with some difficulty to imagine Charlotte, Emily, and Anne engaged in a little game.

'Passing his manuscripts off as their own, of course. They wanted to have him under their noses so that they could steal his work and sell it to buy more drink.'

'Who for – Branwell?'

'No – for themselves. They were all drunkards, but Anne was the worst of the lot. Branwell, who adored her, used to pretend to get drunk at the Black Bull in order to get gin for Anne. The landlord wouldn't let him have it if Branwell hadn't built up – with what devotion, only God knows – that false reputation as a brilliant, reckless, idle drunkard. The landlord was proud to have young Mr Brontë in his tavern; it attracted custom to the place, and Branwell could get gin for Anne on tick – as much as Anne wanted. Secretly, he worked twelve hours a day writing *Shirley* and *Villette* – and, of course, *Wuthering Heights*. I've proved all this by evidence from the three letters to old Mrs Prunty.'

'But do the letters,' inquired Flora, who was fascinated

by this recital, 'actually say that he is writing *Wuthering Heights*?'

'Of course not,' retorted Mr Mybug. 'Look at the question as a psychologist would. Here is a man working fifteen hours a day on a stupendous masterpiece which absorbs almost all his energy. He will scarcely spare the time to eat or sleep. He's like a dynamo driving itself on its own demoniac vitality. Every scrap of his being is concentrated on finishing *Wuthering Heights*. With what little energy he has left he writes to an old aunt in Ireland. Now, I ask you, would you expect him to mention that he was working on *Wuthering Heights*?'

'Yes,' said Flora.

Mr Mybug shook his head violently.

'No – no – no! Of course he wouldn't. He'd want to get away from it for a little while, away from this all-obsessing work that was devouring his vitality. Of course he wouldn't mention it – not even to his aunt.'

'Why not even to her? Was he so fond of her?'

'She was the passion of his life,' said Mr Mybug, simply, with a luminous gravity in his voice. 'Think – he'd never seen her. She was not like the rest of the drab angular women by whom he was surrounded. She symbolized mystery . . . woman . . . the eternal unsolvable and unfindable X. It was a perversion, of course, his passion for her, and that made it all the stronger. All we have left of this fragile, wonderfully delicate relationship between the old woman and the young man are these three short letters. Nothing more.'

'Didn't she ever answer them?'

'If she did, her letters are lost. But his letters to her are enough to go on. They are little masterpieces of repressed passion. They're full of tender little questions . . . he asks her how is her rheumatism . . . has her cat, Toby, "recovered from the fever" . . . what is the weather like at Derrydownderry . . . at Haworth it is not so good . . . how is Cousin Martha (and what a picture we get of Cousin Martha in those simple words, a raw Irish chit, high-cheekboned, with

103

limp black hair and clear blood in her lips!) . . . It didn't matter to Branwell that in London the Duke was jockeying Palmerston in the stormy Corn Reforms of the "forties". Aunt Prunty's health and welfare came first in interest.'

Mr Mybug paused and refreshed himself with a spoonful of orange juice. Flora sat pondering on what she had just heard. Judging by her personal experience among her friends, it was not the habit of men of genius to refresh themselves from their labours by writing to old aunts; this task, indeed, usually fell to the sisters and wives of men of genius, and it struck Flora as far more likely that Charlotte, Anne, or Emily would have had to cope with any old aunts who were clamouring to be written to. However, perhaps Charlotte, Anne, or Emily had all decided one morning that it really *was* Branwell's turn to write to Aunt Prunty, and had sat on his head in turn while he wrote the three letters, which were afterwards posted at prudently spaced intervals.

She glanced at her watch.

It was half past eight. She wondered what time the Brethren came out of the dog-kennel. There was no sign of their release so far; the kennel was thundering to their singing, and at intervals there were pauses, during which Flora presumed that they were quivering. She swallowed a tiny yawn. She was sleepy.

'What are you going to call it?'

She knew that intellectuals always made a great fuss about the titles of their books. The titles of biographies were especially important. Had not *Victorian Vista*, the scathing life of Thomas Carlyle, dropped stone cold last year from the presses because everybody thought it was a boring book of reminiscences, while *Odour of Sanctity*, a rather dull history of Drainage Reform from 1840 to 1873, had sold like hot cakes because everybody thought it was an attack on Victorian morality.

'I'm hesitating between *Scapegoat; A Study of Branwell Brontë*, and *Pard-spirit; A Study of Branwell Brontë* – you know . . . A pard-like spirit, beautiful and swift.'

Flora did indeed know. The quotation was from Shelley's

'Adonais'. One of the disadvantages of almost universal education was the fact that all kinds of persons acquired a familiarity with one's favourite writers. It gave one a curious feeling; it was like seeing a drunken stranger wrapped in one's dressing-gown.

'Which do you like best?' asked Mr Mybug.

'*Pard-spirit*,' said Flora, unhesitatingly, not because she did, but because it would only lead to a long and boring argument if she hesitated.

'Really . . . that's interesting. So do I. It's wilder somehow, isn't it? I mean, I think it does give one something of the feeling of a wild thing bound down and chained, eh? And Branwell's colouring carries out the analogy – that wild reddish-leopard colouring. I refer to him as the Pard throughout the book. And then, of course, there's an undercurrent of symbolism . . .'

He thinks of everything, reflected Flora.

'A leopard can't change his spots, and neither could Branwell, in the end. He might take the blame for his sisters' drunkenness and let them, out of some perverted sense of sacrifice, claim his books. But in the end his genius has flamed out, blackest spots on richest gold. There isn't an intelligent person in Europe to-day who really believes Emily wrote the *Heights*.'

Flora finished her last biscuit, which she had been saving, and looked hopefully across at the dog-kennel. It seemed to her that the hymn now being sung had a sound like the tune of those hymns which are played just before people come out of church.

In the interval of outlining his work, Mr Mybug had been looking at her very steadily, with his chin lowered, and she was not surprised when he said, abruptly:

'Do you cah about walking?'

Flora was now in a dreadful fix, and earnestly wished that the dog-kennel would open and Amos, like a fiery angel, come to rescue her. For if she said that she adored walking, Mr Mybug would drag her for miles in the rain while he talked about sex, and if she said that she liked it only in moderation, he would make her sit on wet stiles, while he tried to kiss her. If, again, she parried his question and said that she loathed walking, he would either suspect that she suspected that he wanted to kiss her, or else he would make her sit in some dire tea-room while he talked more about sex and asked her what she felt about it.

There really seemed no way out of it, except by getting up and rushing out of the shop.

But Mr Mybug spared her this decision by continuing in the same low voice:

'I thought we might do some walks together, if you'd cah to? I'd better warn you – I'm – pretty susceptible.'

And he gave a curt laugh, still looking at her.

'Then perhaps we had better postpone our walks until the weather is finer,' said she, pleasantly. 'It would be too bad if your book were held up by your catching a cold, and if you really have a weak chest you cannot be too careful.'

Mr Mybug looked as though he would have given much to have brushed this aside with a brutal laugh. He had planned that his next sentence should be, in an even lower voice:

'You see, I believe in utter frankness about these things – Flora.'

But somehow he did not say it. He was not used to talking to young women who looked as clean as Flora looked. It rather put him off his stroke. He said instead, in a toneless voice: 'Yes . . . oh, yes, of course,' and gave her a quick glance.

Flora was pensively drawing on her gauntlets and keeping her glance upon the stream of Brethren now issuing from the dog-kennel. She feared to miss Amos.

Mr Mybug rose abruptly, and stood looking at her with his hands thrust into his pockets.

'Are you with anybody?' he asked.

'My cousin is preaching at the Church of the Quivering Brethren opposite. He is driving me home.'

Mr Mybug murmured his, 'dear, how amusing.' He then said:

'Oh ... I thought we might have walked it.'

'It is seven miles, and I am afraid my shoes are not stout enough,' countered Flora firmly.

Mr Mybug gave an ironical smile and muttered something about 'Check to the King', but Flora had seen Amos coming out of the kennel and knew that rescue had come, so she did not mind who was checked.

She said, pleasantly, 'I must go, I am afraid; there is my cousin looking for me. Good-bye, and thank you so much for telling me about your book. It's been so interesting. Perhaps we shall meet again sometime ...'

Mr Mybug leapt on this remark, which slipped out unintentionally from Flora's social armoury, before she could prevent it, and said eagerly that it would be great fun if they could meet again. 'I'll give you my card.' And he brought out a large, dirty, nasty one, which Flora with some reluctance put into her bag.

'I warn you,' added Mr Mybug, 'I'm a queer moody brute. Nobody likes me. I'm like a child that's been rapped over the knuckles till it's afraid to shake hands – but there's something there if you cah to dig for it.'

Flora did not cah to dig, but she thanked him for his card with a smile, and hurried across the road to join Amos, who stood towering in the middle of it.

As she came up to him he drew back, pointed at her, and uttered the single word:

'Fornicator!'

'No – dash it, Cousin Amos, that wasn't a stranger; it was a person I'd met before at a party in London,' protested Flora, her indignation a little roused by the unjustness of the accusation, especially when she thought of her real feelings for Mr Mybug.

''Tes all one – aye, and worse too, comin' from London, the devil's city,' said Amos, grimly.

However, his protest had apparently been a matter more of form than of feeling. He said nothing more about it, and they drove home in silence, save for a single remark from him to the effect that the Brethren had been mightily stirred by his preaching and that Flora had missed a good deal by not staying for the quivering.

To which Flora replied that she was sure she had, but that his eloquence had been altogether too much for her weak and sinful spirit. She added firmly that he really ought to see about going round on that Ford van; and he sighed heavily, and said that no doubt she was a devil sent to tempt him.

Still, the seeds were sown. Her plans were maturing.

It was not until she glanced at Mr Mybug's card in the candle-light of her own room that she discovered that his name was not Mybug, but Meyerburg, and that he lived in Charlotte Street – two facts which were not calculated to raise her spirits. But such had been the varied excitements of the day that her subsequent sleep was deep and unbroken.

CHAPTER 10

It was now the third week in March. Fecund dreams stirred the yearlings. The sukebind was in bud. The swede harvest was over; the beet harvest not yet begun. This meant that Micah, Urk, Amos, Caraway, Harkaway, Mizpah, Luke, Mark and four farm-hands who were not related to the family had a good deal of time on their hands in one way and another. Seth, of course, was always busiest in the spring. Adam was employed about the beastenhousen with the yearling lambs. Reuben was preparing the fields for the harvest after next; he never rested, however slack the season of the year. But the other Starkadders were simply ripe for rows and mischief.

As for Flora, she was quite enjoying herself. She was mixed up in a good many plots. Only a person with a candid mind, who is usually bored by intrigues, can appreciate the full fun of an intrigue when they begin to manage one for the first time. If there are several intrigues and there is a certain danger of their getting mixed up and spoiling each other, the enjoyment is even keener.

Of course, some of the plots were going better than others. Her plot to make Adam use a little mop to clean the dishes with, instead of a thorn twig, had gone sour on her.

One day, when Adam came into the kitchen just after breakfast, Flora had said to him:

'Oh, Adam, here's your little mop. I got it in Howling this afternoon. Look, isn't it a nice little one? You try it and see.'

For a second she had thought he would dash it from her hand, but gradually, as he stared at the little mop, his expression of fury changed to one more difficult to read.

It was, indeed, rather a nice little mop. It had a plain handle of white wood with a little waist right at the tip, so that it could be more comfortably held in the hand. Its head was of soft white threads, each fibre being distinct and comely instead of being matted together in an unsightly lump like the heads of most little mops. Most taking of all, it had a loop of fine red string, with which to hang it up, knotted round its little waist.

Adam cautiously put out his finger and poked at it. ''Tes mine?'

'Aye – I mean, yes, it's yours. Your very own. Do take it.'

He took it between his finger and thumb and stood gazing at it. His eyes had filmed over like sightless Atlantic pools before the flurry of the storm breath. His gnarled fingers folded round the handle.

'Aye ... 'tes mine,' he muttered. 'Nor house nor kine, and yet 'tes mine ... My little mop!'

He undid the thorn twig which fastened the bosom of his shirt and thrust the mop within. But then he withdrew it again, and replaced the thorn. 'My little mop!' He stood staring at it in a dream.

'Yes. It's to cletter the dishes with,' said Flora, firmly, suddenly foreseeing a new danger on the horizon.

'Nay ... nay,' protested Adam. ''Tes too pretty to cletter

those great old dishes wi'. I mun do that with the thorn twigs; they'll serve. I'll keep my liddle mop in the shed, along wi' our Pointless and our Feckless.'

'They might eat it,' suggested Flora.

'Aye, aye, so they might, Robert Poste's child. Ah, well, I mun hang it up by its liddle red string above the dish-washin' bowl. Niver put my liddle pretty in that gurt old greasy washin'-up water. Aye, 'tes prettier nor apple-blooth, my liddle mop.'

And shuffling across the kitchen, he hung it carefully on the wall above the sink, and stood for some time admiring it. Flora was justifiably irritated, and went crossly out for a walk.

She was frequently cheered by letters from her friends in London. Mrs Smiling was now in Egypt, but she wrote often. When abroad in hot climates she wore a great many white dresses, said very little, and all the men in the hotel fell in love with her. Charles also wrote in reply to Flora's little notes. Her short, informative sentences on two sides of deep blue note-paper brought details in return from Charles about the weather in Hertfordshire and messages from his mother. What little else he wrote about, Flora seemed to find mightily satisfying. She looked forward to his letters. She also heard from Julia, who collected books about gangsters, from Claud Hart-Harris, and from all her set in general. So, though exiled, she was not lonely.

Occasionally, while taking her daily walk on the Downs, she saw Elfine: a light, rangy shape which had the plastic contours of a choir-boy etched by Botticelli, drawn against the thin cold sky of spring. Elfine never came near her and this annoyed Flora. She wanted to get hold of Elfine and to give her some tactful advice about Dick Hawk-Monitor.

Adam had confided to Flora his fears about Elfine. She did not think he had done it consciously. He was milking at the time, and she was watching him, and he was talking half to himself.

'She's ay a-peerin' at the windows of Hautcouture Hall' (he pronounced it 'Howchiker', in the local man-

ner) 'to get a sight of that young chuck-stubbard, Mus'
Richard,' he had said.

Something earthly, something dark and rooty as the bar-
ran that thrust its tenacious way through the yeasty soil
had crept into the old man's voice with the words. He was
moved. Old tides lapped his loins.

'Is that the young squire?' asked Flora, casually. She
wanted to get to the bottom of this business without seeming inquisitive.

'Aye – blast un fer a capsy, set-up yearling of a womanizer.' The reply came clotted with rage, but behind the rage
were traces of some other and more obscure emotion; a
bright-eyed grubbing in the lore of farmyard and bin, a
hint of the casual lusts of chicken-house and duck-pond, a
racy, yeasty, posty-toasty interest in the sordid drama of
man's eternal blind attack and woman's inevitable yielding
and loss.

Flora had experienced some distaste, but her wish to tidy
up Cold Comfort had compelled her to pursue her inquiries.

She asked when the young people were to be married,
knowing full well what the answer would be. Adam gave a
loud and unaccustomed sound which she had with some
difficulty interpreted as a mirthless laugh.

'When apples grow on the sukebind ye may see lust buy
hissen a wedding garment,' he had replied meaningfully.

Flora nodded, more gloomily than she felt. She thought
that Adam took too black a view of the case. Probably,
Richard Hawk-Monitor was only mildly attracted by Elfine, and the thought of behaving as Adam feared had
never occurred to him. Even if it had, it would have been
instantly dismissed.

Flora knew her hunting gentry. They were what the
Americans, bless them! call dumb. They hated fuss.
Poetry (Flora was pretty sure Elfine wrote poetry) bored
them. They preferred the society of persons who spoke
once in twenty minutes. They liked dogs to be well trained
and girls to be well turned out and frosts to be of short

duration. It was most unlikely that Richard was planning a Lyceum betrayal of Elfine. But it was even less likely that he wanted to marry her. The eccentricity of her dress, behaviour, and hairdressing would put him off automatically. Like most other ideas, the idea would simply not have entered his head.

'So, unless I do something about it,' thought Flora, 'she will simply be left on my hands. And heaven knows nobody will want to marry her while she looks like that and wears those frocks. Unless, of course, I fix her up with Mr Mybug.'

But Mr Mybug was, temporarily at least, in love with Flora herself, so that was another obstacle. And was it quite fair to fling Elfine, all unprepared, to those Bloomsbury-cum-Charlotte-Street lions which exchanged their husbands and wives every other week-end in the most broad-minded fashion? They always made Flora think of the description of the wild boars painted on the vases in Dickens's story – 'each wild boar having his leg elevated in the air at a painful angle to show his perfect freedom and gaiety'. And it must be so discouraging for them to find each new love exactly resembling the old one: just like trying balloon after balloon at a bad party and finding they all had holes in and would not blow up properly.

No. Elfine must not be thrown into Charlotte Street. She must be civilized, and then she must marry Richard.

So Flora continued to look out for Elfine when she went out for walks on the Downs.

Aunt Ada Doom sat in her room upstairs . . . alone.

There was something almost symbolic in her solitude. She was the core, the matrix; the focusing-point of the house . . . and she was, like all cores, utterly alone. You never heard of two cores to a thing, did you? Well, then. Yet all the wandering waves of desire, passion, jealousy, lust, that throbbed through the house converged, web-like, upon her core-solitude. She felt herself to be a core . . . and utterly, irrevocably alone.

The weakening winds of spring fawned against the old house. The old woman's thoughts cowered in the hot room where she sat in solitude ... She would not see her niece ... Keep her away ...

Make some excuse. Shut her out. She had been here a month and you had not seen her. She thought it strange, did she? She dropped hints that she would like to see you. You did not want to see her. You felt ... you felt some strange emotion at the thought of her. You would not see her. Your thoughts wound slowly round the room like beasts rubbing against the drowsy walls. And outside the walls the winds rubbed like drowsy beasts. Half-way between the inside and the outside walls, winds and thoughts were both drowsy. How enervating was the warm wind of the coming spring ...

When you were very small – so small that the lightest puff of breeze blew your little crinoline skirt over your head – you had seen something nasty in the woodshed.

You'd never forgotten it.

You'd never spoken of it to Mamma – you could smell, even to this day, the fresh betel-nut with which her shoes were always cleaned – but you'd remembered all your life.

That was what had made you ... different. That – what you had seen in the tool-shed – had made your marriage a prolonged nightmare to you.

Somehow you had never bothered about what it had been like for your husband ...

That was why you had brought your children into the world with loathing. Even now, when you were seventy-nine, you could never see a bicycle go past your bedroom window without a sick plunge at the apex of your stomach ... in the bicycle shed you'd seen it, something nasty, when you were very small.

That was why you stayed in this room. You had been here for twenty years, ever since Judith had married and her husband had come to live at the farm. You had run away from the huge, terrifying world outside these four walls against which your thoughts rubbed themselves like drowsy yaks. Yes, that was what they were like. Yaks. Exactly like yaks.

Outside in the world there were potting-sheds where nasty things could happen. But nothing could happen here. You saw to that. None of your grandchildren might leave the farm. Judith might not leave. Amos might not leave. Caraway might not leave. Urk might not leave. Seth might not leave. Micah might not leave. Ezra might not leave. Mark and Luke might not leave. Harkaway might leave sometimes because he paid the proceeds of the farm into the bank at Beershorn every Saturday morning, but none of the others might leave.

None of them must go out into the great dirty world where there were cow-sheds in which nasty things could happen and be seen by little girls.

You had them all. You curved your old wrinkled hand into a brown shell, and laughed to yourself. You held them like that... in the hollow of your hand, as the Lord held Israel. None of them had any money except what you gave them. You allowed Micah, Urk, Caraway, Mark, Luke, and Ezra tenpence a week each in pocket-money. Harkaway had a shilling, to cover his fare by bus down into Beershorn and back. You had your heel on them all. They were your washpot, and you had cast your shoe out over them.

Even Seth, your darling, your last and loveliest grandchild, you held in the hollow of your old palm. He had one and sixpence a week pocket-money. Amos had none. Judith had none.

How like yaks were your drowsy thoughts, slowly winding round in the dim air of your quiet room. The winter landscape, breaking upon spring's pressure, beat urgently against the panes.

So you sat here, living from meal to meal (Monday, pork; Tuesday, beef; Wednesday, toad-in-the-hole; Thursday, mutton; Friday, veal; Saturday, curry; Sunday, cutlets). Sometimes... you were so old... how could you know?

... you dropped soup on yourself ... you whimpered ... Once Judith brought up the kidneys for your breakfast and they were too hot and burned your tongue ... Day slipped into day, season into season, year into year. And you sat here, alone. You ... Cold Comfort Farm.

Sometimes Urk came to see you, the second child of your sister's man by marriage, and told you that the farm was rotting away.

No matter. There have always been Starkadders at Cold Comfort.

Well, let it rot ... You couldn't have a farm without sheds (cow, wood, tool, bicycle, and potting), and where there were sheds things were bound to rot ... Besides, so far as you could see from your bi-weekly inspection of the farm account books, things weren't doing too badly ... Anyway, here you were, and here they all stayed with you.

You told them you were mad. You had been mad since you saw something nasty in the woodshed, years and years and years ago. If any of them went away, to any other part of the country, you would go much madder. Any attempt by any of them to get away from the farm made one of your attacks of madness come on. It was unfortunate in some ways but useful in others ... The woodshed incident had twisted something in your child-brain seventy years ago.

And seeing that it was because of that incident that you sat here ruling the roost and having five meals a day brought up to you as regularly as clockwork, it hadn't been such a bad break for you, that day you saw something nasty in the woodshed.

CHAPTER II

THE bull was bellowing. The steady sound went up into the air in a dark red column. Seth leaned moodily on the hoot-piece, watching Reuben, who was slowly but deftly repairing a leak in the midden-rail. Not a bud broke the dark feathery faces of the thorns, but the air whined with spring's passage. It was eleven in the morning. A bird sang his idiotic recitative from the dairy roof.

Both brothers looked up as Flora came across the yard dressed for her walk upon the Downs. She looked inquiringly at the shed, whence issued the shocking row made by Big Business, the bull.

'I think it would be a good idea if you let him out,' she said. Seth grinned and nudged Reuben, who coloured dully.

'I don't mean for stud purposes. I meant simply for air and exercise,' said Flora. 'You cannot expect a bull to produce healthy stock if he is shut up in the smelly dark all day.'

Seth disapproved of the impersonal note which the conversation had taken, so he lounged away. But Reuben was always ready to listen to advice which had the good of the farm at heart, and Flora had discovered this. He said, quite civilly:

'Aye, 'tes true. We mun let un out in the great field tomorrow.' He returned to his repairing of the midden-rail, but just as Flora was walking away he looked up again and remarked:

'So ye went wi' the old devil, eh?'

Flora was learning how to translate the Starkadder argot, and took this to mean that she had, last week, accompanied her Cousin Amos to the Church of the Quivering Brethren. She replied in tones just tinged with polite surprise:

'I am not quite sure what you mean, but if you mean did I go with Cousin Amos to Beershorn, yes, I did.'

'Aye, ye went. And did the old devil say anything about me?'

Flora could only recall a remark about dead men's shoes, which it would scarcely be prudent to repeat, so she replied that she did not remember much of what had been said because the sermon had been so powerful that it had driven everything else out of her head.

'I was advising Cousin Amos,' she added, 'to address his

sermons to a wider audience. I think he ought to go round the country on a lorry, preaching –'

'Frittenin' the harmless birds off the bushes, more like,' interposed Reuben, gloomily.

'– at fairs and on market days. You see, if Cousin Amos were away a good deal it would mean that someone else would have to take charge of the farm, wouldn't it?'

'Someone else will have to take charge of it, in any case, when the old devil dies,' said Reuben. Stark passion curdled the whites of his eyes and his breath came thraw.

'Yes, of course,' said Flora. 'He talks of leaving it to Adam. Now, I don't think that would be at all wise, do you? To begin with, Adam is ninety. He has no children (at least, he has none as far as I know, and, of course, I do not listen to what Mrs Beetle says), and I should not think he is likely to marry, should you? Nor has he the legal type of mind. I shouldn't imagine he would trouble to make a will, for example. And if he did make one, who knows who he would leave the farm to? He might leave it to Feckless, or even to Aimless, and that would mean a lot of legal trouble, for I doubt if two cows can inherit a farm. Then, again, Pointless and Graceless might put in a claim for it, and that could easily mean an endless lawsuit in which all the resources of the farm would be swallowed up. Oh, no, I hardly think it would do for Cousin Amos to leave the farm to Adam. I think it would be much better if he were persuaded to go on a preaching tour round England, or perhaps to retire to some village a long way off and write a nice long book of sermons. Then whoever was left in charge of the farm could get a good grip of affairs here, and when Cousin Amos did come back at last, he would see that the management of the farm must be left in the hands of that person in order to save all the bother of getting things reorganized. You see, Reuben, Cousin Amos could not think of leaving the farm to Adam then, because the person who had been managing it would obviously be the person to leave it to.'

She faltered a little towards the end of her speech as she recalled that the Starkadders rarely did what was obvious, though they were only too embarrassingly ready to do what was natural. Nor did her remarks have the wished-for effect upon Reuben. He said, in a voice thick with fury:

'Meanin' you?'

'No, indeed. I've already told you, Reuben, that I should be no use at all at running the farm. I do think you might believe me.'

'If ye doan't mean you, who do you mean?'

Flora abandoned diplomacy, and said, 'You.'

'Me?'

'Aye, you.' She patiently dropped into Starkadder.

He stared thickly at her. She observed with distaste that his chest was extremely hairy.

''Tes impossible,' he said at last. 'The old lady would never let him go.'

'Why not?' asked Flora. 'Why should he not go? Why does Aunt Ada Doom like to keep you all here, as though you were all children?'

'She – she – she's ill,' stammered Reuben, casting a fleeting glance at the closed, dusty windows of the farm high above his head, where the lin-tits were already building under the eaves. 'If any on us says we'll leave the farm, she gets an attack. There have always been Starkadders at Cold Comfort. None of us mun go, except Harkaway, when he takes the money down to the bank at Beershorn every Saturday morning.'

'But you all go into Beershorn sometimes.'

'Aye, but 'tes a great risk. If she knew, 'twould bring on an attack.'

'An attack? What of?' Flora was getting a little impatient. Unlike Charles she deplored a gloomy mystery.

'Her – her illness. She – she ain't like other people's grandmothers. When she was no bigger than a linnet, she saw –'

'Oh, Reuben, do hurry up and tell me, there's a good

soul. All the sun will be gone by the time I get up on to the Downs.'

'She – she's mad.'

Fat and dark, the word lay between them in the indifferent air. Time, which had been behaving normally lately, suddenly began to spin upon a bright point in endless space. It never rains but it pours.

'Oh,' said Flora, thoughtfully.

So that was it. Aunt Ada Doom was mad. You would expect, by all the laws of probability, to find a mad grandmother at Cold Comfort Farm, and for once the laws of probability had not done you down and a mad grandmother there was.

Flora observed, tapping her shoe with her walking-stick, that it was very awkward.

'Aye,' said Reuben, ''tes terrible. And her madness takes the form of wantin' to know everything as goes on. She has to see all the books twice a week: the milk book an' the chicken book an' the pig book and corn book. If we keeps the books back, she has an attack. 'Tes terrible. She's the head of the family, ye see. We mun keep her alive at all costs. She never comes downstairs but twice a year – on the first of May and on the last day of the harvest festival. If anybody eats too much, she has an attack. 'Tes terrible.'

'It is indeed,' agreed Flora. It struck her that Aunt Ada Doom's madness had taken the most convenient form possible. If everybody who went mad could arrange in what way it was to take them, she felt pretty sure they would all choose to be mad like Ada Doom.

'Is that why she doesn't want to see me?' she asked. 'I've been here nearly a month, you know, and I have never seen her yet.'

'Aye . . . maybe.' said Reuben, indifferently. His long speech seemed to have exhausted him. His face was sodden, sunk in on itself in defensive folds.

'Well, anyway,' said Flora, briskly, 'because Aunt Ada is mad there is no reason why you should not try to persuade Cousin Amos to go on a preaching tour, and then manage the farm while he is away. You have a stab at it.'

'Do you think,' said Reuben, slowly, 'that if I was to look after th' farm while the old devil was away, moitherin' about hell fire to a lot of frittened birds and cows a long way off, he'd come back and see as I could do it, and maybe leave it to me for my own when he's gone?'

'Yes, I do,' said Flora, firmly.

Reuben's face became contorted with a number of emotions, and suddenly, even as she watched him, victory was hers!

'Aye,' he said hoarsely, 'dang me if I doan't din into the old devil how he must be off speechifyin' this very week.'

And much to her surprise he held out his hand to her. She took it and shook it warmly. This was the first sign of humanity she had encountered among the Starkadders, and she was moved by it. She felt like stout Cortez or Sir James Jeans on spotting yet another white dwarf.

She was cheerful as she walked away towards the downland path. If Reuben did not overdo the persuading stunt (and this was a real danger, for Amos was astute and would soon see through any obvious attempt to get rid of him) her plan should succeed.

It was a fresh, pleasant morning and she felt the more disposed to enjoy her walk because Mr Mybug (she could not learn to think of him as Meyerburg) was not with her. For the last three mornings he had been with her, but this morning she had said that he really ought to do some work. Flora did not see why, but one excuse was as good as another to get rid of him.

It cannot be said that Flora really enjoyed taking walks with Mr Mybug. To begin with, he was not really interested in anything but sex. This was understandable, if deplorable. After all, many of our best minds have had the same weakness. The trouble about Mr Mybug was that ordinary subjects, which are not usually associated with sex even by our best minds, did suggest sex to Mr Mybug, and he pointed them out and made comparisons and asked Flora what she thought about it all. Flora found it difficult to reply because she was not interested. She was therefore obliged merely to be polite, and Mr Mybug mistook her lack of enthusiasm and thought it was due to inhibitions. He remarked how curious it was that most Englishwomen (most young Englishwomen, that was, Englishwomen of about nineteen to twenty-four) were inhibited. Cold, that was what young Englishwomen from nineteen to twenty-four were.

They used sometimes to walk through a pleasant wood of young birch trees which were just beginning to come into bud. The stems reminded Mr Mybug of phallic symbols and the buds made Mr Mybug think of nipples and virgins. Mr Mybug pointed out to Flora that he and she were walking on seeds which were germinating in the womb of the earth. He said it made him feel as if he were trampling on the body of a great brown woman. He felt as if he were a partner in some mighty rite of gestation.

Flora used sometimes to ask him the name of a tree, but he never knew.

Yet there were few occasions when he was not reminded of a pair of large breasts by the distant hills. Then, he would stand looking at the woods upon the horizon. He would wrinkle up his eyes and breathe deeply through his nostrils and say that the view reminded him of one of Poussin's lovely things. Or he would pause and peer in a pool and say it was like a painting by Manet.

And, to be fair to Mr Mybug, it must be admitted he was sometimes interested by the social problems of the day. Only yesterday, while he and Flora were walking through an alley of rhododendrons on an estate which was open to the public, he had discussed a case of arrest in Hyde Park. The rhododendrons made him think of Hyde Park. He said that it was impossible to sit down for five minutes in Hyde Park after seven in the evening without being either accosted or arrested.

There were many homosexuals to be seen in Hyde Park. Prostitutes, too. God! those rhododendron buds had a phallic, urgent look!

121

Sooner or later we should have to tackle the problem of homosexuality. We should have to tackle the problem of Lesbians and old maids.

God! that little pool down there in the hollow was shaped just like somebody's navel! He would like to drag off his clothes and leap into it. There was another problem . . . We should have to tackle that, too. In no other country but England was there so much pruriency about nakedness. If we all went about naked, sexual desire would automatically disappear. Had Flora ever been to a party where everybody took off all their clothes? Mr Mybug had. Once a whole lot of us bathed in the river with nothing on and afterwards little Harriet Belmont sat naked in the grass and played to us on her flute. It was delicious; so gay and simple and natural. And Billie Polswett danced a Hawaiian love-dance, making all the gestures that are usually omitted in the stage version. Her husband had danced too. It had been lovely; so warm and natural and *real*, somehow.

So, taking it all round, Flora was pleased to have her walk in solitude.

She passed a girl riding on a pony and two young men walking with knapsacks and sticks, but no one else. She went down into a valley, filled with bushes of hazel and gorse, and made her way towards a little house built of grey stones, its roof painted turquoise-green, which stood on the other side of the Down. It was a shepherd's hut; she could see the stone hut close to it in which ewes were kept at lambing-time and a shallow trough from which they drank.

If Mr Mybug had been there, he would have said that the ewes were paying the female thing's tribute to the Life Force. He said a woman's success could only be estimated by the success of her sexual life, and Flora supposed he would say the same thing about a ewe.

Oh, she *was* so glad he wasn't there!

She went skipping round the corner of the little sheep-house and saw Elfine, sitting on a turf and sunning herself.

Both cousins were startled. But Flora was quite pleased. She wanted a chance to talk to Elfine.

Elfine jumped to her feet and stood poised; she had
something of the brittle grace of a yearling foal. A dryad's
smile played on the curious sullen purity of her mouth, and
her eyes were unawake and unfriendly. Flora thought,
'What a dreadful way of doing one's hair; surely it must be
a mistake.'

'You're Flora – I'm Elfine,' said the other girl simply.
Her voice had a breathless, broken quality that suggested
the fluty sexless timbre of a choir-boy's notes (only choir-
boys are seldom sexless, as many a harassed vicaress knows
to her cost).

'No prizes offered,' thought Flora, rather rudely. But she
said politely: 'Yes. Isn't it a delicious morning. Have you
been far?'

'Yes ... No ... Away over there ...' The vague gesture
of her outflung arm sketched, in some curious fashion,
illimitable horizons. Judith's gestures had the same barrier-
less quality; there was not a vase left anywhere in the farm.

'I feel stifled in the house,' Elfine went on, shyly and
abruptly. 'I hate houses.'

'Indeed?' said Flora.

She observed Elfine draw a deep breath, and knew that
she was about to get well away on a good long description
of herself and her habits, as these shy dryads always did if
you gave them half a chance. So she sat down on another
turf in the sun and composed herself to listen, looking up at
the tall Elfine.

'Do you like poetry?' asked Elfine, suddenly. A pure
flood of colour ran up under her skin. Her hands, burnt and
bone-modelled as a boy's, were clenched.

'Some of it,' responded Flora, cautiously.

'I adore it,' said Elfine, simply. 'It says all the things I
can't say for myself ... somehow ... It means ... oh, I don't
know. Just everything, somehow. It's *enough*. Do you ever
feel that?'

Flora replied that she had, occasionally, felt something of
the sort, but her reply was limited by the fact that she was
not quite sure exactly what Elfine meant.

'I write poetry,' said Elfine. (So I was right! thought Flora.) 'I'll show you some . . . if you promise not to laugh. I can't bear my children being laughed at . . . I call my poems my children.'

Flora felt that she could promise this with safety.

'And love, too,' muttered Elfine, her voice breaking and changing shyly like the Finnish ice under the first lusty rays and wooing winds of the Finnish spring. 'Love and poetry go together, somehow . . . out here on the hills, when I'm alone with my dreams . . . oh, I can't tell you how I feel. I've been chasing a squirrel all the morning.'

Flora said severely:

'Elfine, are you engaged?'

Her cousin stood perfectly still. Slowly the colour receded from her face. Her head dropped. She muttered: 'There's someone . . . We don't want to spoil things by having anything definite and binding . . . it's horrible . . . to bind anyone down.'

'Nonsense. It is a very good idea,' said Flora, austerely, 'and it is a good thing for you to be bound down, too. Now, what do you suppose will happen to you if you don't marry this Someone?'

Elfine's face brightened. 'Oh . . . but I've got it all planned out,' she said, eagerly. 'I shall get a job in an arts and crafts shop in Horsham and do barbola work in my spare time. I shall be all right . . . and later on I can go to Italy and perhaps learn to be a little like St Francis of Assisi . . .'

'It is quite unnecessary for a young woman to resemble St Francis of Assisi,' said Flora coldly; 'and in your case it would be downright suicidal. A large girl like you *must* wear clothes that *fit*; and Elfine, *whatever* you do, always wear court shoes. Remember – c-o-u-r-t. You are so handsome that you can wear the most conventional clothes and look very well in them; but do, for heaven's sake, avoid orange linen jumpers and hand-wrought jewellery. Oh, and shawls in the evening.'

She paused. She saw by Elfine's expression that she had been progressing too quickly. Elfine looked puzzled and extremely wretched. Flora was penitent. She had taken a fancy to the ridiculous chit. She said in a very friendly tone, drawing her cousin down to sit beside her:

'Now, what is it? Tell me. Do you hate being at home?'

'Yes . . . but I'm not often there,' whispered Elfine. 'No . . . it's Urk.'

Urk . . . That was the foxy-looking little man who was always staring at Flora's ankles or else spitting into the well.

'What about Urk?' she demanded.

'He . . . they . . . I think he wants to marry me,' stammered Elfine. 'I think Grandmother means me to marry him when I am eighteen. He . . . he . . . climbs the apple-tree outside my window and tries to watch me going to . . . to bed. I had to hang up three face-towels over the window, and then he poked them down with a fishing-rod and laughed and shook his fist at me . . . I don't know what to do.'

Flora was justly indignant, but concealed her nasty temper. It was at this moment that she resolved to adopt Elfine and rescue her in the teeth of all the Starkadders of Cold Comfort.

'And does Someone know this?' she asked.

'Well . . . I told him.'

'What did he say?'

'Oh . . . he said, "Rotten luck, old girl".'

'It's Dick Hawk-Monitor, isn't it?'

'Oh . . . how did you know? Oh . . . I suppose everybody knows by now. It's beastly.'

'Things are certainly in rather a mess, but I do not think we need go so far as to say they are beastly,' said Flora, more calmly. 'Now, you must forgive my asking you these questions, Elfine, but has the young Hawk-Monitor actually *asked* you to marry him?'

'Well . . . he said he thought it would be a good idea if we did.'

'Bad . . . bad . . .' muttered Flora, shaking her head. 'Forgive me, but does he seem to love you?'

'He . . . he does when I'm there, Flora, but I don't some-how think he thinks much about me when I'm not there.'

'And I suppose you care enough for him, my dear, to wish to become his wife?'

Elfine after some hesitation admitted that she had some-times been selfish enough to wish that she had Dick all to herself. It appeared that there was a dangerous cousin named Pamela, who often came down from London for week-ends. Dick thought she was great fun.

Flora's expression did not change when she heard this piece of news, but her spirits sank. It would be difficult enough to win Dick for Elfine as it was; it would be a thousandfold more difficult with a rival in the field.

But her spirit was of that rare brand which becomes cold and pleased at the prospect of a battle, and her dismay did not last.

Elfine was saying:

'. . . And then there's this dance. Of course, I hate dancing unless it's in the woods with the wind-flowers and the birds, but I did rather want to go to this one, because, you see, it's Dick's twenty-first birthday party and . . . somehow . . . I think it would be rather fun.'

'Amusing or diverting . . . not "rather fun",' corrected Flora, kindly. 'Have you been invited?'

'Oh, no . . . You see, Grandmother does not allow the Starkadders to accept invitations, unless it is to funerals or the churching of women. So now no one sends us invitations. Dick did say he wished that I was coming, but I think he was only being kind. I don't think he really thought for a minute that I should be able to.'

'I suppose it would be of no use asking your grandmother for permission to go? In dealing with old and tyrannical persons it is wise to do the correct thing whenever one can; they are then less likely to suspect when one does something incorrect.'

'Oh, I am sure she would never let me go. She quarrelled with Mr Hawk-Monitor nearly thirty years ago and she hates Dick's mother. She would be mad with rage if she thought that I even knew Dick. Besides, she thinks dancing is wicked.'

'An interesting survival of medieval superstition,' commented Flora. 'Now listen, Elfine, I think it would be an excellent move if you went to this dance. I will try and see if I can manage it. I shall go, too, and keep an eye on you. It may be a little difficult to secure invitations for us, but I will do my best. And when we have got our invitations, I will take you up to Town with me and we will buy you a frock.'

'Oh, Flora!'

Flora was pleased to see that the wild-bird-cum-dryad atmosphere which hung over Elfine like a pestilential vapour was wearing thin. She was talking quite naturally. If this was the good effect of a little ordinary feminine gossip and a little interest in her poor childish affairs, the effect of a well-cut dress and a brushed and burnished head of hair might be miraculous. Flora could have rubbed her hands with glee.

'When is this dance?' she asked. 'Will many people be asked?'

'It's on the twenty-first of April, just a month from to-morrow. Oh, yes, it will be very big; they are holding it in the Assembly Rooms at Godmere, and all the county will be asked, because, you see, it is Dick's twenty-first birthday.'

'All the better,' thought Flora. 'It will be easier to work an invitation.' She had so many friends in London; surely there must be among them someone who knew these Hawk-Monitors? And Claud Hart-Harris could come down to partner her, because he waltzed so well, and who could be an escort for Elfine?

'Does Seth dance?' she asked.

'I don't know. I hate him,' replied Elfine, simply.

'I cannot say that I like him much myself,' confessed Flora, 'but if he dances, I think it would be as well if he came with us. You must have a partner, you know. Or perhaps you could ask some other man?'

But Elfine, being a dryad, naturally knew no other men;

and the only man Flora could think of who would be sure to be available for April 21st was Mr Mybug. She had only to ask *him*, she knew, and he would come bounding along to partner Elfine. It was dreadful to have no choice but Seth or Mr Mybug, but Sussex was like that.

'Well, we can arrange these details later,' she said. 'What I must do now is to find out if anyone in London among my friends know these Hawk-Monitors. I will ask Claud; he knows positive herds of people who live in country houses. I will write to him this afternoon.'

She was well disposed enough towards Elfine, but she really did not wish to spend with her the rest of an exquisite morning. So she rose to her feet and with a pleasant smile (having promised her cousin to let her know how matters were progressing) she went on her way.

CHAPTER 12

CLAUD HART-HARRIS wrote from his house at Chiswick Mall a few days later in reply to Flora's letter. He knew the Hawk-Monitors. Papa was dead, Mamma was a darling old bird whose hobby was the Higher Thought. There was a son who was easy on the eye but slow on the uptake, and a healthy sort of daughter named Joan. He thought he could arrange four invitations for Flora, if she was sure she wanted them. Would it not be rather a tiresome affair? But if she really wanted to go, he would write to Mrs Hawk-Monitor and tell her that a friend of his was in exile in a farm-house at Howling, and that she would love to come to the ball and bring her girl cousin and two young men. He, Claud, would of course be charmed to partner Flora, but, candidly, Seth sounded pretty squalid. Need he come?

'Squalid or not,' said the small, clear voice of Flora, fifty miles away (for she thought she would answer his letter by telephone, as she was in a hurry to get the affair arranged), 'he is all we can find, unless we have that Mr Mybug I told you about. I would really rather we did not have him, Claud. You know how dreadful intelligent people are when you take them to dances.'

Claud twisted the television dial and amused himself by studying Flora's fair, pensive face. Her eyes were lowered and her mouth compressed over the serious business of arranging Elfine's future. He fancied she was tracing a pattern with the tip of her shoe. She could not look at him, because public telephones were not fitted with television dials.

'Oh, yes, we certainly don't want a lot of intelligent conversation,' he said, decidedly. 'I think we will rule out the Mybug. Well, then, I will write to Mrs Hawk-Monitor today, and let you know as soon as I hear. Or perhaps I had better ask her to send the invitations direct to you, shall I?'

And so it was arranged.

Flora came out of the post office at Beershorn into the pleasant sunshine feeling a little ashamed of her schemes. Claud had said Mrs Hawk-Monitor was a darling. Flora was planning to palm off Elfine on the darling's only son. She strained her imagination, but found that it refused to present her with a picture of Mrs Hawk-Monitor welcoming Elfine with joy as a daughter-in-law. Mrs Hawk-Monitor's hobby might be the Higher Thought, but Flora felt sure she would be practical enough when it was a question of considering a wife for Richard. She would not be sympathetic, in spite of her own leanings, with Elfine's artiness. Elfine would have to be transformed, inside and out, before Mrs Hawk-Monitor could consider her suitable; and even if the transformation were made, Mrs Hawk-Monitor could not possibly approve Elfine's family. Who, indeed, could approve of such figures of rugged but slightly embarrassing grandeur as Micah and Judith?

And the Starkadders themselves would be sure, when the engagement was announced, to kick up one hell of a shine.

Difficult times lay ahead.

But this was what Flora liked. She detested rows and scenes, but enjoyed quietly pitting her cool will against opposition. It amused her; and when she was defeated, she withdrew in good order and lost interest in the campaign. She had little or no sporting spirit. Bloody battles to the death bored her, nor did she like other people to win.

But it was no fun to fight a darling. Flora herself, had she been sixty-five and Mrs Hawk-Monitor, would have felt most bitter towards a girl who planted an Elfine into the midst of a quiet country family.

There was only one way of soothing her tiresome conscience. Elfine must be transformed indeed; her artiness must be rooted out. Her mind must match the properly groomed head in which it was housed. Her movements must be made less frequent, and her conversation less artless. She must write no more poetry nor go for any long walks unless accompanied by the proper sort of dog to take on long walks. She must learn to be serious about horses. She must learn to laugh when a book or a string quartet was mentioned, and to confess that she was not brainy. She must learn to be long-limbed and clear-eyed and inhibited. The first two qualities she possessed already, and the last she must set to work to acquire at once.

And there were only twenty-seven days in which to teach her all these things!

Flora walked down the High Street towards the place where the buses started, planning how she would begin Elfine's education. She looked at the clock on the Town Hall, which said twelve, and realized that she had half an hour to wait for a bus. It was a Saturday morning and the town was full of people who had come in from outlying farms and villages to do their shopping for the week-end; some of them were already waiting for the bus, and Flora walked across the Market Place, prepared to wait with them.

But then she became aware that someone, a man, was trying to attract her attention. She was very properly not looking at him when something in his appearance seemed familiar to her; he looked like a Starkadder (there were so many of them that one of her minor worries was a fear of not recognizing one when she met him in the street). Sure enough, it was Harkaway. He had just come out of the bank, into which he had been paying the weekly takings of the farm. In a second Flora recognized him, and said 'Good morning' with a bow and a smile.

He returned her greeting in the Starkadder manner, that is, with a suspicious stare. He looked as though he would have liked to ask her what she was doing in Beershorn. She decided that if he did she would undo the parcel of pale green silk she carried and shake it in his face all down the High Street.

Harkaway stopped in front of her and out-manoeuvred her in her advance on the bus.

'You'm a long way from whoam,' he muttered.

'So are you,' retorted Flora. She was rather cross.

'Aye, but I ha' business to do in Beershorn every Saturday. I comes down every Saturday morning in the year, wi' Viper,' and he jerked his head towards that large and disagreeable beast, which Flora now observed anchored to the buggy a little way farther on.

'Indeed. I came by bus.'

A slow, secret smile crept into Harkaway's face. It was wolfish, ursine, vulpine. He softly jangled some coins in his pocket. He seemed as though he bathed in some secret satisfaction of his own. This was because he had driven down to Beershorn in the buggy, and saved the shilling his grandmother gave him every week for the fare.

'Aye, th' bus . . . ' he repeated, drawlingly.

'Yes, the bus. There isn't another one until half past twelve.'

'Happen I might drive you home with me,' he suggested, as Flora had meant him to do. Her disinclination to sit in the damp, smelly bus had fought with her disinclination to drive home with a Starkadder, and the bus had lost. Besides, she was always glad to see more of the private lives of the Starkadders. Harkaway might be able to tell her something about Urk, who was supposed to be going to marry Elfine.

'That would be very kind of you,' she said, and they moved off together to the buggy.

She looked at him meditatively as the buggy passed rapidly between the hedges. She wondered what was his particular nastiness? She could hardly distinguish him from Urk and Caraway, Ezra, Luke, and Mark. Never mind, probably she would get them sorted out in time.

She began to make conversation.

'How is the well getting on?' (Not that she cared.)

''Tes all collapsed. 'Tes terrible.'

'Oh, I am so sorry! What a pity. The last time I saw it, it was nearly finished. How did it happen?'

''Twas Mark. He and our Micah were argyfyin' who should lay the last brick, and we was all standin' round waitin' to see which would hit t'other first. And Mark, he pushed Micah down th' well, and pushed th' bricks down on top of 'un. Laugh! We fair lay on th' ground.'

'Was – is Micah – er – is he badly hurt?'

'Nay. Mark dived in after un and rescued un. But th' bricks was lost.'

'A pity, indeed,' commented Flora.

She was much surprised when Harkaway burst out:

'Aye, 'tis a pity. There's some at Cold Comfort would do better for a few bricks thrown at their heads. I names no names but I know what I think.'

The coins jingled softly again in his pocket. The ursine smile touched his lips.

'Who?' asked Flora.

'Her . . . th' old lady. My grand-aunt. Her as has us all under her thumb.' He jingled the coins again.

'Ah, yes, my aunt,' said Flora, thoughtfully. She found Harkaway comparatively easy to talk to. Nor did he seem unfriendly.

'I cannot understand,' she resumed, 'why you do not break away from her. I suppose she has all the money.'

'Aye . . . and she's mad. If any on us was to leave th' farm, she'd go madder yet. 'Twould be a terrible disgrace on us. We mun keep the head of the family alive and in her right mind. There have always been – '

'I know, I know,' said Flora, hastily. 'Such a comfort, I always feel, don't you? But really, Harkaway, I do think it is carrying authority a little too far when grown men are prevented from marrying – '

Harkaway laughed shortly, rather to Flora's dismay; she feared he was going to make a farmyard joke. But he said, much more surprisingly:

'Nay, nay. Some of us is married right enough. But th' old lady, she mun never see our women-folk, or she'd go right away mad. The women-folk of the Starkadders keep themselves to themselves. They lives down in the village and only comes up when there's a gatherin' or th' old lady comes downstairs. There's Micah's Susan, Mark's Phoebe, Luke's Prue, Caraway's Letty, Ezra's Jane. Urk, he'm a bachelor. Me . . . I've got me own troubles.'

Flora longed to ask what his own troubles were, but feared that the question might bring forth a flood of embarrassing confidences. Perhaps he was in love with Mrs Beetle? Meanwhile, his news was so surprising that she could only stare and stare again.

'And do you mean to say that they all live down in the village. Five women?'

'Six women,' corrected Harkaway, in a low voice. 'Aye, there's – another. There's poor daft Rennet.'

'Really? What relation is she to the others?'

'She'm own daughter to Micah's Susan by her first marriage. Her marriage to Mark, I mean; and Mark, he's own half-brother to Amos, who is Micah's cousin. So 'tes rather confusin', like. Aye, poor Rennet . . .'

'What is the matter with *her*?' inquired Flora, rather tartly. She was exceedingly dismayed at the news that there was a whole horde of female Starkadders whom she had not seen. It really seemed as though her task would be too much for her.

'She were disappointed o' Mark Dolour, ten years ago. She's never married. She's queer, like, in her head. Sometimes, when the sukebind hangs heavy from the passin' wains, she jumps down th' well. Aye, an' twice she's tried

133

to choke Meriam, the hired girl. 'Tes Nature, you may say, turned sour in her veins.'

Flora was really quite glad when the buggy stopped outside the farm. She wanted to hear no more. She felt that she could not undertake to rescue Susan, Letty, Phoebe, Prue, Jane, and Rennet as well as Elfine. Dash it, the women must take their chance. She would rescue Elfine, and as soon as that was accomplished, she would try to have a show-down with Aunt Ada, but beyond this she would make no promises.

For the next three weeks she was so busy with Elfine that she had no time to worry about the unknown female Starkadders.

She spent most of her time with Elfine. She expected at first that someone would interfere, and try to stop Elfine and her from going for their morning walk along the top of the Downs and from spending the afternoons in Flora's little green parlour. These habits were innocent, but that was not enough to keep the Starkadders from trying to stop them. Nay, their very innocency was more likely to set the grand, rugged Starkadder machinery in motion. For it is a peculiarity of persons who lead rich emotional lives and who (as the saying is) live intensely and with a wild poetry, that they read all kinds of meanings into comparatively simple actions, especially the actions of other people, who do not live intensely and with a wild poetry. Thus you may find them weeping passionately on their bed, and be told that you – you alone – are the cause because you said that awful thing to them at lunch. Or they wonder why you like going to concerts; there must be more in it than meets the eye.

So the cousins usually slipped out for their walks when no one was about.

Flora had learned, by experience, that she must ask permission of the Starkadders if she wanted to go down into Beershorn, or if (as she did a week or so after her arrival) she wanted to buy a pot of apricot jam for tea. On this occasion she had found Judith lying face downwards in the furrows of Ticklepenny's Corner, weeping. In reply to her question, Judith had said that anybody might do anything they pleased, so long as she was left alone with her sorrow. Flora took this generous statement to mean that she might pay for the jam.

And so she did; but on the whole she spent little money at Cold Comfort, and so she had nearly eighty pounds to spend on Elfine. She decided that they would go up to London together the day before the ball and buy her gown and get her hair cut correctly.

She was pleased to be spending eighty pounds on Elfine. If she succeeded in making Dick Hawk-Monitor propose to Elfine it would be a successful *geste* in the face of the Stark-adders. It would be a triumph of the Higher Common Sense over Aunt Ada Doom. It would be a victory for Flora's philosophy of life over the subconscious life-philosophy of the Starkadders. It would be like a splendid deer stepping haughtily across a ploughed field.

For three weeks she forced Elfine as a gardener skilfully forces a flower in a hothouse. Her task was difficult, but might have been much more so. For Elfine's peculiarities of dress, outlook, and behaviour were due only to her own youthful tastes. They had not been ground into her, for years, by older people. She was ready to shed them if something better was shown to her. Also, she was only seventeen years old, and docile; when Flora planed away all the St Francis-cum-barbola-work crust, she found beneath it an honest child, capable of loving calmly and deeply, friendly and sweet-tempered and fond of pretty things.

'Have you always admired St Francis?' asked Flora, as they sat one rainy afternoon in the little green parlour, towards the end of the first week. 'I mean, who told you about him, and who taught you to wear those shocking clothes?'

'I wanted to be like Miss Ashford. She kept the Blue Bird's Cage down in Howling for a month or two last summer. I went in there to tea once or twice. She was very kind to me. She used to have lovely clothes – that is, I mean, they weren't what you would call lovely, but I used to like them. She had a smock – '

'Embroidered with hollyhocks,' said Flora, resignedly. 'And I'll bet she wore her hair in shells round her ears and a pendant made of hammered silver with a bit of blue enamel in the middle. And did she try to grow herbs?'

'How did you know?'

'Never mind, I do know. And she talked to you about Brother Wind and Sister Sun and the wind on the heath, didn't she?'

'Yes . . . She had a picture of St Francis feeding the birds. It was lovely.'

'And did you want to be like her, Elfine?'

'Oh, yes . . . She never tried to make me like her, of course, but I did want to be. I used to copy her clothes . . .'

'Yes, well, never mind that now. Go on with your reading.'

And Elfine obediently resumed her reading aloud of 'Our Lives from Day to Day' from an April number of *Vogue*. When she had finished, Flora took her, page by page, through a copy of *Chiffons*, which was devoted to descriptions and sketches of lingerie. Flora pointed out how these graceful petticoats and night-gowns depended upon their pure line and delicate embroidery for their beauty; how all gross romanticism was purged away, or expressed only in a fold or a flute of material. She then showed how the same delicacy might be found in the style of Jane Austen, or a painting by Marie Laurencin.

'It is that kind of beauty,' said Flora, 'that you must learn to look for and admire in everyday life.'

'I like the night-gowns and "Persuasion",' said Elfine, 'but I don't like "Our Lives" very much, Flora. It's all rather in a hurry, isn't it, and wanting to tell you how nice it was?'

'I do not propose that you shall found a life-philosophy upon "Our Lives from Day to Day", Elfine. I merely make you read it because you will have to meet people who do that kind of thing, and you must on no account be all dewy and awed when you do meet them. You can, if you like, secretly despise them. Nor must you talk about Marie Laurencin to people who hunt. They will merely think she is your new mare. No. I tell you of these things in order that you may have some standards, within yourself, with which secretly to compare the many new facts and people you will meet if you enter a new life.'

She did not tell Elfine of *The Higher Common Sense*, but quoted one or two of the *Pensées* to her, from time to time, and resolved to give her H. B. Mainwaring's excellent translation of *The Higher Common Sense* as a wedding present.

Elfine progressed. Her charming nature and Flora's wise advice met and mingled naturally. Only over poetry was there a little struggle. Flora warned Elfine that she must write no more poetry if she wanted to marry into the county.

'I thought poetry was enough,' said Elfine, wistfully. 'I mean, I thought poetry was so beautiful that if you met someone you loved, and you told them you wrote poetry, that would be enough to make them love you, too.'

'On the contrary,' said Flora, firmly, 'most young men are alarmed on hearing that a young woman writes poetry. Combined with an ill-groomed head of hair and an eccentric style of dress, such an admission is almost fatal.'

'I shall write it secretly, and publish it when I am fifty,' said Elfine, rebelliously.

Flora coldly raised her eyebrows, and decided that she would return to the attack when Elfine had had her hair cut and seen her beautiful new dress.

They entered upon the third week in hopeful spirits. At first, Elfine had been bewildered and unhappy in the new worlds into which Flora led her. But as she grew at home in them, and became fond of Flora, she was happy, and bloomed like a rose-peony. She fed upon hope; and even Flora's confident spirit faltered before the thought of what a weltering ruin, what a desert, must ensue if those hopes were never achieved.

But they must be achieved! Flora wrote as much to her ally, Claud Hart-Harris. She had chosen him, rather than

Charles, as her escort to the Hawk-Monitors' ball, because she felt that she would need all her powers of concentration to see herself and Elfine safely through the evening; and if Charles came to partner her she would be conscious of a certain interest in their own personal relationship, a current of unsaid speeches, which would distract her feelings and perhaps confuse a little her thoughts.

Claud had written to say that she might expect the invitation on April 19th or so. So she came down to breakfast in the kitchen on the morning of the nineteenth with a pleasant sensation of excitement and anticipation.

It was half past eight. Mrs Beetle had finished sweeping the floor and was shaking the mat out in the yard, in the sunshine. (It always surprised Flora to see the sun shining into the yard at Cold Comfort; she had a feeling that the rays ought to be short-circuited just outside the wall by the atmosphere of the farm-house.)

'Ni smorning,' screamed Mrs Beetle, adding that we could do with a bit of it.

Flora smilingly agreed and went across to the cupboard to take down her own little green teapot (a present from Mrs Smiling) and tin of China tea. She glanced out into the yard and was pleased to see that none of the male Starkadders were about. Elfine was out on a walk. Judith was probably lying despairingly across her bed, looking with leaden eyes at the ceiling across which the first flies of the year were beginning monotonously to circle and crawl.

The bull suddenly bellowed his thick, dark-red note. Flora paused, with the teapot in her hand, and looked thoughtfully out across the yard towards his shed.

'Mrs Beetle,' she said firmly, 'the bull ought to be let out. Could you help me do it? Are you afraid of bulls?'

'Yes,' said Mrs Beetle, 'I am afraid o' bulls. And you don't let 'im out, miss, not if I stand 'ere till midnight. In all respect, Miss Poste, though you was to kill me for it.'

'We could guide him towards the gate with the bull-fork, or whatever it is called,' suggested Flora, glancing at the implement which lay across two hooks at the side of the shed.

'No, miss,' said Mrs Beetle.

'Well, I shall open the gate and try to drive him through it,' said Flora, who was utterly terrified of bulls, and cows too, for that matter. 'You must wave your apron at him, Mrs Beetle, and shout.'

'Yes, miss. I'll go up to your bedroom window,' said Mrs Beetle, 'and shout at 'im from there. The sound'll carry better.'

And she nipped away like lightning before Flora could stop her. A few seconds later Flora heard her shouting shrilly from the window overhead.

'Go on, Miss Poste. I'm 'ere!'

Flora was now rather dismayed. The situation seemed to have developed much more quickly than she had thought it would. She was extremely afraid. She stood there, idly waving the teapot, and trying to remember all she had ever read about the habits of bulls. They ran at red. Well, they would not run at her; she was all green. They were savage, especially in spring (it was the middle of April, and the trees were in bud). They gored you . . .

Big Business bellowed again. It was a harsh, mournful sound; there were old swamps and rotting horns buried in it. Flora ran across the yard and pushed open the gate leading into the big field facing the farm, fastening it back. Then she took down the bull-prong, or whatever it called itself, and, standing at a comfortable distance from the shed, manoeuvred the catch back, and saw the door swing open.

Out came Big Business. It was a much less dramatic affair than she had supposed it would be. He stood for a second or two bewildered by the light, with his big head swaying stupidly. Flora stood quite still.

'Eeee-yer! Go on, yer old brute!' shrieked Mrs Beetle.

The bull lumbered off across the yard, still with his head down, towards the gate. Flora followed cautiously, holding the bull-prong. Mrs Beetle screeched to her for the dear's sake to be careful. Once Big Business half turned towards her, and she made a determined movement with the prong. Then, to her relief, he went through the gate into the grassy field, and she swung it to and shut it before he had time to turn round.

'There!' said Mrs Beetle, reappearing at the kitchen door with the speed of a newspaper proprietor explaining his candidate's failure at a by-election. 'I told you so!'

Flora replaced the bull-prong and went back into the kitchen to make her breakfast. It was nine o'clock. The postman should arrive at any minute now.

So she sat down to her breakfast in a position that gave her, through the kitchen window, a view of the path leading up to the farm, for she did not want any one of the Starkadders to get the letters from the postman before she had seen whether the invitation to the Hawk-Monitor ball was among them.

But, to her dismay, just as the figure of the postman appeared at that point of the path where it curved over the hill towards the farm-house, it was joined by another figure. Flora craned her eyes above her cup to see who it might be. It was somebody who was hung about with a good many dead rabbits and pheasants in one way and another, so that his features were obscured from view. He stopped, said something to the postman, and Flora saw something white pass from hand to hand. The rabbit-festooned Starkadder, whoever he might be, had forestalled her. She bit crossly into a piece of toast and continued to observe the approaching figure. He soon came close enough for her to see that it was Urk.

She was much disconcerted. It could not have been worse.

'Turns you up, don't it, seein' ter-day's dinner come in 'anging round someone's neck like that?' observed Mrs Beetle, who was loading a tray with food to take up to Mrs Doom. 'Ter-morrer's, too, for all I know, and the day after's. Give me cold storage, any day.'

Urk opened the door of the kitchen and came slowly into the room.

140

He had been shooting rabbits. His narrow nostrils were slightly distended to inhale the blood-odour from the seventeen which hung round his neck. Their cold fur brushed his hands lightly and imploringly like little pleas for mercy, and his buttocks were softly brushed by the draggled tail-feathers of five pheasants which hung from the pheasant-belt encircling his waist. He felt the weight of the twenty-five dead animals he bore (for there was a shrew or two in his breast pocket) pulling him down, like heavy, dark-blooded roots into the dumb soil. He was drowsy with killing, in the mood of a lion lying on a hippopotamus with its mouth full.

He held the letters in front of him, looking down at them with a sleepy stare. Flora saw, with a start of indignation, that his thumb had left a red mark upon an envelope addressed in Charles's neat hand.

This was quite intolerable. She rose quickly to her feet, holding out her hand.

'My letters, please,' she said, crisply.

Urk pushed them across the table to her, but he kept one in his hand, turning it over curiously to look at a crest upon the back of the envelope. ('Oh, Lord!' thought Flora.)

'I think that one is for me, too,' she said.

Urk did not answer. He looked at her, then down at the letter, then across at Flora again. When his voice came, it was a throaty snarl:

'Who's writing to you from Howchiker?'

'Mary, Queen of Scots. Thanks,' said Flora, with deplorable pertness, and twitched it out of his hand. She slipped it into the pocket of her coat, and sat down to finish her breakfast. But the low, throaty snarl cut once more across the silence:

'Ye're smart, aren't yer? Think I don't know what's going on ... wi' books from London and all that rot. Now you listen to me. She's mine, I tell you ... mine. She's my woman, same as a hen belongs to a cock, and no one don't have her except me, ye see? She were promised to me the day she were born, by her Grandmother. I put a cross in water-vole's blood on her feedin'-bottle when she was an hour old, to mark her for mine, and held her up so's she might see it and know she was mine ... And every year since then, on her birthday, I've taken her up to Ticklepenny's Corner and we've hung over th' old well until we see a water-vole, and I've said to her, I've said, "Remember". And all she would say was: "What, Cousin Urk?" But she knows all right. She knows. When the water-voles mate under the may trees this summer I'll make her mine. Dick Hawk-Monitor ... what's he? A bit of a boy? Playin' at horses in a red coat, like his daddy afore him. Many a time I've lay and laughed at 'em ... fools. Me and the water-voles, we can afford to wait for what we want. So you heed what I say, miss. Elfine's mine. I doan't mind her bein' a bit above me' (here his voice thickened in a manner which caused Mrs Beetle to make a sound resembling 't-t-t-t-'), ''cause a man likes his piece to be a bit dainty. But she's mine –'

'We heard,' said Flora; 'you said it before.'

'– and God help the man or woman who tries to take her from me. Me and the water-voles, we'll get her back.'

'Are those water-voles round your neck?' asked Flora, interestedly. 'I've never seen any before. What a lot of them all at once!'

He turned from her, with a peculiar stooping, stealthy, swooping movement, and padded out of the kitchen.

'Well, I never,' said Mrs Beetle, loudly; 'there's a narsty temper for you.'

Flora placidly agreed that it was, but she made up her mind that Elfine must be taken up to Town that very day, instead of to-morrow, as she had planned.

She had meant to take Elfine up on the day before the ball, but there was no time to be lost. If Urk suspected that they were going to the ball he would probably try to stop them. They must be sure of the dress, and of Elfine's shorn head, whatever happened. They must go at once. She rose, leaving her breakfast unfinished, and hurried upstairs to

Elfine's room. She found Elfine just returned from her walk.

Flora quickly told her of the change in their plans and left her to get ready while she hurried downstairs to try to find Seth, and to ask him to drive them down to the station. They could just catch the ten fifty-nine to Town.

Seth was hanging over the fence round the great field, looking sullenly at Big Business, who was cantering round and round bellowing.

'Someone's let the bull out,' said Seth, pointing.

'I know. I did. And quite time, too,' said Flora. 'But never mind that now. Seth, will you drive Elfine and me down to Beershorn, to catch the ten fifty-nine?'

Her request was made in a cool, pleasant voice. Yet the softly burning, perpetual ruby flame of romance in Seth responded to some tremor of urgency in her tones. Besides, he wanted to go to the Hawk-Monitors' dance, and see if it was at all like the hunt ball scene in 'Silver Hoofs', the stupendous drama of English country life which Intro-Pan-National had made a year or two ago, and he guessed that Flora was taking Elfine up to London to buy her dress. He did not want anything to interfere with the preparations for the ball.

He said 'Aye', he would, and lounged away with his curious animal grace to get out the buggy.

Adam appeared at the door of the cow-shed, where he had been milking Graceless, Pointless, Feckless, Aimless, and Fury. His old body was bent like a thorn against a sharp dazzle of sticky buds bursting from the boughs of a chestnut-tree which hung over the yard.

'Eh, eh – someone's let the bull out,' he said. ''Tes terrible ... I – I mun soothe our Feckless. She'm not herself. Who let un out?'

'I did,' said Flora, buckling the belt of her coat.

And distant shouts came from the back of the farm, where Micah and Ezra were busy setting up the hitten-piece which supported the bucket above the well.

'Th' bull's out!'

'Who let out Big Business?'

'Who let un loose?'

'Ay, 'tes terrible!'

Flora had been writing on a leaf from her pocket-diary, which she now gave to Adam, and instructed him to pin it on the door of the kitchen where it could be seen by everyone as they came hurrying into the yard. It said:

'I did. F. Poste.'

The buggy came out into the yard with Viper in the shafts and Seth holding the reins, just as Elfine, wearing a deplorable blue cape, appeared at the kitchen door.

'Jump up, my dear. We have no time to waste,' cried Flora, mounting the step of the buggy.

'Who let th' bull out?' thundered Reuben, starting from the pig-pen, where he had been delivering a sow who was experienced enough, heaven knows, to deliver herself, but who enjoyed being fussed over.

Flora pointed silently to the note pinned upon the kitchen door. Seth signed to Adam to open the gate of the yard, which Adam did.

'Who let th' bull out?' screamed Judith, putting her head out from an upper window. The question was repeated by Amos, who burst from the chicken-run where he had been collecting eggs.

Flora hoped that they would all see the note and have their curiosity satisfied, or else they would all go blaming each other, and when she came home there would be a shocking atmosphere of rows and uncomfortableness.

But now they were off. Seth struck Viper on the flanks, and they shot forward. Flora repressed an inclination to raise her hat and bow from side to side as they passed through the gate. She felt that someone should have shouted loyally: 'God bless the young squire!'

CHAPTER 13

THEY passed a pleasant day in London.

Flora first took Elfine to Maison Viol, of Brass Street, in Lambeth, to have her hair cut. Short hair was just coming back into fashion, yet it was still new enough to be distinguished. M. Viol himself cut Elfine's hair, and dressed it in a careless, simple, fiendishly expensive way that showed the tips of her ears.

Flora then took Elfine to Maison Solide. M. Solide had dressed Flora for the last two years and did not despise her as much as he despised most of the women whom he dressed. His eyes widened when he saw Elfine. He looked at her broad shoulders and slim waist and long legs. His fingers made the gestures of a pair of scissors, and he groped blindly towards a roll of snow-coloured satin which a well-trained assistant put into his arms.

'White?' ventured Flora.

'But what else?' screamed M. Solide, ripping the scissors across the satin. 'It is to wear white that God, once in a hundred years, makes such a young girl.'

Flora sat and watched for an hour while M. Solide worried the satin like a terrier, tore it into breadths, swathed and caped and draped it. Flora was pleased to see that Elfine did not seem nervous or bored. She seemed to take naturally to the atmosphere of a world-famous dressmaker's establishment. She bathed delightedly in white satin, like a swan in foam. She twisted her neck this way and that, and peered down the length of her body, as though down a snow slope, to watch the assistants like busy black ants pinning and rearranging the hem a thousand feet below.

Flora opened a new romance, and became absorbed in it, until Julia arrived at one o'clock to take them to lunch.

M. Solide, pale and cross after his orgy, assured Flora that the dress would be ready by to-morrow morning. Flora said that they would call for it. No, he must not send it. It was too rare. Would he post a picture by Gauguin to Australia? A thousand evils might befall it on the way.

But, secretly, she wished to protect the dress from Urk. She was sure that he would destroy it if he got a glimmer of a chance.

'Well, do you like your dress?' she asked Elfine, as they sat at lunch in the New River Club.

'It's heavenly,' said Elfine, solemnly. She, like M. Solide, was pale with exhaustion. 'It's better than poetry, Flora.'

'It is not at all like the sort of thing St Francis of Assisi wore,' pointed out Julia, who considered Flora was doing a lot for Elfine and should be appreciated.

Elfine blushed, and bent her head over her cutlet. Flora looked at her benignly. The dress had cost fifty guineas, but Flora did not grudge the sum. She felt at this moment that any sum would have been sacrificed by her to score off the Starkadders.

This feeling was increased by the pleasure she felt in the casual yet delicate appointments of the New River Club. It was the most haughty club in London. No one with an income of more than seven hundred and forty pounds a year might join. Its members were limited to a hundred and twenty. Each member must be nominated by a family with sixteen quarterings. No member might be divorced; if he or she were, membership was forfeited. The Selection Committee was composed of seven of the wildest, proudest, most talented men and women in Europe. The club combined the austerities of a monastic order with the tender peace of a home.

Flora had engaged rooms for Elfine and herself at the club; it was necessary for them to spend the night in Town as they had to call for Elfine's dress the next morning. Flora welcomed the opportunity to indulge herself in some civilized pleasures, from which she had long been absent, and, accordingly, went in the afternoon to hear a concert of Mozart's music at the State Concert Hall in Bloomsbury, leaving Julia to take Elfine to buy a petticoat, some shoes and stockings and a plain evening coat of white velvet. In

the evening she proposed that the three of them should
visit the Pit Theatre, in Stench Street, Seven Dials, to see a
new play by Brandt Slurb called 'Manallalive-O!', a Neo-
Expressionist attempt to give dramatic form to the mental
reactions of a man employed as a waiter in a restaurant
who dreams that he is the double of another man who is
employed as a steward on a liner, and who, on awakening
and realizing that he is still a waiter employed in a restaurant and not a steward employed on a liner, goes mad and
shoots his reflection in a mirror and dies. It had seventeen
scenes and only one character. A pest-house, a laundry, a
lavatory, a court of law, a room in a lepers' settlement, and
the middle of Piccadilly Circus were included in the scenes.

'Why,' asked Julia, 'do you want to see a play like
that?'

'I don't, but I think it would be so good for Elfine, so
that she will know what to avoid when she is married.'

But Julia thought it would be a much better idea if they
went to see Mr Dan Langham in 'On Your Toes!' at the
New Hippodrome, so they went there instead and had a
nice time instead of a nasty one.

In that entranced pause when the lights of the theatre
fade, and upon the crimson of the yet unraised curtain the
footlights throw up their soft glow, Flora glanced at Elfine,
unobserved, and was pleased with what she saw.

A noble yet soft profile was lifted seriously towards the
stage. The light wings of gold hair blew back from either
cheek towards the ears; this gave the head a classic look
like that of a Greek charioteer pressing his team forward to
victory in the face of a strong wind. The beautiful bones,
the youth of the face were now revealed.

Flora was satisfied.

She had done what she had hoped to do. She had
made Elfine look groomed and normal, yet had preserved
in her personality a suggestion of cool, smoothly blowing
winds and of pine trees and the smell of wild flowers. She
had conceived just such a change, and M. Viol and M.
Solide, her instruments, had carried it out.

An artist in living flesh could ask for no more, and the auguries for the evening of the dance were good.

She leaned back in her seat with a contented sigh as the curtains parted.

The cousins reached the farm about five o'clock on the evening of the next day. Much to Flora's surprise. Seth had been at the station to meet their train with the buggy, and he drove them back. They stopped at a large garage in the town on the way home to arrange for a car to call at the farm on the following evening to take them to Godmere. It was to be at Cold Comfort at half past seven, but first it was to meet the six-thirty train and pick up a Mr Hart-Harris, who was arriving at that time.

Having made these arrangements, Flora hopped cheerfully back into the buggy and settled herself into her own black and green plaid rug at Seth's side. Elfine tucked her in. (By this time Elfine was quite devoted to her, and divided the time between devising schemes for Flora's comfort and looking with delight at the picture of her own altered head in the shop windows which they passed.)

'Are you looking forward to it, Seth?' asked Flora.

'Aye,' he drawled softly, in his warm voice, ''twill be th' first time I've ever been to a dance wheer all the women wasn't after me. Happen I can enjoy meself a bit, fer a change.'

Flora doubted whether he really would, for the county would probably fall for Seth as inevitably as did the villages. But there was no point in alarming him beforehand.

'But I thought you liked having girls after you?'

'Nay. I only likes the talkies. I don't mind takin' a girl out if she will let me, but many's the girl I've niver seen again because she worried me in the middle of a talkie. Aye, they're all the same. They must have yer blood and yer breath and ivery bit of yer time and yer thoughts. But I'm not like that. I just likes the talkies.'

Flora reflected, as they drove home through the lanes, that Seth's problem was the next one to tackle. She thought of a letter in her handbag. It was from Mr Earl P. Neck, and it said that he would be motoring down within the next few days to see some friends who lived at Brighton, and he proposed to motor over and see her, too. She was going to introduce Seth to him.

It was five o'clock on the afternoon of the next day. The weather favoured the cousins. Flora had pessimistically presumed that it would be pelting with rain, but it was not. It was a mild, rosy spring evening in which blackbirds sang on the budding boughs of the elms and the air smelled of leaves and freshness.

The cousins were having a fiendish business getting themselves dressed.

The intelligent and sensitive reader will doubtless have wondered at intervals throughout this narrative how Flora managed about a bathroom. The answer is simple. At Cold Comfort there was no bathroom. And when Flora had asked Adam how the family themselves managed for baths, he had replied coldly: 'We manages w'hout,' and the vision of dabblings and chillinesses and inadequacies thus conjured had so repelled Flora that she had pursued her inquiries no further.

She had discovered, however, that that refreshing woman, Mrs Beetle, owned a hip-bath, in which she would permit Flora to bathe every other evening at eight o'clock for a small weekly sum, and this Flora did, and the curtailment of her seven weekly baths to four was by far the most unpleasant experience she had so far had to endure at the farm.

But this evening, just when baths were needed, baths were impossible. So Flora put two enormous noggins of water on the stove in the kitchen to get hot, and hoped for the best.

Her absence from the farm with Elfine had not been commented upon. She doubted if they had noticed it. What with the bull getting out, and Meriam, the hired girl, having so far got through the spring without entering upon her annual interesting condition, and the beginning of the carrot harvest which was even longer and more difficult to do than the swede harvest, the Starkadders had enough to absorb them without noticing where a couple of girls had got to. Besides, it was their habit to avoid seeing each other for days at a time, and the absence of Flora and Elfine seemed fortunately to have coincided with one of these hibernations on the part of the family.

But Aunt Ada – did she know? Elfine said she knew everything. She shuddered as she spoke. If Aunt Ada found out that they were going to the ball...

'She had best not pull any Cinderella stuff on me,' said Flora coldly, peering into the nearest noggin to see if the water were done.

'It is just possible that she may come downstairs one of these evenings,' said Elfine timidly. 'She sometimes does, in the spring.'

Flora said that she hoped it kept fine for her.

But she did rather wonder why the kitchen was decorated with a wreath of deadly nightshade round the mantelpiece and large bunches of the evil-smelling pussy's dinner arranged in jam-jars on the mantelpiece. And round the dim, ancient portrait of Fig Starkadder, which hung above the fireplace, was a wreath of a flower which was unfamiliar to Flora. It had dark green leaves and long, pink, tightly closed buds. She asked Elfine what it was.

'That's the sukebind,' said Elfine fearfully. 'Oh, Flora, is the water done?'

'Just on, my dove. Here, you take one,' and she handed it to Elfine. 'So that's sukebind, is it? I suppose when it opens all the trouble begins?'

But Elfine was already away with the hot water to Flora's room, where her dress lay upon the bed, and Flora must follow her up.

CHAPTER 14

PERHAPS something, some pregnant quality, in the mildly restless air of the spring evening had infused itself into the room where old Mrs Starkadder sat before the huge bed of glowing cinders in the grate. For she struck suddenly, fiercely, upon the little bell that stood ever at her elbow (at least, it was at her elbow whenever she sat in that particular chair).

A plan which she had been pondering for days, and had even hinted at to Seth, had suddenly matured. The shrill sound leapt through the tepid air of the room. It roused Judith, who was standing at the window looking with sodden eyes at the inexorable fecundity of the advancing spring.

'I mun go downstairs,' said the old woman.

'Mother ... you're mistaken. 'Tes not the first o' May nor the seventeenth o' October. You'd better bide here,' protested her daughter.

'I tell you I mun go downstairs. I mun feel you all about me – all of you: Micah, Urk, Ezra, Harkaway, Caraway, Amos, Reuben, and Seth. Aye and Mark and Luke. None of you mun ever leave me. Give me my liberty bodice, girl.'

Silently Judith gave it her.

The old house was silent. The dying light lay quietly upon its walls, and the sound of the blackbird's song came into the still, empty rooms. Aunt Ada's thoughts spun like Catherine wheels as she laboriously dressed herself.

Once ... when you were a little girl ... you had seen something nasty in the woodshed. Now you were old, and could not move easily. You leaned heavily on Judith's shoulder as she pressed her foot into the small of your back to lace your corsets.

Flora drew the curtains and lit the lamp. Elfine's dress lay on the bed, a lovely miracle, and Elfine must be dressed before Flora could begin to think of her own toilet.

It took an hour to dress Elfine. Flora washed her young

cheeks with scalding water until they burned with angry roses, and brushed back the wings of hair, slipped the foam of the petticoat over her head and brushed again, stood on a chair to drop the dress over her head, and then brushed again. Then she put on the stockings and shoes, and wrapped Elfine in the white coat, put the fan and bag into her waiting hands, and made her sit on the bed, out of dust and danger.

'Oh, Flora . . . do I look nice?'

'You look extremely beautiful,' returned Flora, solemnly looking up at her. 'Mind you behave properly.'

But to herself she was thinking, in the words of the Abbé Fausse-Maigre, 'Condole with the Ugly Duckling's mother. She has fathomed the pit of amazement.'

Flora's own dress was in harmonious tones of pale and dark green. She wore no jewels, and her long coat was of viridian velvet. She would not permit Elfine to wear jewels, either, though Elfine begged for at least her little string of pearls.

Now they were ready. It was only half past six. There was a whole hour to wait before they could creep down to the waiting car. In order to calm their nerves, Flora seated herself upon the bed and read aloud from the *Pensées*:

'Never arrive at a house at a quarter past three. It is a dreadful hour; too early for tea and too late for luncheon . . .'

'Can we be sure that an elephant's real name is elephant? Only mankind presumes to name God's creatures; God himself is silent upon the matter.'

Yet the *Pensées* failed to have their usual calming effect. Flora was a little agitated. Would the car arrive safely? Would Claud Hart-Harris miss the train? (He usually did!) How would Seth look in a dinner-jacket? Above all, would Richard Hawk-Monitor propose to Elfine? Even Flora did not dare to imagine what would happen if they returned from the ball and he had not spoken. He *must* speak! She conjured the god of love by the spring evening, by the blackbird's song, by the triumphant beauty of Elfine.

(Now you were putting on your elastic-sided boots. You had not worn them since Fig died. Fig . . . a prickly beard, a smell of flannel, a stumbling, urgent voice in the larder. Your boots smelled nasty. Where was the lavender water? You made Judith sprinkle some, inside and out. So. Now your first petticoat.)

'Flora,' said Elfine, 'I am afraid I feel sick.'

Flora looked sternly at her and read aloud: 'Vanity can rule the queasiest stomach.'

Suddenly there was a tap at the door. Elfine looked at Flora in terror, and Flora noted how her eyes became dark blue when she was moved. It was a good line.

'Shall I open it?' whispered Elfine.

'I expect it's only Seth.'

Flora got off the bed and tiptoed to the door, which she opened an eighth of an inch. Indeed, it was Seth in a ready-made dinner-jacket which in no way destroyed his animal grace; he merely looked like a panther in evening dress. He whispered to Flora that a car was coming up the hill and that perhaps they had best come downstairs.

'Is Urk anywhere about?' asked Flora, for she knew that if he could mess things up he would.

'I saw un hanging over th' well up at Ticklepenny's talkin' to the water-voles an hour ago,' replied Seth.

'Oh, then, he is safe for another half-hour at least,' said Flora. 'I think we might go down, then. Elfine, are you ready? Now, not a sound! Come along.'

By the light of a candle which Seth carried they made their way safely down into the kitchen, which was deserted. The door leading into the yard was open, and they saw a big car, just visible in the twilight, drawn up outside the gate at the other end of the yard. The chauffeur was just getting down to open the gate, and Flora saw, much to her relief, that another person, who must be Claud, was peering out of the car window. She waved reassuringly to him, and caught the words '*too* barbarous' floating across the still evening air. She motioned frantically to him not to make a noise.

'I'll carry Elfine. She mustn't spoil them shoes,' whispered Seth, with unexpected thoughtfulness, and picked his sister up and strode off with her across the yard. He made a second journey for Flora, and she hardly had time to decide whether or not he was holding her unnecessarily tightly when she found herself safely popped into the car, and squeezing the outstretched hands of Claud, with Elfine smiling prettily in the corner.

'My dear, why all this Fall-of-the-House-of-Usher stuff?' inquired Claud. 'I mean, this is too good to be true. Where do we go from here?'

Seth was giving the chauffeur his instructions, and in this pause just before their adventure really began, Flora gazed up searchingly at the windows of the farm-house. ***They were dead as the eyes of fishes, reflecting the dim, pallid blue of the fading west. The crenellated line of the roof thrust blind ledges against a sky into which the infusion of the darkness was already beginning to seep. The livid silver tongues of the early stars leaped between the shapes of the chimney-pots, backwards and forwards, like idiot children dancing to a forgotten tune. As Flora watched, a dim light flowered slowly behind a drawn blind in the window of a room immediately above the kitchen, and she saw a shadow move hesitatingly, as though it had lost a bootlace and was searching dumbly for it, across the blind. The light was like the waxing and waning of the eye in the head of a dying beast. The house seemed to settle deeper into the yard as darkness came. Not a sound broke its quiescence. But the light, strangely naked and innocent, burned waveringly on in the deepening gloom.

The car moved forward, and Flora, for one, was immensely bucked to be off.

'Well, Flora, you look extremely nice,' said Claud, studying her. 'That dress is quite charming. As for your protégée,' he added in a lower tone, 'she is beautiful. Now tell me all about it.'

So, also lowering her voice, Flora told him. He was amused and interested, but a little discontented with his own role. 'I feel,' he complained, 'like a minor character out of "Cinderella".'

Flora soothed him by telling him that this excursion into the hinterland of Sussex should afford him a pleasant change from the excessive urbanity of those circles in which he habitually moved, and the rest of their journey passed pleasantly enough. Seth was inclined to swagger, as he was nervous of Claud's tail coat and white waistcoat and irritated by his casual voice, but he was too excited and looking forward too much to the dance to make himself really disagreeable.

The Assembly Rooms at Godmere were reached by the party without mishap. The High Street was crowded with traffic, for most of the guests had come in from outlying villages and houses in their cars, and a big crowd had come in by bus, from miles round, to gather outside the doors in the Market Place to see the guests going in.

The party from Cold Comfort was fortunate in being in the hands of a competent chauffeur. He actually found a site in a narrow cul-de-sac just round a turning close to the Rooms where he parked their car. Flora instructed him to return at twelve o'clock, when the ball was over, and inquired how he proposed to spend the rest of his evening.

'I shall go to the talkies, madam,' he replied respectfully.

'Aye, there's Marie Rambeau in "Red Heels" at th' Orpheum,' broke in Seth eagerly.

'Yes, well, that will do very well,' said Flora graciously, frowning slightly at Seth; and she slipped her fingers within the arm of Claud, and they moved slowly off through the crowd to the Rooms.

A red carpet had been placed down the flight of steps leading up to the entrance and along the pavement as far as the kerb. On either side of this carpet was assembled a large crowd of sightseers, whose interested and admiring faces were illuminated by two flambeaux which burned at either side of the entrance.

Just as Flora's party was mounting the first steps amid a murmur of admiration from the crowd, she thought she heard someone say her name, and, looking in the direction from which the sound came, she perceived none other than Mr Mybug, perilously poised upon the plinth of a lamp-post, and accompanied by another gentleman of disordered dress and wild appearance, whom she judged to be one of his intellectual peers.

Mr Mybug waved gaily to Flora, and he looked cheerful enough, but she (foolish creature) felt a little sorry for him because he was rather fat and his clothes were not very good, and when she compared his personal appearance with that of Charles, who was always so neat except when a lock of his black hair descended over his forehead while he was playing tennis or otherwise agitated, she felt that Mr Mybug was one of our more desolate figures, and almost wished that he were coming to the ball.

'Who is that?' inquired Claud, glancing in the direction of her gaze.

'A Mr Mybug. I met him in London.'

'Good God!' observed Claud, in a tone of deep distaste.

Had Flora been alone, she would have called pleasantly to Mr Mybug across the heads of the crowd:

'How do you do? . . . How amusing to see you here! Are you copy-hunting?'

But she felt that upon this occasion she stood in the relation of a chaperone and sponsor to Elfine, and that her own conduct must be carefully regulated so as not to give rise to a breath of adverse comment.

She contented herself, therefore, with bowing very pleasantly to Mr Mybug, who looked rather miserable and tried to pull down his cardigan, which had worked up all wrinkly round his waist.

Mr Aubrey Featherweight, who had designed the Assembly Rooms of Godmere in the year 1830, had not been content to provide them with one broad and not unshapely flight of steps as an approach. He had constructed another flight leading down into the large ballroom, which was built slightly below the level of the street.

Now when Flora, emerging from the draughty ladies'

cloak-room immediately within the entrance hall of the Rooms accompanied by the stately and beautiful Elfine, saw this second staircase and realized that it led down into the ballroom, so intense a glow of gratitude filled her heart that she could have fallen upon her knees and thanked Fate.

Did not the Abbé F.-M. say: 'Lost is that man who sees a beautiful woman descending a noble staircase,' and were not both these ingredients here, and ready to her hand? What else but a staircase could so perfectly set off the jewel she had made of Elfine?

A handsome lady of some sixty years stood at the head of the staircase to welcome those guests who passed from the hall on their way to the ballroom, and at her side, aiding her in the task of welcoming each guest, stood a large young woman in a cruel shade of electric blue, whom Flora rightly judged to be Mrs Hawk-Monitor's daughter Joan.

The four young people slowly approached their hostess.

Flora's fine eyes, that were so observant, noticed how propitious was this moment for their entry.

The hour was nearly nine. All the guests of importance had already arrived, and the fine flower of the county of Sussex was circling to the strains of the 'Twelve Sweet Hours' waltz in the ballroom below, the gowns of the young women and the elegant dark purple and white of the young men's clothes being admirably set off by the florid crimson walls, the slender white pillars capped by gold acanthus leaves, and the banks of dark green foliage which decorated the alcoves of the room.

Claud moved forward to present Flora and Elfine to Mrs Hawk-Monitor, who received Flora with a gracious smile, and whose sudden, startled glance at Elfine was all that Flora could wish; and then Elfine, in response to a gentle motion from Flora (who had been detained for a moment in conversation by Joan Hawk-Monitor), began to descend the crimson-covered stairs.

It was at this moment that the sweet, leisurely last notes of the 'Twelve Hours' waltz ceased, and the dancers below slowly came to a standstill and stood clapping and smiling.

Then a startled hush fell upon the clapping. All eyes were turned upon the staircase. A low hum of admiration, the most delightful sound in the world that a woman's ears can receive, rose into the stillness.

Here was beauty. It silenced all comment except that of eager praise. A generation that had admired piquante women, boyish women, ugly, smart, and fascinating women was now confronted by simple beauty, pure and undeniable as that of the young Venus whom the Greeks loved to carve; and responded immediately, in delighted and surprised homage, to its challenge.

Just as no human creature who has eyes to see can deny the beauty of an almond-tree in full flower, no human eyes could deny beauty to Elfine. The slow descent of this young girl down the staircase was like the descent of a sunlit cloud down the breast of a mountain. Her candid beauty, set off by the snowy-silver of her simple dress, refreshed the dancers who stood silently looking up at her as the sight of a cluster of flowers or a moonlight expanse of sea refreshes the eyes.

And Flora, silently watching from the head of the stair-case, saw that a tall young man who stood just at its foot was looking up at Elfine as the young shepherd must once have looked at the moon goddess; and she was satisfied.

The entranced pause was broken by music. The orchestra began to play a gay polka, and the young man (who was Richard Hawk-Monitor himself) came forward to give his hand to Elfine and lead her into the mazes of the dance.

Flora and Claud (who was much amused by all this) came down the stairs into the ballroom a little later and also joined the dancers.

Flora had every reason to feel smug and satisfied with her evening's work as she floated round the room in the arms of Claud, who danced admirably. Without seeming to take so obvious an interest in the movements of Elfine and her part-ner that her gaze became ill-bred, she observed their every action.

What she saw pleased her much. Richard appeared to be deeply in love. It is usual to see a young man looking down into the face of a girl with whom he is dancing with an expression of soft admiration, and Flora was used to such spectacles. But she had not often seen a young man's face so rapt, so almost awed, with adoration and another emotion which can only be defined as gratitude, as was the face of Richard Hawk-Monitor. Wonder, too, was in his expression. He held Elfine preciously, as a man might hold a flowering branch of some rare tree which he has seen for the first time and is bringing back to his cave.

The miracle for which she had conjured the love god had befallen. Richard had realized, not that Elfine was beautiful, but that he loved Elfine. (Young men frequently need this fact pointed out to them, as Flora knew by observing the antics of her friends.)

Now she must wait patiently until the end of the ball, when Elfine would tell her whether Richard had proposed marriage. She felt that the anxiety of waiting to know whether her diplomacy had succeeded might impair the pleasure of the evening for her, but resolved to bear the trial with calmness.

However, as it turned out, she began to enjoy the ball so much that she almost forgot her anxiety.

The ball was, indeed, a very agreeable one. Perhaps it was more by luck than by judgement that Mrs Hawk-Monitor had combined two of the essentials for a successful ball (too many guests in a smallish room), but both were there, and then these were combined with the elegance and lavishness of the supper-tables and the sober richness of the appointments, and the fact that most of the people who were present knew each other slightly, all the ingredients for success were present, and success was achieved.

Flora overheard many comments upon Elfine's beauty, and was asked several times who her lovely companion was. She smilingly replied that she was a cousin, a Miss Starkadder, and would say no more save that Elfine lived in the neighbourhood. She did not make the mistake of snobbishly embroidering upon Elfine's ancestry and charm. She let Elfine's serious beauty do its own work, and very well it did it. Elfine danced most of the dances with Richard Hawk-Monitor, but she gave many others to the group of eager young men who gathered round her as soon as the music paused.

Flora observed that Mrs Hawk-Monitor, from her position in an alcove on the balcony above the ballroom, was beginning to look vaguely anxious, especially during those dances that Elfine gave to Richard.

Flora divided her dances chiefly between Claud and Seth. Seth appeared to be enjoying the evening immensely. In one way and another he had nearly as spectacular a success as Elfine. A group of some nine young persons whose dress proclaimed that they had come down from London for the ball took possession of Seth early in the evening, and would not let him go. Flora overheard two or three of the young women telling each other that their dears, he was *too* creditable, and *merely* body-thrilling, and Seth just smiled his slow, warm smile and drawled: 'Aye' and 'Nay' when asked if he did not adore farming, and what he wanted from life, and didn't he think the important thing was to experience *everything*?

Several young men approached Flora, and seemed anxious to appropriate her company after they had danced with her, and all this was very satisfactory, but she had resolved that for this evening at any rate she must keep herself in the background and make no attempt to rival Elfine. So she danced mostly with Claud, after Seth had been carried off to supper by his adoring tribe of young girls. Flora knew that she did not look so beautiful as Elfine, but, then, she did not want to. She knew that she looked distinguished, elegant, and interesting. She asked for nothing more.

Only one disagreeable incident marred the pleasure of the evening. Just as she and Claud were making their way to the supper-tables in an adjoining room a disturbance broke out in the balcony above their heads, and Flora looked up in time to see the back of a gentleman, which was only too familiar to her, being hustled out through the entrance with some haste by two of the flunkeys.

'Somebody tried to gate-crash,' called a laughing young man to Claud, in passing, as he came running down the stairs. He had been giving the flunkeys a hand.

Flora felt rather distressed. She sat down at the little table which Claud had reserved for them, which was charmingly wreathed with spring leaves and flowers, with a sober expression on her face.

'My dear Flora, was that a friend of yours?' asked Claud, motioning the waiter to open some champagne.

'It was Mr Mybug,' said Flora, simply; 'and I cannot help feeling, Claud, that if I had thought of trying to get him an invitation he would not have had to try and gate-crash.'

'It is a good thing that everybody who hasn't got invitations for things doesn't have to try and gate-crash,' observed Claud.

'I cannot help feeling,' pursued Flora, picking up her fork to begin on the crab *mousse*, 'rather sorry for Mr Mybug.'

'We are purified by suffering,' said Claud, helping himself to crab.

But Flora went on: 'You see, he is rather fat. I always feel sorry for people who are fat. And I haven't got the heart to tell him that's why I won't let him kiss me. He thinks it's because I'm inhibited.'

'But, my dear, he would. Don't distress yourself. Have some more crab.'

And Flora did, and telling herself that it was her duty to look pleasant, for Elfine's sake, she thought no more of Mr Mybug that evening.

Flora and Claud lingered long over the supper-table, enjoying the spectacle of the brilliantly lit, elegantly decorated apartment filled with young persons of both sexes, most of them handsome and all of them happy. Claud, who had served in the Anglo-Nicaraguan wars of '46, was at his ease in the comfortable silence in which they sat, and allowed the irony and grief of his natural expression to emerge from beneath the mask of cheerful idiocy with which he usually covered his sallow, charming face. He had seen his friends die in anguish in the wars. For him, the whole of the rest of his life was an amusing game which no man of taste and intelligence could permit himself to take seriously.

Much as Flora was enjoying the ball, she was doing so more as a spectator than as a participant. She wished regretfully that some others of her friends might have been present: Mrs Smiling, looking vague in a white gown; the handsome Julia; Charles, in the severe tail coat of darkest blue which so well became his height and gravity.

As at all good parties, an atmosphere, impalpable as a perfume yet as real, rose above the heads of the laughing guests. It was the aroma of enjoyment and gaiety. No one could inhale it without instinctively smiling and glancing good-naturedly round the room. Gay voices rose every second above the roar of the general conversation like individual rills of water from the rush of a stream in spate. A laughing mouth, three youthful heads gathered together, while a fourth, distorted with laughter, uttered gasping protests; chins lifted and eyes narrowed between lashes with mirth; an azalea plant revealed as two persons drew back from the table to shout with laughter: such were the outward signs of a Good Party. And above them floated this invisible glittering cloud of success.

Suddenly Flora gave a slight start. Elfine had appeared at the door of the supper-room, accompanied by Richard Hawk-Monitor. They were glancing round the room as if in search of someone, and when Elfine caught sight of Flora's raised hand, in its pale-green glove, she smiled eagerly and said something over her shoulder to the young Hawk-Monitor, and they began to make their way between the tables to where Flora and Claud sat.

Flora's spirits, already excited by the pleasure of the ball, rose still higher. Richard must have proposed, and have been accepted. Nothing else could have made the two look so peculiarly radiant.

They came towards her, threading their way between the laughing groups, who looked up from their talk to smile at

Dick and to look curiously at Elfine; and then Elfine had paused at their table, and Claud had risen to his feet, and Elfine, reaching backwards for Richard's hand, drew him forward and said:

'Oh, Flora, I do so want you to meet Dick.'

Flora bowed and smiled, and said: 'How do you do? I have heard so much about you and I am so pleased to meet you'; but she found her hand taken into a friendly clasp and met the beam of a wind-reddened, open, boyish countenance. She noticed that he had perfect teeth, white as those of a young lion, and a little black moustache.

'I say, I'm awfully glad to meet you. Elf has told me all about you, too. I say, this is jolly, isn't it? Marvellous idea of the mater's, having the orgy here instead of in the family crematorium, what? I say, Miss Poste, it was awfully decent of you to bring Elfine. I simply can't thank you enough, you know. I mean, it's made all the difference in the world. We're engaged, as a matter of fact.'

'My dear! How charming! I am delighted! I congratulate you!' cried Flora, who was indeed overcome with relief and satisfaction.

'Charming,' murmured Claud, in the background.

'We're going to announce it at the end of the evening,' Richard went on. 'Good opportunity, what?'

Claud, sardonically wondering what the feelings of Mrs Hawk-Monitor would be when she heard the news, said that the occasion might have been made for the announcement of the event. Flora then introduced him to Richard, and there was some general conversation, made interesting by the aura of happiness which hovered over the betrothed pair and the smiling sympathy with which Claud and Flora listened to their talk.

CHAPTER 15

IT was now nearly twelve o'clock, and a general movement was made to return to the ballroom. The orchestra had been refreshed by some supper, and broke immediately into a jolly tune to which the 'Lancers' could be danced, and away pranced everybody, and danced until every cheek was crimson and the floor was scattered with fans, hairpins, shoe-buttons, and wilting flowers.

Claud was as light on his feet as the harlequin he somewhat resembled, and while Flora was springing round the room, just guided by the cool touch of his hands, she observed Elfine in Richard's arms, and saw with satisfaction how marvellously happy she looked and how beautiful. Flora glowed with content. Her aim was achieved. She felt as though she had shaken her fist in the face of Aunt Ada Doom. Elfine was rescued. Henceforth, her life would be one of exquisite, sunny, natural content. She would bear children and found a line of pleasant, ordinary English people who were blazing with poetry in their secret souls. All was as it should be.

And Flora, energetically prancing herself to a standstill as the Lancers ended, clapped her hands vigorously, half with the desire for an encore, but more for the joy she felt in her evening's work.

'How you do enjoy yourself, don't you, Florence Nightingale?' observed Claud.

'I do,' retorted Flora; 'and so do you.'

It was true; he did. But never without a pang of exquisite pain in his heart, and a conviction that he was a traitor.

In the pause that followed the music, Flora observed that Richard was leading Elfine to the staircase, and they went slowly up it, to where his mother sat on the balcony with a number of her old friends. Flora moved forward also, in case she should be needed, but before she could begin to mount the stairs Richard left his mother, over whom he had been bending in conversation, and, coming forward to the balcony rail, held up his hand for silence. Elfine stood beside him, but slightly in the background. Flora could not see the expression on the face of Mrs Hawk-Monitor, who was hidden by Richard's body, but she observed that the face of Joan Hawk-Monitor bore an expression which was a curious blend of dismay and interest and envy. ('But then, that shade of blue would do anything to anybody's face,' Flora comforted herself.)

'Ladies and gentlemen,' said Dick. 'It's been awfully jolly seeing you all here to-night. I'm awfully glad you could all come. I mean, I shall always be glad to remember you were all here on my twenty-first birthday. It makes it all so much jollier somehow ... I mean, I do like a cheery mob around me, what?'

He paused. There was laughter and some clapping. Flora held her breath. He must – he *must* announce the engagement! If he did not, she would know (whatever might happen afterwards) that her plot had failed.

But it was all right. He was speaking again. He was drawing Elfine forward to face the guests, and taking her hands in his.

'And this is a particularly jolly evening for me, because I've got something else to tell you all. I want to tell you that Miss Starkadder and I are engaged.'

There! It was out! A storm of clapping and excited comment broke forth, and people began streaming up the staircase to offer their congratulations. Flora, feeling quite weak after the nervous excitement of the past five minutes, turned to Claud, and said: 'There, that's over. Oh, Claud, but do you think we ought to go up and speak to Mrs Hawk-Monitor? I must confess that I would rather not.'

Claud, however, said decidedly that he thought it would be most incorrect if Flora did not do so, for she was there, after all, in the capacity of Elfine's chaperone, and the whole course of affairs had already been so irregular that anything Flora could do to give a colouring of convention to the situation would count in Elfine's favour.

So Flora, reluctantly agreeing, went up the staircase to tackle Mrs Hawk-Monitor.

She found the poor lady looking dazed. She was sitting in an alcove, receiving the thanks and congratulations upon the success of the ball from those guests who were already departing. Flora was relieved to notice that the healthy Joan was standing at some distance away, by the door, so she would not have to cope with *her*, as well as with Mamma H.-M.

Flora went forward with outstretched hand.

'Thank you so much . . . such a lovely party, and so nice of you to let us come.'

But Mrs Hawk-Monitor had risen, and was looking very gravely at her. She might be a vague woman and a darling, but she was not a fool. She took an eyeful of Flora, and knew that here was a young woman of good sense. Her heart longed for some reassurance in the midst of the dismay and doubt which possessed her. She said, almost pleadingly:

'Miss Poste, I will be frank with you. I cannot pretend that I am delighted at this engagement. Who is this young lady? I have only met her once before. I know next to nothing of her family.'

'She is a gentle, docile person,' said Flora, earnestly. 'She is only seventeen. I think she can be moulded into exactly what you would wish her to be. Dear Mrs Hawk-Monitor, pray do not be distressed. I am sure that you will learn to like Elfine. Do believe me when I say that she has excellent qualities. As for her family, if I may venture to offer you some advice, I should take steps at once to see that she sees next to nothing of them for the next few weeks. There will probably be strong opposition to the match.'

'Opposition? What imperti – '

She checked herself. She was amazed and at a loss. She had assumed that Elfine's family would be overjoyed at their offspring's luck.

'Indeed, yes. Mrs Starkadder, her grandmother, has always intended Elfine to marry her cousin, Urk. I am afraid

166

there may be some opposition from him too. In fact, the sooner you can arrange for the marriage to take place the better it will be for Elfine.'

'Oh, dear! I had hoped for a year's engagement, at least. Dick is still so young.'

'The more reason why he should begin at once to be utterly happy,' smiled Flora. 'Indeed, Mrs Hawk-Monitor, I do really think it will be better if you can arrange for the wedding to take place in a month at the latest. Things at the farm are sure to be very unpleasant for Elfine until she leaves, and I am sure you do not want a lot of interference and discussion from the Starkadders, do you?'

'Such a dreadful name, too,' mused Mrs Hawk-Monitor.

At this moment, the arrival of Seth and Claud, dressed ready to depart, made it impossible to discuss the matter any further. Mrs Hawk-Monitor had only time to press Flora's hand, murmuring in a friendlier tone than she had yet used: 'I will think over what you say. Perhaps, after all, everything is for the best.'

So Flora went off in comparatively high spirits.

They found Elfine, looking like a white rose-peony, waiting for them at the door; Dick was with her, tenderly saying good night to her. Flora could see their car, with the chauffeur at the door, waiting for them at the foot of the steps, so after a pleasant farewell to Dick they got away at last.

Flora felt quite desolate after they had dropped Claud outside the Crown of Roses, where he was staying the night. She was rather sleepy and cross and suffering from a reaction after the evening's excitement. So she shut her eyes and slept more or less successfully until the car was within two miles or so from home. Then she woke with a little start. Voices had roused her. Seth was saying, in a tone which was distinctly tinged with gloating:

'Aye, th' old un'll have summat to say about this night's work.'

'Grandmamma can't stop me getting married!'

'Maybe not, but she'll have a dom good try.'

'She cannot do much in a month,' broke in Flora, coldly,

'and possibly Elfine will be staying with the Hawk-Monitors for most of the time. She must just avoid Aunt Ada while she is in the house, that's all. Heaven knows it ought not to be very difficult to do, considering that Aunt Ada never leaves her bedroom.'

Seth gave a low, gloating laugh. An animal quality throbbed in the sound like the network of veins below a rat's fur. The car was just drawing up at the gate leading into the yard, and Seth, leaning past Flora, pointed through the window with one thick finger at the farm-house.

Flora stared in the direction to which he pointed and saw, with a thrill of dismay, that the windows of the farm were ablaze with light.

CHAPTER 16

PERHAPS 'ablaze' is too strong a word. There was a distinct suggestion of corpse-lights and railway-station waiting-rooms about the lights which shone forth from the windows of Cold Comfort. But compared with the heavy, muffling darkness of the night in which the country-side was sunk, the lights looked looked positively rorty.

'Oh, my goodness!' said Flora.

'It's Grandmamma!' whispered Elfine, who had gone very white. 'She must have chosen this night, of all nights, to come downstairs, and have the family party.'

'Nonsense! You don't have parties at places like Cold Comfort,' said Flora, taking notes from her bag with which to pay the chauffeur. She got out of the car, stretching a little and inhaling the fresh, sweet night air, and put them into his hand.

'There. Thank you very much. Everything went off most satisfactorily. Good night.'

And the chauffeur, having thanked her respectfully for his tip, backed the car out of the yard, and away down the lane towards the road.

The headlights swept the hedges and touched the grass to livid green.

They heard him change into top, in the dead, eerie silence and darkness.

Then the friendly sound of the engine began to/recede, until it was absorbed into the vast quiet of the night.

They turned and looked towards the house.

The lights in the windows had a leering, waiting look, like that on the faces of old pimps who sit in the cafés of Holborn Viaduct, plying their casual bartery. A thin wind snivelled among the rotting stacks of Cold Comfort, spreading itself in a sheet of flowing sound across the mossed tiles. Darkness whined with the soundless urge of growth in the hedges, but that did not help any.

'Ay, 'tes Grandmother,' said Seth, sombrely. 'She'm holding the Counting. Ay, 'tes her, all right.'

'What on earth,' said Flora, peevishly, beginning to pick her way across the yard, 'is the Counting, and why in the name of all that's inconvenient should it be held at half past one in the morning?'

''Tes the record of th' family that Grandmother holds ivery year. See – we'm violent folk, we Starkadders. Some on us pushes others down wells. Some on us dies in childerbirth. There's others as die o' drink or goes mad. There's a whole heap on us, too. 'Tes difficult to keep count on us. So once a year Grandmother she holds a gatherin', called the Counting, and she counts us all, to see how many on us 'as died in th' year.'

'Then she can count me out,' retorted Flora, raising her hand to knock at the kitchen door.

Then a thought struck her.

'Seth,' she whispered, 'had you any idea that your grandmother was going to hold this infernal Counting tonight?'

She saw the gleam of his teeth in the dimness.

'Reckon I had,' he drawled.

'Then you're a crashing bounder,' said Flora, vigorously, 'and I hope your water-voles die. Now, Elfine, brace up.

We are, I am afraid, for it. You had best not say a word. I will do the talking.'

And she knocked at the door.

The silence which swayed softly out from within to meet them was a tangible thing. It had plangency. It moulded and compelled. It imposed and awed.

It was broken by heavy footsteps. Someone was crossing the kitchen floor in hob-nailed boots. A hand fumbled with the bolts. Then the door was slowly opened, and Urk stood looking up at them, his face twisted into a Japanese Nō-mask of lust, fury, and grief. Flora could hear Elfine's terri-fied breathing behind her, in the darkness, and put out a comforting hand. It was clasped and held convulsively.

The great kitchen was full of people. They were all silent, and all painted over by the leaping firelight with a hellish red glow. Flora could distinguish Amos, Judith, Meriam, the hired girl; Adam, Ezra, and Harkaway; Caraway, Luke, and Mark, and several of the farm-hands. They were all grouped, in a rough semicircle, about someone who sat in a great high-backed chair by the fire. The dim gold lamp-light and the restless firelight made Rembrandt shadows in the remoter corners of the kitchen, and threw the dwarf and giant shadows of the Starkadders across the ceiling.

A pungent scent came swooning out to meet the inrush of night air. It was sickly sweet, and strange to Flora. Then she saw that the heat of the fire had caused the long, pink buds of the sukebind to burst; the wreath which hung round the portrait of Fig Starkadder was covered with large flowers whose petals sprang back, like snarling fangs, to show the shameless heart that sent out full gusts of sweetness.

Everybody was staring at the door. The silence was ter-rific. It seemed the air must burst with its pressure, and the flickering movement of the light and the fireglow upon the faces of the Starkadders was so restlessly volatile that it emphasized the strange stillness of their bodies. Flora was trying to decide just what the kitchen looked like, and came to the conclusion it was the Chamber of Horrors at Madame Tussaud's.

'Well, well,' she said, amiably, stepping over the doorstep and drawing off her gloves, 'the gang *is* all here, isn't it? Is that Big Business I see there in the corner? Oh, I beg your pardon, it's Micah. I suppose there aren't any sandwiches?'

This cracked the social ice a bit. Signs of life were observed.

'There's food on the table,' said Judith, lifelessly, coming forward, with her burning eyes fixed upon Seth; 'but first, Robert Poste's child, you must greet your Aunt Ada Doom.'

And she took Flora's hand (Flora was very bucked that she had shed her clean gloves) and led her up to the figure which sat in the high-backed chair by the fire.

'Mother,' said Judith, 'this is Flora, Robert Poste's child. I have spoken to you of her.'

'How d'ye do, Aunt Ada?' said Flora, pleasantly, putting out her hand. But Aunt Ada made no effort to take it. She folded her own hands a little more closely upon a copy of the *Milk Producers' Weekly Bulletin and Cowkeepers' Guide*, which she held on her lap, and observed, in a low, toneless voice:

'I saw something nasty in the woodshed.'

Flora turned to Judith, with raised and inquiring eyebrows. A murmur came from the rest of the company, which was watching closely.

''Tes one of her bad nights,' said Judith, whose gaze kept wandering piteously in the direction of Seth (he was wolfing beef in the corner). 'Mother,' she said, louder, 'don't you know me? It's Judith. I have brought Flora Poste to see you – Robert Poste's child.'

'Nay ... I saw something nasty in the woodshed,' said Aunt Ada Doom, fretfully moving her great head from side to side. ' 'Twas a burnin' noonday ... sixty-nine years ago. And me no bigger than a titty-wren. And I saw something na – '

'Well, perhaps she likes it better that way,' said Flora soothingly. She had been observing Aunt Ada's firm chin, clear eyes, tight little mouth, and close grip upon the *Milk Producers' Weekly Bulletin and Cowkeepers' Guide*, and she came to the conclusion that if Aunt Ada was mad, then she, Flora, was one of the Marx Brothers.

'Saw something nasty in the woodshed!!!' suddenly shrilled Aunt Ada, smiting Judith with the *Milk Producers' Weekly Bulletin and Cowkeepers' Guide*, 'something nasty! Take it away. You're all wicked and cruel. You want to go away and leave me alone in the woodshed. But you never shall. None of you. Never! There have always been Stark-adders at Cold Comfort. You must all stay here with me, all of you: Judith, Amos, Micah, Urk, Luke, Mark, Elfine, Caraway, Harkaway, Reuben, and Seth. Where's Seth? Where's my darling? Come – come here, Seth.'

Seth came pushing his way through the crowd of relations, with his mouth full of beef and bread. 'Here, grandma,' he crooned, soothingly. 'Here I am. I'll niver leave 'ee – niver.'

('Do not look at Seth, woman,' whispered Amos, terribly, in Judith's ear. 'You are always looking at him.')

'That's my good boy ... my mommet ... my pippet ...' the old woman murmured, patting Seth's head with the *Milk Producers' Weekly Bulletin and Cowkeepers' Guide*. 'Why, how grand he is to-night! What's this? What's all this?' And she jerked at Seth's dinner-jacket. 'What've you been doing, boy? Tell your granny.'

Flora could see, from the way in which Aunt Ada's remarkably shrewd eyes beneath their heavy lids were examining Seth's person, that she had rumbled their little outing. There was just time to save their faces before the deluge. So she took a deep breath and said loudly and clearly:

'He's been to Godmere, to Richard Hawk-Monitor's twenty-first birthday dance. So have I. So has Elfine. So has a friend of mine called Claud Hart-Harris, whom none of you know. And, what is more, Aunt Ada, Elfine and Richard Hawk-Monitor are engaged to be married, and *will* be married, too, in about a month from now.'

There came a terrible cry from the shadows near the sink. Everybody started violently and turned to stare in the direction whence it came. It was Urk – Urk lying face downward, in the beef sandwiches, with one hand pressed upon his heart in dreadful agony. The hired girl, Meriam, laid her rough hand upon his bowed head and timidly patted it, but he shook her off with a movement like a weasel in a trap.

'My little water-vole,' they heard him moan. 'My little water-vole.'

A babel broke out, in which Aunt Ada could dimly be discerned beating at everybody with the *Milk Producers' Weekly Bulletin and Cowkeepers' Guide*, and shrilly screaming: 'I saw it . . . I saw it! I shall go mad . . . I can't bear it . . . There have always been Starkadders at Cold Comfort. I saw something nasty in the woodshed . . . something nasty . . . nasty . . . nasty . . .'

Seth took her hands and held them in his, kneeling before her and speaking wooingly to her, as though she were a sick child. Flora had dragged Elfine up on a table in a corner near the fireplace, out of the racket, and was pensively feeding the two of them on bread and butter. She had given up all hope of getting to bed that night. It was nearly half past two, and everybody seemed sitting pretty for the sunrise.

She observed several females unknown to her flitting dejectedly about in the gloom, replenishing plates with bread and butter and occasionally weeping in corners.

'Who's that?' she asked Elfine, pointing interestedly at one who had a perfectly flat bust and a face like a baby bird all goggle eyes and beaky nose. This one was weeping half inside a boot cupboard.

''Tes poor Rennet,' said Elfine, sleepily. 'Oh, Flora, I'm so happy, but I do wish we could go to bed, don't you?'

'Presently, yes. So that's poor Rennet, is it? Why (if it be not tactless to ask) are all her clothes sopping wet?'

'Oh! she jumped down the well, about eleven o'clock, Meriam, the hired girl, told me. Grandmamma kept on mocking at her because she's an old maid. She said Rennet couldn't even keep a tight hold on Mark Dolour when she *had* got him, and poor Rennet had hysterics, and then Grandma kept on saying things about – about flat bosoms and things, and then Rennet ran out and jumped down the well. And Grandma had an attack.'

'Serve her right, the old trout,' muttered Flora, yawning. 'Hey, what's up now?' For a renewed uproar had broken out in the midst of the crowd gathered round Aunt Ada.

By standing on the table and peering through the confusing flicker of the firelight and lamplight, Flora and Elfine could distinguish Amos, who was bending over Aunt Ada Doom's chair, and thundering at her. There was such an infernal clatter going on from Micah, Ezra, Reuben, Seth, Judith, Caraway, Harkaway, Susan, Letty, Prue, Adam, Jane, Phoebe, Mark, and Luke that it was difficult to make out what he was saying, but suddenly he raised his voice to a roar, and the others were silent:

'... So I mun go where th' Lord's work calls me and spread th' Lord's word abroad in strange places. Ah, 'tes terrible to have to go, but I mun do it. I been wrestlin' and prayin' and broodin' over it, and I know th' truth at last. I mun go abroad in one o' they Ford vans, preachin' all over th' countryside. Aye, like th' Apostles of old, I have heard my call, and I mun follow it.' He flung his arms wide, and stood with the firelight playing its scarlet fantasia upon his exalted face.

'No ... No!' screamed Aunt Ada Doom, on a high note that cracked with her agony. 'I cannot bear it. There have always been Starkadders at Cold Comfort. You mustn't go ... none of you must go ... I shall go mad! I saw something nasty in the woodshed ... Ah ... ah ...'

She struggled to her feet, supported by Seth and Judith, and struck weakly at Amos with the *Milk Producers' Weekly Bulletin and Cowkeepers' Guide* (which was looking a bit the worse for wear by this time). His great body flinched from the blow, but still he stood rigid, his eyes fixed triumphantly upon some far-off, ecstatic vision, the red light wavering and flickering across his face.

'I mun go ...' he repeated, in a strange, soft voice. 'This very night I mun go. I hear th' glad voices o' angels callin' me out over th' ploughed fields where th' liddle seedlings is

clappin' their hands in prayer; and besides, I arranged wi'
Agony Beetle's brother to pick me up in th' Lunnon milk-
van at half past three, so I've no time to lose. Aye, 'tes good-
bye to you all. Mother, I've broken yer chain at last, wi' th'
help of th' angels and the Lord's word. Wheer's my hat?'

Reuben silently handed it to his father (he had had it
ready for the last ten minutes).

Aunt Ada Doom sat huddled in her chair, breathing
feebly and fast, striking impotently at the air with the *Milk
Producers' Weekly Bulletin and Cowkeepers' Guide*. Her
eyes, slots of pain in her grey face, were turned on Amos.
They blazed with hate, like flaring candles that feel the
pressing dark all about them and flare the brighter for their
fear.

'Aye ...' she whispered. 'Aye ... so you go, and leave me
in the woodshed. There have always been Starkadders at
Cold Comfort ... but that means nothing to you. I shall go
mad ... I shall die here, alone, in the woodshed, with nasty
– things' – her voice thickened; she wrung her hands dis-
tractedly, as though to free them of some obscene spiritual
treacle – 'pressing on me ... alone ... alone ...'

Her voice trailed into silence. Her head sank into her
breast. Her face was drained of blood: grey, broken.

Amos moved with great, slow steps to the door. No one
moved. The hush which froze the room was broken only by
the idle rippling dance of the flames. Amos jerked open the
door, and there was the vast, indifferent face of the night
peering in.

'Amos!'

It was a screech from her heart-roots. It buried itself in
his plexus. But he never turned. He stepped blunderingly
out into the dark – and was gone.

Suddenly there was a wild cry from the corner in the
shadows by the sink. Urk came stumbling forward, dragging
the hired girl, Meriam, in his wake.

(Flora woke up Elfine, who had gone to sleep with her
head on her shoulder, and pointed out that some more fun
was just beginning. It was only a quarter past three.)

Urk was chalk-white. A trail of blood drooled down his chin. His eyes were pools of pain, in which his bruised thoughts darted and fed like tortured fish. He was laughing insanely, noiselessly. Meriam shrank back from him, livid with fear.

'Me and the water-voles ... we've failed,' he babbled in a low, toneless voice. 'We're beaten. We planned a nest for her up there by Ticklepenny's well, when the egg-plants was in bloom. And now she's given herself to him, the dirty stuck-up, lying – ' He choked, and had to fight for breath for a second. 'When she was an hour old, I made a mark on her feeding bottle, in water-vole's blood. She was mine, see? Mine! And I've lost her ... Oh, why did I iver think she were mine?'

He turned upon Meriam, who shrank back in terror.

'Come here – you. I'll take you instead. Aye, dirt as you are, I'll take you, and we'll sink into th' mud together. There have always been Starkadders at Cold Comfort, and now there'll be a Beetle too.'

'And not the first neither, as you'd know if you'd ever cleaned out the larder,' said a voice tartly. It was Mrs Beetle herself, who, hitherto unobserved by Flora, had been busily cutting bread and butter and replenishing the glasses of the farm-hands in a far corner of the long kitchen. She now came forward into the circle about the fire, and confronted Urk with her arms akimbo.

'Well ... 'oo's talking about dirt? 'Eaven knows, you should know something about it, in that coat and them trousers. Enough ter turn up one of yer precious water-voles, you are. A pity you don't spend a bit less time with yer old water-voles and a bit more with a soap and flannel.'

Here she received unexpected support from Mark Dolour who called in a feeling tone from the far end of the kitchen:

'Aye, that's right.'

'Don't you 'ave 'im, ducky, unless you feel like it,' advised Mrs Beetle, turning to Meriam. 'You're full young yet, and 'e won't see forty again.'

'I don't mind. I'll 'ave him, if un wants me,' said Meriam,

176

amiably, 'I can always make 'im wash a bit, if I feels like it.'

Urk gave a wild laugh. His hand fell on her shoulder, and he drew her to him and pressed a savage kiss full on her open mouth. Aunt Ada Doom, choking with rage, struck at them with the *Milk Producers' Weekly Bulletin and Cowkeepers' Guide*, but the blow missed. She fell back, gasping, exhausted.

'Come, my beauty – my handful of dirt. I mun carry thee up to Ticklepenny's and show 'ee to the water-voles.' Urk's face was working with passion.

'What! At this time o' night?' cried Mrs Beetle, scandalized.

Urk put one arm round Meriam's waist and heaved away, but could not budge her from the floor. He cursed aloud, and, kneeling down, placed his arms about her middle, and heaved again. She did not stir. Next he wrapped his arms about her shoulders, and below her knees. She declined upon him, and he, staggering beneath her, sank to the floor. Mrs Beetle made a sound resembling 't-t-t-t-t'.

Mark Dolour was heard to mutter that th' Fireman's Lift was as good a hold as any he knew.

Now Urk made Meriam stand in the middle of the floor, and with a low, passionful cry, ran to her.

'Come, my beauty.'

The sheer animal weight of the man bore her up into his clutching arms. Mark Dolour (who dearly loved a bit of sport) held open the door, and Urk and his burden rushed out into the dark and the earthy scents of the young spring night.

A silence fell.

The door remained open, idly swinging in a slow, cold wind which had risen.

As though frozen, the group within the kitchen waited for the distant crash which should tell them that Urk had fallen down.

Pretty soon it came; and Mark Dolour shut the door.

It was now four o'clock. Elfine had gone to sleep again.

So had all the farm-hands except Mark Dolour. The fire had sunk to a red, lascivious bed of coals, that waned, and then, on the other hand, waxed again in the slow wind which blew under the door.

Flora was desperately sleepy: she felt as though she were at one of Eugene O'Neill's plays; that kind that goes on for hours and hours and hours, until the R.S.P.C. Audiences batters the doors of the theatre in and insists on a tea interval.

There was no doubt that the fun was wearing a bit thin. Judith, huddled in a corner, was looking broodingly at Seth from under her raised hand. Reuben was brooding in another corner. The sukebind flowers were fading. Seth was studying a copy of *Photo Bits* which he had produced from the pocket of his evening jacket.

Only Aunt Ada Doom sat upright, her eyes fixed upon the distance. She was rigid. Her lips moved softly. Flora, from her refuge on the table, could make out what she was saying, and it sounded none too festive.

'Two of them ... gone. Elfine ... Amos ... and I'm alone in the woodshed now ... Who took them away? Who took them away? I must know ... I must know ... That chit. That brat. Robert Poste's child.'

The great bed of red coals, slowly settling into its last sleep towards extinction, threw a glare on her old face, and gave her the look of a carving in a Gothic cathedral. Rennet had crept forward until she was within a few feet of her great-aunt (for such was the relationship between Rennet and Ada Doom), and stood looking down at her with a mad glare in her pale eyes.

Suddenly, without turning round, Aunt Ada struck at her with the *Milk Producers' Weekly Bulletin and Cowkeepers' Guide*, and Rennet flew back to her corner.

A withered flower fell from the sukebind wreath into the coals.

It was half past four.

Suddenly, Flora felt a draught at her back. She looked round crossly, and found herself staring into the face of Reuben, who had opened the little concealed door behind the great bulge of the chimneypiece, which led out into the yard.

'Come on,' whispered Reuben, soundlessly. ''Tes time 'ee were in bed.'

Amazed and grateful, Flora silently woke Elfine, and with breathless caution they slid off the table and tiptoed across to the little door. Reuben drew them safely through it, and closed it noiselessly.

They stood outside in the yard, in a bitter wind, with the first streaks of cold light lying across the purple sky. The way to their beds lay clear before them.

'Reuben,' said Flora, too drunk with sleep to articulate clearly, but remembering her manners, 'you are an *utter* lamb. Why did you?'

'You got th' old devil out of th' way for me.'

'Oh . . . *that*,' yawned Flora.

'Aye . . . an' I doan't forget. Eh, th' farm'll be mine, now, surelie.'

'So it will,' said Flora amiably. 'Such fun for you.'

Suddenly a shocking row broke out in the kitchen behind them. The Starkadders were off again.

But Flora never knew what it was about. She was asleep where she stood. She walked up to her room like an automaton, just stayed awake long enough to undress, and then fell into bed like a log.

CHAPTER 17

THE next day was Sunday, so thank goodness everybody could stay in bed and get over the shocks of the night before. At least, that is what most families would have done. But the Starkadders were not like most families. Life burned in them with a fiercer edge, and by seven o'clock most of them were up and, to a certain extent, doing. Reuben, of course, had much to do because of Amos's sudden departure.

He now thought of himself as master of the farm, and a slow tide of satisfied earth-lust indolently ebbed and flowed in his veins as he began his daily task of counting the chickens' feathers.

Prue, Susan, Letty, Phoebe, and Jane had been escorted back to Howling by Adam, at half past five that morning, and he had returned in time to begin the milking. He was still bewildered by the fact of Elfine's betrothal. The sound of old wedding-bells danced between the tufts of hair in his withered ears, and catches of country rhymes sung before George the Fourth was born:

> 'Come rue, come snow,
> So maidies mun go'

he sang, over and over again to himself as he milked Feckless. He saw, yet did not see, that Aimless had lost another hoof.

The dawn widened into an exquisite spring day. Soft, wool-like puffs of sound came from the thrushes' throats in the trees. The uneasy year, tortured by its spring of adolescence, broke into bud-spots in hedge, copse, spinney, and byre.

Judith sat in the kitchen, looking out with leaden eyes across the disturbed expanse of the teeming country-side. Her face was grey. Rennet huddled by the fire, stirring some rather nasty jam she had suddenly thought she would make. She had decided to stay behind when the other female Starkadders had gone off with Adam; her flayed soul shrank, obliquely, from their unspoken pity.

So noon came, and passed. A rude meal was prepared by Adam, and eaten (some of it) by the rest in the great kitchen. Old Ada Doom kept to her room, whither she had been carried at six o'clock that morning, by Micah, Seth, Mark Dolour, Caraway, and Harkaway.

None dared go in to her. She sat alone, a huddled, vast ruin of flesh, staring unseeingly out between her wrinkled lids. Her fingers picked endlessly at the *Milk Producers' Weekly Bulletin and Cowkeepers' Guide*. She did not think or see. The sharp blue air of spring thundered silently on window-panes fogged by her slow, batrachian breath. Powerless waves of fury coursed over her inert body. Sometimes names burst out of her green lips: 'Amos... Elfine... Urk...' Sometimes they just stayed inside.

No one had seen anything of Urk since he had gone galloping out into the night carrying Meriam, the hired girl. It was generally assumed that he had drowned her and then himself. Who cared, anyway?

As for Flora, she was still asleep at half past three in the afternoon, and would have slept on comfortably enough until tea-time, but that she was aroused by a knocking at her door and the excited voice of Mrs Beetle proclaiming that there was two gentlemen to see her.

'Have you got them there?' asked Flora, sleepily.

Mrs Beetle was much shocked. She said indeed not, they was in Miss Poste's parlour.

'Well... who are they? I mean, did they tell you their names?'

'One's that Mr Mybug, miss, and the other's a gentleman 'oo says 'is name's Neck.'

'Oh, yes... of course, how delightful. Ask them both to wait till I come. I won't be long,' and Flora began slowly to dress, for she would not make herself feel ill by bounding vigorously out of bed, even though she was delighted at the idea of seeing her dear Mr Neck again. As for Mr Mybug, he was a nuisance, but could be coped with easily enough.

She went downstairs at last, looking as fresh as a leaf, and as she entered her little parlour (wherein Mrs Beetle had kindled a fire) Mr Neck advanced to meet her, holding out both his hands and saying:

'Well, well, sweetheart. How's the girl?'

Flora greeted him with warmth. He had already had some conversation with Mr Mybug, who was looking rather sulky and miserable because he had hoped to find Flora alone and have a lovely long scene with her, apologizing for his behaviour last night, and talking a lot about

himself. He became more sulky at first on hearing Mr
Neck address Flora as sweetheart, but after listening to a
little of their conversation, he decided that Mr Neck was
the sort of Amusing Type that calls everybody sweetheart,
and did not mind so much.

Flora instructed Mrs Beetle to bring them some tea,
which soon came, and they sat very pleasantly in the sunlight which streamed through the window of the little
green parlour, drinking their tea and conversing.

Flora felt sleepy and amiable. She had made up her
mind that Mr Neck must not go without seeing Seth, and
quietly told Mrs Beetle to send him to the parlour as soon
as he could be found; but apart from this decision, she was
not worrying about anything at all.

'Are you over here looking for English film stars, Mr
Neck?' asked Mr Mybug, eating a little cake that Flora
had wanted for herself.

'That's so. I want to find me another Clark Gable. Yeah,
you wouldn't remember him, maybe. That's twenty years
ago.'

'But I have seen him at a Sunday Film Club Repertory
Show, in a film called "Mounting Passion",' said Mr
Mybug eagerly. 'Do you know the work of the Sunday
Film Club Repertory people at all?'

'I'll buy it,' said Mr Neck, who had taken a dislike to
Mr Mybug. 'Well, I want a second Clark Gable, see? I
want a big, husky stiff that smells of the great outdoors,
with a golden voice. I want passion. I want red blood. I
don't want no sissies, see? Sissies give me a pain in the neck,
and they're beginning to give the great American public a
pain in the neck, too.'

'Do you know the work of Limf?' asked Mr Mybug.

'Never heard of 'em,' said Mr Neck. 'Thank you, sweetheart' (to Flora, who was feeding him cake). 'You know,
Mr Mybug, we gotta responsibility to the public. We gotta
give them what they want, yet it's gotta be clean. Boy,
that's difficult. I'll tell you it's difficult. I want a man who
can give them what they want, yet give it them so's it don't

leave a taste in their mouths.' He paused and drank tea. The sunshine, vivid as a Kleig light, revealed every wrinkle in his melancholy little monkeyish face and lit the fresh red carnation in his button-hole. For Mr Neck was a great dandy, who usually changed his button-hole twice a day.

'I want a man to fetch the women,' he went on. 'I want a new Gary Cooper (but, lessee, thass twenty years ago), only more ritzy. Someone who can look good in a tuxedo, and yet handle one of them old-world ploughs. (Say, I seen four ploughs since I been over this trip.) Well, who've I got? I got Teck Jones. Yeah, well, Teck's a good kid; he can ride all right, but he's got no body-urge. I got Valentine Orlo. Well, he looks like a wop. They won't stand for no more wops since poor Morelli went to the chair in '42. No, wops is off. Well, I got Peregrine Howard. He's a Britisher. No one can't say his first name right, so he's no good. There's Slake Fountain. Yeah, I'll say there is, too. We keep a gang of hoodlums on their toes at twenty a week each to sober him up every morning before he comes on the set. Then there's Jerry Badger, the sort of nice egg you'd like your kid sister to marry, but nothing to him. Nothing *at* all. Well, what do I get out of it? Nothing. I gotta find somebody, that's all.'

'Have you ever seen Alexandre Fin?' asked Mr Mybug. 'I saw him in Pepin's last film, "La Plume de Ma Tante", in Paris last January. Very amusing stuff. They all wore glass clothes, you know, and moved in time to a metronome.'

'Oh, yeah?' said Mr Neck. 'A frog, eh? Frogs is all under five feet. I want a big, husky fella; the kinda fella that would look good cuddling a kid. Is there another cup, sweetheart?'

Flora poured him some.

'Yeah,' he went on. 'I seen that film in Paris, too. It gave me a pain. Gave me a lot of new dope, though. What not to do, and all that. I've met Pepin, too. The poor egg's cuckoo.'

'He is much admired by the younger men,' said Mr Mybug, daringly, glancing at Flora for approval.

'That helps a whole heap,' said Mr Neck.

'Then your interest in the cinema, Mr Neck, is *entirely* commercial? I mean, you think nothing of its aesthetic possibilities?'

'I gotta responsibility. If your frog friend had to fill fifteen thousand dollars' worth of movie seats every day, he'd have to think of a better stunt than a lot of guys wearin' glass pants.'

He paused and reflected.

'Say, though, that's an idea. A guy buys a new tuxedo, see? Then he offends some ritzy old egg, see? A magician, or something, and this old egg puts a curse on him. Well, this egg (the guy in the tuxedo) goes off to a swell party, and when he comes in all the girls scream. That kind o' stuff. Well, he can't see his pants is turned into glass by this other old egg (the magician, see?), and he says: "Whattha hell", and all the rest of it. Yeah, that's an idea.'

While he was speaking, Seth had come silently, with his graceful, pantherish tread, to the door of the room; and now stood there, looking down inquiringly at Flora. She smiled across at him, motioning him to be silent. Mr Neck's back was towards the door, so that he could not see Seth, but when he saw Flora smile he turned half round, and looked across at the doorway to see at whom her gesture was directed.

And he saw Seth.

A silence fell. The young man stood in the warm light of the declining sun, his bare throat and boldly moulded features looking as though they were bathed in gold. His pose was easy and graceful. A superb self-confidence radiated from him, as it does from any healthy animal. He met Mr Neck's stare with an impudent stare of his own, his head lowered and slightly forward. He looked exactly what he was, the local sexually successful bounder. Millions of women were to realize, in the next five years, that Seth could be transported in fancy to a Welsh mining village, a shoddy North Country seaside town, a raw city in the plains of the Middle West, and still remain eternally and unchangeably the local irresistible bounder.

Is it any wonder that Mr Neck broke the silence by flinging up his hand and saying in a hoarse whisper: 'That's it, sweetheart! That's got it! Hold it!'

And Seth was so soaked in movie slang that he held it, for another second or so in silence.

Flora broke in by saying: 'Oh, Seth, there you are. I wanted Mr Neck to see you. Earl, this is my cousin, Seth Starkadder. He's very interested in the talkies. Mr Neck is a producer, Seth.'

Mr Neck, forgetful of everything else, was craning forward with his head slightly bent downwards, to hear Seth speak. And when that deep, warm drawl came – 'Pleased to meet you, Mr Neck' – Mr Neck looked up with an expression of such relief and delight that it was just as though he had clapped his hands.

'Well, well,' said Mr Neck, surveying Seth rather as though Seth were his dinner (as indeed he was to be for some years to come). 'How's the boy? So you're a fan, eh? You and me must get acquainted, huh? Maybe you'd thought of going in for the game yourself?'

Mr Mybug tilted comfortably back in his chair, choosing a little cake to eat, and prepared to enjoy the sight of Seth being roasted. But he had (as we know) backed the wrong horse.

Seth scowled and drew back. Mr Neck almost patted his face with rapture as he observed how Seth's every mood was reflected, like a child's, in his countenance.

'No . . . No, I'm not kidding,' he observed, amiably. 'I mean it. Would you like to go on the talkies?'

A great cry broke from Seth. Mr Mybug lost his balance and fell over backwards, choking with cake. No one noticed him. All eyes were on Seth. A glory lit his face. Slowly, lingeringly, the words broke from him:

'More than anything else in the world.'

'Well, ain't that dandy?' said Mr Neck, looking round proudly for agreement and support. 'He wants to be a movie star and I want to make him one. What do you know about that? Usually, it's just the other way about. Now, sweetheart, get your grip, and we'll be off. We're catching the Atlantic flier from Brighton at eight to-night. Say, though, what about your folks, huh? What about Momma? Will she need squaring?'

'I will tell you all about that, Earl. Seth, go and pack a bag with everything you need for the journey. Put on a big coat – you are going to fly, you know, and it may be cold at first.'

Seth obeyed Flora without a word, and when he had gone she explained his circumstances to Mr Neck.

'So it's all right if Grandma don't give it the razz, huh? Well, we must go out quiet, thass all. Tell Grandma not to fuss. We'll send her five grand out of the first picture he makes. Oh, boy' – and here he smote Mr Mybug, who was still choking over his little cake – 'I got him! I got him! Whaddya say his name is – Seth? Thassa sissy sort of a name, but it'll do. It's kinda different. Keep 'em guessing. Oh, boy, wait till I get him a tuxedo! Wait till I start his publicity. We must find a new angle. Lessee ... Maybe he'd better be shy. No ... poor Charley Ford ran that to death. Maybe he hates women ... yeah, thass it. He hates women and he hates the movies. Like hell he does. Oh, boy, that'll fetch 'em! It 'ud take more than anyone's grandma to stop me now.'

CHAPTER 18

WHEN Seth returned, wearing his best hat and his overcoat and carrying a suit-case, everybody moved towards the door. Mr Neck's car was waiting for him in the yard, and he hung on to Seth's arm every step of the way there as though he feared Seth would change his mind.

He need not have. Seth's face had the usual expression it bore of repose: an insolent complacency. Of course, he was going to be a film star. When once he had got over the first shock, he wanted to look as if the whole affair seemed perfectly natural to him. He was too conceited to show the fierce joy that surged deep within him. Yet there it surged, a tide of dark gold splendour, deep below the crust of his complacent acceptance.

Well, everything was bowling along swimmingly, and Flora was just patting the still-choking Mr Mybug on the back while they all stood round the door of the car saying good-bye, when the ominous sound of a window being pushed up was heard, and before they could all look up a voice floated out into the quiet air of the late afternoon. It was observing that it had seen something nasty in the woodshed.

Everybody looked up. Flora in some dismay.

Sure enough, it was Aunt Ada Doom. The window of her room, which was directly above the kitchen door, was open, and she was leaning heavily out, supporting herself upon her hands. A shape hovered in the dusty room behind her left shoulder, endeavouring to see over her vasty bulk. By the untidiness of its hair, it was Judith. Another shape hovered behind the right shoulder. Going by nothing but a woman's intuition, it was Rennet.

'Oh, mercy!' said Flora, hastily, in an undertone to Mr Neck. 'Hurry up and go!'

'What ... is that Grandma?' inquired Mr Neck. 'And who's the platinum blonde at the back? Come on, sweetheart' – he hustled Seth into the car – 'we've got to make that flier.'

'Seth ... Seth ... where are you going?' Judith's voice was a throbbing rod of terror and anguish.

'I saw something nasty in the woodshed!' screamed Aunt Ada Doom, flapping about her with something which Flora recognized as all that was left of the *Cowkeepers' Weekly Bulletin and Milk Producers' Guide*. 'My baby ... My darling. You mustn't leave me. I shall go mad. I can't bear it!'

'Can it!' muttered Mr Neck; but aloud he called

politely, waving his hand at Aunt Ada, 'Well, well, how's
the girl?'

'Seth . . . you mustn't go!' Judith implored, her voice a
dry whine of terror. 'You can't leave your mother. There's
the spring-onion harvest, too. 'Tes man's work . . . You
mustn't go.'

'I saw something in the woodshed!'

'Did it see you?' asked Mr Neck, tucking himself into
the car beside Seth. The engine started, and the chauffeur
began to back out of the yard.

'Gee, ma'am, I know it's raw,' shouted Mr Neck, craning
out of the window of the car and peering up at Aunt Ada.
'I know it's tough. But, gee, that's life, girl. You're living
now, sweetheart. All that woodshed line . . . that was years
ago. Young Woodley stuff. Aw, I respect a grandmother's
feelings, sweetheart, but honest, I just can't give him up.
He'll send you five grand out of his first film.'

'Good-bye,' said Seth to Flora, who returned his con-
descending smile with a friendly one of her own.

She watched the car drive away. It was going to Cloud
Cuckoo Land; it was going to the Kingdom of Cockaigne;
it was going to Hollywood. Seth would never have a
chance, now, of becoming a nice, normal young man. He
would become a world-famous, swollen mask.

When next she saw him, it was a year later and the mask
smiled down at her in the drowsy darkness from a great
silver screen: 'Seth Starkadder in "Small Town Sheik".'
Already, as the car receded, he was as unreal as Achilles.

'Seth . . . Seth . . .'

The car turned the curve, and was gone.

Still the wailing voices of the women wound through the
air like strung wires. It was hours before the stars would
begin their idiot dance between the chimney-pots. There
was nothing to do in between except wail.

Aunt Ada had now retreated from the window. Flora
could hear Judith having hysterics. She went on quietly
banging Mr Mybug, who was still choking, and saying,
'There . . . there . . .' and wondering if she ought to go up-

stairs to her Aunt Ada's room and diffuse a spot of *The Higher Common Sense.*

But no. The hour for that was not yet.

She was roused from her reverie by Mr Mybug, who peevishly dodged away from her hand, exclaiming, between chokes: 'I'm quite all right now, thanks,' and went on choking in an irritating manner at some distance away.

Suddenly his chokes ceased. He was staring up at Aunt Ada's window, where Rennet had suddenly appeared and was peering palely out into the evening.

'Who's that?' asked Mr Mybug, in a low voice.

'Rennet Starkadder,' replied Flora.

'What a marvellous face,' said Mr Mybug, still staring. 'She has a brittle, hare-like quality . . . Don't you feel it?' He waved his fingers about. 'She has that untamed look you see sometimes in newly-born leverets. I wish Kopotkin could see her. He'd want to put her into plaster.'

Rennet was staring down at him, too. Flora could see it was quite a case. Oh, well, it would be quite a good thing if he carried Rennet off to Fitzroy Square and set a new fashion in hare-faced beauties . . . except that she, Flora, must make quite sure before they went that he would be kind to poor Rennet, and be a good husband to her. Probably he would be. Rennet was very domesticated. She would mend Mr Mybug's clothes (which nobody had ever done for him before, because, though all his girl friends could embroider beautifully, none of them ever dreamed of mending anything), and cook him lovely nourishing dinners, and fuss over him and simply adore him, and he would become so comfortable he would not know himself, and would be very grateful to her.

From these schemes she was aroused by Mr Mybug. He walked across the yard until he stood directly beneath the window, and called boldly up to Rennet:

'I say! Will you come for a walk with me?'

'What . . . now?' asked Rennet, timidly. Nobody had ever asked her to do such a thing before.

'Why not?' laughed Mr Mybug, looking boyishly up at

her, with his head flung back. Flora thought it *was* a pity he was rather fat.

'I must ask Cousin Judith,' said Rennet, glancing timidly over her shoulder into the darkened room. Then she withdrew into the shadows.

Mr Mybug was very pleased with himself. This was his idea of romance, Flora could see. She knew from experience that intellectuals thought the proper – nay, the only – way to fall in love with somebody was to do it the very instant you saw them. You met somebody, and thought they were 'A charming person. So gay and simple.' Then you walked home from a party with them (preferably across Hampstead Heath, about three in the morning) discussing whether you should sleep together or not. Sometimes you asked them to go to Italy with you. Sometimes they asked you to go to Italy (preferably to Portofino) with them. You held hands, and laughed, and kissed them and called them your 'true love'. You loved them for eight months, and then you met somebody else and began being gay and simple all over again, with small-hours' walk across Hampstead, Portofino invitation, and all.

It was very simple, gay, and natural, somehow.

Anyway, Flora was beginning to feel that things were happening a little too quickly at Cold Comfort Farm. She had not yet recovered from the Counting last night (was it only last night? – it seemed a month ago) and the departure of Amos; and already Seth had gone, and Mr Mybug was falling in love with Rennet, and doubtless planning to carry her off.

If things went on at this rate there would soon be nobody left at the farm at all.

She was extremely sleepy all of a sudden. She thought she would go and sit by the fire in her little green parlour and read until supper-time. So she told Mr Mybug she hoped he would have a pleasant walk, and added casually that Rennet had had a pretty septic life of it, on the whole, and hinted that she would probably appreciate a little gaiety and simplicity, in the Fitzroy Square manner.

Mr Mybug said he quite understood. He also attempted to take her hand, but she foiled him. Since seeing Rennet at the window he seemed to have a vague feeling that his one-sided affair with Flora was at an end, and that it was up to him to make some appropriate farewell remarks.

'We're friends, aren't we?' he asked.

'Certainly,' said Flora, pleasantly, nor did she trouble to inform him that she was not in the habit of thinking of persons whom she had known for five weeks as her friends.

'We might dine together in Town some time?'

'That would be delightful,' agreed Flora, thinking how nasty and boring it would be.

'There's a quality in you ...' said Mr Mybug, staring at her and waving his fingers. 'Remote, somehow, and nymph-like ... oddly unawakened. I should like to write a novel about you and call it *Virginal*.'

'Do, if it passes the time for you,' said Flora; 'and now I must really go and write some letters, I am afraid. Good-bye.'

On her way to her parlour she passed Rennet, coming downstairs, dressed to go out. She wondered how she had managed to obtain permission from Aunt Ada Doom to do so, but Rennet did not wait to be questioned. She darted past Flora with a stare of terror.

Flora was extremely glad to get back to her parlour and to sink into a comfortable little arm-chair covered in green tapestry, which stood by the fire. The refreshing Mrs Beetle was there, clearing away the tea-things.

'Miss Elfine sent you 'er best love, Miss Flora, and she's gone over to spend six weeks at Howchiker Hall. Mr Dick came for her at lunch-time to-day in 'is motor,' said Mrs Beetle. 'Nice-looking boy, ain't he?'

'Very,' said Flora. 'So she's gone, has she? Oh, well, that's splendid. Now the family will have time to settle down and get over the engagement. And where's Urk? Is it true he's drowned Meriam?'

Mrs Beetle snorted.

'It 'ud take more than 'im to drown 'er. No, 'e's as large

as life and twice as natural, down at mine, playin' with the kids.'

'What . . . the jazz-band? I mean, with Meriam's children?'

'Yes. Givin' 'em rides on 'is back and pretendin' 'e's a water-vole (nasty things). Oh, you *should* 'ave 'eard 'ow Agony created when I let on that our Meriam was goin' to marry one of them Starkadders! Create! I thought 'e'd 'ave to be picked off the ceiling.'

'So she really is going to marry him?' asked Flora, leaning languidly back in her chair and enjoying the gossip.

Mrs Beetle gave her a look.

'So I should 'ope, Miss Poste. I don't say as there's been Anything Wrong between them yet, but there ain't goin' to be, neither, until they're safely married. Agony stands firm by that.'

'And what does old Mrs Starkadder say to Urk marrying Meriam?'

'She said she saw something narsty, as usual. Well, if *I*'d 'ad sixpence for all the narsty things I've seen since I bin working at Cold Comfort I could buy the place up (not that I'd want to, come to that).'

'I suppose,' asked Flora idly, 'you haven't any idea of what she really *did* see?'

Mrs Beetle paused in the act of folding the tablecloth, and regarded Flora earnestly. But all she said, after the pause, was that she couldn't say, she was sure. So Flora pursued her inquiries no further.

'So I 'ear that there Seth's gone, too,' was Mrs Beetle's next remark. 'Coo! 'is mother won't 'alf take on!'

'Yes, he's gone to Hollywood to be a film star,' said Flora, sleepily.

Mrs Beetle said sooner 'im than 'er, and added that she wouldn't 'alf 'ave a lot to tell Agony when she got home.

'So Agony likes a spot of gossip, does he?'

'If it ain't spiteful, 'e does. 'E always creates at 'ome something awful when I've finished telling 'im anything spiteful. Oh, well, I must be off now and get Agony's supper. Good night, Miss Poste.'

Flora passed the rest of the evening quietly and pleasantly, and was in bed by ten. Her satisfaction with the way matters were progressing at the farm was completed by the arrival of a postcard for herself by the nine o'clock post.

It represented Canterbury Cathedral. The postmark was Canterbury. On the back was written:

Praise the Lord! This morning I preached the Lord's Word to thousands in the market-place. I am now going out to hire one o' they Ford vans. Tell Micah if he wants to drive it he must come with me out of charity. I mean, no wages. Praise the Lord! Send my flannel shirts. Fond love to all.

A. STARKADDER

CHAPTER 19

AFTER the departure of Seth, life at the farm settled down and became normal again (at least, as normal as it ever was), and Flora was quite glad to have a rest after the strenuous weeks during which she had drilled Elfine, and the series of shocks which had resulted in the whisking of Seth and Amos away from Cold Comfort.

The first of May brought a burst of summer weather. All the trees and hedges came into full leaf overnight; and from behind the latter, in the evenings, cries could be heard of: 'Nay, doan't 'ee, Jem', and 'Nay, niver do that, soul', from the village maidens who were being seduced.

***At the farm, life burgeoned and was quick. A thick, shameless cooing was laid down, stroke on stroke, through the warm air from the throats of the wood-pigeons until the very atmosphere seemed covered with a rich patina of love. The strident yellow note of the cockerel shot up into the sunshine and wavered there, ending in a little feather-tuft of notes. Big Business bellowed triumphantly in the great field. Daisies opened in sly lust to the sun-rays and rain-spears, and eft-flies, locked in a blind embrace, spun radiantly through the glutinous light to their ordained death. Mrs Beetle appeared in a cotton dress, well skewered up at the neck by a brooch with 'Carrie' engraved on it. Flora wore green linen and a shady hat.

The first rays of May fell into the room where Judith lay on her bed in silence; and were withered. The sordid flies, intent on their own selfish pleasure, buzzed in idiotic circles above her head with as much noise and as little meaning as life itself, and their sound drew a web of scarlet pain into her withdrawn darkness. She had veiled each of the two hundred photographs of Seth with a little black crêpe curtain. This done, what else did life hold? The flies buzzed in answer above the dirty water standing in the washbasin, in which floated a solitary black hair.

It, too, was like life – and as meaningless.

The old woman kept her room also, seated before the fire that danced palely in the thick, coarse sunlight, and muttering at intervals. Flares of hate lit her darkness. She sensed the insolence of summer heating on the window-panes and wooing away, with its promises, all the Starkadders from Cold Comfort. Where was Amos? The sunlight answered. Where was Elfine? The ring-doves crooned in reply. Where – last blow of agony – was Seth? She did not even know where he had gone or why. Mrs Beetle said he had gone on them there talkies. What was a talkie? Was Mrs Beetle mad? Were they all mad – all except you, who sat on here alone, in the old crumbling tower of your body? And Urk – a Starkadder – saying he was going to marry the paid slut, Meriam, and openly defying you when you forbade him, and jingling three and sixpence in his pocket which he had earned by selling water-vole skins to a furrier in Godmere . . .

This room was your citadel. Outside, the world you had built up so fiercely for twenty years was crumbling into fantastic ruin.

It was she, Robert Poste's child. The wrong done to him had come back to roost. 'Curses, like rookses, comes home to rest in bosomses and barnses.' She had poured poison into the ears of your family and sent them out into the world, leaving you alone. They would all go: Judith, Micah, Ezra, Harkaway, Caraway, Luke, and Mark, and Adam Lambsbreath. Then ... when they had all gone ... you would be alone – at last – alone in the woodshed.

Flora was having quite a nice time.

It was now the second week in May and the weather was still superb. Reuben was now looked upon by everybody as the owner of Cold Comfort, and had at once (much to Flora's pleasure) set about making improvements in it, and had asked her if she would go into Godmere with him and help him choose fertilizers and new grinders and what not. Flora told him she did not know anything about grinders, but that she would try anything once; so, accordingly, they drove off together one Wednesday morning in the buggy, armed with a copy of the *Internationally Progressive Farmers' Guide and Helpmeet*, which Flora had ordered from London, where it was printed by some Russian friends of hers living in West Kensington.

'Where did you get the money to buy all these lovely grinders, Reuben?' asked Flora, as they sat at lunch in the coffee-room of the Load of Beets, after a busy morning's shopping.

'Stole un,' replied Reuben simply.

'Who from?' asked Flora, who was bored by having to pretend to be shocked at things, and really wanted to know.

'Grandmother.'

'Oh, I say, what a sound scheme. But how did you get hold of it? I mean, did you have to get it out of her stocking, or something?'

'Nay. I falsified th' chicken-book, and when we sold a dozen eggs I writes down we sells two eggs, see? I been doin' that for nigh five years. I had me eye on them grinders for five years, so I plans it all out, see?'

'My dear, I think you're *masterly*,' said Flora. '*Quite*

masterly. If you only keep on as you've begun you will make the farm *too* prosperous.'

'Aye ... if th' old devil don't change his mind and come back,' said Reuben doubtfully. 'Happen he may think America's a long way off – too fur for an old 'un like him to go, eh?'

'Oh, I'm sure he won't,' said Flora decidedly. 'He seems to be – er – main set on the idea.' And she produced from her handbag, for the tenth time that morning, a postcard showing Liverpool Cathedral. It said:

Praise the Lord! I go to spread the Lord's Word among the heathen Americans, with the Rev. Elderberry Shiftglass, of Chicago. Praise the Lord! Tell Reuben he can have the old place. Send clean socks. Love to all except Micah.

A. STARKADDER

'Oh, yes, I am sure he means it,' repeated Flora. 'It's a pity he says "the old place" instead of "the farm", but if any question ever arises, we can always do a spot of forgery, and write "the farm" instead. I wouldn't worry, if I were you.'

So they finished their apple tart in leisurely comfort. Just as he was lifting the last spoonful to his lips, Reuben halted with it in the air and said, looking across at Flora:

'I don't suppose 'ee would marry me, Cousin Flora?'

Flora was much moved. She had grown to like Reuben in the last fortnight. He was worth whole sackfuls of the other male Starkadders. He was really very nice, and kind too, and ready to learn from anyone who would help him to improve the condition of the farm. He had never forgotten that it was she who suggested to Amos that he should go off on the preaching tour; a move which had resulted – after Reuben himself had worked on his father's feelings to take Flora's advice – in Reuben getting possession of the farm; and he was deeply grateful.

She put out her hand across the table. Wonderingly, Reuben took it in his and stared down at it, while the spoonful of apple tart wavered to and fro in his other hand.

'Oh, Reuben, that *is* nice of you. But I am afraid it would never do, you know. Think a moment. I am not at all the kind of person to make a good wife for a farmer.'

'I like yer pretty ways,' said Reuben gruffly.

'That's charming of you. I like yours, too. But, honestly, it wouldn't do. I think somebody like Mark Dolour's Nancy would be much nicer for you – and more useful, too.'

'She'm not fifteen yet.'

'All the better. In three years the farm will be doing really well, and you will have a really nice home to offer her.' Flora's heart faltered as she thought of what Aunt Ada Doom might have to say to such a marriage, but she was beginning to feel a way towards a plan for coping with that old incubus. In three years – who knows? – Aunt Ada might have left the farm!

Reuben reflected, still staring down at Flora's hand.

'Aye,' he said, slowly, at last, 'maybe I'd best have Mark Dolour's Nancy. My chickens have been keeping her dolls in feathers for their 'ats these two years. Reckon it's only right she should have th' chickens too in the end.'

And he released Flora's hand, and finished his spoonful of apple tart. He did not seem at all offended or hurt, and they drove home together afterwards in comfortable silence.

Elfine's visit to the Hawk-Monitors had been extended for a further week, and Flora had twice been over there to tea. Mrs Hawk-Monitor seemed quite won over to Elfine, much to Flora's relief, and described her to Flora as 'a dear little thing. Rather brainy, but quite a nice little thing.' Flora congratulated Elfine in private, and warned her not to talk quite so much about Marie Laurencin and Purcell. The end was achieved; there was no point in overdoing it.

The wedding was fixed for the fourteenth of June. Mrs Hawk-Monitor had decided that it should take place in the church at Howling, which was a beauty. She then stunned Flora by suggesting that the reception should be held at Cold Comfort: 'So much more convenient than coming all the way back here, don't you think?'

'Oh, I say,' said Flora, pulling herself together in response to an agonized glance from Elfine. 'I rather doubt if that would do, you know. I mean, old Mrs Starkadder is a bit of an invalid and what not. The – er – the noise might upset her.'

'She need not come down. A tray of cake can be taken up to her in her room. Yes, I think that would certainly be the best thing to do. Is there a *large* room at the farmhouse, Miss Poste?'

'Several,' said Flora, faintly, thinking about them.

'Splendid. Just the thing. I will write to old Mrs Starkadder to-night.' And Mrs Hawk-Monitor (who was rather wanting to shift some of the botheration of the wedding on to Elfine's family) vaguely but effectively changed the subject.

So there was a new horror on the horizon! Really (thought Flora, riding home in state in the giant Hawk-Monitor Renault) there was no end to her worries. She was beginning to think she would never get the farm tidied up in her life-time. No sooner did she get one person comfortably fixed up than somebody else began to tear up the turf about something, and she had to begin all over again.

It was true, though, that matters were better since Reuben had taken up the position of owner of the farm. Wages were paid regularly. Rooms were swept out occasionally; nay, they were even scrubbed. And though the bi-weekly inspection of the books by Aunt Ada Doom still went on, Reuben had started another set of books of his own, in which he put down the farm's real takings. The books which Aunt Ada saw twice a week were cooked liked Old Harry.

Aunt Ada had not been downstairs since the night of the Counting; and Micah, Ezra, and the other Starkadders had taken advantage of her temporary set-back. They had also been encouraged by the getaway of Seth, Elfine, and Amos. They realized that Aunt Ada, like the rest of us, was only human.

So they commanded Prue, Letty, Jane, Phoebe, and Susan, to say nothing of Rennet, to come up to Cold Comfort from the village and establish themselves and their possessions in some of the empty rooms of the farm-house as far away as possible from Aunt Ada's chamber.

And there they were, all living like fighting cocks; and wherever Flora went she seemed to stumble over hen-faced female Starkadders in cotton dresses. As for Mrs Beetle, she said all them old witches fair gave her the sick, and she was quite glad to get 'ome to Urk and Meriam and the water-voles.

So, on the whole, life at the farm-house was much pleas-anter for the Starkadders than it had ever been before; and they had Flora to thank for it.

But Flora was not satisfied.

She was thinking, as she was borne homewards in the Hawk-Monitor chariot, how much yet remained to be done at Cold Comfort before she could really say that the farm-house was in a condition to satisfy the Abbé Fausse-Maigre.

There was the problem of Judith. There was old Adam. And there was Aunt Ada Doom herself, the greatest prob-lem of all, and the hardest.

She decided that she must tackle Judith next. Judith had been lying in her room with the window shut quite long enough. Twice had Mrs Beetle asked if she could turn out the room; and twice Flora had been forced to reply that it was not yet convenient. But now (Flora decided) things had gone far enough; and she would beard Judith as soon as she got home.

The evening sunlight lay across the corridor in sharp tiger-bars as she approached Judith's room. The door was shut. It was like a forbidding hand, pressed soft and flat against the silence of the corridor. Flora tapped against it, and waited a few seconds for an answer. But there was only the indifferent silence. Oh, well ... she thought, and, turn-ing the handle, walked in.

Judith was standing at the washstand, rinsing one of the two hundred little crêpe curtains which hung over the two hundred photographs of Seth.

***Her blank eyes burrowed through the fetid air be-tween herself and her visitor. They were without content; hollow pools of meaninglessness. They were not eyes, but voids sunk between two jutting pent-houses of bone and two bloodless hummocks of cheek. They suspended two raw rods of grief before their own immobility, like frozen fountains in a bright wintry air; and on these rods the fluttering rags of a futile grief were hung.

'Oh, Cousin Judith, would you care to come up to Town with me to-morrow?' asked Flora pleasantly. 'I want to do some shopping, and I hope to lunch with a very charming Austrian – a Doctor Müdel from Vienna. Do come.'

Judith's laugh shocked even the careless flies that circled above her head into a momentary silence.

'I am a dead woman,' she said simply. Her hands lay piteously at her sides. 'Look . . . the little curtain was dusty,' she murmured. 'I had to rinse the dust off it.'

Flora refrained from pointing out that if you rinsed something that was dusty you merely made it worse. She said patiently that she proposed to catch the ten-thirty to Town, and that she would expect Judith to be ready by nine o'clock.

'I think you will enjoy it, Cousin Judith, when you get there,' she urged her. 'You mustn't carry on like this, you know. It – er – it depresses us all no end. I mean, all this lovely weather and what not. It's a pity to waste it.'

'I myself am a waste,' said Judith stonily. 'I am a used husk . . . a rind . . . a skin. What use am I . . . now he's gone?'

'Well, never mind that now,' said Flora soothingly. 'Just you make up your mind to be ready by nine o'clock to-morrow morning.'

And before she left her that evening, she managed to gain from Judith a vague half-promise that she would be ready as suggested. Judith did not seem to care what happened to her so long as she was not made to talk; and Flora took advantage of her lassitude to impose her fresh will upon her cousin's flaccid one.

After leaving Judith, she sent Adam down into Howling with the following wire:

Herr Doktor Adolf Müdel,
    National Institute Psycho-Analysis,
        Whitehall, S.W.
Interesting case for you can you lunch two of us Grimaldi's one fifteen to-morrow Wednesday hows the baby love F. Poste.

And at nine o'clock that night, while she was sitting at the open window of her little parlour inhaling the fragrance of a may tree and writing to Charles, a telegram was delivered to her (by Mark Dolour's very Nancy herself) which read:

But of course delighted baby has marked paranoiac tendencies nurse assures me quite normal at eight months she knows much more than I do perfect treasure looking forward seeing you what weather eh ... Adolf.

CHAPTER 20

HER day with Judith in London was a complete success, though there were, it is true, some minor disadvantages. Judith's hair, for example, fell down every fifteen minutes and had to be re-pinned by Flora. Then there were the sympathetic and interested inquiries of fellow-travellers to be fobbed off, who were naturally intrigued by hearing Judith refer to herself at intervals as a Used Gourd and a Rind.

But when once their journey was over, Flora's worries were over as well. Seated opposite Dr Müdel and Judith at a quiet table near a window at Grimaldi's, she watched, with a feeling of relief, Dr Müdel taking command of the situation.

It was one of his disagreeable duties as a State psycho-analyst to remove the affections of his patients from the embarrassing objects upon which they were concentrated, and focus them, instead, upon himself. It was true that they did not remain focused there for long: as soon as he could, he switched them on to something harmless, like chess or gardening. But while they *were* focused upon himself, he had rather a thin time of it and earned every penny of the eight hundred a year paid to him by a judicious Government.

And Flora, observing how soon Judith began to glow darkly and do the slumbering volcano act in Dr Müdel's direction, could not help admiring the practised skill with which he had effected the transference in the course of the commonplace conversation throughout lunch.

'She will be oll right now,' he murmured soothingly to Flora, in an undertone, when lunch was over, while Judith was gazing broodingly out of the window at the busy street below. 'I shall take her to the nursing home, and let her talk to me. There she will stay for six months, perhaps. Then I send her abroad for a little holiday. I make her interested in olt churches, I think. Yes, olt churches. There are so many in Europe, and it will take her the rest of her life to see them all. She has money, yes? You must have money in order to see all the olt churches you want. Well, that is oll right, then. Do not distress yourself. She will be quite happy. Oll that energy ... it is a pity, yes. It oll turns *in* instead of *out*. Now I turn it out ... on to the olt churches. Yes.'

Flora felt a little uneasy. It was not the first time she had seen a distraught patient grow calm beneath the will of the analyst, yet she had never grown used to the spectacle. Would Judith *really* be happier? She looked doubtfully at her cousin. Certainly Judith *looked* happier already. Her eyes followed every movement of Dr Müdel as he paid the bill for the lunch; Flora had never seen her look so animated and normal.

'I understand that you are going to stay with Dr Müdel for a while, Cousin Judith?' she said.

'He has asked me. He is very kind ... There is a dark force in him,' returned Judith. 'It beats ... like a black gong. I wonder you do not feel it.'

'Oh, well, we can't all strike lucky,' said Flora amiably. 'But really, Judith, I do think it would be quite a sound scheme if you went. You need a holiday, you know, after all the – er – fuss there's been at home lately. It will do you no end of good. Set you up and what not. And then after a

202

bit you might go abroad and see some of the sights of Europe. Old churches, and all that. Don't worry about the farm. Reuben will look after that for you, and send you a fat piece out of the takings every month.'

'Amos . . .' murmured Judith. She looked as though the threads which bound her to her old life were snapping one by one, yet still held her in a frail tenure.

'Oh, I wouldn't fuss about him,' said Flora easily. 'He's gone off to America with the Reverend Elderberry Shift-glass by now, I shouldn't wonder. He'll let you know when he's coming back. Don't you bother. You enjoy yourself while you're young.'

And this was what Judith evidently decided to do, for she drove off with Dr Müdel in his car looking quite content: at least she looked illumined and transfigured and reft out of herself and all the rest of it, and even when allowances were made for her habit of multiplying every emotion she felt by twice its own weight, she probably *was* feeling fairly chirpy.

Before they said good-bye Flora arranged to send on to the nursing home the five dirty red shawls and sundry bundles of hairpins which seemed to make up the greater part of Judith's wardrobe; and also a comfortable sum of money which should pay for her pleasures during the next six months. Dr Müdel could, of course, be trusted to see that her funds were properly administered.

So that was all settled; and Flora watched the doctor's car drive away with feelings of considerable satisfaction.

It was with a feeling of satisfaction, too, and with something strangely like affection, that she caught her first glimpse of the farm-house on her return that night to Cold Comfort.

It was a mild and lovely evening. The rays of the sun looked heavy, as they frequently do towards the approach of a summer sunset, and lay between the tunnels of green leaves like long rods of gold. There were no clouds in the blue sky, whose colour was beginning to deepen with the advance of night, and the face of the whole country-side was softened by the shadows which were slowly growing in the depths of the woods and hedgerows.

The farm-house itself no longer looked like a beast about to spring. (Not that it ever had, to her, for she was not in the habit of thinking that things looked exactly like other things which were as different from them in appearance as it was possible to be.) But it had looked dirty and miserable and depressing, and when Mr Mybug had once remarked that it looked like a beast about to spring, Flora had simply not had the heart to contradict him.

Now it looked dirty and miserable and depressing no longer. Its windows flung back the gold of the sunset. The yard was swept clean of straws and paper. Check curtains hung crisply at most of the windows, and someone (as a matter of fact it was Ezra, who had a secret yen for horticulture) had been digging and trimming up the garden, and there were already rows of beans in red flower.

'I,' thought Flora simply, as she leant forward in the buggy and surveyed the scene, 'did all that with my little hatchet.' And a feeling of joy and content opened inside her like a flower.

But then she looked upwards at the closed, bland face of the window immediately above the kitchen door, and her face grew pensive again. Aunt Ada's room. Aunt Ada was still there, fighting her losing battle. Aunt Ada, the spirit of Cold Comfort, was hard pressed, but still undefeated. And could she, Flora, really congratulate herself upon her work at the farm, and flatter herself that the end of that work was in sight, while Aunt Ada Doom still brooded aloft in her tower?

'Yer supper's on the table, duck,' said Mrs Beetle, opening the gate to let Reuben lead Viper into the yard. 'Cold veal and salad. I'm off 'ome now. Oh, and there's a blamonge. Pink.'

'Lovely,' said Flora, with a sigh of pleasure, as she climbed down from the buggy. 'Thank you, Mrs Beetle. Miss Judith won't be back to-night. She is going to stay in London for a while. Has everything been all right?'

'*She* took on something awful about Miss Judith going off 'smorning,' said Mrs Beetle, lowering her voice and glancing significantly upwards at the closed window. 'Said she *was* all alone in the woodshed now, and no mistake. She says she don't count Reuben. (She wouldn't, of course – 'im bein' the pick of the bunch.) Still, she keeps 'er appetite, I will say that for 'er. Three 'elpings of veal and two of suet roly for 'er dinner to-day. Can you beat it? Well, this won't buy the baby a new frock. Good night, Miss Flora. I'll be 'ere eight sharp to-morrow.'

And off she went.

Flora went into the kitchen, where a lamp already burned on the table. Its soft light fell into the hearts of a bunch of pink roses in a jam-jar. There was a letter from Charles propped against the jar, too, and the roses threw down a heavy, rounded shadow on to the envelope. It was so pretty that Flora lingered a moment, looking, before she opened her letter.

The serene weather held; and Flora and everybody were hoping that it would last until Elfine's wedding reception at the farm on the fourteenth of June, which was Midsummer Day.

The preparations for this reception were now Flora's chief care. She was anxious that the farm should not disgrace Reuben and his sister; so she went frankly to the former and told him that she must have money to buy decorations and a feast for the wedding guests. Reuben seemed pleased at the idea of holding the reception at the farm, and gave her thirty pounds with which to do her damnedest, but, he added, glancing meaningly up at the ceiling:

'What about the old 'un?'

'Leave her to me,' said Flora decidedly. 'I am thinking out a plan for coping with her, and in a few days I am going to try it out. I will see about decorations and food at once. Oh, and *need* we have all the pictures wreathed with that smelly sukebind? I am afraid it might have a bad effect on Meriam and Rennet. They're so easily upset.'

''Tes no choice o' mine. 'Tes grandmother's choice. Do as you please, Cousin Flora. I niver wants to see a sprig of it again.'

So, armed with his permission, Flora began her preparations.

The days passed pleasantly. She had plenty to do, and even paid three visits to Town, for she was having a new dress made for the reception and it had to be fitted. Mrs Smiling was still abroad; she was not expected home until the day after the wedding, so 1 Mouse Place was shut up. Julia was in Cannes; Claud Hart-Harris at home in Chiswick, whither he repaired every summer, for a month, because he said he could at least be sure of meeting no one he knew there. But Flora could amuse herself; and dined and lunched in pleasant solitude.

In the intervals of fitting her dress and of superintending a simply colossal spring cleaning of the farm (the first it had received for a hundred years) Flora kept a weather eye upon the affair of Mr Mybug and Rennet. She thought it would be best, of course, if they got married; but she was well aware that marriage was not the intellectual's long suit, and she did not want Rennet landed with a shameful bundle.

Mr Mybug, however, did ask Rennet to marry him. He said that, by God, D. H. Lawrence was right when he had said there must be a dumb, dark, dull, bitter belly-tension between a man and a woman, and how else could this be achieved save in the long monotony of marriage? As for Rennet, she accepted him at once and was perfectly happy choosing saucepans. So that was all right; and they were to be married at a register office one week-end in Town and have a share in Elfine's reception on the fourteenth.

As the evenings grew longer towards Midsummer Day, Flora would sit alone in the little green parlour, where the scent of the may tree came in through the open window, reading in *The Higher Common Sense* the chapter on 'Preparing the Mind for the Twin Invasion by Prudence and Daring in Dealing with Substances not Included in the Outline'.

It would help her, she knew, to deal with Aunt Ada Doom. Those long words in German and in Latin were solemn and cragged as Egyptian monoliths; and when the reader peered more closely into the meaning of their syllables that rang like bells, backwards and backwards into Time, they were seen to be frosted with wisdom, cold and irrefutable. Before them, Passion, awed, slunk back to its lair; and divine Reason, and her sister, Love, locked in one another's arms, raised their twin heads to receive the wreath of Happiness.

Aunt Ada was most emphatically one of the Substances not Included in the Outline. As Flora read on, evening after evening, she was aware that a conviction was growing in her mind that this was one of the cases (the chapter warned the student that such might exist) in which she must meekly await the help of a flash of intuition. The chapter would help her to prepare her mind for the invasion, but it could do no more. She must await the moment.

And on an evening of more than common peace and beauty the moment came. She had put aside *The Higher Common Sense* for half an hour while she partook of her supper, and had opened *Mansfield Park* at random to refresh her spirits.

'It was over, however, at last; and the evening set in with more composure to Fanny . . .'

And suddenly – the flash! It was over indeed: her long indecision and her bewilderment about how to deal with Aunt Ada Doom. In a few seconds she had her plan clearly in her head, with every detail as distinct as though the scheme had already been carried through. Calmly she detached a leaf from her pocket-book and wrote the following telegram:

Hart-Harris,
    Chauncey Grove,
        Chiswick Mall.
Please send at once latest number vogue also prospectus hotel miramar paris and very important photographs fanny ward love Flora.

Then she summoned Mark Dolour's Nancy, who had come in to help with the spring cleaning, and sent her down to the post office in Howling with the telegram.

As Nancy ran off through the clear summer twilight, Flora reverently shut the covers of *The Higher Common Sense*. She needed it no longer. It could remain closed until the next time she encountered a Substance not Included in the Outline. And she retired to bed that night in the calm confidence that she had found the way to deal with Aunt Ada Doom.

There was now only a week to go before the wedding, so Flora hoped very much that Claud would send at once the papers for which she had asked. It would probably take time to deal with Aunt Ada, and no time must be wasted if her aim was to be achieved by the day of the wedding.

But Claud did not fail her. The papers arrived by air-mail at noon next day. They were dropped neatly into the great field by the air-postman, and were accompanied by a plaintive note from Claud asking her what in heck she was up to now? He said that except for the fact that she was larger, she reminded him of a mosquito.

Flora undid the parcel and made quite sure that all the things for which she had asked were there. She then re-coiled her hair and put on a fresh linen dress and (as it was luncheon time) directed Mrs Beetle to give to her the tray upon which was arranged Aunt Ada's lunch.

'Go on. You'll strain yourself,' said Mrs Beetle. 'It weighs about 'alf er 'undredweight.'

But Flora quietly took the tray and (under the awed eyes of Mark Dolour's Nancy, Reuben, Mrs Beetle and Sue, Phoebe, Jane and Letty) she arranged upon it the copy of *Vogue*, the prospectus of the Hotel Miramar in Paris, and the photographs of Fanny Ward.

'I am going to take her lunch up to Aunt Ada,' she announced. 'If I have not come down by three o'clock, Mrs Beetle, will you kindly bring up some lemonade. At half past four you may bring up tea and some of the currant cake Phoebe made last week. If I am not down by seven o'clock, please bring up a tray with supper for two, and we will have hot milk and biscuits at ten. Now, good-bye, all of you. I beg of you not to worry. All will be well.'

And slowly, before the fascinated gaze of the Starkadders and Mrs Beetle, Flora began to mount the stairs which led to Aunt Ada's chamber, bearing the tray of lunch steadily before her. They heard the light sound of her footsteps receding along the corridor; they paused, and the listeners heard, in the airy summer stillness of the house, her tap on the door and her clear voice saying: 'I have brought your lunch, Aunt Ada. May I come in? It is Flora.'

There was a silence. Then the door was heard to open, and Flora and the tray of lunch passed therein.

That was the last that anyone heard or saw of her for nearly nine hours.

At three o'clock, at half past four, and at seven o'clock Mrs Beetle took up the refreshments as she had been instructed. Each time she returned she found the empty plates and cups packed neatly outside the closed door. From within there came the steady rise and fall of voices; but though she listened for many minutes she could not distinguish a word; and this disappointing piece of information was all she had to carry back to the eagerly waiting group downstairs.

At seven o'clock Mr Mybug and Rennet joined the band of watchers, and after waiting until nearly eight o'clock for Flora to come downstairs, they decided that it would be best to begin without her, and made their supper of beef, beer, and pickled onions, pleasantly spiced by anxiety and speculation.

After supper they settled down once more to watch and wait. Mrs Beetle wondered a dozen times if she should not just run up with a few sandwiches and some cocoa at nine, in order to see whether there were any developments to be observed. But Reuben said no, she was not to; she had been told to take up hot milk at ten o'clock, and hot milk at ten she should take; he would not have Flora's instructions disobeyed by the tiniest detail. So she stayed where she was.

They all got very cosy, sitting round the open door in the lingering twilight; and presently Mrs Beetle made them all some barley water, flavoured with lemon, and they sat sipping it comfortably, for their throats were quite sore with talking and wondering what on earth Flora could be saying to Aunt Ada Doom, and recalling details of the farm's history for the past twenty years, and reminding each other what a nuisance old Fig Starkadder had always been, and wondering how Seth was getting on in Hollywood and whether he would run into Amos there, and saying how lovely Elfine's wedding was going to be, and wondering how Urk and Meriam would get on when they were married, and speculating as to what on earth Judith was doing in London, and, if so, why, and who with? It grew slowly dark and cooler outside, and the summer stars came out.

They were talking away so hard that they never heard the clock strike ten, and it was not until nearly a quarter past that Mrs Beetle suddenly made them all jump by leaping from her chair and saying loudly: 'There now! I fergot the milk! I'll forget me own name next. I'll take it up at once.'

And she was just going over to the range to put wood on to the ashes, when a sound outside made them all start, and turn their heads in the direction of the dark doorway of the kitchen.

Someone was coming slowly downstairs, with light steps that dragged a little.

Reuben stood up and lit a match, which he held above his head. The light grew, and into it, through the dark doorway, walked Flora ... at last.

She looked composed enough, but rather pale and sleepy, and a curl of her dark gold hair hung loose against her cheek.

'Hullo,' she said, pleasantly, 'you're all here, then? (Hullo, Mr Mybug, surely it's time you were in bed?) Can I have that milk now, please, Mrs Beetle? I'll drink it down here. You need not take any up to Aunt Ada. I've put her to bed. She's asleep.'

There was a gasp of wonder from everybody.

Flora sank into Reuben's empty chair, with a long yawn.

'We was feared for 'ee, soul,' said Letty, reprovingly, after a pause in which lamps were lit and the curtains drawn. Nobody liked to ask any questions, though they were all pop-eyed with curiosity. 'Duna-many times we near came up to fetch 'ee down again.'

'Too nice of you,' said Flora, languidly, with one eye on the preparation of the milk. 'But it was quite all right, really. Everything's settled now. You need not worry, Reuben; there will be no fuss at the wedding or anything. We can go right ahead with the food and the decorations. In fact, everything ought to be rather good, in one way and another.'

'Cousin Flora, no one but 'ee could have done it,' said Reuben simply. 'I – I suppose 'ee wouldn't tell us how 'twas done?'

'Well,' said Flora, diving into the milk, 'it's a long story, you know. We talked for hours. I can't possibly tell you all we said. It would take all night.' Here she repressed a vast yawn. 'You'll see, when the time comes. On the wedding day, I mean. You wait. It will be a surprise. A lovely surprise. I can't tell you now. It would spoil things. You just wait and see. It will be simply lovely. Surprise!'

Her voice had been growing sleepier and sleepier towards the end of her speech, and just as it finally dwindled into silence, Mrs Beetle darted forward and was just too late to catch the glass of milk as it fell from her hand. She was asleep.

'Like a tired child,' said Mr Mybug, who, like most of your brutal intellectuals, was as soft as a cheese underneath. 'Just like a little tired child,' and he was just reaching out in a dreamy, absent kind of way to stroke Flora's hair when Mrs Beetle gave a sharp dab at his hand, exclaiming:

'Paws off, Pompey!' which so much upset him that he marched off home, pursued by the wailing Rennet, without pausing to make any farewells.

Mrs Beetle then shoved Susan, Letty, Phoebe, Prue, and

Jane off to their own chambers, and with the assistance of Reuben roused Flora from her slumber.

She stood up, still very sleepily, and smiled at Reuben as she took her candle from his hand.

'Good night, Cousin Flora. 'Twere a good day for Cold Comfort when first 'ee came here,' he said, looking down at her.

'My dear soul, don't name it. It's been the most enormous diversion to me,' said Flora. 'Just you wait until the wedding day, though. That *is* going to be fun, if you like. Mrs Beetle, you know how I dislike making complaints, but the cutlets Mrs Starkadder and I had for supper were slightly underdone. We both noticed it. Mrs Starkadder's, indeed, was almost *raw*.'

'I'm sorry, I'm sure, Miss Poste,' said Mrs Beetle.

And then everybody went sleepily up to bed.

CHAPTER 21

MIDSUMMER DAY dawned with a thick grey haze in the air and a heavy dew on the meadows and trees.

Down among the little gardens of the still-sleeping cottages of Howling an idyllic procession might have been observed making its way from flower-bed to flower-bed, like ravaging bees. It was none other than the three members of Mrs Beetle's embryo jazz-band, shepherded by the patriarchal form of Agony Beetle himself.

They had been commissioned to pick the bunches of flowers which were to decorate the church and the refreshment-tables up at the farm. A lorry load of pink and white rose-peonies, from Covent Garden, had already been discharged at the gates of the farm; and even now, Mrs Beetle and Flora were crossing and re-crossing the yard with their arms full of sleeping flowers.

Flora noted the heat-haze with joy. It would be a day of heat; brilliant, blue, and radiant.

Adam Lambsbreath had been even earlier astir, making wreaths of wallflowers with which to garland the horns of Feckless, Pointless, Graceless, and Aimless. It was not until he actually came to affix the decorations that he observed that none of the cows had any horns left, and had been forced to fasten the wreaths round their necks and tails instead. This done, he led them forth to their morning pasture, singing a smutty wedding song he had learnt for the marriage of George IV.

As the day emerged from the heat-haze, and the sky grew blue and sunny, the farm buzzed with energy like a hive. Phoebe, Letty, Jane, and Susan were whisking syllabubs in the dairy; Micah carried the pails of ice, in which stood the champagne, down into the darkest and coolest corner of the cellar. Caraway and Harkaway were fixing the awning across from the gate of the yard to the door of the kitchen. Ezra was putting his rows of beans under a net to protect them from damage during the festivities. Mark and Luke were arranging the long trestle tables in the kitchen, while Mrs Beetle and Flora unpacked the silver and linen sent down in crates from a London store. Reuben was filling with water the dozens of jars and vases in which the flowers were to be arranged. Mark Dolour's Nancy was superintending the boiling of two dozen eggs for everybody's breakfast. And upstairs on her bed lay Flora's new dress, a wonder of frilled and quilted, ruffled and tucked, pinked and shirred green batiste, and her plain hat of white straw.

At half past eight everybody sat down to breakfast in the dairy, for the kitchen was being prepared for the reception, and could not be used for meals to-day.

'I'll just take up '*er* breakfast,' said Mrs Beetle. 'She'll 'ave to 'ave it cold to-day. There's 'alf an 'am and a jar of pickled onions. I won't be a jiff.'

'Oh, I've just been in to see Aunt Ada,' said Flora, looking up from her breakfast. 'She doesn't want anything for breakfast except a Hell's Angel. Here, give me an egg. I'll mix it for her.' She rose and went over to the newly stocked store cupboard.

Mrs Beetle stared, while Flora tossed an egg, two ounces of brandy, a teaspoonful of cream and some chips of ice in a jam-jar, and everybody else was very interested, too

'There,' said Flora, giving Mrs Beetle the foaming jam-jar. 'You run along upstairs with that.'

So Mrs Beetle ran; but was heard to observe that it would take more than a mess like that to keep *her* stomach from rumbling before one o'clock. As for the other Starkadders, they were considerably intrigued by this dramatic change in Aunt Ada's diet.

'Is the old un gone off again?' asked Reuben anxiously. 'Will she come down and upset everything after all, do 'ee think, Cousin Flora?'

'Not on your sweet life,' said Flora. 'Everything will be all right. Remember, I told you there was going to be a surprise. Well, it's just beginning.'

And the Starkadders were satisfied.

Breakfast over, they all fell to work like demons, for the ceremony was at half past twelve and there was much to be done.

Agony Beetle and the jazz-band arrived with their arms full of nasturtiums, sweet-william, and cherry-pie; and were sent off on a second journey for more.

Reuben, obeying a request from Flora, pulled out from the cupboard in which it was usually kept the large carved chair in which Aunt Ada had sat on the night of the Counting; and Mark and Luke (who were so stupid that they could have been relied upon to lay a mine under the house without commenting upon it) were told to decorate it with wreaths of rose-peonies.

It was half past ten. The awning was up, looking immediately festive, as awnings always do. And in the kitchen the two long trestle tables were decorated and ready.

Flora had arranged two kinds of food for the two kinds of guests she was expecting. For the Starkadders and such of the local thorny peasantry as would attend there were syllabubs, ice-pudding, caviare sandwiches, crab patties, trifle, and champagne. For the County there was cider, cold home-cured ham, home-made bread, and salads made from local fruit. The table from which the County were to feed was rich with cottage flowers. The rosy efflorescence of the peonies floated above the table from which the peasantry would eat.

Wreaths of little flowers, like chains of little gems, hung from the rafters. Their reds, oranges, blues, and pinks glowed against the soft, sooty-black of the ceiling and walls. The air smelled sweet of cherry-pie and fruit salad. Outside the sun flamed in glory; and inside the kitchen there were these sweet smells and cool, delicious-looking food.

Flora took a last look round, and was utterly satisfied.

It was eleven o'clock.

She went upstairs to Aunt Ada's room, knocked at the door, and in response to a crisp: 'Come in, my dear,' entered and shut the door carefully behind her.

Phoebe, who was on her way to her room to put on her wedding array, nudged Susan.

'Did 'ee see that, soul? Ah! there's somethin' strange in the air to-day, love 'ee. And to think on it . . . our Rennet is no more a maid! Last night, as ever was, un came to say good-bye to me before un took the twelve-thirty train from Godmere with un's husband-to-be.'

'Was un weepin', poor soul?' inquired Susan.

'Nay; but un said un would feel safer when once the words was said, and un's man could not get away. Well . . . 'tes done now, Lord love 'ee. And they will be here for th' breakfast, man and wife, as ever was.'

A hush now fell upon the cool, flower-garlanded, sweet-smelling farm. The sun climbed royally towards his zenith, and the shadows grew shorter. In a dozen bedrooms the Starkadders struggled with their wedding garments. Flora came out of Aunt Ada's room exactly at half past eleven, and went along to her own room.

She was soon dressed. A bathe in cold water, ten minutes brushing of her hair and some business with her make-up boxes, and she emerged, serene, gay, and elegant, and ready for the pleasures of the day.

She went straight down into the kitchen, to reassure herself that everything was still as it should be; and arrived just in time to prevent Mr Mybug, who had arrived unexpectedly early, from picking a cherry off one of the cakes. Rennet was imploring him not to, and he was laughing like a boyish faun (or so *he* thought) and just about to pick at it when Flora sailed in.

'Mr *My*bug!' exclaimed Flora.

He jumped as though he had been stung and gave a boyish laugh.

'Ah, dear lady ... there you are!'

'Yes. And so are you, I see,' said Flora. 'There is plenty for *everybody*, Mr Mybug. If you are hungry, Mrs Beetle will cut you some bread and butter. How are *you*, Mrs Mybug?' and Flora pressed Rennet's hand graciously, and congratulated her upon her striking toilette, which had been borrowed from one of Mr Mybug's girl friends who drank rather a lot in one way and another and kept a tame boxer in her studio for the sheer love of the thing.

The other Starkadders now began to come downstairs; and as the sound of the church clock coming across the sunny fields now warned them it was twelve, they thought it time to go down to the church.

After a last glance round the flowery kitchen, Flora floated out with one hand on Reuben's arm, and the others followed.

They found quite a big crowd already assembled outside the church, for the wedding had aroused much interest in neighbouring villages, as well as in Howling itself. The little church was crammed, and the only empty seats were those for the County and those in which the party from the farm now took their places.

On rising from her knees, Flora had leisure to study the decorations. They were really charming. Agony Beetle had done them, with the help of Mark Dolour. They had agreed with pleasing unanimity that only white flowers were suitable to Elfine's extreme youth and undoubted purity. So the pews were hung with chains of marguerites, and two tall lilies stood like archangelic trumpets at the end of each pew, lining the aisle. There were many jars filled with white pinks, and the altar steps where the bride would kneel were banked with snowy geraniums.

Flora repressed the unworthy reflection that it reminded her of a White Sale at Messrs Marshall & Snelgrove's, and turned her attention to Letty, Jane, Phoebe, Prue, and Susan, who had all begun to cry. Silently she fitted them all out with clean handkerchiefs from a store previously laid in for this very purpose.

Reuben, very nervous, stood at the door, waiting for Elfine. The sun blazed down outside, the organ wandered softly through a voluntary, and the crowd respectfully buzzed at the County as it came in, bursting with curiosity and wearing its direst hats. The hands on the clock tower jumped on, minute by minute, to the half-hour.

Flora took one cautious glance round the church before she settled down to wait in decorous quietude for the last few minutes.

The church seemed full of Starkadders. They were all there; and all there by her agency, except the four whom she had helped to escape.

There they all were. Enjoying themselves. Having a nice time. And having it in an ordinary human manner. Not having it because they were raping somebody, or beating somebody, or having religious mania or being doomed to silence by a gloomy, earthly pride, or loving the soil with the fierce desire of a lecher, or anything of that sort. No, they were just enjoying an ordinary human event, like any of the millions of ordinary people in the world.

Really, when she thought what they had all been like, only five months ago . . .

She bowed her head. She had accomplished a great work; and had much to be thankful for. And to-day would see her achievements crowned!

At last! The organ struck bravely into 'Here Comes the Bride!' and every head turned towards the door, and every eye fixed itself upon the large car which had just drawn up outside the church. A low murmur of interest went up.

And now the crowd was cheering. Something tall, white, and cool as a cloud detached itself from the car, and floated quickly along the path to the church door.

Here comes the bride! Here is Elfine, pale and serious and starry-eyed, as a bride should be, leaning upon the arm of Reuben. Here is Dick Hawk-Monitor, his pleasant red face betraying none of the nervousness he must feel. Here is Mrs Hawk-Monitor, looking vague in grey; and the healthy Joan Hawk-Monitor in pink organdie (a deplorable choice – quite deplorable, thought Flora, regretfully).

The procession reached the altar steps, and halted.

The music ceased. Into the hush that fell, the vicar's voice broke quickly yet gravely: 'Dearly beloved . . .'

It was not until she was standing in the vestry, smilingly watching the best man (Ralph Pent-Hartigan) kiss the bride, that Flora felt an unusual sensation in the palm of her right-hand glove. She looked down at it, and saw to her surprise and amusement that it was split right across.

She realized then that she had been extremely nervous lest anything should go wrong. But nothing had; and now she was extremely happy.

Susan, Letty, Phoebe, Prue, and Jane were still roaring away like town-bulls, and Flora had to tell them rather sharply not to make such a noise. Several persons had already asked them, in kindly concern, if they were in pain, or had had bad news.

'Of course,' Mr Mybug was explaining to Rennet, who was also crying because she had had only a nasty register-office wedding and no lovely dress or wreath – 'of course, this is all the sheerest barbarism. It's utterly pagan . . . and a bit obscene, too, if we only look below the ritual. That business of throwing the shoe, for instance – '

'Mr Mybug, we are all going up to the farm now. Of course you're coming too?' Flora had interrupted him, she felt, just at the right moment. He hastily promised Rennet another wedding, a proper one, if she would only stop crying, and rushed away with her under his arm after the rest of the party.

CHAPTER 22

In fifteen minutes they were all going in at the farm gate, chattering and laughing and experiencing that curious exultation which always follows a wedding or a funeral.

And how gay and cheerful the farm looked, with the awning all bravely white and crimson in the sun, and the wreaths of flowers and the rosy clouds of peonies shining out of the darkness of the kitchen, through the open door. And, oh, look! Someone had put a rope of wallflowers and geraniums round the neck of Big Business, who was proudly stamping round the big field, and pausing to stare over the hedge at the wedding guests with his huge, soft eyes.

'What a charming idea. So original,' said Mrs Hawk-Monitor, thinking it was rather indelicate. 'And the cows, I see, are also wreathed. Quite an idea.'

Adam came forward; the desolate Atlantic pools that were his eyes were filmed with the ready tears of ninety years. He stopped in front of Elfine, who looked kindly down at him, and held out to her his cupped hands.

'A wedding present for 'ee, maidy,' he crooned (much to Flora's annoyance, who was afraid the ice would melt and the champagne be tepid). 'A gift for my own wild marsh-tigget.'

And he opened his hands, revealing a marsh-tigget's nest with four pink eggs in it.

'Oh, Adam ... how sweet of you,' said Elfine, pressing his arm affectionately.

'Put it in thy bosom. 'Twill make 'ee bear four children,' advised Adam, and was proceeding to give further instruction when Flora broke up the meeting by sweeping Adam before her towards the kitchen, with the soothing assurance that Elfine would certainly do as he suggested when she had had something to eat.

She led the way into the room, followed by the bride and bridegroom, Mrs Hawk-Monitor and Joan, Ralph

Pent-Hartigan, Reuben, Micah, Mark, and Luke, Caraway, Harkaway, Ezra, Phoebe, Susan, Letty, Mr Mybug and Rennet, Jane, and, following somewhat in the rear, such minors as Mrs Beetle, Mark Dolour's Nancy, Agony and the jazz-band, Mark Dolour himself, and Urk and Meriam, to say nothing of Mrs Murther from the Condemn'd Man and a number of other worthies whom Reuben considered were entitled, by their connection with the farm, to come to the feast. These included the three farm-hands who worked directly under Mark Dolour, and old Adam himself.

As she crossed the threshold and passed from the hot sunshine into the cool room, Flora suddenly stepped aside, to let the guests have a clear view of the kitchen, and of somebody who rose from a chair wreathed in peonies, greeting them with a ringing cry:

'So here you all are! Welcome to Cold Comfort!'

And a handsome old lady, dressed from head to foot in the smartest flying kit of black leather, advanced to meet the astounded party. Her hands were stretched out in welcome.

A roar of amazement broke from Micah, who never did have any tact, anyway.

''Tes Aunt Ada! 'Tes Aunt Ada Doom!'

And the others, released from their first frozen shock of surprise, broke also into ejaculations of amazement:

'Why, so 'tes!'

''Tes terrible!'

''Tes flying in the face of Nature!'

'Aye ... and in trousers, too! Do 'ee mark 'em, lovee?'

'The first time these twenty year ...'

'She'm rising eighty.'

''Tes enough to kill her.'

'Dear me ... how delightful ... so unexpected. How do you do, Miss Doom ... or should I say Mrs Starkadder? ... so confusing.'

'Oh, *Grandmother*!'

''Tes the old un herself!'

'Well, you could knock me down with a warming-pan! Miracles will never cease!'

'Aye . . . fruit and flower, by their growth 'ee shall know 'em! That I should live to see this day!'

Aunt Ada stood in smiling silence while the roar of voices gradually subsided. She glanced once or twice at Flora, with raised eyebrows, and her friendly smile deepened into one of amusement.

At last she held up her hand. Silence immediately fell. She said:

'Well, good people, all this is very flattering, but if I am to spend any time with my granddaughter and the rest of you, we must hurry up and begin the wedding breakfast. I leave for Paris by air in less than an hour.'

On this, confusion broke forth again. The Starkadders were so flabbergasted, so knocked clean out of the perpendicular by the bosom-shattering stupendosity of the event, that nothing but a good deal of food could persuade them to shut their mouths.

So Flora and Ralph Pent-Hartigan (she was beginning to approve of that young man: he had the rudiments) caught up plates of crab patties and began to circulate among the guests, persuading everybody to begin to eat and keep up their strength.

Then Elfine, roused from her fascinated stare at her grandmother by a gentle touch from Flora, cut the wedding cake; and the feast officially began.

Soon everybody was enjoying themselves tremendously. The shattering surprise of Aunt Ada's appearance gave everybody something to talk about, and enhanced the delicious flavours of the food they ate. It would, of course, have been even more stimulating to the appetite if she had appeared in her usual clothes and with her usual manner, and tried to stop the wedding, and had been defied by the Starkadders in a body. That *would* have been worth seeing, if you like. However, one cannot have everything, and what there was, was good.

After she had moved around a little among the guests,

and said a few pleasant phrases to everyone, Aunt Ada sat down again in her flowery chair, and addressed herself to champagne and some caviare sandwiches.

Flora sat by her side, also eating caviare. She thought it best to watch over her handiwork up to the last minute. In only half an hour the aeroplane which was to take Aunt Ada to Paris would land in Ticklepenny's Field. But a lot of things could happen in half an hour. Apparently, Aunt Ada had thoroughly realized what a nasty time she had had for twenty years, and had now made up her mind to have a nice one. But you never knew.

So there Flora sat, watching her aunt, smiling occasionally at people from under the brim of her hat, and seeking an opening in the conversation with her aunt to introduce her rights; those mysterious rights Judith had mentioned in her first letter to Flora nearly six months ago.

Soon it came. Aunt Ada was in excellent spirits. She thanked Flora for the hundredth time for pointing out to her what a nice time was had by Miss Fanny Ward, who looked so much younger than she really was; and for telling her how luxurious was the Hôtel Miramar in Paris, and emphasizing what a pleasant life could be had in this world by a handsome, sensible old lady of good fortune, blessed with a sound constitution and a firm will.

'And I will remember, my dear,' she was saying, 'to preserve my personality, as you advise. You shall not find me plucking my eyebrows, nor dieting, nor doting on a boy of twenty-five. I am very grateful to you, my pippet. What pretty thing shall I send you from Paris?'

'A work-box, please. Mine is wearing out,' said Flora, promptly. 'But, Aunt Ada, there is something else you can do for me, too, if you will. What was the wrong that Amos did to my father, Robert Poste? And what are my "rights", of which Judith used to speak? I feel that I cannot let you go off on your tour without asking you.'

Aunt Ada's face grew grave. She glanced round the kitchen, and observed with satisfaction that everybody was eating much too hard and talking much too fast to take any notice of anyone else. She put her wrinkled hand over Flora's cool young one, and drew her towards her, until aunt and niece were both sheltered by the curving brim of Flora's hat. Then she began to speak in a quick murmur. She spoke for several moments. An observer would not have noted much change in Flora's attentive face. At last the murmur ceased. Flora lifted her head, and asked:

'And did the goat die?'

But at this very second Aunt Ada's attention was distracted by Elfine and Dick, who came up to her accompanied by Adam. Flora's question went unheard, and she did not care to repeat it in front of the others.

'Grandmother, Adam wants to come to live at Hautcouture Hall with us, and look after our cows,' said Elfine. 'May he? We should so like him to. He knows all about cows, you know.'

'By all means, my dear,' said Aunt Ada, graciously. 'But who will care for Feckless, Graceless, Pointless, and Aimless if he deserts them?'

A piercing cry broke from Adam. He flung himself forward. His gnarled hands were knotted in anguish.

'Nay, niver say that, Mrs Starkadder, ma'am. I'll take 'em wi' me, all four on 'em. There's room for us all at Howchiker Hall.'

'It sounds like the finale of the first act in a musical comedy,' observed Aunt Ada. 'Well, well, you may take them if you want to.'

'Bless 'ee. Now bless 'ee, Mrs Starkadder, ma'am,' crooned Adam, and hurried away to tell the cows to make ready for their journey that very afternoon.

'And did the goat die? And what about my rights?' asked Flora, a little louder this time. Dash it, the thing must be straightened out.

But it was no use. Mrs Hawk-Monitor chose that identical second to come up to Aunt Ada, murmuring that she was so sorry that Mrs Starkadder was going away at once, and that none of them would have an opportunity of seeing her during the summer, but that she must come to dinner the very moment she returned from her world-tour, and Aunt Ada said that *she* was so sorry, too, but would be delighted to.

So Flora's question was not answered.

And it was fated never to be answered. For the next interruption was the high, sinister drone of an aeroplane engine, so near that it could be heard even above the roar of conversation in the kitchen; and the youngest member of the jazz-band (who had gone out into Ezra's bean rows to be quietly sick from too many crab patties) came rushing in, his sickness forgotten, proclaiming that there was an aeroplane, an aeroplane, falling into Ticklepenny's Field.

Everybody at once charged out into the garden to look at it, except Mrs Hawk-Monitor, Flora, the bride and bridegroom, and Aunt Ada. In face of the bustle of buckling Aunt Ada into her kit, and exchanging embraces and messages and promises to write and to meet at Hautcouture Hall at Christmas, Flora could not put her question a third time. It would have been ill-bred. She must just relinquish her rights — whatever they might be — and be resigned never to know whether the goat died or not.

Everybody streamed out across the fields to see Aunt Ada off. The pilot (a dark, cross-looking young man) was presented, to his obvious repugnance, with a piece of wedding cake. They all stood round the machine laughing and talking, while Agony Beetle dashed somebody else's glass of champagne over the propeller, and Aunt Ada made her farewells.

Then she climbed into the cockpit and settled herself comfortably. She tucked her chin deeper into her helmet, and looked down with smiling benevolence on the assembled Starkadders. Flora, standing close to the machine, had her shoulder patted, and was thanked again, in a low voice, for the transformation she had achieved in her aunt's life.

Flora smiled prettily; but could not help feeling a bit disappointed about the goat and the rights.

The propeller began to revolve. The machine trembled.

'Three cheers for Aunt Ada!' cried Urk, flinging his voleskin cap into the air. They were just at the beginning of the third 'Hurrah!' when the machine took a run forward and rose from the ground.

It skimmed the hedge, and rose to the level of the elms and above them. The crowd had a last glimpse of Aunt Ada's confident face turned over her shoulder to smile. She waved; and, still waving, was carried from their sight into the heavens.

'Now let's go back and drink a good deal more,' suggested Ralph Pent-Hartigan, taking Flora's hand in a familiar but rather pleasing way. 'Dick and the *sposa* will be taking off in half an hour, you know. Their plane is timed for three-thirty.'

'Goodness . . . it's nothing but people going off in aeroplanes,' said Flora, rather crossly. 'I had best go and help Elfine change her dress.'

And so, while all the others flowed back into the kitchen and sank their fangs into what was left of the provender, she slipped upstairs to Elfine's room, and helped her to put on her blue going-away suit. Elfine was very happy and not at all tearful or nervous.

She embraced Flora warmly, thanked her a thousand times for her goodness, and promised solemnly never to forget all the good advice Flora had given her. The latter placed in her hands a copy of *The Higher Common Sense*, suitably inscribed, and they went downstairs together affectionately entwined.

The second aeroplane came down in the Big Field opposite the farm, punctual to the second. (Big Business had been led away by Micah a few moments previously – a suggestion from some of the blither spirits to the effect that it should be left there 'to see what he makes of the aeroplane' having been vetoed by Flora.)

The second departure was noisier than the first. The Starkadders were not used to drinking champagne. But they liked it all right. There was a great deal of cheering, and some tears from Susan, Prue, Letty, Phoebe and Jane, and Meriam, and some thunderings from Micah warning Dick to be good to his lily-flower.

Flora took advantage of the scrimmage to slip back to the kitchen and warn Mrs Beetle, who was sombrely beginning to tidy up, not to open any more champagne.

'Only in case of illness, Miss Poste,' promised Mrs Beetle.

When Flora got back to the field the aeroplane was just rising from the ground. She smiled up at Elfine's lovely little face framed by the black flying-cap, and Elfine blew her a tender kiss. The roar of the engine swelled to a triumphant thunder. They were gone.

'Well, *now* will you come back and drink a good deal more?' asked Ralph Pent-Hartigan, showing an inclination to put his arm round Flora's waist.

Flora dodged him, with her prettiest smile. She *was* so wishing that everybody would go home. The wedding breakfast seemed to have been going on for ever. Except that this was a cheerful occasion and the other had been a dismal one, it reminded her of the Counting...

('Oh,' she thought, 'and I shall never know what it was that Aunt Ada saw in the woodshed. How I wish I had asked her about that as well.')

In the kitchen the party was at last showing signs of breaking up. All the food was eaten. All the drink had gone long ago. The pretty ropes of flowers were fading in the heat. The floor was littered with crumpled paper napkins, cigarette stubs, crushed flowers, champagne corks, spilt water. The air seemed to sink under its burden of tobacco smoke and mingled smells. Only the rose-peonies were unharmed. The heat had made them open to their full extent, so that they showed their hearts of gold. Flora put her nose into one. It smelled sweet and cool.

She endeavoured to compose her spirits. She was conscious that for the last hour they had been agitated and melancholy. What could be the matter with her? She wished only to be alone.

It was with some difficulty that, in saying good-bye to everybody at the door of the kitchen, she maintained an air of cheerfulness. But she was comforted by the fact that everybody seemed to have had a perfectly lovely time. Everyone, especially Mrs Hawk-Monitor, congratulated her upon the organization of the wedding breakfast and the deliciousness of the food and the elegance of the decorations.

She received invitations to dine with the Hawk-Monitors next week, to visit Mr Mybug and Rennet at the studio (with sink) in which they proposed to live in Fitzroy Square. Urk and Meriam said that they would be honoured if Miss Poste would come to tea at 'Byewaies', the villa which Urk had bought out of his savings from the water-vole trade, and into which he and his bride would move next week.

Flora thanked them all smilingly, and promised to go to all of them.

One by one the guests departed, and the Starkadders, sleepy with champagne and the novelty of enjoying themselves in a normal manner, slipped away to their bedrooms to sleep it off. The figure of the last guest, Agony Beetle, disappeared over the curve of the hill on the path that led down to Howling, accompanied by the jazz-band. Quiet, which had been driven from the farm at six o'clock that morning, began timidly to creep out of shadowy corners and to take possession of it once more.

'Miss Poste. You look done up. Come for a run in the old bouncer?' said Ralph Pent-Hartigan, who was about to start up his eight-cylinder Volupté which stood in the yard.

Flora came down the two little steps leading from the kitchen door and crossed the yard to the car.

'I don't think I'll come for a run, thanks,' she said. 'But it would be very kind of you if you would take me down into the village. I want to telephone.'

He was delighted. He made her get in beside him at once, and soon they were spinning down the hill into Howling. The speed made a wind of grateful coolness that fanned their flushed cheeks.

'I suppose you wouldn't care to dine with me in Town

to-night? Marvellous evening. We might dance at the New River, if you like?'

'I would have loved it, but the fact is I've just made up my mind to leave the farm to-night. I shall have packing and things to do. I'm so sorry. Some other time it would be delightful.'

'Well ... but ... look here, couldn't I run you back?'

The car stopped outside the post office. Flora got out.

'Again, I'm so sorry,' she said, smiling into his disappointed young face, 'but I think my cousin is going to fetch me. I'm just going to see if he is at home. We made the arrangement months ago.'

Fortunately there was only a delay of a few minutes to the Hertfordshire exchange. Flora, waiting in the stuffy telephone box, was not in the mood to be sensible about delays. She had not even started to fume when the bell rang, sounding deafening in that narrow space.

She took off the receiver, and listened.

'Hullo,' said Charles's quiet, deep voice, seventy miles away. It was made tiny by distance, but not less musical.

She gave a little gasp.

'Oh ... hullo, Charles. Is that you? This is Flora. Look here, are you doing anything to-night?'

'Not if you want me.'

'Well ... could you be an absolute angel, and come and fetch me away from the farm to-night in Speed Cop the Second? We've had a wedding here to-day, and I've tidied everything up. I mean there's nothing left for me to do here. And I really am tired. I would like to be fetched ... if you could ...'

'*I'm coming*,' said the deep voice. 'What time may I be there? Is there a big field near the house?'

'Oh, yes, just outside. Can you be here by eight, do you think? It's nearly five o'clock now.'

'Of course. I'll be there at eight.'

There was a pause.

'Charles,' said Flora.

'Yes?'

'Charles . . . I mean, it isn't putting you out or anything?'

Smiling, she hung up the receiver to the tiny distant sound of Charles's laughter.

CHAPTER 23

YOUNG Pent-Hartigan drove her back to the farm. She said good-bye to him and promised to dine with him very soon. Then he drove off; and with the retreating noise of his engine the last invader of the farm's quietude was gone. Quiet flowed back into the sunny empty rooms like the returning sea. The only sounds were the tiny ones of a summer's day that is drawing towards evening.

Flora went upstairs and changed from her party dress into a tweed suit in which she could fly without feeling cold. She brushed her hair and cooled her hands and forehead with eau-de-Cologne. Then she packed, and labelled her trunk for 1 Mouse Place. It would be sent off to-morrow. She took with her only the *Pensées*, *The Higher Common Sense*, and what Chaucer has summed up for all time as 'a bag of needments'.

It was six o'clock when she came slowly downstairs again. The kitchen was tidy and empty. All signs of the feast had been cleared away. Only the awning was left, its stripes of red and white glowing against the deep blue sky of early evening. The shadows of the bean rows were long across the garden, and their flowers were transparent red in the sunlight. All was cool, quiet, blessedly peaceful. Flora's supper was neatly laid, and of the Starkadders there was not a sign. She supposed that they must all be asleep upstairs or else gone a-mollocking off to Godmere. She hoped they would not come downstairs before she left. She loved them all dearly, but this evening she just did not want to see them any more.

She sat down, with a sigh, in a comfortable deep chair, and relaxed her limbs. She would sit here, she thought, until half past six; then she would eat her supper; and then go out into the Big Field and sit on the stile under the may-tree and wait for Charles.

Her dreamy musings were interrupted by the distant soft jangling of bells. She recognized the sound: it was made by the bells that (copying a heathen foreign fashion he had once seen demonstrated on the talkies) Adam had hung round the necks of Graceless, Pointless, Feckless, and Aimless.

Even as she listened a procession came into sight. It wound across the winding path which she could see, silhouetted against the blue sky and held as if in a frame by the open door, from where she sat.

It was Adam and the cows, on their way to Hautcouture Hall.

Adam went first, wearing his ancient hat and his age-green corduroys. The liddle mop was slung round his neck. His head was lifted to the sinking sun, whose strong rays turned him to gold. He was singing the bawdy song he had learned for the wedding of George IV.

Behind him came the cows in single file, still wreathed with their wedding garlands of wallflowers. They swung their heads in lowly content, and their bells chimed in time to Adam's singing.

Slowly they passed across the frame of the doorway. Then they were gone. Nothing could be seen save the green path, rising away into the empty blue of the evening sky. The dying sound of the bells came back to Flora, softly and more softly until it was lost in silence.

Smiling, Flora drew her chair to the table and ate her supper. She did not think of anything, except that in an hour she would see Charles, and tell him about everything she had done, and hear what he had to say about it all.

When she had finished her supper she wrote an affectionate little letter to Reuben, explaining that her work at the farm was now finished, and that she felt she would like to go back to Town. She promised to come down again

230

very soon to see them all, and enclosed a pound note and her earnest thanks for Mrs Beetle.

She left the note open on the table, where everybody could read it, and not even a Starkadder could be alarmed by it or mysterious about it. Then she slipped on her coat, picked up her bag of needments, and sauntered out into the cool evening.

The Big Field was covered with long, fresh grass which threw millions of tiny lengthening shadows. There was not a breath of wind. It was the loveliest hour of the English year: seven o'clock on Midsummer Night.

Flora crossed the grass to the stile, the cool grass swishing against her ankles. She sat down on the step of the stile, leaning back comfortably against the gate part, and stared up into the black boughs of the may-tree. Beneath, they were in shadow. Above, they held their white flowers and green leaves up into the gold of the last sun-rays. She could see the flowers and leaves dazzling against the pure sky.

The shadows grew slowly longer. A cold, fresh smell came up out of the grass and fell from the trees. The birds began their sleep song.

The sun had almost disappeared behind the black traceries of the may-hedge on the far side of the field. Such of his rays as struck through the branches were still, heavy, and of the softest gold.

The air cooled slowly. Flowers shut before Flora's very eyes, but gave out fragrance still. Now there were more shadows than light. The last blackbird that always flies chattering across a summer evening's quiet came dashing down the meadow and vanished in the may-hedge.

The country-side was falling asleep. Flora drew her coat round her, and looked up into the darkening vault of the sky. Then she glanced at her watch. It was five to eight. Her ears had caught a steady, recurrent murmur that might or might not have been the beating of her own blood.

In another moment the sound was the only one in the whole heaven. The aeroplane appeared over the top of the may-hedge, swooping downwards. The under-carriage touched the earth, and then it was taxi-ing comfortably to a standstill.

Flora had stood up as it came in sight. Now she went down the field towards it. The pilot was getting out of the cockpit, loosening his helmet, looking towards her. He came across the grass to meet her, swinging his helmet in his hand, his black hair ruffled by the way he had dragged off the cap.

It was purest happiness to see him. It was like meeting again a dearest friend whom one has loved for long years, and missed in silence. Flora went straight into his open arms, put her own round his neck, and kissed him with all her heart.

Presently Charles said:

'This is for ever, isn't it?'

And Flora whispered: 'For ever.'

It was nearly dark. The stars and moon were out, and the may-trees glimmering. Flora and Charles sighed at last, looked at one another and laughed, and Charles said:

'Look here, I think we ought to go home, you know, darling. Mary's waiting for us at Mouse Place. She got back a day earlier. What do you think? We can talk when we get there.'

'I don't mind,' said Flora, placidly. 'Charles, you do smell nice. Is it stuff you put on your hair, or what? Oh, it is nice to think what years we have got in which to find out things like that! Quite fifty years I should think, wouldn't you, Charles?'

Charles said he hoped so; and added that he did not put stuff on his hair. He also added inconsequently that he was glad he had been born.

They were both in rather a state of dither, but Charles finally pulled himself together, and began to jab purposefully at the interior of the aeroplane, while Flora hovered round telling him all about what she had done at Cold Comfort, and also about Mr Mybug; and Charles laughed, but he said Mr Mybug was a little tick and Flora ought to be more careful. He also said she was the Local Busybody, adding that he did not approve of people who interfered with other people's lives.

Flora heard this with delight.

'Shall I be allowed to interfere with yours?' she asked. Like all really strong-minded women, on whom everybody flops, she adored being bossed about. It was so restful.

'No,' said Charles. And he grinned at her disrespectfully, and she noticed how white and even his teeth were.

'Charles, you have got *heavenly* teeth.'

'Don't fuss,' said Charles. 'Now, are you ready, my dearest darling? Because I am, and so's Speed Cop. We'll be home in half an hour. Oh, Flora, I'm so unbearably happy. I can't believe it's true.' He snatched her roughly into his arms, and looked longingly down into her face. 'It *is* true, isn't it? Say "I love you".'

And Flora, unutterably moved, told him just how much she did.

They climbed into the aeroplane. The roar of the propeller rose into the exquisite stillness of the night. Soon they were rising above the elms, that were faintly silvered by the moon, and the country-side lay spread beneath them.

'Say it again.'

She saw Charles's lips move, as the farm dropped away beneath them, and guessed what he was saying.

He was fully occupied with keeping the machine clear of the topmost branches of the elms, and could not look at her, but she saw by his troubled profile that he feared (so fantastically beautiful was the night and this discovery of their love) that it might be some cruel mistake.

Flora put her warm lips close to his cap.

'I love you,' she said. He could not hear her very well, but he turned for a second, and, comforted, smiled into her eyes.

She glanced upwards for a second at the soft blue vault of the midsummer night sky. Not a cloud misted its solemn depths. To-morrow would be a beautiful day.

Discover more about our forthcoming books through Penguin's FREE newspaper...

READ MORE IN PENGUIN

In every corner of the world, on every subject under the sun, Penguin represents quality and variety – the very best in publishing today.

For complete information about books available from Penguin – including Puffins, Penguin Classics and Arkana – and how to order them, write to us at the appropriate address below. Please note that for copyright reasons the selection of books varies from country to country.

In the United Kingdom: Please write to *Dept. JC, Penguin Books Ltd, FREEPOST, West Drayton, Middlesex UB7 OBR*

If you have any difficulty in obtaining a title, please send your order with the correct money, plus ten per cent for postage and packaging, to *PO Box No. 11, West Drayton, Middlesex UB7 OBR*

In the United States: Please write to *Penguin USA Inc., 375 Hudson Street, New York, NY 10014*

In Canada: Please write to *Penguin Books Canada Ltd, 10 Alcorn Avenue, Suite 300, Toronto, Ontario M4V 3B2*

In Australia: Please write to *Penguin Books Australia Ltd, 487 Maroondah Highway, Ringwood, Victoria 3134*

In New Zealand: Please write to *Penguin Books (NZ) Ltd,182–190 Wairau Road, Private Bag, Takapuna, Auckland 9*

In India: Please write to *Penguin Books India Pvt Ltd, 706 Eros Apartments, 56 Nehru Place, New Delhi 110 019*

In the Netherlands: Please write to *Penguin Books Netherlands B.V., Keizersgracht 231 NL–1016 DV Amsterdam*

In Germany: Please write to *Penguin Books Deutschland GmbH, Friedrichstrasse 10–12, W–6000 Frankfurt/Main 1*

In Spain: Please write to *Penguin Books S. A., C. San Bernardo 117–6° E–28015 Madrid*

In Italy: Please write to *Penguin Italia s.r.l., Via Felice Casati 20, I–20124 Milano*

In France: Please write to *Penguin France S. A., 17 rue Lejeune, F–31000 Toulouse*

In Japan: Please write to *Penguin Books Japan, Ishikiribashi Building, 2–5–4, Suido, Bunkyo-ku, Tokyo 112*

In Greece: Please write to *Penguin Hellas Ltd, Dimocritou 3, GR–106 71 Athens*

In South Africa: Please write to *Longman Penguin Southern Africa (Pty) Ltd, Private Bag X08, Bertsham 2013*

READ MORE IN PENGUIN

A CHOICE OF FICTION

Changes at Fairacre Miss Read

'Miss Read understands and loves the country and can write tenderly and humorously about the minutiae of village life without distortion or sentimentality' – *The Times Educational Supplement*

Lucia Rising E. F. Benson

Outrageously funny and wickedly satirical, E. F. Benson's portrait of society in the glamorous 1920s is as endlessly entertaining today as when it was first published.

Travels with My Aunt Graham Greene

In *Travels with My Aunt* Graham Greene not only gives us intoxicating entertainment but also confronts us with some of the most perplexing of human dilemmas.

The Folks That Live on the Hill Kingsley Amis

'In this utterly entertaining piece, Kingsley Amis proves once more that no one can hold a candle to his blistering command of contemporary life – and letters' – *Mail on Sunday*

A Gentleman of Leisure P. G. Wodehouse

Redolent with the sights, sounds and smells of rural English life, *A Gentleman of Leisure* also contains all the wit and vivacity we have come to expect from the inimitable Wodehouse.

READ MORE IN PENGUIN

A CHOICE OF FICTION

London Fields   Martin Amis

'*London Fields*, its pastoral title savagely inappropriate to its inner-city setting, vibrates, like all Amis's work, with the force fields of sinister, destructive energies. At the core of its surreal fable are four figures locked in lethal alignment' – Peter Kemp in the *Sunday Times*

A Bottle in the Smoke   A. N. Wilson

'Stunningly funny ... Wilson's knowing mockery of the viler aspects of the London literary world and the "insane vanity" of authors is spot-on ... But there is a redeeming idea behind it all, about the fantasies people live by' – Victoria Glendinning in *The Times*

Brazzaville Beach   William Boyd

'A most extraordinary parable about mankind ... quite unlike anything else I have ever read' – *Sunday Express*. 'Boyd is a brilliant storyteller ... a most serious book which stretches, tantalises and delights' – Mary Hope in the *Financial Times*

Paradise News   David Lodge

'Lodge could never be solemn and the book crackles with good jokes ... leaves you with a mild and thoughtful glow of happiness' – *Sunday Telegraph*. 'Amusing, accessible, intelligent ... the story rolls, the sparks fly' – *Financial Times*

That Darcy, That Dancer, That Gentleman   J. P. Donleavy

'Marvellously funny and poetic, as if James Joyce had sat down to write a Tom Sharpe novel ... he is able to mix a lovely lyricism with the broadest of bawdy farce' – Stanley Reynolds in the *Guardian*

READ MORE IN PENGUIN

A CHOICE OF FICTION

A Sense of Guilt   Andrea Newman

Felix Cramer, famous author and notorious womanizer, is faced with a temptation he can't resist – an affair with Sally, the teenage stepdaughter of his best friend... 'From the first toe-tingling sentence ... I couldn't put this bulky, breathless, beanfeast of a novel down' – *Daily Mail*

Mrs Hartley and the Growth Centre   Philippa Gregory

Statuesque Alice Hartley can no longer arouse the interest of her pompous husband, the adulterous professor. Just as she is compelled to face this chilling truth, she meets Michael, a young gullible student with an excessive libido. In Michael, Alice discovers an endless supply of all she has sought: revenge, sex and a large house suitable for conversion.

Closed at Dusk   Monica Dickens

'Creepy ... a story of love, hate, and murder, tinged with the super-natural' – *Sunday Express*. 'Monica Dickens's prose is evocative ... [her] talents for storytelling have, if anything, improved over the years' – *Daily Mail*

Varying Degrees of Hopelessness   Lucy Ellmann

'Funny and furious ... what the author is interested in is the hopelessness of life. Her merry little novel is a vehicle for disgust. Lucy Ellmann is clever, and very angry' – *The Times*. 'An irresistible cocktail of satire, slapstick and tenderness' – *Cosmopolitan*

The Invisible Worm   Jennifer Johnston

'This quietly ambitious novel is one of Jennifer Johnston's more persuasive parables of cruelty and the need to defy it' – *Irish Times*. 'A powerful, moving novel, and beautifully written' – *Sunday Express*